Stories from Western Canada

Stories from Western Canada

a selection by
RUDY WIEBE

Macmillan of Canada

© Macmillan Company of Canada
Limited 1972

ISBN 7705-0872-3

Library of Congress Catalogue
Card No. 79-186433

Printed in Canada for
The Macmillan Company of Canada
70 Bond Street, Toronto

10c

to Dick Harrison,
Dave Carpenter and the others
in English 590B, 1970-71,
who helped

ACKNOWLEDGEMENTS

For permission to reprint copyright material grateful acknowledgement is made to the following:

Victor Carl Friesen for "Old Mrs. Dirks."

A. Leonard Grove for "The First Day of an Immigrant" by Frederick Philip Grove.

Henry Kreisel for "The Broken Globe."

Robert Kroetsch for "Earth Moving."

Dorothy Livesay for "A Week in the Country."

McClelland and Stewart Limited for "The Move" from *The Road Past Altamont* by Gabrielle Roy, and "Horses of the Night" from *A Bird in the House* by Margaret Laurence; both reprinted by permission of The Canadian Publishers, McClelland and Stewart Limited.

Edward McCourt for "Cranes Fly South." First published in *Weekend Magazine,* April 9, 1955.

Ken Mitchell for "The Great Electrical Revolution" from *Prism international,* Vancouver, Spring, 1970.

W. O. Mitchell for "Hercules Salvage."

Estate of Mary Pauline Niven, for "Indian Woman" by Frederick Niven. Originally published by William Collins Ltd., in *The Flying Years,* 1942.

Howard O'Hagan for "The Tepee." Published by Swallow Press in *The Woman Who Got on at Jasper Station, and Other Stories.*

Sinclair Ross for "A Day with Pegasus." Originally published in *Queen's Quarterly,* Summer, 1938.

Stephen Scobie for "Streak Mosaic."

W. D. Valgardson for "Dominion Day." Originally published in *Fiddlehead,* Spring, 1971.

The Viking Press Inc., for "Carrion Spring" from *Wolf Willow* by Wallace Stegner. Copyright © 1968 by Wallace Stegner. First appeared in *Esquire.*

Sheila Watson for "The Black Farm." Originally published in *Queen's Quarterly,* Summer, 1956.

Wilfred Watson for "The Lice." Originally published in *Prism international,* Fall, 1960.

Jon Whyte for "Peter Pond, His True Confession."

Rudy Wiebe for "Did Jesus Ever Laugh?" Originally published in *Fiddlehead,* March-April, 1970.

Ethel Wilson for "A Visit to the Frontier." Originally published in *Tamarack Review,* No. 33, 1964.

CONTENTS

INTRODUCTION

Beyond the river to the east . . . was another gradual
rise, which gathered breath for several miles and
heaved up finally with a tremendous effort to a
double-crested hill that dominated the eastern landscape. To Isaac the land seemed like a great arrested
movement, petrified in time, like his memories, and
the city crawled about its surface in a counterpoint
of life.

— Adele Wiseman

One Thursday morning near the end of May, 1971, I walked
through the bush to the homestead where my mother says
I was born. The night before one of the two farmers left in
the district had shown me where the place must be. I did not
remember being there since before I began school; my memory rests largely on two snapshots, one showing over-exposed
horses belly-deep in grass with our family in a wagon behind
them, the other a log building on a distant hill with what is
today called snowfencing for a roof. Against it stands a dark
figure outlined in a large white apron yoke: my mother; and
another not quite up to the rectangular window—that is me.

The farmer pointed out a bluff on a small hill across a long
hayslough. The plastic card in my pocket had the necessary
numbers all right, but where the iron marker should have

been only slender poplars and mounds, endless mounds under leaves that had nothing to do with the civilization of survey, only the busy ants. But on the south face of the hill, I knew it. I found the depression which had once been the well, the patch of weeds still growing thicker, taller in the perimeter of the vanished barn. North under huge poplars was the depression left by the icehouse, and on the field slope to the east a scattering of "zooroump" plants my mother had to use in borscht until the cabbage headed, if ever. On the hill was the cellar over which the house had stood. Tiny as always in actuality, woodchuck holes in its caving sides and poplars, one six inches through.

Simply the work of time undisturbed. What made the hill truly unrecognizable was the surrounding landscape. I have no idea why that hill itself had been spared, no doubt momentarily, but it rose in a bluff perhaps an eighth of a mile square and on three sides around the land had been scraped bare to its very rocks. Instead of the inevitable birch, pine, poplar forests, haysloughs, bullrushed lakes and spruce muskegs, south and west and north all that could be seen was the humpy land naked with incredible windrows of bulldozed trees crushed into parallels a hundred yards apart, endless bloated welts flogged upon the land as far as could be seen. When a month later I described it to one of the writers in this collection, she burst into tears. What was happening?

Progress. The other farmer explained that since the rocky bush soil was good for nothing (my father could have told them), a community pasture organization was clearing it, sowing grass between the windrows to summer pasture cattle and sheep; when the wood dried the windrows would be burned and more grass sown. Simple. But to me, having climbed up those slashed trees with the sweet rotting earth still tangled in their roots but in their branches and dead leaves also, it was obscene.

Which standard contemporary environmental thought (I can afford it since I'm not trying to feed a family digging that land, as my father tried and failed thirty years ago), does finally bring me to the collection of stories in hand.

For it is a collection of *stories*; each has not only a beginning but also a middle and an end, has sequential relationships between its differing events (though the events do not necessarily appear in chronology), has characters that sometimes have moments of recognition, sometimes have insights, sometimes learn, sometimes even change their behaviour slightly but probably permanently. In other words, they are not pieces but stories made of character with discoverable plots. And that is not contemporary at all.

Cultural ages ago, before the sixties, we were already told that "plot, in the Dickensian sense, is obsolete" (Hugh Kenner, *The Poetry of Ezra Pound*, 1951). If any 'now' writer or critic reads the above paragraph, he'll be smiling. Everybody knows the Canadian West (i.e., between the Shield and the Rockies, not swingin' B.C.) consists of equal parts of Puritanism, Monotony, Farmers, and Depression; the closest you come to non-guilty sex is the grain elevator as phallic symbol and the closest to culture is the ice arena used either for hockey or hellfire preaching. So its stories have plots, what else is new?

Still, one could think that the world of anti-story would find some place in the West. For if, as Henri Peyre suggests *(New York Times Book Review,* January 12, 1969) these most-now efforts, which have no sequence, no characters and aggressively no point, are concerned "to retain the totality and diversity of the world in space while neglecting the diversity and the movement of the world in time," why, we must have more space than Paris or even New York. If, as Kenner insists, "the place of plot is taken by interlocking large-scale rhythms of recurrence," why, just drive fast across Saskatchewan.

A story tells as much by its form as by any other of its characteristics. One mark of authenticity in these stories about Western Canada is that they do not pretend to trendiness. As Civic Square is a place so is Rocky Mountain House a place; though the latter is harder to find, and certainly less newsworthy, it could for those very reasons be the more exciting to the story-maker. And, no matter what the visitor transient across the land may feel, the world of the prairie human being is dominated not only by the great space around him, but also by time. Just as I, with a visit every two decades, can afford to get bothered by a community pasture, so the person who has always known the water tap dripping beside his electric stove and the supermarket open around the corner six days a week can afford to forget about time. But no man on the Canadian prairie.

For those people who do live in space close to nature are genuinely dominated by time; not by invented city hours, certainly, but the cycles of their bodies, and of the seasons. There is no way the story-maker on the prairies can ignore that; it is there implicit in form and content even in the city stories since, Winnipeg perhaps excepted, prairie cities are only now beginning to grow a genuine urban generation. Almost everyone in them until now has moved in from the land. And no matter how large they have become, none can yet isolate its people from the space of land. Stand on a fifteenth-floor balcony of a Regina hotel or drive twenty minutes in any direction from Calgary's city centre and you'll believe.

Like the railroad-builder, the story-maker may have to import some materials necessary to his structure (steel, a certain discipline of language); basically, however, like the engineer he builds of the stuff he finds where he chooses to build. Chief Dan Kennedy of the Assiniboine Reserve near Qu'Appelle told it long ago straighter than ever I can. Many of his tales can be found in the Saskatchewan Archives, as is this one.

The Legend of Grandfather Buffalo

. . . before treaty number 4 was signed at Fort Qu'Appelle [1874] some people were camping around Troy, as south Qu'Appelle was called then, and doing this and hunting ducks, rabbits, and deer. One morning one of the young men was rounding up the ponies, and rounding one big bluff he saw an animal, who seeing him ran away northwards towards the lakes of the Qu'Appelle Valley. So he immediately raced back, being on horseback, and told the men in the camp that he saw a big black animal. The older people at once knew what was the animal. "Buffalo," they said.

At that time the buffalo were simply disappearing and there would be an odd one seen and killed. The men of the camp, having rounded their ponies and getting their muzzle-loading guns, gave chase, but did not catch up with the buffalo till one of the younger men sighted something on the lake and he shouted and pointed to the lake. Sure enough, it was the buffalo swimming across, northwards. They raced around the lake and forded the river and raced eastward to try and head the buffalo, but alas they went along the lake and tracked the animal where he had landed on the shore and they raced up in different directions, but one of the older men stayed back and walked his pony following the tracks till he came halfway up on the side hill and the tracks ended around where a big blue-black rock was, long, resembling an animal lying down. He was puzzled, and in the meantime two of the chasers had gone up the hill to try and intercept the animal, but they saw no sign of tracks. They were bitterly disappointed and the old man of the party told his fellow chasers to get off the ponies and they sat around the rock and he took the sweet grass and incensing his head and hands, he prayed to the Great Spirit, that He take pity on them, and after his prayer gave vent to his feelings by crying; and the rest of them did the same. Ever afterwards, the people passing along the road would stop and visit the rock and left some sacrifice tobacco, sweet grass, cloth.

Afterwards, the railroad passed through and they, with their big machines, cut the side hills and Grandfather Buffalo was cut down and made a road-bed for the iron road that passes along the valley.

The story-teller, like the engineer, is a maker of new things out of old. The difference is, he does it without violence to the originals. Perhaps that's why his things only seem to be new.

This is almost my ideal collection of western stories; a very few could not be included for what seem to me sufficient human reason, and several authors are not represented for reasons that verge on the inhuman. Every story included I have enjoyed for itself, as a thing made, and seeing them together I believe they do, by their range of complexity, subject, season, terrain, mood, character, indicate the richness of story telling that has come out of, been stimulated by, Western Canada. One was written in the 1920s, one in the 30s, two each in the 40s and 50s, eight in the 60s and seven in the 70s; four appear in print here for the first time. However, this collection does not attempt to be an historical survey of anything; it hopes to provide the varieties of pleasure that stories still give those who care to listen.

R. W.
November 8, 1971.

Ethel Wilson

A
VISIT
TO THE
FRONTIER

Lucy turned from looking out of the window of the train.

The appearance of the country has changed since we left Saskatoon, hasn't it? she said, but Charles did not answer. He remained concealed by the weekend review which he was reading; so, since the question was of the kind which neither requires nor demands an answer, Lucy returned her gaze to the window.

Rivers flow through, or near, four of the five cities of the Canadian north and middle west. The fifth city, which has no large adjacent body of water, has courageously made itself a spacious lake in the dry prairies, and planted trees. The small northern city of Saskatoon on the high banks of the Saskatchewan River had given Lucy a great deal of pleasure. True, in summer the weather was very hot and in winter the weather was very cold. But the far spread of prairie, the vast span of sky with wildness of sunrise and sunset and aurora, the felt nearness of the northland, the grave majestic sweep of the tawny Saskatchewan River, the clarity and stimulation of the air delighted her—a dweller by the western ocean. So did the neatness of the heart of the small city; the dignity of the

1

surprisingly large hotel upon the high river bank; the austere elegance of the large red brick churches on the river road, outlined clean against the clean sky as by some northern Canaletto; and those churches which terminated, also with elegance, in Byzantine onions.

By this time the train had left behind the flat prairies, and any suggestion of a town or even a dwelling was so improbable as to make one wonder, Will the curve of any small hill or valley here ever become home and significant and a part of memory to people who will live here and die here— all so empty of life now? (Yet see, a hawk!) Lucy sat wondering. The broad land slid behind them and now the country was broken, curved, into innumerable forested or bushy valleys and headlands, with stretches of intermediate green. Streams appeared around distant curves or near at hand, and vanished again, left behind. Was it the same stream? Were they many streams? And beyond the horizon disclosed by the speeding train, was there more of this softly moulded, recklessly planted and treed, mildly watered greenish brownish country, or did it change with suddenness into the true north? And what did the true north look like? she wondered. Perhaps this was the true north, momentarily kind, just before the end of autumn.

It is impossible to guess, so why guess, said Lucy, partly to herself and partly aloud and unheeded, whether this everlasting empty country will ever be settled with people and activity, will ever, in fact, be covered with towns and cities? We haven't seen a dwelling for hours. There are a great many factors of climate, water, soil, oil, minerals, transportation that must enter, of course. If you and I, two hundred years ago—which is nothing at all in time—should have found ourselves on the empty banks of the Saskatchewan River where Saskatoon now stands, we would have seen nothing to suggest the establishment of a town or city there, and the same is true now, and here.

A quiver of the weekend review caused Lucy to stop her soliloquy for the moment. There was nothing in what she had to say just then to warrant Charles's breaking off his reading and coming out of his private world to listen.

She turned her attention to him, and away from the window. How heavenly fortunate I am, she thought—and this time she kept her soliloquy to herself, as there are many things that do not translate into mutual speech and this was one— that ever since we first loved each other, every day has renewed our love. Never never have we taken it for granted but have always known, without saying, that it is our greatest thing and that it might be removed at any moment (although not in essence) by death, which comes once and forever to each person on earth, on this continent, on this train, and we are no exception. And so, now, as I sit across from Charlie and see him lounging there, and see his elbows sticking out each side of his paper, and his legs sprawled across, one boot touching my shoe, the contentment and joy of his presence is greater than when my heart first leapt to see him. And one wonders why most of the books that have ever been written and most of the tales that have been told (for the oldest tales were tales of fighting or of love) have been of nascent love, tragic love, deceived, faithless or unlawful love, but not of perfect and lasting fulfilment. There is no literature of perfect and lasting fulfilment of happy love. That must be because continuing fulfilment does not lend itself to the curiosity that is impelled to read a story and because in any case this fulfilment can never be revealed.

Charles came out from behind the paper. Listen to this, he said, it's funny. He had come to the end of the paper where the competitions are. He read, and his French was pleasantly bad. 'An English Member of Parliament who belonged to the M.R.A. related his confessions at a house party in France. He said *"Quand je regarde mon derrière, je vois qu'il est divisé en deux parties."* ' Lucy laughed a lot at this and at some similar stories in the competition, and Charles turned to the serious beginning of the review again and fell silent. Lucy now saw his face above the paper, intent and grown serious again.

The scenery had slipped behind the train unobserved, and the rather spectacular changes in the nature of the scenery had escaped Lucy's notice as she sat, still smiling at the derrière which was divisé. The roadbed appeared to be rough here and so the train gave the impression of hurrying. It was actually slower and rocked a good deal, and soap and glasses and bags and coats slipped and rattled and swayed in the compartment as the train ran on.

I'm glad, said Lucy out loud and still amused at the story, that now I've discovered—

Charles came up over the top of his paper again and looked at her. What on earth are you chunnering about now? he said.

I'm not chunnering, said Lucy. I'm simply saying—but she never said what she was simply saying because of the crash.

If it was a crash. It was a shattering, a physical impact, a screeching, a settling, a cessation in which she was seized and shaken and lost. It was for a millionth of a second—or forever —fear and helpless panic to the obliteration of everything that had been Lucy. There was at last this settling down again to the irregular motion of the train and the assumption that something had happened and something was over. Lucy, who had so lately been in the middle of her laughing, had been banged about (it seemed), with sudden pain like thunder and lightning, and sat now with her eyes closed because she was afraid to open them. She remembered like a quick dream that once, in the sage-brush country, the train had run into a small herd of cattle. The train, at that time, had stopped, and there was a long wait while the poor beasts were removed from the rails. Evidently—and her first emotion was gladness—they had not run over anybody or any animal because they still kept on their way; probably one of the large boulders which so often overhang the railway cuttings had timed its falling to the vibrations of the train passing below and had knocked them about. Still a little fearful, Lucy opened her eyes and saw, but hazily, Charles sitting on the opposite seat, still read-ing. Really, Charlie, this is carrying imperturbability too far.

Darling, what was that? she said.

What was what? said Charles indifferently.

That crash, said his wife.

I don't know, said Charles and went on reading.

Sometimes you do infuriate me! said Lucy, and now I'm sure that you just pretend when you put it over me as you often do—being imperturbable like that. What *did* happen?

Charles looked up at her and the familiar look flowed between them. He said amiably, The train is slowing up. And it was.

Lucy still felt shaken. It's possible, she thought, that nothing happened at all, except inside my head. Dear me, I hope I'm not starting to have fits like a cat. Do people? she said out loud.

Do people what? asked Charles who had got up and was putting on this tweed jacket over his sweater.

Start having fits, she said.

At that moment the conductor put his head in at the compartment door. Cut Off. This stop is Cut Off, he said. An hour and a half at Cut Off. You'll have time to go up to the settlement. They say it's worth seeing. And he went on and made his announcement along the train.

Lucy put on her leather jacket because they were pretty far north and the air would no doubt be nippy. They both went out.

She stepped on to the platform, glad to be free of the train for a long prospect of time, and stood before the sign of the railway station. The station was wooden, primitive, and so was the sign. It spelled CUT OFF. Lucy turned to the coloured porter who stood beside the steps. He was particularly nice and seemed to know the answers to all railroad questions.

Porter, she said, what an odd name. What does it mean?

The porter shrugged and regarded her with his slow gentle smile. Ah doan know, lady, he said. They's mighty odd names all over this country. They's The Leavings and Ah guess that kinda speaks for itself, n they's Dog Pound n Jumpn Pound n Ghost River n Spirit River but Ah doan no nuthn about Cut Off. Tell you the truth lady, it's the first time Ah done this run. And he helped down another passenger.

The air was brilliantly fresh after the train smell. Lucy breathed deep. She noticed the passenger who had followed them off the train. He was tall. His face was serious and perhaps sad. He regarded his surroundings with slow sweeping glances which were also inward glances and he appeared anxious.

Who's that, Charles? breathed Lucy. I've seen him or seen his picture and why is he so sad?

That is Proker, said Charles, and he has lost his fountain pen. Perhaps he lost it when we changed trains.

Changed trains? said Lucy. (Changed trains *changed trains changed trains* changed trains.) Her head clanged. She put her hand to her eyes, closing them, and then it was better and she stepped out with Charlie because they had no time to waste.

They left behind the little wooden station and the people standing about and walked into the open space to see what they could of the settlement of Cut Off.

Impressions flowed in on Lucy like a newly tasted wine, and yet taste was the only faculty unemployed. Simultaneously, simultaneously, they flowed in, ravishing her. The prospect revealed itself to the north towards which they looked as an open stretch of brisk grass in front of them, crossed by paths and wagon trails and sloping down to a near river which cut foaming across the landscape. This river which was large enough to be spectacular and powerful and yet not useful for navigation was of water so whitely brilliant as to be quite dazzling in its motion. It had a strange peculiarity which Lucy had never seen before in picture or story; and now she marvelled that this attribute of the river had not already become famous. At intervals in the course of the river, both on its banks and springing up through the waters of the river itself, were fountains, rising buoyantly and joyously several feet in the air. Only to look at these fountains of bright perpetual water refreshed and revived Lucy—and perhaps other watchers too, for some of the other passengers were standing, gazing—so that her sense of well-being was beyond anything she had ever felt before. They stood, and then looked beyond the river, where lay the settlement proper. The river was crossed by two simple wooden bridges that led to the settlement.

Wood seemed to be abundant here. Spreading trees which still held their leaves and large dark comely firs and shapely cedars grew, not very crowded, on either side of the sloping river banks. Indians and other people walked here, separately or together, or stood looking at the fountains of springing waters, or sat upon the pine and cedar scented earth. A look to right and left showed the country folded away and away further and further into hills and valleys behind hills and valleys, wild yet embowered in trees; away until soft brown and green hills of wiry tawny grass and light and dark trees became dun-coloured, mauve, and then deeply purple. Lucy turned back to look at the river. Across the river flew one after another of small western blue-birds, bluer than forget-me-nots in flight, and there came continuous bird-song from the trees.

She was soon aware that the air which they were breathing was different from the air she customarily breathed and whose quality she used not to notice particularly unless it was exceptionally bad. This air, at Cut Off, was vigorous, so vigorous that Lucy felt herself different, stronger, and gayer. She said to Charles, Don't you feel as if the air we used to breathe was more like earth and stone than air—solid and heavy, I mean—and I feel as if it was only water that I used to have in my veins. This must be the true north.

But Charles did not answer.

She turned and looked up but he was not there. She looked back. Perhaps he had gone to hunt for the fountain pen. Or was it possible—but not likely—that Charles had walked on alone or with some other people?

Charles! Darling! Charlie! she called, but he cannot have heard her.

Well, she thought, how strange, but he must have gone on ahead. I'll hurry after, I mustn't wait here, we'll meet at the train. She found it much easier than usual not to worry. She was aware as she walked on quickly, and with a delight in walking, that she had shed some accompanying emotion (the emotion was anxiety). Even the unaccountable absence of Charles did not make her anxious.

This delicious air, strong and pine-scented, which she drew in gave her active pleasure. It *was* like water or wine compared to earth or stone. She came to the nearer footbridge and stood for a few moments watching the lively river and the strange crystalline fountains that shot vertically upwards and sprayed down again into the rushing sparkling stream whose noise was strangely agreeable. She watched, too, some of the people who seemed to be inhabitants enjoying the river and its banks. These people walked quickly, or strolled, or sat on the ground. But whether they walked or wandered or rested, whether moving or in repose, there was a lively look of well-being and pleasure upon them. They talked to each other in passing and laughed spontaneously. Even a crippled man whom she saw making his way on crutches by the river-bank seemed to swing along in an easy debonair fashion and whistled as he swung. They feel as I do, thought Lucy; this is certainly a very healthy place.

On the footbridge as she stopped to look down at the water racing radiant and broken under the bridge, a man and woman leaned upon the railing. Lucy heard them talking and found that their language was strange to her; but she had a vague sentiment of knowing what they were talking about, although she did not understand the words, only the feeling. They looked at her in friendly fashion and seemed as if they would include her in the conversation only that they knew she could not converse with them. Lucy wondered if this were one of the many foreign settlements to be found in the Canadian northwest—Ukrainians, Hutterites. No, not Hutterites; these people had no uniformity of dress.

She realized that time (was it time?) was passing, and that if she were to climb the far slope and see the buildings which the trees partly disclosed, she could no longer stand there water-gazing. So she crossed the footbridge, and leaving the river bank she climbed the gradual slope of the hill, following a trail which led up among the trees.

She felt no shortness of breath, as she sometimes did, but an increased exhilaration in this climbing. People in twos and threes climbed, too, or walked down the hill and towards the river. She was struck by the freedom and elasticity of their steps, and the certainty and serenity of their faces. They were not like the crowds she knew. She did not recognize the absence of anxiety or preoccupation in them or in herself, because there was no anxiety to recognize. This is a country of truth! she thought, surprised. We are free like birds.

She now saw through the trees, which had become fewer,

a long low building of dark stained rough wood. The building was pleasing in its simple proportions. There was a long verandah which faced west. The settlement of Cut Off must be unexpectedly large, she thought, for already she had seen more people than would usually constitute a village, and she found that more were coming and going in and out of the unusually large doors of the building which was perhaps some kind of lodge or village centre. As she went up to the broad, shallow, wooden steps towards the entrance, she saw that there were, higher up the trail, other buildings among the trees. Is there a church? she wondered. If I could see a church, that would tell me something.

She was about to cross the threshold of the lodge quite eagerly, without any customary shyness, and to mingle with the people amongst whom friendliness seemed to blow like a breeze—although no-one appeared to notice her—when there sounded the very loud ringing of a bell. She turned quickly. Something in her spirit and spirits descended and became confused, and she remembered the time, and the train, and above all she remembered Charles. Without looking further inside the lodge she went with an attempt at haste down the hill. So far from buoying her up as the bright air had heretofore done, the bright air was too strong for her and now pressed her down, so that she made her way with some difficulty until she reached a low rectangular stone, seat high. She looked down upon the stone, and on it was chiselled a finely sweeping double curve. She bent down and followed this curve with her finger, murmuring The Line of Beauty, The Line of Beauty. She thought, I must sit down for a moment on this stone for I am very tired and I am confused. So she sank down and sat on the stone, and looked towards the dazzling jets of water which no longer invigorated her but were far too strong, as some strong drink might be too strong. A man walked up to her and stood over her, and she looked up at him and was grateful for something in his face. He spoke to her, and although she could not understand his words she knew that he wished to be kind. I am like a dog who is lost, she thought, and he is like a man who is kind to the dog and powerful; but because he is a man and I am a dog, however kind and powerful he is, we cannot communicate except on the level of pity. He helped her to rise, and she hurried on, labouring as she ran.

After she crossed the footbridge, her mind and body freshened a little, and some of her calm and pleasure seemed to be restored, so that she did not race and press on to the railway station with anxiety. There were new sounds in the air. She heard from her right, behind the brow of a curving hill, the galloping of hooves. And there was this peculiarity in this air, that one sound did not overlay or drown out another sound; so that the sound of galloping hooves which drew nearer and nearer did not at all drown the sound of light and laughing voices calling to one another.

Around the curve swept into view one, two, seven, twelve horses and their riders. Lucy stood entranced.

The girls who raced their horses round the concealing curve of the hill, into the clearing and across the clearing to a spinney of thin trees, turned to each other as they galloped, and seemed to be in a kind of laughing harmony. They wore bright scarves which fluttered behind them in the wind; so that these merry riders galloping towards the spinney with their bright scarves flowing behind them were a beautiful sight. The heavy hooves pounded, the gay voices sounded, the scarves streamed and fluttered, all in the brilliant air. Lucy stood like a radiant statue, watching. When the riders reached the spinney, they slid down off their horses, while the sound of their light voices crossed and criss-crossed. They threw the reins forward over their horses' heads and the horses stood, tossing their long manes, switching their tails, and moving only a step or two towards a patch of grass or a green bough.

Lucy was so enchanted with the girl riders that she had again forgotten her urgency. Some of the girls wore full divided skirts such as a riding gypsy might wear (but they were not gypsies), and walking lightly, talking and laughing together, they set out quickly for the footbridge by which Lucy had just crossed the river, some in blue jeans, some in gypsy skirts, all with their scarves fluttering. One bright-eyed Indian girl saw Lucy standing there and waved to her as they passed. Lucy waved back, very much pleased at this. Where do they come from behind those hills? What is it, there? Why do they come? But the girls had gone towards the bridge and only the horses remained in the spinney, resting, pawing, and shaking their heads. Lucy heard again the loud station bell. The train was pulling out. Oh! she gasped, and began to run.

She ran, and caught a handle beside a step; a hand from a dark blue sleeve clutched her and she swung onto the train.

Oh thank you, she gasped to the conductor, and made her way into the train. There was no-one there. The train was very old. Not a single passenger. There was no sign at all that Charles had ever been there. It was not the same train. Oh! she cried desperately, and found her way to the conductor. I'm on the wrong train! Where is my husband?

The conductor said You must have changed trains (changed trains *changed trains changed trains* changed trains).

If you want to get off, said the conductor, you'd better jump before the train gets up speed. Her one desire was to get off. She stood on the lowest step of this old-fashioned train, still holding on and—divided between the desire to leave the train at once before it got up speed, and the desire to choose a good place on which to jump out so that she would not disable herself—she jumped, onto a soft grassy mound. She scrambled up, and in raising herself she leaned her weight on a soft but firm object that moved beneath her hand. She looked down in a hurry and saw that her hand rested upon the flat head of a large polar bear. She drew her hand away in alarm, but not before she had felt the texture of the crisp, coarse, gleaming, cream-coloured hair. The bear looked at her with humourless animal eyes and extended its head this way that way—this way, that way—and then paid her no attention. She thought as she regained her equilibrium and started to run the short distance back to the station, Yes, this must be the true north, yet something is wrong about that bear.

And as she ran she began to be aware that living in this country would, of itself, inescapably exclude the memory of much sorrow and much joy that made up the uneven fabric of her life as she had known it. She began to pray as she ran, panting, stumbling. Oh God just this. Let me find him. Where is he? Let me find him. Just to be together. Only that. Oh God, oh God!

When she reached the station she saw that their own train was beside the little platform. She stood and scanned the windows anxiously. There, looking out of a window was the serious face of the passenger who had lost his fountain pen. She mounted the steps and hurried to their compartment. Charles was not there. The weekend review lay upon the seat where he had put it down. For some reason she clutched the paper and held it tightly crumpled in her hand. She made her way down the car—the train had begun to move—to where their fellow-passenger sat. She supported herself at his open compartment door.

Please, she said to the poet—for she felt somehow that he was a poet or kin to a poet—have you seen my husband? I have lost him.

I saw him, said the passenger, but he is not here now. He came back to the train and looked for you. He told me, She always likes water and she must have followed the river. So he took the far footbridge and followed down the stream. I am very sorry, said the passenger deliberately and with compassion.

Lucy turned and went back with great difficulty to the steps. It seemed as though she fell, and lay there, on the tawny prairie.

In the course of time, or of time and a time, all memory and strange pictures and confusion of human experience left her, and she died.

When those who were killed in the train wreck had at last recovered from the fatigues of death, it may be that some of them met again with a transfigured delight in that beautiful and happy country, with death past and over. We do not know.

SUCH
PEOPLE

Frederick Niven INDIAN WOMAN

The end of it all was that in the spring of 1858 young Angus
Munro (just nineteen then) took his woman—it was never
my wife; my woman it was—to the factor, her father and
mother with them, to have an entry made of his union with
Minota Red Shield in the company's books.

He did not ask himself insistently why that was all, why
he did not go to the mission and have a white man's marriage. He silenced the inquiry by telling himself that some
white men took their woman to wife without even the formality of an entry in the books, no more formality than the present
of a gun or a few horses to the father.

What was the depth of his love? What was the depth of
hers? Her eyes had clouded when, her promise to be his
woman given, he had said that they had better have it written down at the Fort; but she had not asked, instead, for a
prayer-book ceremony. Minota would have gone with him
even without that. He offered neither gun nor horses to old
Red Shield. She did not want that; her father, she said, did
not want that. That savage, Chief Red Shield, and his squaw
looked upon it as an honour to have their daughter wed to a
white man. Minota's mother was a sonsy woman, coming to
the age when those of her race have a tendency to broaden in
a very definite "middle-age spread," a sonsy woman with
genial eyes and a happy laugh. She was a Stony (which is to

say an Assiniboine of the west, a Rocky Mountain Assiniboine) whom Red Shield had met once at the House when both her tribe and his were camped closeby there to trade.

No—no gun, no horse for the girl but, not as the purchase price, merely as a gift—as the phrases went, *a prairie gift, a gift cut off, a gift in itself,* meaning not given in hope of any return or exchange—he presented Chief Red Shield (on the sober advice of Captain Buchanan) with a silk hat, a second-hand top hat, with a second-hand ostrich feather round it, for the trade-room at Rocky Mountain House had a queer miscellaneous stock of goods.

Within the palisades were two or three cabins from an earlier period, uninhabited, and in one of these, new-caulked in chinks between the logs, with a Franklin stove from the trade-room, Angus took up house with Minota, making the third at that time in the Fort with an Indian woman. He had moved, as it were, another step away from Loch Brendan. This log cabin was not like those at Red River, thatched, but had a roof of split cedar—*cedar shakes.*

Speedily his Cree talk improved. He discovered that there was not only pidgin-English but pidgin-Cree, and that many white people who imagined that they spoke Cree spoke only that. Minota unfolded for him the tenses of the verbs, and he learnt how pliant were the sentence formations, how full the vocabulary, and that often with one word could be conveyed what necessitated the use of half a dozen English to express. He came to respect *les sauvages* more and more.

As she taught him her language his mind often went back to Sabbath evenings in Scotland, Sabbath evenings at Red River, and the voice of his father (or of Fraser) would be with him again, reading in the Scriptures. For to the same simple, elemental, eternal things did the Crees go for imagery as the Hebrews. *The winter is past, the rain is over and gone, the flowers appear on the earth, the time of the singing birds is come and the voice of the turtle is heard in the land,* might have been one of Minota's songs. *Like as a hen gathering her chickens under her wings* was pure Cree, it struck him. When she taught him the sign language even more did he recall the voice of his father rolling out the Hebraic metaphor in the candlelight at Brendan. If one would signify in the sign language *I am happy,* so Minota showed him, one made the signs for *day* and *my heart,* meaning: *The day is in my heart.* There seemed to be no giving of orders in the talk of the hands. There was no *Do that,* no *Do not do that.* Instead there was *I think it good for you to do that,* or *I think it not good to do that.*

The names of the months, the moons, she told him, beginning with the moon before winter; the moon when the leaves fall; the moon when deer rut; the moon when deer shed their horns; the moon that is hard to bear; the moon when the buffalo cow's foetus is large; the moon of sore eyes (because of the sunlit snow then); the moon when the geese lay eggs; the moon of growing grass; the moon when strawberries ripen; the moon when the buffalo bulls are fat; the moon when the buffalo cows are in season; the moon of red plums. She showed him games, gambling games with little pegs, peeled wands; and one that was simply cup-and-ball Indian fashion.

Well though she could speak English she could read neither print nor script, nor did she know the Cree syllabics devised at Norway House by the Methodist missionary there, James Evans, for her people. Pictograph she could have translated, with the symbolic colourings among the figures represented, but not these symbols. The Woods Crees speedily learnt them but the Plains Crees, roving about in bands, buffalo hunters chiefly, had not the same need to leave missives behind as those who split up into small parties and families for their hunting and trapping in the Land of Little Sticks. The day was to come when Angus would regret that he had not taught her to write.

Like most white men he had looked upon *savages* as signifying something ceaselessly vindictive and treacherous. Red River had corrected that. Like most white men he had looked upon the religion of his people as the only true faith —and discarded that view while living with Minota. Very tenderly he came to think of her as she lost her shyness before him and revealed what lived behind these dark, deer-like eyes, behind that soft-moving and graceful exterior. She reminded him at times, by reason of her innocence, her naïveté, of his mother, and occasionally, with her heresies, of his father. She could not understand, for example, simple though it is to the civilized mind, how the company that sold firearms to the Crees was the same that sold firearms to the Blackfeet, Blackfeet and Cree being hereditary enemies. The shareholders in armament firms that gaily, in our days, manufacture lethal weapons for any who will buy she could not have understood.

There were moments when, in place of feeling that he had condescended, or descended, in this alliance, he felt that he was in the presence of something far superior. She was credulous, pathetically so, he thought often, but that credulity, he realized, was from her honesty and truthfulness. She told him of the Blackrobe that came to the Piegans southward with what was called the seventh day ceremonials.

"And one day," said she, "a Piegan went out to hunt, and the Blackrobe saw him going and called to him that it was the Rest Day. The Indian laughed at him and——" her eyes were solemn as she continued, "he was killed that day by a grizzly bear. So the Blackrobe stood up before all the people and told them that God had sent the bear to punish that man, and the next time he rang his bell and called that it was the Day of Rest he had a great gathering in his lodge for the ceremonial. Do you think," she ended, "that God would send a grizzly to kill the man for not resting on His Day?"

Angus shook his head slowly, saying nothing.

"After that Blackrobe left them he went through the Flathead country and there he baptized a great many, all under the water in a river. And after he had baptized them they went on a war party against the Crows and got many horses, without any being killed. The Blackfeet heard of it and waited for him to come back and got him to baptize a lot of them, and then they went out horse-stealing into the Gros Ventre country, and it was the most successful raid they had had for many snows."

She looked into his eyes.

"You think there is nothing in it?" she asked, trying to read his thoughts.

He was in a quandary similar to that of parents who have had formal religious upbringing and wonder, grown to years of questioning, whether they should bring their children up to a belief in all the old stories or not. She pressed the point.

"You think there is nothing in it?" she repeated.

"I do not know," he said.

It was clear to her he would not say any more than that.

Of her own people's medicine-men she had been rendered somewhat skeptical. They demanded much when they came to shake their rattles, beat their drums, blow their whistles and sing over sick people. She thought that many men and women could do more for illness with herbs and certain roots made into plaisters. Not but what she herself knew of a medicine-man who did a wonderful thing. He cut with a flint a crack in the side of an ailing woman, sucked some of the bad blood there, spat it forth, and lo, he had sucked a little frog from her inside.

"Did she recover?" Angus asked.

"Yes, she recovered at once, and her man gave the medicine-man ten ponies, for he was very fond of her."

She told him the medicine-men were paid chiefly with ponies and buffalo robes. But when anyone was dead their powers ended. The good Father Lacombe at Fort Edmonton had power even after men died. That beautiful black horse he rode he had received from a widow for getting the soul of her dead husband out of purgatory.

"All round us is mystery," said Minota.

Angus nodded slowly, listening.

"Yes," he replied.

"We have the same belief," she said.

There came to Rocky Mountain House news of the Sepoy Mutiny. What was it all about? they wondered. The first emotion was, no doubt, that whatever its cause, enemies of Britain, and rebels, must take their punishment. But soon there was sympathy at the Fort with the mutineers when they heard more. Living among a people prone to superstitions and respecting these if for no other reason than that the amenities might continue and Trade go well, the general view was that British arrogance had made a mess among the Sepoys. Angus, after hearing the talk, explained to Minota thus: Much as in the way that the Crees will eat dog, a dish that is abhorrent to the Blackfeet, it was *bad medicine* to some of the people away off there to touch pig and to others the cow was sacred. A new sort of rifle was issued to these people, the cartridges of which needed to be greased, and they had found out that the grease used was that of pig and cow. They objected, and their objection was unheeded—hence the Indian Mutiny.

"Could they not have let beaver fat, or some other fat, be used?" asked Minota. "That would have put the matter well."

"They would never think of that," replied Angus, deep in him a hatred of tyranny, of the arrogant.

He would talk to her of his early home on Loch Brendan, of how his people had been driven first from fruitful soil to barren soil by the salt-water edge, and then harried even from that. Her eyes had fear in them.

"There are some of my people," said she, "who think that the day will come when we will be treated that way by yours, but I cannot think so. I think there are many more good than bad white people, enough good to keep the bad from doing that to us. I think if they tried to my people would die fighting. Did your people fight?"

"Not where I was. Our medicine-men said we were to go and that if we offered resistance we would sizzle in hell."

"You do not believe in hell fire?"

"I—do—not!" he replied.

The year slipped past. There came the moon when the deer shed their horns, December, and preparations were made for Christmas Day (Big Sunday) with Oregon grape branches in place of holly. The doings of Big Sunday somewhat puzzled the innocence and directness of Angus's woman. According to an old usage of his Highland home he set a lit candle in the window on Christmas eve, and hearing the significance of that—a light for the dead to see—Minota took it much more seriously than he. All night she was hushed, thinking of, as she called them, *the shadows* seeing that signal—his father, his mother, his brother who had been drowned in the big water. Angus had difficulty in explaining to her that he was not sure if the shadows would really see. She thought they would—and they left it at that.

At the Fort the Nativity was celebrated in the usual way. *Braw claes* were worn as they had been worn on high-days and days of celebration all across that land, from the Great Lakes and from Hudson Bay to the Pacific, from the beginnings of the fur trade. A prospector from the mountains (there were many such in the land, much gold having been found the year before far west in the Cariboo Country, by white men who had wandered all that way from California) drank so much rum that he died of alcoholic poisoning next day. Minota was troubled over that.

"Did they get drunk," she asked, "at the last feast before He was nailed up on the cross?"

"I should hardly think so."

"My father once got drunk and spewed in the lodge and was very much ashamed. I think Jesus Christ would not like His friends to get drunk and be sick on their last feast together. It was a cruel way to kill Him," she added. "That is a sad story."

The new year came and the new year slipped along. The moon of the sore eyes was none too bad because of a warm wind (the Chinook) which wiped the snow away. The moon when the geese lay eggs came, geese and ducks honking over, driving their wedges into the north; and Minota sang:

> "The ice has broken in the rivers,
> The geese and the ducks fly over,
> All day—and even at night."

But with the spring she grew restless. Her people were moving out of their winter camps, setting up sweat lodges by the river sides and taking baths both wet and dry, as she explained—that is to say, steaming themselves in the low brush cages (the sweat lodges), with hot stones thrust in to them, and then either cooling outside wrapped in blankets (a dry bath) or plunging into the river afterwards (a wet bath).

The desire to move was agony to Minota. One morning

she asked Angus if he would object if she went on a visit to her people who were going from the woods to the plains soon.

"Why, no," said he.

She was troubled lest he should think she loved them more than she loved him, but after more parley and mutual assurances of devotion, and assurance of understanding from him, she took off her white woman's clothes, attired herself in the deerskin kirtle and leggings, wrapped herself in a blanket, and prepared to go. On the point of departure almost she remained. Her people, said she, would come into the Fort some day, and she could see them then. So it was his part to beg her to go and tell her he knew how she felt. As he spoke she looked long in his eyes, loving and troubled.

After she had gone, Tom Renwick must needs chaff him about his woman.

"Well, your woman has gone back to the blanket!" he said.

Angus felt he had either to take that remark as friendly jest, or to fell him. He wished that Tom's smile had been pleasanter as he spoke, to make the acceptance of his speech as a joke more easy.

"That's it," he answered, "that's it," and lightly laughed as one does when humouring another with whom for this or that reason he has to associate and would hide with amicably, though at heart he would fain see far.

Minota came back within a month, after many sweat-baths, smelling of sweet-grass which she carried in a little sack hanging from a thin raw-hide string round her neck.

In the moon when the strawberries ripen there was a suggestion by Buchanan that they might soon have finished all their work there and have to go to Fort Edmonton; and then arrived at Rocky Mountain House—Sam Douglas. He had been far beyond Edmonton into the mountains by the Howse Pass and Tête Jaune Cache Pass. He had made thorough survey of the foothill country between the ranges and Edmonton, wintering (for his first year) with Macaulay at Jasper House and (for his second) with Colin Fraser at St. Ann's. He was well content. There was coal "almost anywhere," said he. He was going back to *the Old Country* to "interest capital," and had come to Rocky Mountain House because he had been told there might be those there who could convoy him to Fort Brenton on the Missouri River.

No! Impossible! Attempts had been made to open a transport route that way—and failed. The Blackfeet to the south contested the passage of all. Even in mid-summer when they would be out on the plains none could risk that traverse. Angus could see, at that, that Douglas was perturbed. He evidently had no desire to cross the thousand miles to Fort Garry alone. The Crees were friendly, but there was always the risk of coming on some Blackfoot raiding party in their country. He smoothed a hand over his head, meditating. Angus laughed, surmising Douglas's cogitations.

"Yes," said he, "you have a fine, fair scalp-lock trophy there to deck the lodge of a Blackfoot on the South Saskatchewan!"

"That's just the trouble," said Sam, "that and the loneliness. I am not a man that can live alone. I've been alone enough of late, since last we parted. I was alone in the mountains till I heard voices there. Oh, man, man, I have heard the water-kelpies—and no use to assure me it was but a boulder rumbling down in the spate, or the freshets, as some of them say here, or the rise and fall of a wind that made the creeks cry loud and then hush. No, I canna thole the loneliness."

"When the voices of the dead are heard," explained Minota, "those who have been to the Catholic Mission make this sign," and she showed him. "The Methodist ones just pray without a sign. We pray and make the sign of *I pity you* to them, like this—or like this, *I bless you.*"

The grace of her motions held Douglas's eye with admiration, and then——

"Aye," said he. "Well, I think I would make all the signs." She agreed to that suggestion.

"The more signs the better," said she.

"Would you," began Sam, turning again to Angus, "think of accompanying me across the plains? In fact, I was wondering if you would come all the way with me, seeing the boat-building is nearly finished. Since seeing the coal fires here I have been thinking that evidence of a person living here would

be of great help. They might look upon me as a mere pro-
moter, ye ken, but if I had one of the men of the land wi'
me——"

There came to Angus what, in Minota's absence with her
people that spring, had often come to him. He saw, he heard,
he smelt the old land. Often, while she had been away, he
had looked at the Rockies to west and seen a peak there like
Ben Chattan that stands over the head of Loch Brendan.
The forests along the slopes he had, by half shutting his eyes,
turned into heather and moors. At Douglas's suggestion he
saw, in memory, the seaweed fringe of Scotland undulating to
the tides that pound in from the Atlantic, in his reverie saw
the silver reflection of the weaving gulls in the dark waters of
the loch. The wood smoke and coal smoke odours of the
Mountain House were changed to the smell of smouldering
peat.

"I would pay all expenses," said Douglas. "We could even
arrange something in the manner of a stipend. You have
conned your book"—(it was his father's phrase too,)—"and
you could be of great service secretarially, too, I have nae
doot." He always broadened his speech when he was engaged
upon a special pleading.

Angus turned to his woman.

"Minota," said he. "It is as you felt in the spring when
you had to go and see your people."

"I know it," she replied.

"If I went, what would you do till I came back?" he asked
her.

She did not answer at once and Sam, with a manner as of
stealth, clearing his throat, stepped to the door, looked out,
the girl's dark eyes gazing after him—reproachfully, it
seemed.

"I could arrange for you to have everything here you would
want while I was away," said Angus.

She shook her head.

"No. It would be easier with my people. Here——" she
hesitated.

Douglas went strolling out, his hands clasped behind his
back.

"Some of the white men while you were away," she began, then hesitated again. "I could wear a protection string," she said, "though with my people I think my conduct would be enough; no one would ever learn that I wore one. With the white men—some of them—especially on Big Sunday, or at the new year, well, they would not then respect even a protection string. No, I would go to my people until," she looked at him with doubt in her eyes, he thought, "you come back."

Angus wondered if among her people would be some, like Tom Renwick, who would jest at her that her white man would never return. That look of doubt on her face hurt him. He had an inspiration how to wipe it away. On the impulse he withdrew the collet-ring of his forebears and, taking her hand in his, put it on her third finger. He had compromised between a Blackrobe ceremony and the less ritualistic Indian ceremony of marriage—which was none at all, unless the delivery of a string of horses at the father's door be called ceremony. He had only had the union entered in the Company's books. If she had desired more, now did he abruptly atone.

She was surely his by the light in her eyes then. Had he never before realized how deep was her devotion—her fealty—he knew it at that moment.

"I will wait for you," she said, "till you come back from the country of your people. I will wait for you—with my people."

Howard O'Hagan THE TEPEE

I went into that valley, tributary to the Athabaska, to look at the timber. It was not big timber. Timber does not grow big on the Arctic slope of the Rockies. It was big enough, though, and clean, the branches beginning high up, tall, lean, black lodge-pole pines, with the hard look of hunger on them —hundreds of them, thousands of them, rank after rank by the river, column after column coming down to it.

I am a short man, thick in the calf and forearm, deep in the chest; among those trees, slim and aspiring, I felt smaller and shorter than ever. I walked so that scarcely a pine needle creaked under my hobnailed boots—carefully as a child who searches for God in an empty church I walked, wondering what lumber the timber would yield for poles and railroad ties.

That was the idea we had, my partner and I, to float logs down the river in the spring to the tie camp on the railroad. It was September and my partner had not come with me. He had gone into Edmonton to see his girl. Bruce had no notion of who his girl was, or where she lived, or if she had brown eyes or blue. The less of her he knew, the easier she could be found. He was to return in October, by which time I would have looked over the timber and picked a site for the cabin we were to build. We would take out the logs for poles and ties in the winter, skid them down to the river over the snow to be ready for the breakup in April.

25

I had been in the valley three weeks or more when I saw fresh, unshod hoof marks on the trail above my camp. My roan saddle horse and the two pack horses were shod. I knew the tracks of each of them. These tracks I found were strange. It was in the afternoon and I was riding my roan bareback, driving the other two horses before me along a ridge of willow which led into the timber and towards a meadow I had found two days before. Feed in that valley was scant. I had to drive my horses a mile before turning them loose to graze.

The number of strange tracks showed there were six or seven head of horses ahead of me—and only just ahead, for, dropping from the ridge and crossing a small stream, I saw water still seeping into those tracks along its edge. Probably, too, being unshod, they were Indian ponies. Bands of Cree Indians moved along that eastern slope of the Rockies, between the railroad and their hunting and trapping grounds at Grande Cache on the Smokey. I knew them, had worked with them on fall hunting parties, had visited with them in their tepees.

We were only a few yards from the timber when I saw the woman. She came out of it riding a small, wild-eyed pinto. She sat him close as a burr, holding with a high hand the lines of her rawhide bridle. She wore buckskin trousers, not fringed, but fitting her leg tightly, and a man's blue woollen shirt open at the throat.

She came onto me suddenly, with no warning at all, so that my roan jumped, hardened his muscles, as she swung off the trail to let me by. She appeared, passed, left me twisting on my horse, staring at her back, before a word had gone from my lips or my tongue had formed a word to greet her. She came so near that the breath of her passage brushed me and I felt hard earth on my shin, spattered from her horses' hoofs. Her long black hair was free, and flowed back until her forehead shone in the evening light. Her eyes, squeezed into slits against the sun, gave no sign of having seen me. Only her nostril, like a small autumn leaf fingered by the wind, flinched as she went by. She passed me as though I were a stump and she a woman riding on a fateful mission.

I watched her blue shirt vanish towards the river, her appearance in itself an act of disappearance. She would not go far. She had brought her horses upstream to loose them in the meadow. She was going back now to her camp and it would not be distant from my own. I saw her ford the river. The gleam of her shirt died before my eyes as she entered the forest on its other side.

A river ran between us. But a river could be forded. It could be crossed on foot on one of the many spruce trees the wind or winter snow had laid across it. The valley, which had been empty, which was wide enough to hold and to shield from each other's eyes, two hostile armies, now with one woman in it was crowded. Our horses fed from the same poor crop of grass. The air I breathed was shared between us. And there would be others, too. There would be her husband. Or many others. She might be camped in a tepee with her family. It was that which I set out to learn. Not that, at the moment, I especially desired to. I had enough on my hands to keep me occupied. But she had come close to me, to spatter hard mud on my leg. She had, so to speak, touched me, and I had lived long enough to know that the one escape from woman was to go towards her.

I dismounted, slipped the bridle from my roan, lashed the lines across his long, smooth haunches, sent him and the two pack horses with him, racing up the trail. I returned quickly to my tent in its clearing. There the tea water was boiling on the tin heater stove, but instead of preparing supper, I took down my hunting glasses. I climbed the small rise separating me from a view down the river. From behind some willows I observed the tepee. It was less than half a mile away, a brown, up-ended funnel.

Firewood was stacked neatly beside the closed flap of hairy moose hide which served for its door. Inside, a fire was burning and grey smoke puffed slowly from the cluster of poles at the tepee's tip. Pitched low and broad in the Indian style, it gave me the impression of having pushed itself up out of the ground while my back was turned. I had, during the day, heard no sounds of arrival, no whinnying of horses, no shouts, no chopping, none of the strife of making camp in the wilderness. It had simply sprouted, as a mushroom would sprout, and seemed as much a part of its surroundings.

The tepee was on a point in the river, commanding a view upstream and down. When a man stepped out its door, he held the valley in his vision. The dark forest opened two arms about it and beside it grew a young poplar tree, its leaves already scorched yellow by the frost. Above, a mountain rose. It rose in ledges and great hanging cliffs. It thrust itself urgently up out of the earth and was still shaking from its shoulders rocks and struggling timber, and white cascades of water whose rumble reached me where I stood.

I took my glasses from their case, sat down, putting my elbows on my knees, holding the glasses steady to examine more closely what was before me. At first the yellow poplar tree filled the lens, flaring like flame from the soil. Leaves dropped about its roots shed a glow upon the ground.

Dusk was in the valley, but the sun, topping the western range, held the tepee, the poplar tree, the narrow point of shingle jutting into the river, in a pool of light.

The woman's pinto horse was tethered downstream on a goose-grass flat. As I watched, the haired flap of the tepee was pushed back and the woman emerged. She had tied her hair with a red ribbon. She began to carry firewood inside. The glasses brought her near to me so that when she bent over I saw the hang of her brown, heavy breasts. I saw the pebbles pressing against her moccasined feet and, glinting in the sun's light, what might have been a gold ring on her finger. Once coming out, she straightened and looked up the valley, into my eyes as it were, and she seemed so close to me that I expected her lips to open and speak my name. I slipped lower until I was lying flat on the ground. When I raised myself again, she was gone. The flap of the tepee closed. Smoke swirled more heavily from the tepee top.

I lay there until all the stars were out, until, one by one, they vanished behind a storm cloud rising in the east. I waited. I supposed her man would be about. But I had seen no one but her. I heard no voices. In the tepee for a while the fire burned and between the black lines of the poles a woman's form was outlined on the canvas, grotesque and slow-moving, as if a giant-winged bat, half stupefied with smoke, fluttered between the walls. The fire inside died down.

I heard the river throbbing in the dark. At first a gentle flow of streaming waters. Then an endless advance and an endless receding of ripples over shallows and the beat of the conflict filled the night, fell against my ears so that I no longer knew if it was the river I listened to, or the throb of my heart, or the throb of a woman's heart, lying like mine close against the ground and echoing from the stolid rock of mountains.

I crossed the river on a spruce log and walked towards the tepee, at first no more than a ghostly blur in my vision. No stir came from within it. No sputter of a half-extinguished fire. I thought, "Perhaps she has gone."

When I came closer I smelled dried hides and old wood smoke and grease burned on the fire. I knocked the back of my hand against the flap of moose hide.

"Hello!" I said. I paused. I hit the flap again. "Hello! Hello!" I said. "May I come in?" The wind ran through the dry leaves of the poplar tree beside me.

I reached my hand in front of me and my fingers ran against coarse new wood. I pulled them back, startled at the palpable shape of an opened doorway. I put forth my hand again. I shoved it in and knocked a piece of wood, from about my shoulder level, into the tepee, rolling it into the coals of the fire.

A wall of wood prevented my entrance. She had piled firewood from inside before the doorway and fortified herself against me.

I commenced to unbuild what she had done. One by one I took those slim pieces of wood and laid them outside by the wall of the tepee. I worked with care, with precision, feeling myself involved with her in a deep scheme of silence. Not one of those pieces of wood should fall from my hands to disturb the spell. And while I worked I heard the mutter of the river, closer, and closer behind me, until at last in the dark my feet felt wet with its water.

I removed the last stick of firewood. I entered. The flap dropped behind me. I turned, fumbled with its cord, but my fingers, studded with splinters, failed to tie the knot to hold it to its pole.

The coal still gleamed red in the fireplace, made of a circle of stones on the ground, and rain tapped on the canvas above me. After the rain would come the snow. Soon snow would lie over all the mountains.

I sat down by the wall of the tepee. I leaned over, stirred with a piece of kindling the coals of the fire, until a flame leaped up, lighted the woman's face where she waited under a robe of grey marmot skins across from me. For some time she did not speak.

Finally she said, "You were slow. I have been waiting."

I told her I had taken my time. For one thing I hadn't been sure that she was alone.

"Oh, yes," she said, "I am alone."

She reached up and touched a fringed shirt of caribou hide, worn almost black from use, which hung from the stub of a branch on the slanted pole above her hide.

"He has gone down to the railroad. Maybe he will come back tomorrow, and maybe not until one or two days later," she said.

"Who's gone down to the railroad? Who's coming back?" I asked.

"Felix," she said. "My husband—with a pack horse for some flour and tea. Then he will look for a place with better feed. He always takes good care of the horses." She drew in her breath. "He is a very strong man," she said. "I have seen him lift a horse on his shoulders."

A mountain cayuse weighs six or seven hundred pounds. The feat was one to be regarded with respect.

"He sounds like quite a fellow," I said. "Does he do that very often?"

She shook her head. "No, not very often. Just when he feels good and there are people around. . . . But I knew before he came back, you would be down to see me."

"You did, eh?"

"You were behind the willow bushes, watching me," she said. "The sun flashed on your hunting glasses."

"Then why did you pile your firewood in the door of the tepee?"

She turned her head and looked up into the night through the funnel above us, where the wind whined through the tapering tepee poles. She put the back of her hand across her mouth and dug her teeth into its flesh. Her cheeks creased and hid her eyes in their folds. She tossed on the bed and giggled, lying on her back, moving her black head of hair from side to side. Her knees rose up under the robe of skins. They spread and came together, then spread again.

One of her legs escaped from its covering, knee and thigh rising, brown and smooth and glistening as with oil in the firelight, round and firm, commanding as the shape of my desire.

The edge of the marmot robe fell between her knees. I saw that she lay naked.

As I went towards her, around the edge of the fire, I thought of her working in the narrow tepee, piling those sticks of wood by the door, one by one above the other, and realized, what I had sensed before, that it had been no more than a gesture, the gesture of a woman who in another place would have hid her face behind a shawl, have drawn the curtain across her window, have said that she was busy and would I come around another day.

Later I learned her name was Marie Lapierre. Marie and Felix Lapierre—names not without their brave connotations. They recalled the days when French voyageurs and Scottish traders of the great fur companies travelled through the country with flags and sound of harness bells, with drums and bugles, and mixed their blood with that of the native Cree Indians, as if so to atone for the ingenious rascality of their trading.

Marie and her husband had arrived, only the day before, from somewhere close to the Peace River in the North. The season was now too advanced for them to return with their horses and they would stay in the valley for the winter. After all it mattered little where they were, so long as the woods gave cover for game and fur. They were vagrant as a puff of wind and came and went for no more apparent reason. They were not seeking life, nor fleeing from it, nor interested in building a larger tepee than their neighbours. They lived by what they had, and not, in the white man's way, for what they lacked. The future did not intrude into their present, but their lifelong present endured into the future. They had rifles, traps and horses, and the skill to use them.

The next day I settled on a cabin site for my partner and myself. I cleared a bit of ground and cut a few logs for the cabin. Snow had fallen lightly during the early morning and, coming back to my tent, I saw Marie's small footprints among my own. Before entering the tent, she had carefully circled it, as though stalking a piece of game. She had taken a few pounds of flour from the bag hung from the ridge-pole at the back and emptied about half of my tea from its tin.

Two nights later Felix Lapierre returned and came to see me.

It was late, after eight o'clock, when I saw his portentous form against my tent. The moon was out and the canvas above me so drenched with light that it seemed, when he touched it, it would commence to drip and the drops to hiss upon the low, round stove, glowing and panting with its heat in a corner by the door.

Felix threw back the flap and, awaiting no invitation, seated himself on a grub-box just inside. He took papers and tobacco from his vest pocket and set to rolling himself a smoke. I watched him from where I lay on my blankets, head upon my packsack. He was a tall man, broad-shouldered. A stronger man than I was. His black hair, its tips appearing silvered in the moonlight filtering through the canvas, hung down over his eyes. From behind it, his face looked out—the driven, hollow-cheeked face of a man who has travelled far through the mountains.

Then he dropped his eyes to his task, where his long fingers weaved and coaxed until suddenly from among them the cigarette emerged, completed as by sleight of hand.

I lifted myself and sat with my arms buckled over my knees.

"Well," I said, "you got through all right."

"Sure, I always get through," he said. He spoke to me in

English—English learned in some mission school, at the foot of a black-robed priest. He spoke with caution, correctly, and in monotone.

After a minute, he asked, "She has been around, eh?"

"Who?"

"Her down there at the tepee. My wife."

I told him I had seen her three or four days before when I was putting my horses up into the meadow. "She rode by me," I said. This, at least, was literal truth.

Felix said, "Usually she stops to talk."

A puff of smoke from his mouth spread along the canvas wall. From under it he stared at me coldly and, as it were, slowly—the gaze of an ancestry foreign to my own, of blood and hunger, hunt and knife, of forest and hill, stream and lake. I wondered how much he knew, and if he did not know, what he would do when he did know. Marie—she needed to tell him nothing. The marks of my hobnailed boots, in three nights of going and coming in the snow about the tepee, would speak a logic of their own. There was, further, my remark about his "getting through." It had hardly passed unnoticed.

For what must have been a minute he stared at me. We did not speak. The stillness was a third self in the tent. Through it our eyes became locked in a contest of wills. Then I glanced quickly, as with stealth, to my left. There, within arm reach of Felix, my rifle in its scabbard rested against a pile of horse blankets. Ashes fell and settled in the stove.

His eyes followed mine. He dragged deeply on his cigarette, took it from his mouth. As he exhaled, the smoke spread along the canvas wall, lay for a while long and flat beneath the shadow of the pine tree branch moving forth and back in the night wind. I waited for what he would say.

"You have found good feed for your horses?" he asked me quietly, studying his cigarette stub, flicking it from the end of his thumb against the stove. It was a conventional question.

"Pretty good feed," I said.

He half rose, as if about to leave, thought better of it, and settled himself again on the grub-box.

He said, "She told me." Then after a pause, he added, "About you and her." It seemed he smiled, or perhaps it was a mere curl of his lip, but I caught a glimpse of white teeth like a light that glimmered and dimmed in his mouth. Marie had told him—Marie, who with her careful speech, her tossing head, stayed with me less as a woman than as a place where I had been.

I failed to answer him, not knowing what answer to give.

He stood up. I rose quickly to stand beside him. In the narrow tent we were so close that our chests almost touched, and feeling his breath warm upon my forehead I was aware of fear, wondering what he might do. He was a strong man. He had lifted a horse on his back.

He held out his hand. "I am not mad," he said.

We shook hands. His was the wide, sinewy hand of the horseman. Taking me by surprise, he tightened his grip around my knuckles, bore upon them with a pressure I could not resist. The joints cracked. I lowered my elbow, bent my knee to relieve the pain rising as sound to my lips.

"No," he said, without relaxing his grip. "I am not mad. This winter I will camp here or up the valley where the feed is better for my horses. I will be away a lot of the time on my trapping line. You and my wife . . . it will be all right, see?"

Then he let go, turned, ducked out the tent flap and was gone, having shown me the contempt of his strength and the disdain of his charity. From the doorway I watched him go along the ridge and down it, wading through the willows that in the moonlight rose around him, around his legs, his hips, his shoulders until at last, when against the gleaming river his head dropped from view, it was as though he had walked down among the roots, under the faded grasses, into the earth to which he was closer neighbour than I.

Jon Whyte

PETER POND, HIS TRUE CONFESSION

The document presented herewith for the first time may be a late writing of Peter Pond, the Connecticut Yankee who has long intrigued historians of Canada's fur trade.

Pond's mercurial disposition, his strength of character, and his dreadful spelling create an image of willfulness, inquisitiveness and straightforward nastiness. He may be a noble villain in our history; he is probably also a whitewashed blackguard. Nevertheless, as Harold Innis has demonstrated, Pond's discovery of the Methye Portage, a traversible link between the Saskatchewan and Mackenzie River systems, was a major contribution to the geographic possibility of Canada *a mari usque ad mare.*

Of Pond's overweening desire to excel in the struggle of aggrandizement and survival that marked relations between the Nor-Westers (Canadians) and the Hudson's Bay Company (largely Englishmen) in the years following the American Revolution, little need here be said. His manner is clear from the one duel that is authenticated, about which he himself writes:

35

Beaing Exposed to all Sorts of Cumpaney it Hapend
that a parson who was in trade himSilf to Abuese
me in a Shamefull manner Knowing that if I Resont
he Could Shake me in Peacis at th same tim Sup-
poseing that I Dair not Sea him at the Pints ar at
Leas I would not But the Abuse was two grate we
met the Nex Morning Eairley and Dischargd Pistels
in which the Pore fellow was unfortennt

It has long been suspected that Pond was responsible for
the deaths of Jean Etienne Waden in the Saskatchewan and
John Ross in the Athabasca country. It may be that relatives
suppressed the brutal ending, if brutal it was, of Pond's
famous "Narrative" (see *Five Fur Traders of the Northwest,*
Minnesota Historical Society, 1933), and it may be that the
fragment which follows is that possibly suppressed ending.
It does seem to capture the energy and spirit of a man vital
to an understanding of Canadian history; almost American
though he may be.

A. Harrison Abre,
Head, Department of History,
Kameisto-waysit University, Saskatchewan.

. . . new and Haveing strivd Mitely wyth them it is nott My
Intenton to conetend with thm Dead. Wadenne was a Man
ilPrepaird to liv in the Wids of the Ston Naton [country of
the Assiniboine or Stone Indians] Week and Yillow and short
of Injinuitee that sarv to kip a Man aLiv he Moar inClinde
to lissin to his Wif whan he otter hav Lissent two himSil
Pairhaips I should heav Brott mySel Doun Riverr to tryl at
Montryl if I feld thar wair deMand for sutch a Pearans But
reasin thare war none for the Gud Maddam and Wif to
Wadenn dirs not speik of wat discours and a Bues I was
ofendd by It is eneff I hav bin soarely Malined by thoze hoo
New mea in the Arathpeskow Cuntrey [here the manuscript is
torn] must be denide my Dinity a woumen hwo thot two spiek
hilye of me whan hair husbund was knot abowt
    She wair a gud Woumen Hevvy a Bout the middul But furm

and Fleshd like a sheBare in the fall and the onely wummen
uthr then Indeen a Bowt in ye Cuntrarey   Shee twict and
[ms. again torn] ranklt ye Foart and fund hair buzzynis at
owr Cabben nair two the dusk of ege dai and Temptaton
groweing the Bettir of me I fownde ocashin to inveit the
Ladie in Litel nowing wat to egxpect when Wadein had gon
to find wethr the Riverrs wair aFlud in March and Sum
daze Laiter wen Waiden ritarnd Shee wud naithr Luk my
way or Gnollig [acknowledge] my Presens till shay met me
won dai by the Crike and askd cud I fined Som Waye of
getting Rid of hair Housbin an Axiden sed she so nun could
gess othrways and thenne Shee tost hur hare coily as a skule-
girl and winkte to me and Disaperde

I hadde by this tym [ie. about 1781-82] Venturd to ye
Athabaskiwia taretores and was ingagd delvupping the
rootes thar to inlarg and istablish owr biznes ye wch Wadenn
was opozd two and Whil we wair sposed to wirk togithair
I fownde his litl goles and wiek Ambition tuff to stummick
He wair Happie two daipend on wat we cannued from Lacla
Rong and wair not dizirus of increesing the traid   Of al the
menne I New in my muskrat daze he wair the porest in
Speerit   So it Hapend that Spurd bye my Desairs I fownde
mySil inClind to think moar Particewlarily of the laydees
boalde rekwesst and maid my Planes to a Firm owre Traide
and lae my Worees to Rest

Thair wair no Problim in gitting Wadinne to vizit me of
an Eaving four matirs thare wair ful Menny two kepe us
tauking lait into the nit   Wee Dranke fully of a cag of Rumm
a Bowt and spok at lainth of the poor suits of the Sumr
to com   Whan tempirs Flaird apon sum Mattir I hav now
forgot contending mysil to argew with my Clark Toussin wo
was Prisint we dru Pistells and sot to have the a Fair owt
thenne and Thar   Toosane two drunk to holde his pistole
steddy swange and branDishd the barl in al Dire actions
fewming so mutch I thot in eror he might agily [actually]
shut Mee i hidd a moamint

He showted and cride to his Godde I should nott be a
courde and thate I should faice him like a manne and thenne
he lett owt a Blasst that shuk the loggs and toar the chingking

owt letting the coald air in Tussain I showted foar Gods
saik and min man Keepe yoar Peice   But it was two lait foar
Wadding inter Posd himSilf and toque the fyer to dispell the
arme from Twosen ful in ye nee   I ment to hitt him hire

No suner hadd ye secinct blasst rang owt thain Birchy
[Bertier] anithr clairk caim running in and seaing the blud
aloavr [all over] the floar rust to Wadenns sied asting himm
wu hadd doan this to ye wch Waiden replide My Frind I am
ded   Thenne it wair thayt Maddim Wadin who Secritly had
hald hair bidn in the rume A jacint caim in scrimming and
weaping laik hair owne deth was a Pon hir come foarting
hair hasbin crine vilaneys at Me for having murdrid hir
mann and how would she liv and al the tyme wayting for Him
to Dye   We beried himm the neg day

In the daiz subSegwent to his daeth Shee did not takk to
ma a Tall and than I be Gain to bea a Fird for it caim a Parint
she tuk me all to Blaim for ye Murdir of hair HasBin and
would no Pairt herSil be raisponsibyl it baying as it wair
my ConSarn ownly and non of hair   Yule pai for yer Yll
tempir Peter Pond she would go abowt mutring and sun aftr
she touk it ap on hairsel to live the plais at ye tym of the
brak upp and retarn to Mantryal by the furst cannue donstrim
in ye Spryng and laide a Charg a gayn me   For mye pairt I
new wye her mainer changd for it wair clair shee was wursr
for hair instigaton off the Creim and new I wair no gayn for
suner I would be up the Rivr not haild bak by Waddaine
than hold a Bowte by a Wommin and ye con Fines of ye
Forrt [ms. torn]

. . . depairtd for Arobaskia But ye Poax [smallpox] wair
so badd in that Plais as wayerevair in ye planes that ye Trad
was not Gud and hwat beevr and muskrat we Obtand could
not sooFise for ye End Ever [endeavour]   This wair an awl
ful tyme the Indyanns feevrd and crine as the Dis eeas feld
them lik pin treas in a forst fier and Thay would not a Proach
owre cannews for thai bleevd we brout the sikness a Pon them
I sawe at that tym Peepl thro themSelfs in the coled waitr
of the laikes till thay wair so num thay could not Fele or
Moav and drownded be Cowse thier Harts seezd or thai frozd
And othrs wair hoo Brennt themsailves with Brans from there

Fiers hue casst in to ye Fyers and scremt all daye and nait oar withrd bnethe thair Robes   Wee caim acros a Bandnd [abandoned] villig wair ownly the Old wair lefft Dyine and a Thurst a Pon peeple werevr fleeing the skurg and smelt the Stinke of the dying evvywair I hoap Hell hoalds no toar Mints laik these pore Devls undargoan

We wintrd in ye Aro Baski that yair meating at that tim sum of the Savidges hu traveld with Hern to the Copr Rivr ten yairs befour Devillipping a traid to Hudsins Baye from the plaise whar ye Riverrs runn noward and [ms. torn] . . . now ingiged in Drect Combaditon with ye Engelsh and by mye indaivors we hade fownd ruots to Mantrayal from Arabiska to Kikischewon [Saskatchewan River] and thens to Grand portag   All I larnd was of moar valu than ye fir that yair and . . . [ms. torn] I was praypard to ventr doan to ye Sante Laorens to fais watevr Charg hade ben laied a Gain foar wan wee gott to Lak La Rong we haird that Waddens wief sed I should dey fore my part in hair hasbens Deth

At Graind Portag the neckst yair sartin men detarmind to aprahand me Butt my relaton of the mattair two thar satisfacton thai sayd I should Nott have too apir in Thare Cusstidy But I went doan ennywai to por Chase Suplies and fined the news   My nollig of the new cowntree I was toled wass of moar Importans than my passed Involvmnt in a strai Deth in the Distant Land wair Nuthing would be non that the Wind and ye Sno could not covir   I nevr Came to Triall

Thar was mutch Takk of the traide of consarn to ye rivvers in the Norwest and of wair the Prospicts would be Besst to wch I aded only that wch I could safely tail for I nue then I wanted a whil yett in the Westren Lainds and if I sayd two much I mit yett cum to trail   I droppt to Milford [Connecticut] to se my gud wif who hadde not seen in tin or eleavn Yairs   I war hoam for onely won dai or to whan shee sed we musst to Chuarch for she sed It would doo my sole Gud   I hadd not atindd a Sarvis in alle the wile I had bin gon   In spit of this I thot to see hair moar and ye childern whan I retird from the furrs

I hadde pripard a Mappe shown the Lanes I hadd explord Butt had not giv it Two any of the traid in Canaday   No

mann at that tim undrstud the Continet as I daid for I hadd
not bin fair from the Pesific ye lasst Wintre I spennd in the
Arapescha   It beaing at the mossed fiev or six daiz gurny
[journey] from owr Fort and allso the Root from ye Laik
Athrapeskow noarth to Herrin [Hearne's] See   Wat I hade
larned risintly in Cannade I could not plais aPon the maip
that I have discovrd the Sors of Couks Rivver and nue the
Waye from see to Sae   It war my pleashe to prisint two the
congers [Congress] of mye callanes the mapp I hade prpard
for watevr yews thay mite mak of it   It hade bin my be leef
that ye Amarkins would pursoo the welth of the farre landes
desirous of Traid wyth ye Frinch wh wair now cutt off from
ye Newe Wurl by ye Anglis

It was not my ink Linaton two sitt abow the Hows whan
thar ware moar Impurtnt devilipmints afut   My frinds and
cuntreymen havving gan thru the resint uprizing and I tost
in wyth ye Canaydeens I fownd I no loongr hade a hoam

I indeverd to fined saport fore my Traid in the Norwes
in Conn [ecticut] or Amarycai travling evven to Bostin But
siport was Nott forth coming So I retirnd to Montrayal and
mett with Magil and praypard for an ither Cumpny   Itt ware
a tarn of fait that I who hadd born armes agaynst the frinsh
shud git my asistans in that difited toun and Nott from my
feloe Colinists

W. O. Mitchell HERCULES SALVAGE

Precisely out of the city's centre, the Devonian Tower thrust its stiff arrogance fully a third higher than the tallest office buildings near it. From the broad cylindrical base the concave sides soared six hundred feet so that its glass revolving restaurant, boutiques, gift shop and broadcasting station CSFA, floated above traffic smog. Unique. Pretty nearly the only six-hundred-foot concrete erection in the British Commonwealth. With a May basket balanced on its tip. North America. And with a red oil derrick to spear the last fifty feet. The world.

Two blocks south of the tower, and an hour earlier in the spring afternoon, Archie Nicotine had stood before the Ladies and Escorts entrance of the Empress Hotel Beer Parlour, in his hip pocket forty-eight dollars he had been paid by Moon for cutting poles. Forty-eight dollars—rings for the half-ton truck—sixteen—rebuilt carburetor from Hercules Salvage—maybe eighteen—thirty—thirty-two—maybe fifteen over—ten anyway. Forty-eight. He could feel it almost warm against his left cheek—in his pocket there. Also he could use a beer. Way a man's tongue stuck to the roof of his mouth and his throat got stiff for the tickle of beer and the earth taste of beer!

A Hutterite passed him, turned into the Men's door; funny for them to be so religious, but you still saw a lot of black

41

pail hats in any beer parlour all the same. Another man pushed past. Denim smock—flat boots—farmer. Forty-eight —rings sixteen—carburetor eighteen. Twenty—fifteen dollars of beer was one hell of a lot of beer. Beer never hurt him— never hurt anybody. Let everyone suck it down and not a drop for him!

Red luck right from the start. There was the difference. How you were born was the whole situation. You either got born a horse or a fool-hen or a link. Red or white. His luck he got dropped in the corner of a reservation bull field, laced into moss in a yo-kay-bo, weaned on an elk bone. Tag around the tent or cabin—beans and bannock and tea when it was there—roll in or out when you felt like it—colt roping or grabbing hold of girls from thirteen on and Onward Christian Soldiers washed in the blood and all the white religions said no beer at all. With their flower-pot hats and their long noses and twang, Latter Day Saints said it loudest. Mormon missionaries could ride and they could rope all right—got the coal oil onto their fire over beer—even tea and coffee—coke. So that washed up the LDS. How sweet the name of Jesus and the taste of beer—beer—beer—beer—the salt taste of beer cooling down your hot throat!

He caught a smell sweet as wolf willow from the woman who pushed past him and into the Ladies and Escorts door, her perfume winning over the bloom of beer—beer—beer— buh-beer—buh-beer—buhbeer! It beat in him like a chicken dance drum!

Rings and rebuilt carburetor after!

Three bottles later he sat at the table in the middle of the slop and clink and bung and banter of the Ladies and Escorts room. He'd bought the first round for Norman and Gloria Catface and himself. Then the young man with the brush cut and acne all over his face like purple yarn bits, had joined their table, bought two rounds. His entire interest was for Gloria.

Five years ago, when she had been seventeen, she had rightfully won the zircon diadem of Miss North-west Fish and Game of 1954. Her blackberry eyes were large and lovely; she was dark madonna beautiful still. Just as she poured the rest of her bottle into her glass, there was a signal look from Norman, a suggesting movement of his head; it seemed to include the young man. Norman's hair was a black aster centred in the middle of his very round head, falling in thin points above the tilted seeds of his eyes. His face had the oval grace of his sister's, but also fixed derision because of the old knife-scar slicing up from one corner of his mouth to a vanishing point just below and in front of his right ear. He did not know, had never known, just who had given his face extra mouth value. In the middle of Stampede Week, the same year that his sister had won her contest, he had lost a drunken one. He'd passed out in the lantern dusk of the chuck-wagon horse barn; before all life could bleed from the severed facial artery, Gloria had found him lying in the sweet alfalfa. Twenty-nine stitches. One half Cheshire cat. It was not a completely frightening face. He and Gloria were almost inseparable, not only because they were brother and sister, but because he pimped for her as well. From time to time whenever need was great.

Gloria set down her empty glass. She stood up. "I got to go."

"Sit down," the young man said. "Buy you another."

Gloria shook her head and turned away.

"Hey, Taffy, over here!" Norman called. The young man stood up. "Hold on for us, Taffy," Norman said. "You said you was buyin' . . ."

"I changed my mind."

"I already called him."

"You can pay him too. I bought two." The door was closing behind Gloria.

"Archie and me could use another . . ."

But the young man had left the table.

Norman stared at the empty glasses and bottles. "You gonna buy a couple?"

"No," Archie said.

"I can't. We didn't even eat too good this week."

"Haven't you sold her much?"

"They stopped her four times. How you fixed?"

"I can't help you."

"Next time he takes her in . . . and me." He looked up to the waiter, who stood now with a tray holding beer bottles. "Never mind."

"If you're all through, don't hold up the table."

"I'm just talkin' with my friend. We may change our mind later." To Archie he said, "Next time they'll lay a charge against her . . . me. It's spring."

Archie stood up, put his chair back. "I can't help you any."

"I just thought you might have something."

"It's for rings and a rebuilt carburetor." Surprise, very near consternation, showed on Norman's face.

"Jeses! You got enough for rings and a carburetor!"

"Hey-up."

"Hey, Taffy—a couple here! Hold on." Norman hooked Archie's belt with his hand, the other raised high with four fingers extended.

"I'm not buyin', Norman . . . let go."

Norman jumped up. "You can't leave when you still got...."

"Let go my arm, Norman. Sit down. I'm goin' to Hercules Salvage now."

"Sure . . . sure." Norman put his arm over Archie's shoulder. "Let's . . ."

Archie shoved Norman away, but Norman turned and grabbed at him again. Archie pushed Norman's chest, so that the chair caught the backs of Norman's knees. Norman sat down.

"All right . . . none of that!" It was Taffy—but without a tray this time.

"Alone," Archie said. He left Norman.

In the Men's all the china stalls were full of backs and spraddled legs. He went out to walk down the narrow back hallway, then opened a door to the bright alleyway. He walked along the brick back of the hotel building till he came to the parking lot. There he paused in the shelter of a truck to relieve himself. It was half ton too. But green.

He felt the hand on his shoulder almost as soon as he heard. "What the hell you doin'!" He turned his head—carefully, for there had been three bottles. Behind the policeman was a black and white car with the red gum drop of its light on top.

"I just had three and that is the whole situation," Archie said. A policeman partner sat behind the steering wheel, the motor still running.

"Better come with us."

"Just a minute," Archie said.

In front of the Pioneer War Surplus, one block down from the Empress Hotel, one block the other way from the Devonian Tower, Gloria Catface faced the young man with the pitted face, who had caught up with her, then asked her the question. She answered him. "Ten."

"Ten!"

"That's right."

"Hell . . ."

"If you got it."

"I got it."

"All right."

"Yeah . . . but most the time smoked gash is free."

"Crabs free too?"

"Now look . . . no sense gettin' unfriendly about it!"

"You started it."

"I just said ten seems kind of high."

"It's been higher . . . lots."

"It couldn't!"

"Sure as hell could . . . when I was Miss Fish and Game . . ."

"You aren't now and ten's steep!"

"Uh-huh."

"Five."

"Ten."

"For all night?"

"Middle the afternoon—two o'clock," Gloria explained to him.

"Then ten is too goddam . . ."

"Ten is for once. You want more? Buy supper—beer— then all night?" He considered. She said, "Twenty-seven fifty."

"Hell, no!"

"You don't want all night. Maybe you don't want once either."

"It's just that ten . . ."

"Go on over to Ninth east where they got the head in the window."

"Huh?"

"Two bucks."

"Nobody gets screwed for two bucks in this town . . ."

"The gipsy girl there . . ."

"I don't want some money blessed."

"They charge five for that . . . but for two she'll let you take a look at it."

"Hell, I need more'n a peek at . . ."

"All right. Ten bucks. Make up your mind."

"I did."

"Then let's have it."

"Don't be funny. Where's your place?"

"Couple blocks."

"Hotel? Which one?"

"Just a room . . . like a room. Let's have the ten."

"Look, you may of been Miss Fish and Game an' I'm game but I'm no fish. Ten's the deal . . . when we get there . . . after."

She shrugged and turned and walked away from him. He caught up with her in front of the Brenda Kaye Savoir Faire Model School and Agency. "Complete Courses in Modelling and Self Improvement . . . Fashion Shows . . . Hostessing . . . Television Promotion . . . Advertising." Through the spring sunshine they walked on together past the Devonian Tower.

In Studio B of CSFA-TV, "high atop the Devonian Tower," the Reverend Heally Richards unbuckled his belt and pulled down his fly zipper enough to drop the mike cord inside his trousers. He wiggled it down and along his leg, retrieved it from his pant cuff. This extra care was necessary because when he worked he liked to pace back and forth; a black cord showing would flaw his white totality. The Burning Bush Hour pulpit was white as well.

On discreet rubber casters, the camera glided sideways, then wheeled and aimed on the evangelist. The camera man with shoulders hunched and an eye at the lens, said "Three minutes, Reverend," and then softly, "Carl, come here." He stepped aside when the other man came over. "Take a look."

Carl leaned down to look at a miniature, white Heally Richards before a white pulpit, with white Bible in his dark hand, white crest of hair above his dark face.

"Hit you too, Carl?"

"Yeah—yeah." Eye still at the lens, Carl emitted a light, incredulous laugh. He whispered, "Looks just like a goddam photograph negative!"

Gloria Catface and her young customer passed the Liberty Café, then the high fenced space to the corner. They turned and walked along the great sign: BLACKFOOT BUILDING SUPPLIES, with its huge black foot, the giant and boney toe pivotting on the rest of the foot, activated by a small motor behind the sign, moving slowly up and down with its rabbit-eared bandage bow. SPECIALIZING IN RUMPUS AND GAME ROOMS. . . . POLYNESIAN IS IN EVERYONE'S BUDGET.

She led the young man round the end of the sign, then down the narrow space between it and the south wall of the Liberty Café.

"Room! Call this a room!" He looked at the space canopied by two orange war surplus parachutes, sheltered under them, a nest of Arctic down sleeping bags, two Coleman gas camp stoves, a rank of olive coloured canisters.

"We're campin' here," Gloria said.

"Shee-yit!"

"You Blood?" the Constable at the receiving desk said to Archie Nicotine.

"No."

"Sarcee?"

"No."

"Blackfoot?"

"No."

The Constable laid down his pencil, looked at Archie. "Sure as hell aren't Hooterite."

"You're correct," Archie said. "Stony."

"Thanks, Chief."

"I'm not."

"Friendly form of address."

"It isn't."

"All right. Honest mistake then."

"I'm a duly elected band councillor. This time is wrong. I just had three in the Empress and that's the whole situation."

"That isn't the problem. In this case it was haulin' out that smoked John Donacker of yours in public."

"How much does that one generally cost?"

"With a kind magistrate maybe ten and costs. Empty your pockets please."

"That's easy," Archie said as he began to comply. "I got forty-five—still have enough left over for . . ."

"Keep goin'," the Corporal said. Then, "What's the matter, Chief?"

"I been robbed out of my rings and rebuilt carburetor!"

"You can lay your own charge later. Right now . . ."

"I got to make a phone call."

"Sure—you can call your agency . . ."

"Reverend Heally Richards."

"We are all sinners—we're humans—we're mortals an' therefore we are sinners. Congratulations. Now—I did not say hopeless sinners. No—I did not. For Jeeesusss Christ was cruceeeefied for us—poor—mortal—sinners. Those spikes were hammered through His Dear Palms for us sinners. Sin. Ay word—sin. Ay old-fashioned word, isn't it. It is not ay in-word—today—not with wife-swappin' parties—not when our young are rottin' their bodies an' minds with dope. Sin is not in. I should say—the *word*—sin—is not in. But sin itself is in! Sin is very, very popular! Don't you tell me it isn't! My friends, sin is today—more popular than it ever was—more popular than it was when Jeesuss of Galilee healed the sick —more popular than when the Caesars held sway! Oh—I know—the word sin can bring gales of laughter from our leaders and from our legislators and from our modern clergy and from our teachers and from our professors in their tickley tossel swingin' mortar boards! Sin is taught today . . . kindergarten sin . . . grammar school sin . . . college sin . . . graduate

sin . . . sweet sin-uh . . . rotten delicious sin-uh . . . deeelightful
sin-uh . . . !

"Easy—easy!" Gloria said. "Take your time! You wanta tear
my pants! Godammit—it isn't gonna go away!"

"Now then—Hell is another unpopular word today! You don't
like it—so just forget it—then it'll go away! Hell will go away!
There just simply isn't any Hell anymore! You don't want
there to be a Hell, so just you close your eyes and it will
vanish! You don't want Hell—nobody wants Hell—so—there
—is—no Hell. Isn't that dandy? No Hell—no sin—well then,
I guess I can just go right out and loot and riot and smoke pot
and rape my neighbour's wife and teach sin and preach sin
and legislate sin and encourage sodomy between consentin'
adults and butcher unborn children—because there is no Hell
and there is no sin!"

"That'll be thirteen ninety-five," Gloria Catface said to the
young man with the acne-ravaged face.
"Our deal was ten."
"I said it before."
"What's different now?"
"You tore my pants . . . that's what's different now!"
He turned away from her. "So just clip another pair next
time you're in Ladies' Underwear . . ."
"I paid! Three-ninety-five just last week!"
"Don't bother showin' me the receipt." He had begun to
walk away. "Our deal was ten."
He was halfway to the alley when she called after him, "All
right . . . you're right! Maybe ten was too much! No charge at
all for rabbits!"
He kept on walking.
"Your face may heal up," she called after him, "when
you're older!"
That stopped him. He wheeled, took several quick steps
towards her before he saw the knife in her hand. Then he
stopped again. He stared uncertainly at her, at the knife.
"Tight ass!"

He grinned with sudden relief. "You sure as hell wasn't, Miss Fish an' Game." He was still grinning as he turned to leave.

". . . tell that to Jacob gruntin' and sweatin' and strivin' to lock a full Nelson round the neck of the angel of the Lord! Don't tell Lot's wife because she can't hear you, but you tell Abraham about the God that spoke to him and said to him, 'Abraham hold back on that knife there!' Tell that to Jacob and his brother Esau eatin' his bread an' pottage of lentils! Tell it to all the children of Israel fleein' over the wet sand floppin' an' gaspin' with needle fish an' mullet—with prisoner fish an' sting-rays an' whip-a-rays all wonderin' what happened to their Red Sea the Lord dried up under them! Tell it to Daniel an' all those prowlin' lions! Pull open that fiery furnace door and tell the news to Mischak, Shadrack and Abednego. Tell Jeesussss—tell Him!"

The Reverend Healy Richards stopped, turned full to the camera, which slowly dollied to close-up on his face.

"Jeesuss," Healy Richards said, "I got a bereavin' message for you—Your Daddy is dead."

The red light on Camera One blinked off. The evangelist unclipped the mike from the vee of his white vest, unbuckled his belt and pulled down the zipper on his fly part way, then wiggled the mike down his white pant leg, extricated it from his white pant cuff.

Freddy, the floorman, said, "Reverend Richards—I got a telephone message for you—city police—somebody name of Archie Nicotine."

"I'd like to pay this man's fine," Reverend Healy Richards said to the red-headed corporal with the pale eye. "Nicotine."

The corporal pulled a sheet over to himself. "His name, Mr. Nicotine?"

"It is Nicotine. I'm the Reverend Healy Richards."

"Sure." The finger moved slowly down the page.

"Archie Nicotine," Archie said.

"Sure—sure—ah—yeah—ten and costs—and the charge—indec . . ."

"We already know that," Archie said quickly.

The evangelist dropped a twenty-dollar bill on the desk, turned, began to walk towards the outer door.

He was halfway there when the corporal called after him, "Hold on. You got change coming."

"How much?" Archie said.

"Two-fifty."

Archie glanced at the broad white back at the door now. "You're new on here. I come frequent. Just put it down for a credit on my account."

"I don't keep any—I can't put . . ."

The door had closed behind the evangelist.

"Sometime I may want to fart when I'm in this civilized city."

LAND

Wallace Stegner   CARRION SPRING

The moment she came to the door she could smell it, not really rotten and not coming from any particular direction, but sweetish, faintly sickening, sourceless, filling the whole air the way a river's water can taste of weeds—the carrion smell of a whole country breathing out in the first warmth across hundreds of square miles.

Three days of chinook had uncovered everything that had been under snow since November. The yard lay discoloured and ugly, gray ashpile, rusted cans, spilled lignite, bones. The clinkers that had given them winter footing to privy and stable lay in raised gray wavers across the mud; the strung lariats they had used for lifelines in blizzardy weather had dried out and sagged to the ground. Muck was knee deep down in the corrals by the sod-roofed stable, the whitewashed logs were yellowed at the corners from dogs lifting their legs against them. Sunken drifts around the hay yard were a reminder of how many times the boys had had to shovel out there to keep the calves from walking into the stacks across the top of them. Across the wan and dishevelled yard the willows were bare, and beyond them the floodplain hill was brown. The sky was roiled with gray cloud.

Matted, filthy, lifeless, littered, the place of her winter imprisonment was exposed, ugly enough to put gooseflesh up her backbone, and with the carrion smell over all of it. It was

54

like a bad and disgusting wound, infected wire cut or proud
flesh or the gangrene of frostbite, with the bandage off. With
her packed trunk and her telescope bag and two loaded grain
sacks behind her, she stood in the door waiting for Ray to
come with the buckboard, and she was sick to be gone.

Yet when he did come, with the boys all slopping through
the mud behind him, and they threw her trunk and telescope
and bags into the buckboard and tied the tarp down and there
was nothing left to do but go, she faced them with a sudden,
desolating desire to cry. She laughed, and caught her lower
lip under her teeth and bit down hard on it, and went around
to shake one hoof-like hand after the other, staring into each
face in turn and seeing in each something that made it all the
harder to say something easy: Goodbye. Red-bearded, black-
bearded, gray-bristled, clean-shaven (for her?), two of them
with puckered sunken scars on the cheekbones, all of them
seedy, matted-haired, weathered and cracked as old lumber
left out for years, they looked sheepish, or sober, or cheerful,
and said things like, 'Well, Molly, have you a nice trip, now,"
or "See you in Malta maybe." They had been her family. She
had looked after them, fed them, patched their clothes, un-
ravelled old socks to knit them new ones, cut their hair, lanced
their boils, tended their wounds. Now it was like the gathered-
in family parting at the graveside after someone's funeral.

She had begun quite openly to cry. She pulled her cheeks
down, opened her mouth, dabbed at her eyes with her
knuckles, laughed. "Now you all take care," she said. "And
come see us, you hear? Jesse? Rusty? Slip? Buck, when you
come I'll fix you a better patch on your pants than that one.
Goodbye, Panguingue, you were the best man I had on the
coal scuttle. Don't you forget me. Little Horn, I'm *sorry* we
ran out of pie fixings. When you come to Malta I'll make you
a peach pie a yard across."

She could not have helped speaking their names, as if to
name them were to insure their permanence. But she knew
that though she might see them, or most of them, when Ray
brought the drive in to Malta in July, these were friends who
would soon be lost for good. They had already got the word:
sweep the range and sell everything—steers, bulls, calves,

cows—for whatever it would bring. Put a For Sale sign on the ranch, or simply abandon it. The country had rubbed its lesson in. Like half the outfits between the Milk and the CPR, the T-Down was quitting. As for her, she was quitting first.

She saw Ray slumping, glooming down from the buckboard seat with the reins wrapped around one gloved hand. Dude and Dinger were hipshot in the harness. As Rusty and Little Horn gave Molly a hand up to climb the wheel, Dude raised his tail and dropped an oaty bundle of dung on the singletree, but she did not even bother to make a face or say something provoked and joking. She was watching Ray, looking right into his gray eyes and his sombre dark face and seeing all at once what the winter of disaster had done to him. His cheek, like Ed's and Rusty's, was puckered with frost scars; frost had nibbled at the lobes of his ears; she could see the strain of bone-cracking labour, the bitterness of failure, in the lines from his nose to the corners of his mouth. Making room for her, he did not smile. With her back momentarily to the others, speaking only for him, she said through her tight teeth, "Let's git!"

Promptly—he was always prompt and ready—he plucked whip from whipsocket. The tip snapped on Dinger's haunch, the lurch of the buggy threw her so that she could cling and not have to turn to reveal her face. "Goodbye!" she cried, more into the collar of her mackinaw than to them, throwing the words over her shoulder like a flower or a coin, and tossed her left hand in the air and shook it. The single burst of their voices chopped off into silence. She heard only the grate of the tires in gravel; beside her the wheel poured yellow drip. She concentrated on it, fighting her lips that wanted to blubber.

"This could be bad for a minute," Ray said. She looked up. Obediently she clamped thumb and finger over her nose. To their right, filling half of Frying Pan Flat, was the boneyard, two acres of carcasses scattered where the boys had dragged them after skinning them out when they found them dead in the brush. It did not seem that off there they could smell, for the chinook was blowing out in light airs from the west. But when she let go her nose she smelled it rich and rotten, as if it rolled upwind the way water runs upstream in an eddy.

Beside her Ray was silent. The horses were trotting now in the soft sand of the patrol trail. On both sides the willows were gnawed down to stubs, broken and mouthed and gummed off by starving cattle. There was floodwater in the low spots, and the sound of running water under the drifts of every side coulee.

Once Ray said, "Harry Willis says a railroad survey's coming right up the Whitemud valley this summer. S'pose that'll mean homesteaders in here, maybe a town."

"I s'pose."

"Make it a little easier when you run out of prunes, if there was a store at Whitemud."

"Well," she said, "we won't be here to run out," and then immediately, as she caught a whiff that gagged her, "Pee-you! Hurry up!"

Ray did not touch up the team. "What for?" he said. "To get to the next one quicker?"

She appraised the surliness of his voice, and judged that some of it was general disgust and some of it was aimed at her. But what did he want? Every time she made a suggestion of some outfit around Malta or Chinook where he might get a job he humped his back and looked impenetrable. What *did* he want? To come back here and take another licking? When there wasn't even a cattle outfit left, except maybe the little ones like the Z-X and the Lazy-S? And where one winter could kill you, as it had just killed the T-Down? She felt like yelling at him, "Look at your face. Look at your hands—you can't open them even halfway, for calluses. For what? Maybe three thousand cattle left out of ten thousand, and them skin and bone. Why wouldn't I be glad to get out? Who *cares* if there's a store at Whitemud? You're just like an old bulldog with his teeth clinched in somebody's behind, and it'll take a pry-bar to make you unclinch!" She said nothing; she forced herself to breathe evenly the tainted air.

Floodwater forced them out of the bottoms and up onto the second floodplain. Below them Molly saw the river astonishingly wide, pushing across willow bars and pressing deep into the cutbank bends. She could hear it, when the wheels went quietly—a hushed roar like wind. Cattle were balloonily afloat in the brush where they had died. She saw a brindle longhorn waltz around the deep water of a bend with his legs in the air, and farther on a whiteface that stranded momentarily among flooded rosebushes, and rotated free, and stranded again.

Their bench was cut by a side coulee, and they tipped and rocked down, the rumps of the horses back against the dashboard, Ray's hand on the brake, the shoes screeching mud from the tires. There was brush in the bottom, and stained drifts still unmelted. Their wheels sank in slush, she hung to the seat rail, they righted, the lines cracked across the muscling rumps as the team dug in and lifted them out of the cold, snowbank breath of the draw. Then abruptly, in a hollow on the right, dead eyeballs stared at her from between spraddled legs, horns and tails and legs were tangled in a starved mass of bone and hide not yet, in that cold bottom, puffing with the gases of decay. They must have been three deep— piled on one another, she supposed, while drifting before some one of the winter's blizzards.

A little later, accosted by a stench so overpowering that she breathed it in deeply as if to sample the worst, she looked to the left and saw a longhorn, its belly blown up ready to pop, hanging by neck and horns from a tight clump of alder and black birch where the snow had left him. She saw the wind make catspaws in the heavy winter hair.

"Jesus," Ray said, "when you find 'em in *trees!*"

His boots, worn and whitened by many wettings, were braced against the dash. From the corner of her eye Molly could see his glove, its wrist-lace open. His wrist looked as wide as a doubletree, the sleeve of his Levi jacket was tight with forearm. The very sight of his strength made her hate the tone of defeat and outrage in his voice. Yet she appraised the tone cunningly, for she did not want him somehow butting his bullheaded way back into it. There were better things they could do than break their backs and hearts in a hopeless country a hundred miles from anywhere.

With narrowed eyes, caught in an instant vision, she saw the lilac bushes by the front porch of her father's house, heard the screen door bang behind her brother Charley (screen doors!), saw people passing, women in dresses, maybe all going to a picnic or a ballgame down in the park by the river. She passed the front of McCabe's General Store and through the window saw the counters and shelves: dried apples, dried peaches, prunes, tapioca, Karo syrup, everything they had done without for six weeks; and new white-stitched overalls, yellow horsehide gloves, varnished axe handles, barrels of flour and bags of sugar, shiny boots and workshoes, counters full of calico and flowered voile and crepe de chine and curtain net, whole stacks of flypaper stuck sheet to sheet, jars of peppermints and striped candy and horehound...She giggled.

"What?" Ray's neck and shoulders were so stiff with muscle that he all but creaked when he turned his head.

"I was just thinking. Remember the night I used our last sugar to make that batch of divinity, and dragged all the boys in after bedtime to eat it?"

"Kind of saved the day," Ray said. "Took the edge off ever'body."

"Kind of left us starving for sugar, too. I can still see them picking up those little bitty dabs of fluff with their fingers like tongs, and stuffing them in among their whiskers and making faces, *yum yum,* and wondering what on earth had got into me."

"Nothing got into you. You was just fed up. We all was."

"Remember when Slip picked up that pincushion I was tatting a cover for, and I got sort of hysterical and asked him if he knew what it was? Remember what he said? 'It a doll piller, ain't it, Molly?' I thought I'd die."

She shook her head angrily. Ray was looking sideward at her in alarm. She turned her face away and stared down across the water that spread nearly a half-mile wide in the bottoms. Dirty foam and brush circled in the eddies. She saw a slab cave from an almost drowned cutbank and sink bubbling. From where they drove, between the water and the outer slope that rolled up to the high prairie, the Cypress Hills made a snow-patched, tree-darkened dome across the west. The wind came off them mild as milk. Poisoned! she told herself, and dragged it deep into her lungs.

She was aware again of Ray's gray eye. "Hard on you," he said. For some reason he made her mad, as if he were accusing her of bellyaching. She felt how all the time they bumped and rolled along the shoulder of the river valley they had this antagonism between them like a snarl of barbed wire. You couldn't reach out anywhere without running into it. Did he blame her for going home, or what? What did he expect her to do, come along with a whole bunch of men on that round-up, spend six or eight weeks in pants out among the carcasses? And then what?

A high, sharp whicker came downwind. The team chuckled and surged into their collars. Looking ahead, she saw a horse —picketed or hobbled—and a man who leaned on something —rifle?—watching them. "Young Schulz," Ray said, and then here came the dogs, four big bony hounds. The team began to dance. Ray held them in tight and whistled the buggywhip in the air when the hounds got too close.

Young Schulz, Molly saw as they got closer, was leaning on a shovel, not a rifle. He had dug a trench two or three feet deep and ten or twelve long. He dragged a bare forearm across his forehead under a muskrat cap: a sullen-faced boy with eyes like dirty ice. She supposed he had been living all alone since his father had disappeared. Somehow he made her want to turn her lips inside out. A wild man, worse than an Indian. She had not liked his father and she did not like him.

The hounds below her were sniffing at the wheels and testing the air up in her direction, wagging slow tails. "What've you got, wolves?" Ray asked.

"Coyotes."

"Old ones down there?"

"One, anyway. Chased her in."

"Find any escape holes?"

"One. Plugged it."

"You get 'em the hard way," Ray said. "How've you been doing on wolves?"

The boy said a hard four-letter word, slanted his eyes sideward at Molly in something less than apology—acknowledgment, maybe. "The dogs ain't worth a damn without Puma to kill for 'em. Since he got killed they just catch up with a wolf and run alongside him. I dug out a couple dens."

With his thumb and finger he worked at a pimple under his jaw. The soft wind blew over them, the taint of carrion only a suspicion, perhaps imaginary. The roily sky had begun to break up in patches of blue. Beside her Molly felt the solid bump of Ray's shoulder as he twisted to cast a weather eye upward. "Going to be a real spring day," he said. To young Schulz he said, "How far in that burrow go, d'you s'pose?"

"Wouldn't ordinarily go more'n twenty feet or so."

"Need any help diggin'?"

The Schulz boy spat. "Never turn it down."

"Ray . . ." Molly said. But she stopped when she saw his face.

"Been a long time since I helped dig out a coyote," he said. He watched her as if waiting for a reaction. "Been a long time since I did anything for *fun.*"

"Oh, go ahead!" she said. "Long as we don't miss that train."

"I guess we can make Maple Creek by noon tomorrow. And you ain't in such a hurry you have to be there sooner, are you?"

She had never heard so much edge in his voice. He looked at her as if he hated her. She turned so as to keep the Schulz boy from seeing her face, and for just a second she and Ray were all alone up there, eye to eye. She laid a hand on his knee. "I don't know what it is," she said. "Honestly I don't. But you better work it off."

Young Schulz went back to his digging while Ray unhitched and looped the tugs and tied the horses to the wheels. Then Ray took the shovel and began to fill the air with clods. He moved more dirt than the Fresno scrapers she had seen grading the railroad back home; he worked as if exercising his muscles after a long layoff, as if spring had fired him up and set him to running. The soil was sandy and came out in clean brown shovelfuls. The hounds lay back out of range and watched. Ray did not look toward Molly, or say anything to Schulz. He just moved dirt as if dirt was his worst enemy. After a few minutes Molly pulled the buffalo robe

out of the buckboard and spread it on the drying prairie. By
that time it was getting close to noon. The sun was full out;
she felt it warm on her face and hands.

The coyote hole ran along about three feet underground.
From where she sat she could look right up the trench, and
see the black opening at the bottom when the shovel broke
into it. She could imagine the coyotes crammed back at the
end of their burrow, hearing the noises and seeing the growing
light as their death dug toward them, and no way out, nothing
to do but wait.

Young Schulz took the shovel and Ray stood out of the
trench, blowing. The violent work seemed to have made him
more cheerful. He said to Schulz, when the boy stooped and
reached a gloved hand up the hole, "She comes out of there
in a hurry she'll run right up your sleeve."

Schulz grunted and resumed his digging. The untroubled
sun went over, hanging almost overhead, and an untroubled
wind stirred the old grass. Over where the last terrace of the
floodplain rolled up to the prairie the first gopher of the season
sat up and looked them over. A dog moved, and he disappeared with a flirt of his tail. Ray was rolling up his sleeves,
whistling loosely between his teeth. His forearms were white,
his hands blackened and cracked as the charred ends of sticks.
His eyes touched her—speculatively, she thought. She smiled,
making a forgiving, kissing motion of her mouth, but all he
did in reply was work his eyebrows, and she could not tell
what he was thinking.

Young Schulz was poking up the hole with the shovel
handle. Crouching in the trench in his muskrat cap, he looked
like some digging animal; she half expected him to put his
nose into the hole and sniff and then start throwing dirt out
between his hind legs.

Then in a single convulsion of movement Schulz rolled
sideward. A naked-gummed thing of teeth and gray fur shot
into sight, scrambled at the edge, and disappeared in a pin-
wheel of dogs. Molly leaped to the heads of the horses, rearing
and wall-eyed and yanking the light buckboard sideways, and
with a hand in each bridle steadied them down. Schulz, she
saw, was circling the dogs with the shotgun, but the dogs had

already done it for him. The roaring and snapping tailed off. Schulz kicked the dogs away and with one quick flash and circle and rip tore the scalp and ears off the coyote. It lay there wet, mauled, bloody, with its pink skull bare—a little dog brutally murdered. One of the hounds came up, sniffed with its neck stretched out, sank its teeth in the coyote's shoulder, dragged it a foot or two.

"Ray . . ." Molly said.

He did not hear her; he was blocking the burrow with the shovel blade while Schulz went over to his horse. The boy came back with a red willow stick seven or eight feet long, forked like a small slingshot at the end. Ray pulled away the shovel and Schulz twisted in the hole with the forked end of the stick. A hard grunt came out of him, and he backed up, pulling the stick from the hole. At the last moment he yanked hard, and a squirm of gray broke free and rolled and was pounced on by the hounds.

This time Ray kicked them aside. He picked up the pup by the tail, and it hung down and kicked its hind legs a little. Schulz was down again, probing the burrow, twisting, probing again, twisting hard.

Again he backed up, working the entangled pup out carefully until it was in the open, and then landing it over his head like a sucker from the river. The pup landed within three feet of the buckboard wheel, and floundered, stunned. In an instant Molly dropped down and smothered it in clothes, hands, arms. There was snarling in her very ear, she was bumped hard, she heard Ray yelling, and then he had her on her feet. From his face, she thought he was going to hit her. Against her middle, held by the scruff and grappled with the other arm, the pup snapped and slavered with needle teeth. She felt the sting of bites on her hands and wrists. The dogs ringed her, ready to jump, kept off by Ray's kicking boot.

"God a'mighty," Ray said, "you want to get yourself killed?"

"I didn't want the dogs to get him."

"No. What are you going to do with him? We'll just have to knock him in the head."

"I'm going to keep him."

"In Malta?"

"Why not?"

He let go his clutch on her arm. "He'll be a cute pup for a month and then he'll be a chicken thief and then somebody'll shoot him."

"At least he'll have a little bit of a life. Get *away,* you dirty, murdering . . . !" She cradled the thudding little body along one arm under her mackinaw, keeping her hold in the scruff with her right hand, and turned herself away from the crowding hounds. "I'm going to tame him," she said. "I don't care what you say."

"Scalp's worth three dollars," Schulz said from the edge of the ditch.

Ray kicked the dogs back. His eyes, ordinarily so cool and gray, looked hot. The digging and the excitement did not seem to have taken the edge off whatever was eating him. He said, "Look, maybe you have to go back home to your folks, but you don't have to take a menagerie along. What are you going to do with him on the train?"

But now it was out. He did blame her. "You think I'm running out on you," she said.

"I just said you can't take a menagerie back to town."

"You said *maybe* I had to go home. Where else would I go? You're going to be on roundup till July. The ranch is going to be sold. Where on earth *would* I go but home?"

"You don't have to stay. You don't have to make me go back to ridin' for some outfit for twenty a month and found."

His dark, battered, scarred face told her to be quiet. Dipping far down in the tight pocket of his Levis he brought up his snap purse and took from it three silver dollars. Young Schulz, who had been probing the den to see if anything else was there, climbed out of the ditch and took the money in his dirty chapped hand. He gave Molly one cool look with his dirty-ice eyes, scalped the dead pup, picked up shotgun and twisting-stick and shovel, tied them behind the saddle, mounted, whistled at the dogs, and with barely a nod rode off toward the northeastern flank of the Hills. The hounds fanned out ahead of him, running loose and easy. In the silence their departure left behind, a clod broke and rolled into the ditch.

A gopher piped somewhere. The wind moved quiet as breathing in the grass.

Molly drew a breath that caught a little—a sigh for their quarrelling, for whatever bothered him so deeply that he gloomed and grumped and asked something impossible of her —but when she spoke she spoke around it. "No thanks for your digging."

"He don't know much about living with people."

"He's like everything else in this country, wild and dirty and thankless."

In a minute she would really start feeling sorry for herself. But why not? Did it ever occur to him that since November, when they came across the prairie on their honeymoon in this same buckboard, she had seen exactly one woman, for one day and a night? Did he have any idea how she had felt, a bride of three weeks, when he went out with the boys on late fall roundup and was gone ten days, through three different blizzards, while she stayed home and didn't know whether he was dead or alive?

"If you mean me," Ray said, "I may be wild and I'm probably dirty, but I ain't thankless, honey." Shamed, she opened her mouth to reply, but he was already turning away to rummage up a strap and a piece of whang leather to make a collar and leash for her pup.

"Are you hungry?" she said to his shoulders.

"Any time."

"I put up some sandwiches."

"O.K."

"Oh, Ray," she said, "let's not crab at each other! Sure I'm glad we're getting out. Is that so awful? I hate to see you killing yourself bucking this *hopeless* country. But does that mean we have to fight? I thought maybe we could have a picnic like we had coming in, back on that slough where the ducks kept coming in and landing on the ice and skidding end over end. I don't know, it don't hardly seem we've laughed since."

"Well," he said, "it ain't been much of a laughing winter, for a fact." He had cut down a cheekstrap and tied a rawhide thong to it. Carefully she brought out the pup and he buckled the collar around its neck, but when she set it on the ground it backed up to the end of the thong, cringing and showing its naked gums, so that she picked it up again and let it dig along her arm, hunting darkness under her mackinaw.

"Shall we eat here?" Ray said. "Kind of a lot of chewed-up coyote around."

"Let's go up on the bench."

"Want to tie the pup in the buckboard?"

"I'll take him. I want to get him used to me."

"O.K.," he said. "You go on. I'll tie a nosebag on these nags and bring the robe and the lunchbox."

She walked slowly, not to scare the pup, until she was up the little bench and onto the prairie. From up there she could see not only the Cypress Hills across the west, but the valley of the Whitemud breaking out of them, and a big slough, spread by floodwater, and watercourses going both ways out of it, marked by thin willows. Just where the Whitemud emerged from the hills were three white dots—the Mountie post, probably, or the Lazy-S, or both. The sun was surprisingly warm, until she counted up and found that it was May 8. It ought to be warm.

Ray brought the buffalo robe and spread it, and she sat down. One-handed because she had the thong of the leash wrapped around her palm, she doled out sandwiches and hard-boiled eggs. Ray popped a whole egg in his mouth, and chewing, pointed. "There goes the South Fork of the Swift Current, out of the slough. The one this side, that little scraggle of willows you can see, empties into the Whitemud. That slough sits right on the divide and runs both ways. You don't see that very often."

She appraised his tone. He was feeling better. For that matter, so was she. It had turned out a beautiful day, with big fairweather clouds coasting over. She saw the flooded river bottoms below them, on the left, darken to winter and then sweep bright back to spring again while she could have counted no more than ten. As she moved, the coyote pup clawed and scrambled against her side, and she said, wrinkling her nose in her Freckleface smile, "If he started eating me, I wonder if I could keep from yelling? Did you ever read that

story about the boy that hid the fox under his clothes and the
fox started eating a hole in him and the boy never batted an
eye, just let himself be chewed?"

"No, I never heard that one," Ray said. "Don't seem very
likely, does it?" He lay back and turned his face, shut-eyed,
into the sun. Now and then his hand rose to feed bites of
sandwich into his mouth.

"The pup's quieter," Molly said. "I bet he'll tame. I wonder
if he'd eat a piece of sandwich?"

"Leave him be for a while, I would."

"I guess."

His hand reached over blindly and she put another sandwich into its pincer claws. Chewing, he came up on an elbow;
his eyes opened, he stared a long time down into the flooded
bottoms and then across toward the slough and the hills.
"Soon as the sun comes out, she don't look like the same
country, does she?"

Molly said nothing. She watched his nostrils fan in and out
as he sniffed. "No smell up here, do you think?" he said. But
she heard the direction he was groping in, the regret that could
lead, if they did not watch out, to some renewed and futile
hope, and she said tartly, "I can smell it, all right."

He sighed. He lay back and closed his eyes. After about
three minutes he said, "Boy, what a day, though. I won't get
through on the patrol trail goin' back. The ice'll be breakin'
up before tonight, at this rate. Did you hear it crackin' and
poppin' a minute ago?"

"I didn't hear it."

"Listen."

They were still. She heard the soft wind move in the prairie
wool, and beyond it, filling the background, the hushed and
hollow noise of the floodwater, sigh of drowned willows, suck
of whirlpools, splash and guggle as cutbanks caved, and the
steady push and swash and ripple of moving water. Into the
soft rush of sound came a muffled report like a tree cracking,
or a shot a long way off. "Is that it?" she said. "Is that the ice
letting loose?"

"Stick around till tomorrow and you'll see that whole chan-
nel full of ice."

Another shadow from one of the big flat-bottomed clouds chilled across them and passed. Ray said into the air, "Harry Willis said this railroad survey will go right through to Medicine Hat. Open up this whole country."

Now she sat very still, stroking the soft bulge of the pup through the cloth.

"Probably mean a town at Whitemud."

"You told me."

"With a store that close we couldn't get quite so snowed in as we did this winter."

Molly said nothing, because she dared not. They were a couple that, like the slough spread out northwest of them, flowed two ways, he to this wild range, she back to town and friends and family. And yet in the thaw of one bright day, their last together up here north of the Line, she teetered. She feared the softening that could start her draining toward his side.

"Molly," Ray said, and made her look at him. She saw him as the country and the winter had left him, weathered and scarred. His eyes were gray and steady, marksman's eyes.

She made a wordless sound that sounded in her own ears almost a groan. "You want awful bad to stay," she said.

His tong fingers plucked a strand of grass, he bit it between his teeth, his head went slowly up and down.

"But how?" she said. "Do you want to strike the Z-X for a job, or the Lazy-S, or somebody? Do you want to open a store in Whitemud for when the railroad comes through, or what?"

"Haven't you figured that out yet?" he said. "Kept waitin' for you to see it. I want to buy the T-Down."

"You *what?*"

"I want us to buy the T-Down and make her go."

She felt that she went all to pieces. She laughed. She threw her hands around so that the pup scrambled and clawed at her side. "Ray Henry," she said, "you're crazy as a bedbug. Even if it made any sense, which it doesn't, where'd we get the money?"

"Borrow it."

"Go in debt to stay up *here?*"

"Molly," he said, and she heard the slow gather of determination in his voice, "when else could we pick up cattle for twenty dollars a head with sucking calves thrown in? When else could we get a whole ranch layout for a few hundred bucks? That Goodnight herd we were running was the best herd in Canada, maybe anywhere. This spring roundup we could take our pick of what's left, including bulls, and put our brand on 'em and turn 'em into summer range and drive everything else to Malta. We wouldn't want more than three-four hundred head. We can swing that much, and we can cut enough hay to bring that many through even a winter like this last one."

She watched him; her eyes groped and slipped. He said, "We're never goin' to have another chance like this as long as we live. This country's goin' to change; there'll be home-steaders in here soon as the railroad comes. Towns, stores, what you've been missin'. Women folks. And we can sit out here on the Whitemud with good hay land and good range and just make this God darned country holler uncle."

"How long?" she said. "How long have you been thinking this way?"

"Since we got John's letter."

"You never said anything."

"I kept waitin' for you to get the idea yourself. But you were hell bent to get out."

She escaped his eyes, looked down, shifted carefully to accommodate the wild thing snuggled in darkness at her waist, and as she moved, her foot scuffed up the scalloped felt edge of the buffalo robe. By her toe was a half-crushed crocus, palely lavender, a thing so tender and unbelievable in the waste of brown grass under the great pour of sky that she cried out, "Why, good land, look at that!"—taking advantage of it both as discovery and as diversion.

"Crocus?" Ray said, bending. "Don't take long, once the snow goes."

It lay in her palm, a thing lucky as a four-leaf clover, and as if it had had some effect in clearing her sight, Molly looked down the south-facing slope and saw it tinged with faintest green. She put the crocus to her nose, but smelled only a mild freshness, an odour no more showy than that of grass. But maybe enough to cover the scent of carrion.

Her eyes came up and found Ray's watching her steadily. "You think we could do it," she said.

"I know we could."

"It's a funny time to start talking that way, when I'm on my way out."

"You don't have to stay out."

Sniffing the crocus, she put her right hand under the mackinaw until her fingers touched fur. The pup stiffened but did not turn or snap. She moved her fingers softly along his back, willing him tame. For some reason she felt as if she might burst out crying.

"Haven't you got any ambition to be the first white woman in five hundred miles?" Ray said.

Past and below him, three or four miles off, she saw the great slough darken under a driving cloud shadow and then brighten to a blue that danced with little wind-whipped waves. She wondered what happened to the ice in a slough like that, whether it went on down the little flooded creeks to add to the jams in the Whitemud and Swift Current, or whether it just rose to the surface and gradually melted there. She didn't suppose it would be spectacular like the break-up in the river.

"Mumma and Dad would think we'd lost our minds," she said. "How much would we have to borrow?"

"Maybe six or eight thousand."

"Oh Lord!" She contemplated the sum, a burden of debt heavy enough to pin them down for life. She remembered the winter, six months of unremitting slavery and imprisonment. She lifted the crocus and laid it against Ray's dark scarred cheek.

"You should never wear lavender," she said, and giggled at the very idea, and let her eyes come up to his and stared at him, sick and scared. "All right," she said. "If it's what you want."

Frederick Philip Grove THE FIRST DAY OF AN IMMIGRANT

About six miles west of the little prairie town of Balfour, twelve miles south of another little town called Minor, hard on the bank of the Muddy River which gurgles darkly and sluggishly along, there lies a prosperous farm, a very symbol of harvest and ease. Far and wide the red hip-roof of its gigantic barn shows above the trees that fringe the river which hardly deserves that name, seeing that it is no more than a creek. The commodious, white-painted dwelling, with its roofed-over porch and its glassed-in veranda, however, reveals itself for a moment only as you pass the gate of the yard while driving along the east-west road that leads past it, a few hundred feet to the north; for the old, once primeval bush has been carefully preserved here to enclose and to shelter the homestead; and the tall trees, with their small leaves always aquiver, aspen leaves, while screening the yard from view, seem at the same time to invite you to enter and to linger.

The east-west road cuts right through the property, leaving the level fields, at least the greater part of them, three hundred and twenty acres, to the north, while the yard nestles to the south in a bend of the little river which, curiously, makes

71

the impression as if it were introduced into this landscape for the sole purpose of enfolding this home of man. Beyond the river, there is the remainder of another quarter section the greater part of which serves as pasture. Huge, sleek, gaily coloured cows and frisky colts, accompanied by anxious mares, have at all times access to the black-bottomed water.

The gates to both sides of the road—the one leading to the yard, and the other, opposite it, to the fields—stand open; and a black track leads across the grey-yellow highway from one to the other. There, humus from the field is ground together with the clay of the grade into an exceedingly fine and light dust, perfectly dry, which betrays that many loads have already passed from the field to the yard.

It is a beautiful, crisp, and sunny morning of that reminiscent revival of things past which we call the Indian summer. A far corner of the fields, to the north-west, is bustling with the threshing crews. Engine and separator fill the air with their pulsating hum; and the yellow chaff of the straw comes drifting over the stubble and crosses the road and enters even the yard, threading its way through the trees which, apart from the trembling leaves, stand motionless, and through the entrance that winds in a leisurely way through their aisles. Slowly the chaff filters down, like fine, dry, light snow.

Now and then a wagon, drawn by heavy horses and heavily laden with bags of grain, passes slowly over the road; and every now and then an empty wagon—empty except for a pile of bags on its floor—rattles out in the opposite direction, going to the scene of operations in the field. From the gate a diagonal trail leads through the stubble to the engine; it is cut a few inches deep into the soft soil and worn smooth and hard by many haulings.

That happens just now; let us jump on at the back and go with the driver, an elderly, bearded man of unmistakably Scottish cast: broad-shouldered and heavily set, his grave, though not unpleasant face dusted over with grime and chaff. The wagon, being without a load, rattles along; the horses trot.

Twice the driver has to get out of the trail in order to let a load pass on its way to the yard. To the left, the ground now slopes down a grassy slough in which here and there a clump of willows breaks the monotony of the prairie landscape; no doubt this slough holds water in spring; but at present it is perfectly dry. At its far end, beyond the threshing outfit, an enormous hay-stack rises on its sloping bank.

Now we are in the field of operations. All about, long rows of stooks dot the stubble, big stooks of heavy sheaves. Hay-racks drive from one to the other, one man walking alongside and picking up the sheaves with his fork, pitching them up to another who receives and piles them on the load. Here the work proceeds in a leisurely, unhurried way which contrasts strangely with the scene ahead. The horses do not need to be guided; they know their work; a word from the man on the load is enough to tell them what is wanted.

We have reached the vibrating machines now, joined by a huge, swinging belt. But our Scotsman has to wait a few minutes before he can drive up to the spout that delivers the grain, for another teamster is filling the last of his bags.

Two or three hay-racks, loaded high with sheaves, stand waiting alongside the engine that hums its harvest song. The drivers are lazily reclining on their loads while they wait for those who are ahead of them to finish. They do not even sit up when they move a place forward; the horses know as well as their drivers what is expected of them. Here, the air is thick with chaff and dust.

The few older men in the crew set the pace; the younger ones, some of them inclined to take things easy, have to follow. Those who are alongside the feeder platform, pitching the sheaves, do not make the impression of leisurely laziness.

The engineer, in a black, greasy pair of overalls, is busy with long-spouted oil-can and a huge handful of cottonwaste. The "separator-man" stands on top of his mighty machine, exchanging bantering talk with the pitching men.

"Let her come, Jim," he shouts to one of the men, a tall, good-looking youth who works with a sort of defiant composure, not exactly lazily but as if he were carefully calculating his speed to yield just a reasonable day's work and no more; a cynical smile plays in his young, unruffled face. "Let her come," the separator-man repeats. "Can't choke her up."

"Can't?" challenges Jim's partner, a swarthy, unmistakably foreign-looking man.

And from the opposite side of the feeder-platform another foreigner, a Swede, a giant of a man, six feet four inches tall and proportionately built, shouts over, "We'll see about that." He is alone on his load, for, as usual, the crew is short-handed; and he has volunteered to pitch and load by himself.

And this giant, the Swede, starts to work like one possessed, pitching down the sheaves as if his life depended on choking the machine. The Ruthenian, on the near side, follows his example; but Jim, a piece of straw in the corner of his smiling mouth, remains uninfected. He proceeds in his nonchalant way which is almost provoking, almost contemptuous.

All about, the drivers on their loads are sitting up; this is a sporting proposition; and as such it arouses a general interest. Even the Scotsman follows proceedings with a smile.

But apart from these, there has been another looker-on. The outfit stands a few hundred feet from the edge of the slough which stretches its broad trough of hay-land slantways across this end of the field; and there, among some willows, stands a medium-sized man, with a cardboard suit-case at his feet and a bundle hanging from the end of a stout cane that rests on his shoulder. He is neither slender nor stout, five feet and eleven inches tall, and dressed in a new suit of overalls, stiff with newness, his flaxen-haired head covered with a blue-denim cap that, on its band, displays the advertisement of a certain brand of lubricating oil. His clean-shaven face is broadened by a grin as he watches the frantic efforts of the two men on their respective loads. His is an almost ridiculous figure; for he looks so foreign and absurd, the more so as his effort to adapt himself to the ways of the country is obvious and unsuccessful.

But he watches idly for only a very few seconds. Then he drops bundle and cane and runs, circling the engine, to the side of the Swede. There he looks about for a moment, finds a spare fork sticking with its prongs in the loose soil under the feeder-platform, grabs it, vaults up on the load of the giant, and, without a word of explanation, begins to pitch as frantically as the other two. The loads seem to melt away from under their feet.

The grimy separator-man on top of his machine laughs and rubs his hands. His teeth look strangely white in his dust-blackened face; his tongue and gums, when they show, strangely pink, as in the face of a negro. "Let her come, boys," he shouts again, above the din of the machine, "let her come. Can't choke her up, I tell you. She's a forty-two. But try!" From his words speaks that pride which the craftsman takes in his tools and his output. He looks strange as he stands there, in the dust-laden air, on the shaking machine; his very clothes seem to vibrate; and in them his limbs and his body; he looks like a figure drawn with a trembling hand.

A fixed, nearly apologetic grin does not leave the face of the unbidden helper. There is good-nature in this grin; but also embarrassment and the vacancy of non-comprehension.

The elderly Scotsman who came out a little while ago has meanwhile driven up to the grain-spout and is filling his bags. He keeps watching the newcomer, putting two and two together in his mind. And when his load is made up at last, he detaches himself from the group, casting a last, wondering look at the man who is pitching as if he were engaged on piece-work; for, when the Swede has finished his load, this stranger has simply taken his place on the next one that has come along.

Then the Scotsman threads once more the diagonal trail across the field, staying on it this time when he meets another wagon, for the man with the load, such is the rule, has the right-of-way; and finally, when he reaches the gate, he drives through it and across the road, and on into the welcome shade. For the length of a few rods the entrance leads through the gap between the huge, park-like trees, and then it widens out into the yard. Right in front stands the house, a large, comfortable, and easy-going affair with a look of relaxation about it, though, no doubt, at present nobody there has time to relax, for, red from the heat of the ranges, women are frantically preparing the noon-day meal for the many-mouthed, hungry monster, the crew. The huge and towering barn, painted red, occupies the west side of the yard; and beyond it, a smaller building—it, too, painted red—is the granary for which the load is bound.

In its dark interior a man is working, shovelling wheat to the back. He is tall, standing more than six feet high, broad-shouldered but lean, almost gaunt. His narrow face is divided by a grey moustache which, as he straightens his back, he rubs with the back of his hand in order to free it from the chaff that has collected in its hairs. He is covered all over with the dust of the grain.

When the wagon approaches, he looks out and asks, "How many, Jim?"

Jim is backing his load against the open door. "Twenty-four," he answers over his shoulder.

The man inside takes a pencil suspended by a string from a nail and makes note of the number on a piece of card-board tacked to the wall. Thus he keeps track of the approximate number of bushels, counting two and a half to the bag.

Jim, having tied his lines to the seat, tilts the first of the bags, and the man inside receives it on his shoulder and empties it into the bin to the left. That bin is already filled to one third of its height.

Jim speaks. "Got a new hand, Dave?" he asks.

"Not that I know of," replies the man inside with a questioning inflection.

"Fellow came about an hour ago, climbed up on a load, and started to pitch. Good worker, too, it seems."

"That so?" Dave says. "I could use another man well enough. But I didn't know about him."

"Looks like a Swede."

"Better send him over."

So, when Jim, the Scotsman, returns to the field, he shouts to the stranger, above the din of machine and engine, "Hi, you!" And when the stranger turns, he adds, "Boss wants to see you," nodding his head backwards in the direction of the yard.

But the stranger merely grins vacantly and, with exaggerated motion, shrugs his shoulders.

The others all look at Jim and laugh. So he, shrugging his

shoulders in turn, drives on and takes his place behind the wagon at the spout.

Two more hours pass by; and still the stranger goes on with his unbidden work. The sun, on his path, nears the noon. Meanwhile the stranger has been the partner of all the men who drive up on his side of the outfit: but only one of them has spoken to him, that giant of a Swede who was the first man whom he helped. This giant is clean-shaven and dressed with a striking neatness, yes, a rustic foppishness which shows through all the dust and chaff with which he is covered. He does not wear overalls but a flannel shirt and corduroy trousers tucked into high boots ornamented with a line of coloured stitching along their upper edge. Those of the others who address him call him Nelson.

"Aer du Svensk?" he has asked of the stranger. "Are you a Swede?"

"Yo," the stranger has replied in the affirmative.

And further questions have brought out the fact that he has just arrived from the east, on a through-ticket reading from Malmoe in Sweden to Balfour, Manitoba, Canada. "You'll find lots of Swedes up there," the agent had told him at home, at Karlskrona in Blekinge, whence he hails.

Nelson grins when he hears that tale. Three years ago, when he himself left Sweden, he was told the same thing; but when he arrived, he found that the Swedish settlement was small and considerably farther north. Thus he has become wise in the tricks of the steamship-agent's trade. "Did the boss hire you?" he asks, speaking Swedish, of course, while they proceed with the work in hand.

"No. I haven't seen anybody yet. But I do want work."

"Better see him at noon. What's your name?"

"Niels Lindstedt."

"Come with me when the whistle blows," says Nelson as he drives away.

The brief conversation has cheered Niels greatly.

"I am in luck," he thinks, "to meet a Swede right away, a friend to help me in getting started."

In Balfour, where he had landed very early in the morning, he had almost lost courage when he had found that nobody understood him. But at the hardware store a man—the same who had made him a present of the cap he was wearing—had made signs to him as if pitching sheaves, meanwhile talking to him, tentatively, in short monosyllables, apparently asking questions. Niels had understood this sign language sufficiently to know that he was trying to find out whether he wanted work in the harvest fields; and so he had nodded. Next the hardware dealer had made clear to him, again by signs, that his clothes were unsuitable for work; for he had been dressed in a black cloth suit, stiff and heavy, the kind that lasts the people at home a lifetime, so strong that even years of wearing do not flatten out the seams. He had shown him the way to a store where he had acquired what he needed, till he thought that now he looked exactly like a Canadian. Then he had once more returned to the hardware store, and the friendly man had put him on the road, pushing him by the shoulder and pointing and shouting directions till he had picked up his suitcase and the bundle with the clothes he had been wearing and had started out. When, after a few hundred yards, he had looked back, the hardware man had still been standing at the corner of his street and nodding and waving his arm, for him to go on and on, for many miles. And he had done so.

Most of the men with whom he has been working are foreigners themselves. Niels knows the English or Canadian type sufficiently already to recognize that. Some are Slavonic, some German; though they, too, seem to have Russian blood.

Niels exults in the work. After the enforced idleness of the passage across the ocean and the cramped trip in the train, it feels good to be at work in the open. He wonders whether he will be paid for what he does. He is hungry, for he has had no breakfast; and so he hopes he will get his dinner at least. Probably, he thinks, that will be all he is entitled to. He has heard, of course, of the fabulous wages paid to the working-man in America. But possibly that is no more than idle talk. As hunger and the consequent exhaustion lay hold of him, he begins to view things pessimistically.

The size of the field about him dazes him. The owner, he thinks, must be some nobleman. Will a field one tenth, one fiftieth of the size of this one some day be within his own reach, he wonders? The mere thought of it sends him once more into a fury of work; again he pitches the sheaves like one possessed.

Then, suddenly, startlingly, the noon whistle blows from the engine; and when he sees Nelson, the giant, just arriving on top of a load of sheaves, he runs over and helps him to unhitch his horses.

"Come on," says Nelson and starts off, running and galloping his horses, in order to snatch a ride on a hay-rack which is returning empty to the yard. The rack waits for them, and they climb on, Nelson leading his horses behind.

When the team is stabled in the huge barn where Niels looks about and marvels, the two go over to the granary and find Dave Porter, the boss. Dave looks Niels over and asks a few questions, Nelson interpreting for his new friend.

A few minutes later the newcomer is hired at current wages of four dollars a day till threshing is over; and if he cares to stay after that, at a dollar and fifty a day for plowing till it snows or freezes up. Niels gasps at the figures and has to recalculate them in Swedish money, multiplying them by four: sixteen and six kroner a day! There must be a mistake, he thinks; he cannot have heard right. The wages must be for the week. But when Dave turns away and Niels asks Nelson, the giant laughs and says, "No. No mistake."

So they turn and walk over to the house for dinner.

Niels is quick to learn; and by the time he has had his dinner and gone over the yard with Nelson while they are waiting for the horses to finish theirs, he has picked up much of the new country's lore.

In the granary where they return Niels shows him the figures jotted down on the piece of card-board which show that already the huge bins hold eight thousand bushels of oats, four thousand of barley, and three thousand of wheat. Niels is awed by the enormity of these quantities. There is a strange sort of exhilaration in them. He merely pronounces the figures and has to laugh; and something very like tears comes into his eyes. Nelson chimes in with his throaty bass. No, Niels does not feel sorry that he has come out into this west.

Yes, when the horses are taken out again and the two new friends once more find room on an empty hay-rack, to return to the field, there is a shadow on his consciousness. At dinner, in the house, he has become aware of a certain attitude towards himself, an attitude assumed by those who were unmistakably Canadian. After all, this is not home; it is a strange country; and he is among strange people who look down upon him as if he were something inferior, something not to be taken as fully human. He does not understand that, of course. He has heard Jim, the cynical, good-looking young fellow say something to a number of the men who, like Niels himself, were apparently recent immigrants. Jim had contemptuously addressed them as "You Galishans!" And it had been clear that they resented it. Niels does not quite see why they should; if they are Galicians, why should they mind being called by that name? But he also understands that what they really resent is the tone in which it was said.

He wonders as he looks about while the horses trot briskly over the stubble whether in a few years' time this country will seem like home to him, as apparently it does to Nelson, his newly-won friend.

And with that he turns his mind away from his critical thoughts and back to his dreams. He sees himself established on a small farm of his own, with a woman in the house; and he sees the two of them sitting by lamp-light in a neat little living room of that house while from upstairs there sounds down to them the pitter-patter of little children's feet—his own little children's, romping before they crawl into their snug little beds.

That is his vision: the vision that has brought him into these broad plains. And that vision is destined to shape his whole life in the future.

Ken Mitchell   THE
GREAT
ELECTRICAL
REVOLUTION

I was only a little guy in 1937, but I can still remember
Grandad being out of work. Nobody had any money to pay
him and as he said, there wasn't much future in brick-laying
as a charity. So mostly he just sat around in his suite above
the hardware store, listening to his radio. We *all* listened to it
when there was nothing else to do, which was most of the
time unless you happened to be going to school like me.
Grandad stuck right there through it all—soap operas, weather
reports and quiz shows—unless he got a bit of cash from
somewhere. Then he and Uncle Fred would go downtown to
the beer parlour at the King William Hotel.

Grandad and Grandma came from the old country long
before I was born. When they arrived in Moose Jaw, all they
had was three children: Uncle Fred, Aunt Thecla, and my
Dad; a trunk full of working clothes; and a 26-pound post
mall for putting up fences to keep "rogues" off Grandad's
land. Rogues meant Indians, Orangemen, cattle rustlers and
capitalists. All the way out on the train from Montreal, he
glared out the Pullman window at the endless flat, saying to
his family:

"I came out here for land, b'Christ, and none of 'em's goin' to sly it on me."

He had sworn to carve a mighty estate from the raw Saskatchewan prairie, although he had never so much as picked up a garden hoe in his whole life before leaving Dublin.

So when he stepped off the train at the C.P.R. station in Moose Jaw, it looked like he was thinking of tearing it down and seeding the site to oats. It was two o'clock in the morning, but he kept striding up and down the lobby of the station, dressed in his good wool suit with the vest, as cocky as a bantam rooster in a chicken run. My Dad and Uncle Fred and Aunt Thecla sat on the trunk, while Grandma nagged at him to go and find them a place to stay. (It was only later they realized he was afraid to step outside the station.) He finally quit strutting long enough to get a porter to carry their trunk to a hotel down the street.

The next morning they went to the government land office to secure their homestead. Then Grandad rented a democrat and took my Dad and Uncle Fred out to see the land they had come half-way around the world to find. Grandma and Aunt Thecla were told to stay in the hotel room and thank the Blessed Virgin for deliverance. They were still offering their prayers some three hours later, when Grandad burst into the room, his eyes wild and his face pale and quivering.

"Sweet Jesus Christ!" he shouted at them. "There's too much of it! There's just too damn much of it out there." He ran around the room several times in circles, knocking against the walls. "Miles and miles of nothing but miles and miles!" He collapsed onto one of the beds, and lay staring at the ceiling.

"It 'ud drive us all witless in a week," he moaned.

The two boys came in and told the story of the expedition. Grandad had started out fine, perhaps just a little nervous. But the further they went from the town, the more agitated and wild-eyed he got. Soon he stopped urging the horse along and asked it to stop. They were barely ten miles from town when they turned around and came back, with Uncle Fred driving. Grandad could only crouch on the floor of the democrat, trying to hide from the enormous sky, and whispering hoarsely at Fred to go faster. He'd come four thousand miles to the wide open spaces—only to discover he suffered from agoraphobia.

That was his last real excursion onto the open prairie. He gave up forever the idea of a farm of his own. (He did make one special trip to Mortlach in 1928 to fix Aunt Thecla's chimney, but that was a family favour. Even then Uncle Fred had to drive him in an enclosed Ford sedan in the middle of the night, with newspapers taped to the windows so he couldn't see out.) There was nothing left for him to do but take up his old trade of brick-laying in the town of Moose Jaw, where there were trees and tall buildings to protect him from the vastness. Maybe it was a fortunate turn of fate; certainly he prospered from then until the Depression hit, about the time I was born.

Yet—Grandad always felt guilty about not settling on the land. Maybe it was his conscience that prompted him to send my Dad out to work for a cattle rancher in the hills, the day after he turned eighteen. Another point: he married Aunt Thecla off to a Lutheran wheat farmer at Mortlach who actually threshed about five hundred acres of wheat every fall. Uucle Fred was the eldest and closer to Grandad (he had worked with him as an apprentice brick-layer before they immigrated) so he stayed in town and lived in the suite above the hardware store.

I don't remember much about my father's cattle ranch, except whirls of dust and skinny animals dragging themselves from one side of the range to the other. Finally there were no more cattle, and no money to buy more, and nothing to feed them if we *did* buy them, except wild fox-tails and Russian thistles. So we moved into Moose Jaw with Grandad and Grandma, and went on relief. It was better than the ranch where there was nothing to do but watch tumbleweeds roll through the yard. We would have had to travel into town every week to collect the salted fish and government pork, anyway. Grandad was very happy to have us, because when my Dad went down to the railway yard to get our ration, he collected Grandad's too. My Dad never complained about waiting in line for the handout, but Grandad would've starved to death first. "The God damned government drives us all to the edge," he would say. "Then they want us to queue up for the God damned swill they're poisoning us with."

That was when we spent so much time listening to Grandad's radio. It came in a monstrous slab of black walnut cabinet he had swindled, so he thought, from a second-hand dealer on River Street. An incandescent green bulb glowed in the centre to show when the tubes were warming up. There was a row of knobs with elaborate-looking initials and a dial with the names of cities like Tokyo, Madrid, and Chicago. Try as we might on long winter evenings to tune the needle into those stations and hear a play in Japanese or Russian, all we ever got was CHMJ Moose Jaw, The Buckle of the Wheat Belt. Even so, I spent hours lying on the floor, tracing the floral patterns on the cloth-covered speaker while I listened to another world of mystery and fascination.

When the time came that Grandad could find no more bricks to lay, he set a kitchen chair in front of the radio and stayed there, not moving except to go to the King William, where Uncle Fred now spent most of his time. My Dad had managed to get a job with the city, gravelling streets for fifty cents a day. But things grew worse. The Moose Jaw Light and Power Company came around one day in the fall of 1937 and cut off our electricity for non-payment. It was very hard on Grandad not to have his radio. Not only did he have nothing to do, but he had to spend all his time thinking about it. He stared out the parlour window, which looked over the alley running behind the hardware store. There was a grand view of the back of the Rainbow Laundry.

That was what he was doing the day of his discovery, just before Christmas. Uncle Fred and my Dad were arguing about who caused the Depression—R. B. Bennett or the C.P.R. Suddenly Grandad turned from the window. There was a new and strange look on his face.

"Where does that wire go?" he said.

"Wire?" said Uncle Fred, looking absent-mindedly around the room. He patted his pockets looking for a wire.

"What wire?" my Dad said.

Grandad nodded toward the window. "This wire running right past the window."

He pointed to a double strand of power line that ran from a pole in the back alley to the side of our building. It was a lead-in for the hardware store.

"Holy Moses Cousin Harry. Isn't that a sight now!" Grandad said, grinning like a crazy man.

"You're crazy," Uncle Fred told him. "You can't never get a tap off that line there. They'd find you out in nothing flat."

Grandma, who always heard everything that was said, called from the kitchen: "Father, don't you go and do some foolishness will have us all electrinated."

"By God," he muttered. He never paid any attention to a word she said. "Cut off *my* power, will they?"

That night, after they made me go to bed, I listened to him and Uncle Fred banging and scraping as they bored a hole through the parlour wall. My Dad wouldn't have anything to do with it and took my mother to the free movie at the co-op. He said Grandad was descending to the level of the Moose Jaw Light and Power Company.

Actually, Grandad knew quite a bit about electricity. He had known for a long time how to jump a wire from one side of the meter around to the other, to cheat the power company. I had often watched him under the meter, stretched out from his tip-toes at the top of a broken step-ladder, yelling at Grandma to lift the God-damned Holy Candle a little higher so he could see what the Christ he was doing.

The next day, Grandad and Uncle Fred were acting like a couple of kids, snorting and giggling and jabbing each other in the ribs. They were waiting for the King William beer parlour to open so they could go down and tell their friends about Grandad's revenge on the power company. They spent the day like heroes down there, telling over and over how Grandad had spied the lead-in, and how they bored the hole in the wall, and how justice had finally descended on the capitalist leeches. The two of them showed up at home for supper, but as soon as they ate they headed back to the King William where everybody was buying them free beer.

Grandma didn't seem to think much of their efforts, although now that she had electricity again, she could spend the evenings doing her housework if she wanted to. The cord came through the hole in the wall, across the parlour to the hall and the kitchen. Along the way, other cords were attached which led to the two bedrooms. Grandma muttered when she had to sweep around the black tangle of wires and sockets. With six of us living in the tiny suite, somebody was forever tripping on one of the cords and knocking things over.

But we lived with all that because Grandad was happy again. We might *all* have lived happily if Grandad and Uncle Fred could have kept quiet about their revenge on the power company. One night about a week later we were in the parlour listening to Fibber McGee and Molly when somebody knocked at the door. It was Mrs. Pizak, who lived next door in a tiny room.

"Goot evening," she said, looking all around. "I see your power has turnt beck on."

"Ha," Grandad said. "We turned it on *for* 'em. Damned rogues."

"Come in and sit down and listen to the show with us," Grandma said. Mrs. Pizak kept looking at the black wires running back and forth across the parlour, and at Grandad's radio. You could tell she wasn't listening to the show.

"Dey shut off my power, too," she said. "I alvays like listen de Shut-In. Now my radio isn't vork."

"Hmmm," Grandad said, trying to hear Fibber and the Old-Timer. Grandma and my Dad watched him, not listening to the radio any more either. Finally he couldn't stand it.

"All right, Fred," he said. "Go and get the brace and bit."

They bored a hole through one of the bedroom walls into Mrs. Pizak's cubicle. From then on, she was on Grandad's power grid, too. It didn't take long for everybody else in the block to find out about the free power, and they all wanted to hook up. There were two floors of suites above the hardware store, and soon the walls and ceiling of Grandad's suite were as full of holes as a colander, with wires running in all directions. For the price of a bottle of whiskey, people could run their lights twenty-four hours a day if they wanted. By Christmas Day, even those who *paid* their bills had given notice to the power company. It was a beautiful Christmas in a bad year—and Grandad and Uncle Fred liked to take a lot of credit for it. Nobody blamed them, either. There was a lot of celebration up and down the halls, where they always seemed to show up as guests of honour. There was a funny feeling running through the block, like being in a state of siege, or a revolution, with Uncle Fred and my Grandad leading it.

One late afternoon just before New Year's, I was lying on the floor of the front parlour, reading a second-hand Book of Knowledge I had got for Christmas. Grandma and my mother were knitting socks, and all three of us were listening vaguely to the Ted Mack Amateur Hour. Suddenly, out of the corner of my eye, I thought I saw Grandad's radio move. I blinked and stared at it, but the big console just sat there talking about Geritol. I turned a page. Again, it seemed to move in a jerk. What was going on?

"Grandma," I said. "The radio—"

She looked up from her knitting, already not believing a word I might have to say. I gave it up, and glared spitefully at the offending machine. While I watched, it slid at least six inches across the parlour floor.

"Grandma!" I screamed. "The radio's moving! It was sitting there—and it moved over here. All by itself!"

She looked calmly at the radio, then the tangle of wires spread across the floor, and out the front parlour window.

"Larry-boy, you'd best run and fetch your grand-father. He's over at McBrides'. Number eight."

McBrides' suite was down the gloomy hall and across. I dashed down the corridor and pounded frantically at the door. Someone opened it the width of a crack.

"Is my Grandad in there?" I squeaked. Grandad stepped out into the hall with a glass in his hand, closing the door behind him.

"What is it, Larry?"

"Grandma says for you to come quick. The radio! There's something—"

"My radio!" Grandad was not a large man, but he had the energy of a buzz-saw. He started walking back up the hall, breaking into a trot, then a steady gallop, holding his glass of whiskey out in front at arm's length so it wouldn't spill. He burst through the door and screeched to a stop in front of the radio, which sat there, perfectly normal except that it stood maybe a foot to the left of the chair.

"By the Holy toe-nails of Moses—what is it?"

Grandma looked up ominously and jerked her chin toward the window. Her quiet firmness usually managed to calm him, but now, in two fantastic bounds, Grandad stood in front of the window, looking out.

"Larry," he said, glaring outside, "fetch your Uncle Fred." I tore off down the hall again to number eight and brought Uncle Fred back to the suite. The two women were still knitting on the other side of the room. Grandma was doing her stitches calmly enough, but my mother's needles clattered like telegraph keys, and she was throwing terrified glances around the room.

"Have a gawk at this, will you, Fred?"

Uncle Fred and I crowded around him to see out. There, on a pole only twenty feet from our parlour window, practically facing us eye-to-eye, was a lineman from the power company. He was replacing broken glass insulators; God knows why he was doing it in the dead of winter. Obviously, he hadn't noticed our home-made lead-in, or he would have been knocking at the door. We could only pray he wouldn't look at the wire too closely. Once, he lifted his eyes toward the lighted window where we all stood gaping out at him in the growing darkness. He grinned at us, and raised his hand in a salute. He must have thought we were admiring his work.

"Wave back!" Grandad ordered. The three of us waved frantically at the lineman, to make him think we appreciated his efforts, although Grandad was muttering some very ugly things about the man's ancestry.

Finally, to our relief, the lineman finished his work and got ready to come down the pole. He reached out his hand for support—and my heart stopped beating as his weight hung on the contraband wire. Behind me, I could hear the radio slide another foot across the parlour floor. The lineman stared at the wire he held. He tugged experimentally, his eyes following it up to the hole through our wall. He looked at Grandad and Uncle Fred and me standing there in the lit-up window, with our crazy horror-struck grins and our arms frozen above our heads in grotesque waves. Understanding seemed to spread slowly across his face.

He scrambled around to the opposite side of the pole and braced himself to give a mighty pull on our line. Simultaneously, Grandad leaped into action, grabbing the wire on our side of the wall. He wrapped it around his hands, and braced his feet against the baseboard. The lineman gave his first vicious yank, and it almost jerked Grandad smack against the wall. I remember thinking what a powerful man the lineman must be to do that to my Grandad.

"Fred, you feather-brained idiot!" he shouted. "Get over here and haul on this line before the black-hearted son of a bitch pulls me through the wall."

Uncle Fred ran to the wire just in time, as the man on the pole gave another, mightier heave. At the window, I could see the lineman stiffen with rage and determination. The slender wire sawed back and forth through the hole in the wall for at least ten minutes, first one side, and then the other, getting advantage. The curses on our side got very loud and bitter. I couldn't hear the lineman, of course, but I could see him—with his mouth twisted in an awful snarl, throwing absolutely terrible looks at me in the window, and heaving on the line. I know he wasn't praying to St. Jude.

Grandad's cursing would subside periodically when Grandma warned: "Now, now, father, not in front of the boy." Then she would go back to her knitting and pretend the whole thing wasn't happening, as Grandad's violent language would soar to a new high.

That lineman must have been in extra-good condition, because our side very quickly began to play out. Grandad screamed at Grandma and my mother, and even at me, to throw ourselves on the line and help. But the women refused to leave their knitting, and they wouldn't let me be corrupted. I couldn't leave my viewpoint at the window, anyway.

Grandad and Uncle Fred kept losing acreage. Gradually

the huge radio had scraped all the way across the floor and stood at their backs, hampering their efforts.

"Larry!" Grandad shouted. "Is he weakenin' any?"

He wanted desperately for me to say yes, but it was useless. "It doesn't look like it," I said. Grandad burst out in a froth of curses I'd never heard before. A fresh attack on the line pulled his knuckles to the wall and barked them badly. He looked tired and beaten. All the slack in the line was taken up and he was against the wall, his head twisted looking at me. A light flared up in his eyes.

"All right, Fred," he said. "If he wants the God-damned thing so bad—let him have it!" They both jumped back—and nothing happened.

I could see the lineman, completely unaware of his impending disaster, almost literally winding himself up for an all-out assault on our wire. I wanted out of human kindness to shout a warning at him. But it was too late. With an incredible backward lunge, he disappeared from sight behind the power pole.

A shattering explosion of wild noises blasted my senses, like a bomb had fallen in Grandad's suite. Every appliance and electric light that Grandma owned flew into the parlour, bounding off the walls and smashing against each other. A table lamp from the bedroom caromed off Uncle Fred's knee. The radio collided against the wall and was ripped off its wire by the impact. Sparking and flashing like lightning, all of Grandma's things hurled themselves against the parlour wall. They were stripped like chokecherries from an electric vine as it went zipping through the hole. A silence fell—like a breath of air to a drowning man. The late afternoon darkness settled through the room.

"Sweet Jesus Christ!" Grandad said. He had barely got it out, when there came a second uproar: a blood-curdling barrage of bangs and shouts, as our neighbours in the block saw all their lamps, radios, irons and toasters leap from their tables and collect in ruined piles of junk around the "free power" holes in their walls. Uncle Fred turned white as a sheet.

I looked out the window. The lineman sat on the ground at the foot of his pole, dazed. He looked up at me with one more hate-filled glare, then deliberately snipped our wire with a pair of cutters. He taped up the end and marched away into the night.

Grandad stood in the midst of the ruined parlour, trying in the darkness to examine his beloved radio for damage. Grandma sat in her rocking chair, knitting socks and refusing to acknowledge the disaster.

It was Grandad who finally spoke first. "They're lucky," he said. "It's just God-damned lucky for them they didn't scratch my radio."

Henry Kreisel

THE BROKEN GLOBE

Since it was Nick Solchuk who first told me about the opening in my field at the University of Alberta, I went up to see him as soon as I received word that I had been appointed. He lived in one of those old mansions in Pimlico that had once served as town houses for wealthy merchants and aristocrats, but now housed a less moneyed group of people— stenographers, students, and intellectuals of various kinds. He had studied at Cambridge and got his doctorate there and was now doing research at the Imperial College and rapidly establishing a reputation among the younger men for his work on problems which had to do with the curvature of the earth.

His room was on the third floor, and it was very cramped, but he refused to move because he could look out from his window and see the Thames and the steady flow of boats, and that gave him a sense of distance and of space also. Space, he said, was what he missed most in the crowded city. He referred to himself, nostalgically, as a prairie boy, and when he wanted to demonstrate what he meant by space he used to say that when a man stood and looked out across the open prairie, it was possible for him to believe that the earth was flat.

"So," he said, after I had told him my news, "you are going to teach French to prairie boys and girls. I congratulate you." Then he cocked his head to one side, and looked me over and said: "How are your ears?"

92

"My ears?" I said. "They're all right. Why?"

"Prepare yourself," he said. "Prairie voices trying to speak French—that will be a great experience for you. I speak from experience. I learned my French pronunciation in a little one-room school in a prairie village. From an extraordinary girl, mind you, but her mind ran to science. Joan McKenzie —that was her name. A wiry little thing, sharp-nosed, and she always wore brown dresses. She was particularly fascinated by earthquakes. 'In 1755 the city of Lisbon, Portugal, was devastated. 60,000 persons died; the shock was felt in Southern France and North Africa; and inland waters of Great Britain and Scandinavia were agitated.' You see, I still remember that, and I can hear her voice too. Listen: 'In common with the entire solar system, the earth is moving through space at the rate of approximately 45,000 miles per hour, toward the constellation of Hercules. Think of that, boys and girls.' Well, I thought about it. It was a lot to think about. Maybe that's why I became a geophysicist. Her enthusiasm was infectious. I knew her at her peak. After a while she got tired and married a solid farmer and had eight children."

"But her French, I take it, was not so good," I said.

"No," he said. "Language gave no scope to her imagination. Mind you, I took French seriously enough. I was a very serious student. For a while I even practised French pronunciation at home. But I stopped it because it bothered my father. My mother begged me to stop. For the sake of peace."

"Your father's ears were offended," I said.

"Oh, no," Nick said, "not his ears. His soul. He was sure that I was learning French so I could run off and marry a French girl. . . . Don't laugh. It's true. When once my father believed something, it was very hard to shake him."

"But why should he have objected to your marrying a French girl anyway?"

"Because," said Nick, and pointed a stern finger at me, "because when he came to Canada he sailed from some French port, and he was robbed of all his money while he slept. He held all Frenchmen responsible. He never forgot and he never forgave. And, by God, he wasn't going to have that cursed language spoken in his house. He wasn't going to

have any nonsense about science talked in his house either."
Nick was silent for a moment, and then he said, speaking
very quietly. "Curious man, my father. He had strange ideas,
but a strange kind of imagination, too. I couldn't understand
him when I was going to school or to the university. But then
a year or two ago, I suddenly realized that the shape of the
world he lived in had been forever fixed for him by some
medieval priest in the small Ukrainian village where he was
born and where he received an education of sorts when he
was a boy. And I suddenly realized that he wasn't mad, but
that he lived in the universe of the medieval church. The earth
for him was the centre of the universe, and the centre was still.
It didn't move. The sun rose in the East and it set in the West,
and it moved perpetually around a still earth. God had made
this earth especially for man, and man's function was to per-
petuate himself and to worship God. My father never said all
that in so many words, mind you, but that is what he believed.
Everything else was heresy."

He fell silent.

"How extraordinary," I said.

He did not answer at once, and after a while he said, in a
tone of voice which seemed to indicate that he did not want
to pursue the matter further, "Well, when you are in the
middle of the Canadian West, I'll be in Rome. I've been asked
to give a paper to the International Congress of Geophysicists
which meets there in October."

"So I heard," I said. "Wilcocks told me the other day. He
said it was going to be a paper of some importance. In fact,
he said it would create a stir."

"Did Wilcocks really say that?" he asked eagerly, his face
reddening, and he seemed very pleased. We talked for a while
longer, and then I rose to go.

He saw me to the door and was about to open it for me,
but stopped suddenly, as if he were turning something over
in his mind, and then said quickly, "Tell me—would you do
something for me?"

"Of course," I said. "If I can."

He motioned me back to my chair and I sat down again.
"When you are in Alberta," he said, "and if it is convenient

for you, would you—would you go to see my father?"

"Why, yes," I stammered, "why, of course. I—I didn't realize he was still. . . ."

"Oh, yes," he said, "he's still alive, still working. He lives on his farm, in a place called Three Bear Hills, about sixty or seventy miles out of Edmonton. He lives alone. My mother is dead. I have a sister who is married and lives in Calgary. There were only the two of us. My mother could have no more children. It was a source of great agony for them. My sister goes to see him sometimes, and then she sometimes writes to me. He never writes to me. We—we had—what shall I call it—differences. If you went to see him and told him that I had not gone to the devil, perhaps. . . ." He broke off abruptly, clearly agitated, and walked over to his window and stood staring out, then said. "Perhaps you'd better not. I—I don't want to impose on you."

I protested that he was not imposing at all, and promised that I would write to him as soon as I had paid my visit.

I met him several times after that, but he never mentioned the matter again.

I sailed from England about the middle of August and arrived in Montreal a week later. The long journey West was one of the most memorable experiences I have ever had. There were moments of weariness and dullness. But the very monotony was impressive. There was a grandeur about it. It was monotony of a really monumental kind. There were moments when, exhausted by the sheer impact of the land-scape, I thought back with longing to the tidy, highly cul-tivated countryside of England and of France, to the sight of men and women working in the fields, to the steady suc-cession of villages and towns, and everywhere the conscious-ness of nature humanized. But I also began to understand why Nick Solchuk was always longing for more space and more air, especially when we moved into the prairies, and the land became flatter until there seemed nothing, neither hill nor tree nor bush, to disturb the vast unbroken flow of land until in the far distance a thin, blue line marked the point where the prairie merged into the sky. Yet over all there was a strange tranquillity, all motion seemed suspended, and only the sun moved steadily, imperturbably West, dropping finally over the rim of the horizon, a blazing red ball, but leaving a superb evening light lying over the land still.

I was reminded of the promise I had made, but when I arrived in Edmonton, the task of settling down absorbed my time and energy so completely that I did nothing about it. Then, about the middle of October, I saw a brief report in the newspaper about the geophysical congress which had opened in Rome on the previous day, and I was mindful of my promise again. Before I could safely bury it in the back of my mind again, I sat down and wrote a brief letter to Nick's father, asking him when I could come out to visit him. Two weeks passed without an answer, and I decided to go and see him on the next Saturday without further formalities.

The day broke clear and fine. A few white clouds were in the metallic autumn sky and the sun shone coldly down upon the earth, as if from a great distance. I drove south as far as Wetaskiwin and then turned east. The paved highway gave way to gravel and got steadily worse. I was beginning to wonder whether I was going right, when I rounded a bend and a grain elevator hove like a signpost into view. It was now about three o'clock and I had arrived in Three Bear Hills, but, as Nick had told me, there were neither bears nor hills here, but only prairie, and suddenly the beginning of an embryonic street with a few buildings on either side like a small island in a vast sea, and then all was prairie again.

I stopped in front of the small general store and went in to ask for directions. Three farmers were talking to the storekeeper, a bald, bespectacled little man who wore a long, dirty apron and stood leaning against his counter. They stopped talking and turned to look at me. I asked where the Solchuk farm was.

Slowly scrutinizing me, the storekeeper asked, "You just new here?"

"Yes," I said.

"From the old country, eh?"

"Yes."

"You selling something?"

"No, no," I said. "I—I teach at the University."

"That so?" He turned to the other men and said, "Only boy ever went to University from around here was Solchuk's boy, Nick. Real brainy young kid, Nick. Two of 'em never got on together. Too different. You know."

They nodded slowly.

"But that boy of his—he's a real big-shot scientist now. You know them addem bombs and them hydrergen bombs. He helps make 'em."

"No, no," I broke in quickly. "That's not what he does. He's a geophysicist."

"What's that?" asked one of the men.

But before I could answer, the little storekeeper asked excitedly, "You know Nick?"

"Yes," I said, "we're friends. I've come to see his father."

"And where's he now? Nick, I mean."

"Right now he is in Rome," I said. "But he lives in London, and does research there."

"Big-shot, eh," said one of the men laconically, but with a trace of admiration in his voice, too.

"He's a big scientist, though, like I said. Isn't that so?" the storekeeper broke in.

"He's going to be a very important scientist indeed," I said, a trifle solemnly.

"Like I said," he called out triumphantly. "That's showing 'em. A kid from Three Bear Hills, Alberta. More power to him!" His pride was unmistakable. "Tell me, mister," he went on, his voice dropping, "does he remember this place sometimes? Or don't he want to know us no more?"

"Oh, no," I said quickly. "He often talks of this place, and of Alberta, and of Canada. Some day he plans to return."

"That's right," he said with satisfaction. He drew himself up to full height, banged his fist on the table and said, "I'm proud of that boy. Maybe old Solchuk don't think so much of him, but you tell him old Mister Marshall is proud of him." He came from behind the counter and almost ceremoniously escorted me out to my car and showed me the way to Solchuk's farm.

I had about another five miles to drive, and the road, hardly more now than two black furrows cut into the prairie, was uneven and bumpy. The land was fenced on both sides of the road, and at last I came to a rough wooden gate hanging loosely on one hinge, and beyond it there was a cluster of small wooden buildings. The largest of these, the house itself, seemed at one time to have been ochre-coloured, but the paint had worn off and it now looked curiously mottled. A few chickens were wandering about, pecking at the ground, and from the back I could hear the grunting and squealing of pigs.

I walked up to the house and, just as I was about to knock, the door was suddenly opened, and a tall, massively built old man stood before me.

"My name is . . ." I began.

But he interrupted me. "You the man wrote to me?" His voice, though unpolished, had the same deep timbre as Nick's.

"That's right," I said.

"You a friend of Nick?"

"Yes."

He beckoned me in with a nod of his head. The door was low and I had to stoop a bit to get into the room. It was a large, low-ceilinged room. A smallish window let in a patch of light which lit up the middle of the room but did not spread into the corners, so that it seemed as if it were perpetually dusk. A table occupied the centre, and on the far side there was a large wood stove on which stood a softly hissing black kettle. In the corner facing the entrance there was an iron bedstead, and the bed was roughly made, with a patchwork quilt thrown carelessly on top.

The old man gestured me to one of the chairs which stood around the table.

"Sit."

I did as he told me, and he sat down opposite me and placed his large calloused hands before him on the table. He seemed to study me intently for a while, and I scrutinized him. His face was covered by a three-days' stubble, but in spite of that, and in spite of the fact that it was a face beaten by sun and wind, it was clear that he was Nick's father. For Nick had the same determined mouth, and the same high cheek bones and the same dark, penetrating eyes.

At last he spoke. "You friend of Nick."

I nodded my head.

"What he do now?" he asked sharply. "He still tampering with the earth?"

His voice rose as if he were delivering a challenge, and I drew back involuntarily. "Why—he's doing scientific research, yes," I told him. "He's. . . ."

"What God has made," he said sternly, "no man should touch."

Before I could regain my composure, he went on, "He sent you. What for? What he want?"

"Nothing," I said, "Nothing at all. He sent me to bring you greetings and to tell you he is well."

"And you come all the way from Edmonton to tell me?"

"Yes, of course."

A faint smile played about his mouth, and the features of his face softened. Then suddenly he rose from his chair and stood towering over me. "You are welcome in this house," he said.

The formality with which he spoke was quite extraordinary and seemed to call for an appropriate reply, but I could do little more than stammer a thank you, and he, assuming again a normal tone of voice, asked me if I cared to have coffee. When I assented he walked to the far end of the room and busied himself about the stove.

It was then that I noticed, just under the window, a rough little wooden table and on top of it a faded old globe made of cardboard, such as little children use in school. I was intrigued to see it there and went over to look at it more closely. The cheap metal mount was brown with rust, and when I lifted it and tried to turn the globe on its axis, I found that it would not rotate because part of it had been squashed and broken. I ran my hand over the deep dent, and suddenly the old man startled me.

"What you doing there?" Curiosity seemed mingled with suspicion in his voice and made me feel like a small child surprised by its mother in an unauthorized raid on the pantry. I set down the globe and turned. He was standing by the table with two big mugs of coffee in his hands.

"Coffee is hot," he said.

I went back to my chair and sat down, slightly embarrassed.

"Drink," he said, pushing one of the mugs over to me.

We both began to sip the coffee, and for some time neither of us said anything.

"That thing over there," he said at last, putting down his mug, "that thing you was looking at—he brought it home one day—he was a boy then—maybe thirteen-year-old Nick. The other day I found it up in the attic. I was going to throw it in the garbage. But I forgot. There it belongs. In the garbage. It is a false thing." His voice had now become venomous.

"False?" I said. "How is it false?"

He disregarded my question. "I remember," he went on, "he came home from school one day and we was all here in this room—all sitting around this table eating supper, his mother, his sister and me and Alex, too—the hired man like. And then sudden like Nick pipes up, and he says, we learned in school today, he says, how the earth is round like a ball, he says, and how it moves around and around the sun and never stops, he says. They learning you rubbish in school, I say. But he says, no, Miss McKenzie never told him no lies. Then I say she does, I say, and a son of mine shouldn't believe it. Stop your ears! Let not Satan come in!" He raised an outspread hand and his voice thundered as if he were a prophet armed. "But he was always a stubborn boy—Nick. Like a mule. He never listened to reason. I believe it, he says. To me he says that—his father, just like that. I believe it, he says, because science has proved it and it is the truth. It is false, I cry, and you will not believe it. I believe it, he says. So then I hit him because he will not listen and will not obey. But he keeps shouting and shouting and shouting. 'She moves,' he shouts, 'she moves, she moves!' "

He stopped. His hands had balled themselves into fists, and the remembered fury sent the blood streaming into his face. He seemed now to have forgotten my presence and he went on speaking in a low murmuring voice, almost as if he were telling the story to himself.

"So the next day, or the day after, I go down to that school, and there is this little Miss McKenzie, so small and so thin that I could have crush her with my bare hands. What you teaching my boy Nick? I ask her. What false lies you stuffing in his head? What you telling him that the earth is round and that she moves for? Did Joshua tell the earth to stand still, or did he command the sun? So she says to me, I don't care what Joshua done, she says, I will tell him what science has discovered. With that woman I could get nowhere. So then I try to keep him away from school, and I lock him up in the house, but it was no good. He got out, and he run to the school like, and Miss McKenzie she sends me a letter to say she will sent up the inspectors if I try to keep him away from the school. And I could do nothing."

His sense of impotence was palpable. He sat sunk into himself as if he were still contemplating ways of halting the scientific education of his son.

"Two, three weeks after," he went on, "he comes walking in this door with a large paper parcel in his hand. Now, he calls out to me, now I will prove it to you, I will prove that she moves. And he tears off the paper from the box and takes out this—this thing, and he puts it on the table here. Here, he cries, here is the earth, and look, she moves. And he gives that thing a little push and it twirls around like. I have to laugh. A toy, I say to him, you bring me a toy here, not bigger than my hand, and it is supposed to be the world, this little toy here, with the printed words on coloured paper, this little cardboard ball. This Miss McKenzie, I say to him, she's turning you crazy in that school. But look, he says, she moves. Now I have to stop my laughing. I'll soon show you she moves, I say, for he is beginning to get me mad again. And I go up to the table and I take the toy thing in my hands and I smash it down like this."

He raised his fists and let them crash down on the table as if he meant to splinter it.

"That'll learn you, I cry. I don't think he could believe I had done it, because he picks up the thing and he tries to turn it, but it don't turn no more. He stands there and the tears roll down his cheeks, and then, sudden like, he takes the thing in both his hands and he throws it at me. And it would have hit me right in the face, for sure, if I did not put up my hand. Against your father, I cry, you will raise up your hand against your father. Asmodeus! I grab him by the arm, and I shake him and I beat him like he was the devil. And he makes me madder and madder because he don't cry or shout or anything. And I would have kill him there, for sure, if his mother didn't come in then and pull me away. His nose was bleeding, but he didn't notice. Only he looks at me and says, you can beat me and break my globe, but you can't stop her moving. That night my wife she make me swear by all that's holy that I wouldn't touch him no more. And from then on I never hit him again nor talk to him about this thing. He goes his way and I go mine."

He fell silent. Then after a moment he snapped suddenly, "You hold with that?"

"Hold with what?" I asked, taken aback.

"With that thing?" He pointed behind him at the little table and at the broken globe. His gnarled hands now tightly interlocked, he leaned forward in his chair and his dark, brooding eyes sought an answer from mine in the twilight of the room.

Alone with him there, I was almost afraid to answer firmly. Was it because I feared that I would hurt him too deeply if I did, or was I perhaps afraid that he would use violence on me as he had on Nick?

I cleared my throat. "Yes," I said then. "Yes, I believe that the earth is round and that she moves. That fact has been accepted now for a long time."

I expected him to round on me but he seemed suddenly to have grown very tired, and in a low resigned voice he said, "Satan has taken over all the world." Then suddenly he roused himself and hit the table hard with his fist, and cried passionately, "But not me! Not me!"

It was unbearable. I felt that I must break the tension, and I said the first thing that came into my mind. "You can be proud of your son in spite of all that happened between you. He is a fine man, and the world honours him for his work."

He gave me a long look. "He should have stayed here," he

said quietly. "When I die, there will be nobody to look after the land. Instead he has gone off to tamper with God's earth."

His fury was now all spent. We sat for a while in silence, and then I rose. Together we walked out of the house. When I was about to get into my car, he touched me lightly on the arm. I turned. His eyes surveyed the vast expanse of sky and land, stretching far into the distance, reddish clouds in the sky and blue shadows on the land. With a gesture of great dignity and power he lifted his arm and stood pointing into the distance, at the flat land and the low-hanging sky.

"Look," he said, very slowly and very quietly, "she is flat, and she stands still."

It was impossible not to feel a kind of admiration for the old man. There was something heroic about him. I held out my hand and he took it. He looked at me steadily, then averted his eyes and said, "Send greetings to my son."

I drove off quickly, but had to stop again in order to open the wooden gate. I looked back at the house, and saw him still standing there, still looking at his beloved land, a lonely, towering figure framed against the darkening evening sky.

DREAM
AND LIVE

Sinclair Ross   A DAY
WITH
PEGASUS

"Two white stockings and a star," Mrs. Parker called from the kitchen, and in his bare feet, struggling with suspenders, Peter raced downstairs and across the yard to see.

At the stable door, just for an instant, he hesitated. It was some instinct perhaps of emotional thrift, warning him that so fierce and strange a tingle of expectancy ought to be prolonged a little—some vague apprehension that in Biddy's stall there might be less than he had seen already. Then he advanced slowly—a finger raised to forbid the yellow pup that waited for his word to leap and yelp—on furtive tiptoe past the stalls where Mr. Parker and his grown-up brother Dan stood harnessing their horses for the field. This suddenly was important. In what awaited him there was no place for Dan or his father or the pup. The stable with its gloom and rustling mangerfuls of hay had subdued his excitement to a breathless sense of solemnity—a solemnity that was personal, intimately his own—that he knew the others would misunderstand and mar. He even felt a vague resentment that while he was still sleeping they had been here before him. It was his colt—it should have been his first to see and touch. Five months he had been waiting. "Biddy's colt about the end of May," they had promised him at Christmas, and today now was the twenty-eighth. Marvelling a little at the prophecy he reached the box-stall door. There was a moment's stillness while the pup sat watching with his silly head cocked up as if it were a game. Then the mare whinnied to him and he slipped inside.

It was a small colt—disconcertingly small—even though no smaller than the other new-born colts that he had seen. It lay, a black, unprepossessing little heap among the straw, its coat still rough and mangy-looking, its eyes half-closed, its head unsteady. He squatted in front of it, almost in a conversational attitude, as if he were introducing himself and awaiting recognition. But the colt, even before the advent of its owner, showed signs of neither interest nor respect. Even when the owner put out a finger to touch and verify the star. Even when the finger became gently importunate in an effort to prod awake some sign of at least potential speed and grace. The head kept swaying back and forth, the eyes went shut and open blearily—and nothing more.

Then Biddy came up, and with a no-nonsense push of her nose toppled him sprawling off his hunkers into the straw. He lay there still a minute, watching respectfully as she licked the colt between the ears. Nearly all their horses were Biddy's colts or grand-colts. Big, rangy, hairy-footed Clydes, and yet with twice the dash and spirit of the horses that he knew on other farms. Because Biddy had a strain of racing blood. Even after nearly twenty years of foal-bearing and the plough, she herself always pranced a little as they led her out of the stable. And every day of his life young Tim raced the others to the water-trough where, heels twitching and ears flat to his head, he dared them to approach till he had drunk his fill. The same with the bay mares Lulu and Marie, who in town one day last summer had pretended fright at the sight of a truck, and to the scurrying amazement of all Main Street taken off a wheel on the corner of Pandora's Beauty Shop. He remembered gratefully, encouraging himself with the thought that his colt now, for all its poor beginnings, was not likely to prove an exception.

Then Dan came in, and eager for an expert's pronouncement, Peter sprang attentive to his feet. But first, without a word, Dan put his arms around the colt and lifted it. He steadied the shaky body a minute, straightened out one of the white-stockinged legs that was buckling at the knee, and then for a long time—a mercilessly long time—stood thoughtful and appraising.

It would be final, Dan's opinion. Fearfully, as if in the sober, sun-tanned features his own destiny were to be read, Peter scanned his face. "What do you think?" he asked anxiously at last, unable to contain himself longer. "I mean —will he be all right? Is he as good as her other colts?"

Dan smiled in answer—the inarticulate smile of a horse-lover, tender, almost grateful—and pierced with understanding Peter wheeled and fled outside.

It was a strange, almost unbearable moment. The horse that for five months he had lived with, gloried in, and, underneath it all, never quite expected to come true—it was a reality now—alive, warm and breathing—two white stockings and a star.

He ran; the yellow pup rolled tangling at his feet; and on he ran again. The colt ran with him, more swiftly now than it had ever run before. No earth beneath their feet, they leaped across the garden and around the house—around the house and across the garden—then back to stand a moment eager and irresolute before the stable door.

But this time he stayed outside. His colt, grown fleet of limb, possessed a fire and beauty that enslaved him now, that he could not abandon for the bleary-eyed reality in Biddy's stall. "You'll be late for school," Dan warned him as he led out the horses. "Remember, you've got the calves to feed before you go."

Ordinarily it was a trial, the way Dan disciplined him, the twenty-year-old smugness with which he imposed his own standards of cleanliness and decorum, but this time Peter trotted off for breakfast willingly. Partly because he understood that for a while at least it would be better if he kept away from the box-stall. Partly because in Dan's smile as he appraised the colt there had been a quality of reverence that established between them a kinship stronger than the disparity of eleven years.

He swallowed only a few mouthfuls, slipping most of his breakfast to the pup while Mrs. Parker went on working at the stove. "You're quiet," she noticed presently. "What's wrong? Dan says it's the best colt Biddy's ever had."

"I know—I'm just wondering what's a good name." It would be useless trying to explain. His silence belonged to an emotion that he was sure lay outside her experience. "We've got a King already—and Skinny Saunders called his pony Prince—so he'd think I was copying."

"Bill's a good name," she suggested. "Short and sensible. Or Mike, or Joe. We had a Buster once—before your time."

He asked resignedly, "Is the milk ready for the calves?"

"If you've finished your breakfast." She glanced from his empty plate to the pup, but it was an accomplishment of the pup to swallow instantly, without so much as a smack of his chops, and reassured she went on. "Mind there's no milk spilt this morning, and don't stop in to bother the colt again. You've still got to brush your hair and get into your shoes and stockings."

It was the colt, the colt he had raced with before breakfast across the garden, that made the feeding of the calves this morning such a humiliation. They slobbered milk over his feet, dribbled it down his trousers; one of them got its tongue around the bit of shirt-tail that he hadn't yet tucked in, and annoyed to find no nourishment forthcoming, bunted him elbow-deep into the pail. Nigger—Daisy—Dot—as stupid and silly as their names, gurgling and blowing at him till there was no colt left at all—until for beginnings again he had to steal back to the stable and pay another visit to the box-stall.

This time he examined the colt curiously: toy-horse, woolly little tail, trim dainty limbs with both white stockings drawn up neatly to the knees, incredibly small and incredibly perfect hooves. A horse—in astonishing miniature still, but authentically a horse—and this time for just its frail reality he began to feel an enthusiasm that at last made the box-stall too confining, and sent him spinning sky-high to the house to dress for school.

But it was a mile to school, and the reality could not last so far. The white-stockinged legs began to flash more quickly, the long limp neck to arch, the stubby tail to flow. Then suddenly he was mounted, and the still May morning sprang in

whistling wind around his ears. Field after field reeled up
and fell away. The earth resounded thundering, then dimmed
and dropped until it seemed they cleaved their way through
flashing light . . . Until at last he stood quite still, impaled by
the fear and wonder of it, while the sun poured blazing, and
the road stretched white and dusty through the fields of early
wheat. A long time: reader clutched in one hand, red shining
dinner-pail in the other.

He arrived nearly fifteen minutes late. That in itself was
always bad enough: forfeit of mid-morning recess, Miss Kinley "picking" on him for the rest of the day; but this time
there was the additional penalty of isolation. Penalty because
of the sudden ache to tell someone, to share the wonder of
his horse. Across the aisle he tried, "It's here, Skinny—it's
here—two white stockings—" but instant, like the crack of a
sniper's rifle, Miss Kinley's ruler struck the desk. "Indeed,
Peter! Fifteen minutes late and wasting time. I'm sure then
you will be able to explain the lesson to the rest of us who
aren't so clever. Step forward."

An age-long journey. He took a piece of chalk from her
outstretched hand, advanced to the blackboard, then stood
quite still and blind. It was a matter of papering a room in
which there were two doors and three windows, of a careless
paper-hanger who spoiled one foot for every ten he used, and
paper at fifty-seven cents a roll. "We're waiting," Miss Kinley
reminded him, but through the hammer of mortification in
his ears her voice came meaningless and faint. Hammer of
mortification—of despairing certainty that he would never
solve the problem—and at last of galloping hooves.

He couldn't help it. The rhythm persisted, stronger than his
will, than his embarrassment, stronger even than the im-
placability of Miss Kinley's tapping ruler. "We're waiting,
Peter," she repeated, but this time he didn't hear at all. Gradually the classroom fell away. The light flashed golden in his
eyes again. The fields sped reeling young and green.

The withering voice and stony eyes were all wasted. Back
in his seat at last, disgraced, studying the mountains and rivers
of South America, he began thinking again of a name for
his colt. Last summer on a visit to his uncle's ranch he had

met a cowboy with a horse called Tony. A white and sorrel skewbald: two round patches on his hips that shone when the sun was on them just like copper plates, hot bloodshot eyes and a rakish forelock—but somehow, for his horse, Tony wouldn't do. Too light, too easy. No, he wanted a name to match the look that had come into Dan's eyes when he lifted and held the colt, the little smile of marvelling delight. That was it—he wanted a name to match the miracle.

The same with the cowboy. A big, handsome fellow who had taken time off from roping steers to show Peter the spurs and belt and silver-studded chaps he had won in the big rodeos, who had brought him ten plugs of licorice one Saturday night from town, and a fine red silk bandana. But they had called him Slim, this cowboy, nothing but Slim; and not even to commemorate a hero and a friendship could Peter give a name like *that* to his horse.

Slim, though, must have had another name—a real name—so now that he had his own horse why not set out again to find him? Almost a horse—it wouldn't be long. To his uncle's ranch, then farther west and south. Rodeo to rodeo, round-up to round-up, until word at last must find its way to Slim of this young rider and his white-legged horse. Then on again, all four of them. Unequal, yet in total virtue equalling: himself on the horse that was to be called whatever Slim's name really was, and a great cowboy riding Tony.

They rode a long time. With swaggering sombreros, puff-pommelled saddle, gleaming spurs. Even while the class dismissed for recess, and Miss Kinley came again to learn the cost of papering a room with paper fifty-seven cents a roll. To the wonder and acclaim of crowds, and alone across desert wastelands. Even with the spelling lesson under way, and Skinny whispering across the aisle should 'muscle' have one *s* or two?

Until suddenly it was noon around him, with an offer from Skinny before they had even reached their lunch-pails to trade custard pie for gherkins. "That's what keeps you so thin," Peter rebuked him. "Always eating pickles—don't you know they dry up the blood? No—let's sit here on the steps today with the others."

Skinny drove to school, and when the weather was fine they usually sat in his buggy to eat their lunch, just the two of them, working out judicious trades, and for future adjustment keeping strict account of unequal ones. But today, blandly heedless of custom, Peter squeezed his way up to the top step, and left the choice of standing or the bottom one to Skinny. Skinny stood, because on the bottom step one became the irresistible target for everybody's crusts and egg-shells. "Here are the gherkins," Peter offered by way of compensation, holding out his lunch-pail over Rusty Martin's head. "I'm not very hungry so you can keep the pie."

And then, nibbling nervously at a sandwich, he waited. It was wise to wait. Watching the others all intent upon their lunch-pails, he congratulated himself on his foresight and forbearance. Not yet—they were too busy to listen. His announcement would be wasted. Not for at least another five minutes.

For last winter when he told Rusty Martin and the others about the colt they had laughed; and it was to settle that score, not to slight Skinny, that this noon he had chosen the steps for lunch. With the exception of Skinny not one of them had a horse of his own anyway. Not one of their fathers even had a horse that could be compared to Biddy or her colt. They wouldn't laugh now. They wouldn't say it was a funny Christmas present you had to wait five months for. His eyes narrowed as he watched them. It was hard holding back. The blood was pounding in his temples and his stomach felt small and tight. At last, momentously, he began:

"My colt's here, Skinny—the one I told you Biddy's been expecting." It was important to address himself to Skinny, to speak casually, so they would suspect nothing premeditated. Peering into his lunch-pail as if still hungry he went on, "Dan say he's not bad—the best one Biddy's ever had. And he's got a star, and two white stockings."

"A colt that's to be your own?" seven-year-old Willie Thompson squeaked. "Why?"

"Because my father's given him to me, that's why." Peter forgave Willie the absurdity of such a question, because his ear had caught a faint ring of the envy and incredulity he had been hoping for. "Last Christmas he promised. Remember, Skinny! I said all along it was to be May."

"What's two white stockings mean?" Willie squeaked again. "How can a colt—"

"He means white legs," Bud Nicholson broke in, confederate of Rusty in disdain. "I've got a calf with four."

"Me, too," another seven-year-old spoke up. "Three anyway and a foot. I call her Rosie."

Peter flinched. It was the promiscuity that hurt: Biddy's colt in the same breath with a calf called Rosie. To them his announcement could suggest no more than a heap of blear-eyed helplessness not very different from the reality in Biddy's stall before which he even he this morning had stood rather critical and unimpressed; but that, of course, was what he didn't understand. Their indifference as they closed up lunch-pails and flicked away crumbs seemed deliberate, a conspiracy to belittle his colt. He sat still a moment, indignant, tight-lipped; then, determined to exact their respect even at the cost of strict truthfulness:

"My brother says he's got legs to make a runner—and Dan knows horses."

"So brother Dan says," Rusty turned towards him, squinting, "but how do you think a colt out of that old Biddy mare's ever going to make a runner? Too much Clydesdale—you've only got to look at the feet."

"Biddy's not Clydesdale—not *all* Clydesdale. She's got racing blood."

"Maybe," Bud countered, "but the *father* of your colt's a Clydesdale. Pure-bred. I ought to know. Dad's got his papers framed and hanging in the stable. Mother won't have them in the house."

In the past few months faint suspicions of this had already occurred to Peter, but now, roused to defiance of even heredity and its laws, he flared, "I don't care who his father is—he's a runner. Dan says so. You've only got to look at his legs."

"Maybe he's right," Skinny agreed suddenly. "You can't always tell. My mother weighs two hundred and thirty-five and look at me."

"But that's because you're always eating pickles," Rusty

snickered. "There's an idea for you, Peter. Feed your nag pickles, and he'll maybe make a runner after all."

It was the insult "nag" that flashed a blaze of red in Peter's eyes, and hurled him both fists doubled square on Rusty's snickering jaw. They struck at each other wildly a few times, then clinched and rolled clattering off the steps among the lunch-pails. The boys made an instant eager ring around them; the girls ran squealing from the other side of the school to watch. Peter regained his feet first, and unethically pounced again before Rusty was off his knees. Rusty jerked up his head, caught Peter in the midriff, and sent him staggering back among the girls. It was a good fight while it lasted. Rusty had a loose tooth and a skinned cheekbone by the time Miss Kinley forced her way between them. Peter's nose was bleeding creditably, and one of his eyes had started to puff.

They washed, shook hands, said they were sorry, and then till classes were resumed at one o'clock worked long division questions on the blackboard. But Peter was too jubilant to mind. The colt, now that he had actually championed it, seemed more real, more dependable. When school called and the little girls tittered at his eye he smiled deeply. His horse was going to be a runner.

For their next period they were to write a composition. "Something that you'll enjoy," Miss Kinley beamed at them over her glasses. "How you spent last Saturday. Just a little story about the little things you did. Watch your spelling and punctuation—and remember the way to start a paragraph."

For a few minutes Peter conscientiously reviewed last Saturday; then he sat idle, wetting his pencil and thinking about the colt. It was useless. He hadn't done anything Saturday but help Dan plant potatoes. Some composition! "We've had enough nonsense from you already, Peter," Miss Kinley warned a second time. "Now hurry. I'm not going to speak to you again."

She sailed on to her desk at the front of the classroom; there was a moment's stillness round him, clear and isolating like a magic crystal globe; and then suddenly he was writing.

As he had never written before. Writing, writing—the words just pouring. "Early in the morning," this Saturday began, "I saddled my horse and rode over to meet Slim. He's a friend of mine. Then we went to the rodeo in town where everybody was waiting to see Slim ride broncos. He had on his leather chaps with the silver studs all over them, and a blue shirt and a yellow handkerchief—"

He wrote and he wrote. Because on the one hand it was impossible not to write at all, because Miss Kinley's threats were never idle; and because on the other it was equally impossible to write about last Saturday in its long-drawn, potato-planting reality. So he transformed it, soared above the limitations of mere time and distance. All the glamour and bravura of the rodeos he had never seen was there, all the fleet-limbed pride and wonder of the horse that still was but a few hours old, all the steadfastness of his vanished comrade-ship with Slim. Miss Kinley was aghast.

"I'll have to see you at recess," she said tensely; and at recess, white lips and knuckles suppressing tremendous agitation:

"How could you, Peter? Stand up and answer me. How could you? Rodeos—*cowboys*—you surely didn't expect me to believe—"

She was more distressed than angry. It was something she had never encountered before, something that evaded her ordinary, time-tried classifications of good conduct and bad. "You haven't a horse at all. You were at home on Saturday. I drove past your place on my way to town, and you were in the garden with your brother planting potatoes."

"Yes," he nodded quickly, "that was it—Saturday I planted potatoes all day."

"Then why didn't you obey me? Why did you write all this?"

He glanced up and met her eyes, wondering hopelessly how to make her understand. "Because it wasn't worth writing about—because it was just planting potatoes."

"And you think that's excuse enough for all these lies?"

"But they aren't lies, Miss Kinley—not real lies."

She pursed her lips. "You mean you do have a horse—and it did run a race and win a hundred dollars?"

"No—not really—not yet—"

Again she pursed her lips, then turned quickly and spoke over shoulder. "That's all then, for now. You'd better go outside and play for a few minutes. I'll have to keep you after school to write another composition."

But he couldn't play. He was beginning to feel that perhaps he had written lies, and to wonder what Dan or Slim would say if ever they found out. It was all because of Miss Kinley's strange distress. He had never seen it before, and it made him feel guiltier than if she had remained stern and unmoved as usual. "Just the way you spent the day," she pleaded with him after school—"if it's only six or seven lines—" and in response he wrote penitently:

> Saturday morning I had breakfast and fed the calves. Then I cut up potatoes into small pieces for planting with my brother Dan, and then we planted them. It was hot. He plowed furrows and I dropped the potatoes in. Then he plowed them over again with more furrows, but first he helped drop potatoes in too. We had a boiled rooster for dinner, because at this time of the year they're too tough any other way. We planted potatoes in the afternoon too till nearly supper-time and then I had to go for the cows. After supper Dan went to town. He wouldn't take me because he was going to take his girl. My back was stiff, so I went to bed. Dan brought me some gum. He said he bought some candies too, but his girl thought they were for her, so I didn't get them.

"It's very good," Miss Kinley said when he was finished. "Why couldn't you have written it in the first place? There—" With a sharp movement she tore out the two sheets of his scribbler on which he had written his first composition. "Run along now—we'll forget all about it."

He did run—hungry, shame-faced, tired—all his pride in a peerless horse become a humble need to draw comfort from a wobbly-legged one. At top speed every step of the mile. Catercorner over the oat field and garden. Straight past the house and on to the stable. Cuffing the pup away and scattering chickens. Until at the box-stall door he paused again— temples throbbing, eyes for a moment closed.

The box-stall was empty. He stared at it rooted with dread, then slapped down the pup and ran desperate around the stable to the pasture gate. But they were there, both with their ears pricked forward looking at him; and at the sight of the white-stockinged legs again he sprang forward shaking with relief. Biddy was patient. For more than a minute she let him worry and hug the colt, pull at its ears and try to lift its forefeet off the ground. Not till he started searching for teeth did she stretch out and nick him neatly with her own in the behind: a reminder that there were proprieties to be observed towards the newborn of even the equines.

It was getting late now. He flung himself down on the grass to lie watching the colt, but a sudden neigh from Biddy told him that the teams must already be coming in from the field. Supper-time—and he still had to go for the cows. Back at the gate for an instant he took one sandwich for himself from his lunch-pail, tossed out everything else for the pup lest his mother think he needed medicine, then set off slowly towards the far end of the pasture.

Slowly because he was tired now—because he had a black, swollen eye, and knew that at the supper-table there would be interminable questions. First the legitimate and reproachful ones of his mother, then the interfering and sarcastic ones of Dan. Dan was like that of late. Clean hands, good table manners, polite answers—ever since he started going with his girl friend—as if all at once it was his responsibility how the whole family behaved.

Peter wondered a little at this as he started the cows for home: how in the last year Dan could have become such a meddlesome old Miss Kinley, and yet at the same time remain among his horses so infallible and true. Too bad that instead of *riding* horses like Slim he just drove them hitched to a cultivator or plough. Peter himself could now drive six abreast —even climb up in the mangers and put their bridles on. Nothing to it—Dan had wasted himself. The way to a really full and virile life, he decided sagely, was never a girl friend and never a compromise with a plough.

When at last he reached the stable Dan and his father had already gone in for supper. He lingered a few minutes, responsive to the stillness and the nuzzling hunger round him, just as that morning when he tiptoed to Biddy's stall in fearful hope of what awaited him. The same hush, the same solemnity. He looked into the stall again, turned quickly from its emptiness and slipped upstairs to the loft.

To be alone a few minutes longer, to feel his way through and beyond this mystery of beginning—all at once it was important, necessary. A little door in the loft that they used for throwing in feed was open, and he sat down on its sill, his legs dangling out against the stable wall. Before him the prairie spread alight with slanting sun and early grain. For a few miles it fell gently, then with a long slow swell slipped over the horizon. There was a state of mind, a mood, a restfulness, in which one could skim along this curve of prairie floor and, gathering momentum from the downward swing, glide up again and soar away from earth. He succeeded now, borne by a white-limbed steed again. And as they soared the mystery was not solved, but gradually absorbed, a mystery still but intimate, a heartening gleam upon the roof of life to let him see its vault and spaciousness.

"Supper," they called him from the house, "supper—we're waiting—" but he wasn't listening. Biddy had come round the corner of the stable, and slowly, to let the colt keep up with her, was cropping her way towards the well. Trim little white-stockinged legs, toy-horse tail, head up as if in consternation at the windmill and the cock-eared pup. And this time yesterday there had been no colt at all. In a single day he had met the Parkers, seen chickens and cows, smelled grass.

"Supper," they called again, Dan's voice now a boom of warning, but just for a moment longer he sat still. Thinking that beyond a doubt the horses had the best of it, awake the first day, nearly half-grown up as soon as they were born. Legs that could walk—eyes that could see. Able to go into and explore a whole new waiting world. . . . It seemed a pity that a boy was never born that way.

Gabrielle Roy   THE MOVE

I have perhaps never envied anyone as much as a girl I knew
when I was about eleven years old and of whom today I
remember not much more than the name, Florence. Her
father was a mover. I don't think this was his trade. He was
a handyman, I imagine, engaging in various odd jobs; at the
time of the seasonal movings—and it seems to me that people
changed their lodgings often in those days—he moved the
household effects of people of small means who lived near
us and even quite far away, in the suburbs and distant
quarters of Winnipeg. No doubt, his huge cart and his horses,
which he had not wanted to dispose of when he came from
the country to the city, had made him a mover.

On Saturdays Florence accompanied her father on his
journeys, which, because of the slow pace of the horses, often
took the entire day. I envied her to the point of having no
more than one fixed idea: Why was my father not also a
mover? What finer trade could one practice?

I don't know what moving signified to me in those days.
Certainly I could not have had any clear idea what it was
like. I had been born and had grown up in the fine, comfortable house in which we were still living and which, in all
probability, we would never leave. Such fixity seemed fright-
fully monotonous to me that summer. Actually we were
never really away from that large house. If we were going
to the country for a while, even if we were only to be absent

for a day, the problem immediately arose: Yes, but who will look after the house?

To take one's furniture and belongings, to abandon a place, close a door behind one forever, say good-by to a neighbourhood, this was an adventure of which I knew nothing; and it was probably the sheer force of my efforts to picture it to myself that made it seem so daring, heroic, and exalted in my eyes.

"Aren't we ever going to move?" I used to ask Maman.

"I certainly hope not," she would say. "By the grace of God and the long patience of your father, we are solidly established at last. I only hope it is forever."

She told me that to her no sight in the world could be more heartbreaking, more poignant even, than a house moving.

"For a while," she said, "it's as if you were related to the nomads, those poor souls who slip along the surface of existence, putting their roots down nowhere. You no longer have a roof over your head. Yes indeed, for a few hours at least, it's as if you were drifting on the stream of life."

Poor Mother! Her objections and comparisons only strengthened my strange hankering. To drift on the stream of life! To be like the nomads! To wander through the world! There was nothing in any of this that did not seem to me complete felicity.

Since I myself could not move, I wished to be present at someone else's moving and see what it was all about. Summer came. My unreasonable desire grew. Even now I cannot speak of it lightly, much less so with derision. Certain of our desires, as if they knew about us before we do ourselves, do not deserve to be mocked.

Each Saturday morning I used to go and wander around Florence's house. Her father—a big dirty-blond man in blue work clothes, always grumbling a little or even, perhaps, swearing—would be busy getting the impressive cart out of the barn. When the horses were harnessed and provided with nose bags of oats, the father and his little daughter would climb onto the high seat; the father would take the reins in his hands; they would both, it seemed to me, look at me then with slight pity, a vague commiseration. I would feel forsaken, of an inferior species of humans unworthy of high adventure.

The father would shout something to the horses. The cart would shake. I would watch them set out in that cool little morning haze that seems to promise such delightful emotions to come. I would wave my hand at them, even though they never looked back at me. "Have a good trip," I would call. I would feel so unhappy at being left behind that I would nurse my regret all day and with it an aching curiosity. What would they see today? Where were they at this moment? What was offering itself to their travellers' eyes? It was no use my knowing that they could go only a limited distance in any event. I would imagine the two of them seeing things that no one else in the world could see. From the top of the cart, I thought, how transformed the world must appear.

At last my desire to go with them was so strong and so constant that I decided to ask my mother for permission— although I was almost certain I would never obtain it. She held my new friends in rather poor esteem and, though she tolerated my hanging continually about them, smelling their odour of horses, adventure, and dust, I knew in my heart of hearts that the mere idea that I might wish to accompany them would fill her with indignation.

At my first words, indeed, she silenced me.

"Are you mad? To wander about the city in a moving wagon! Just picture yourself," she said, "in the midst of furniture and boxes and piled-up mattresses all day, and with who knows what people! What can you imagine would be pleasant about that?"

How strange it was. Even the idea, for instance, of being surrounded by heaped-up chairs, chests with empty drawers, unhooked pictures—the very novelty of all this stimulated my desire.

"Never speak of that whim to me again," said my mother. "The answer is no and no it will remain."

Next day I went over to see Florence, to feed my nostalgic envy of their existence on the few words she might say to me.

"Where did you go yesterday? Who did you move?"

"Oh I'm not sure," Florence said, chewing gum—she was always either chewing gum or sucking a candy. "We went over to Fort Rouge, I think, to get some folks and move them way to hell and gone over by East Kildonan."

These were the names of quite ordinary suburbs. Why was it that at moments such as these they seemed to hold the slightly poignant attraction of those parts of the world that are remote, mysterious, and difficult to reach?

"What did you see?" I asked.

Florence shifted her gum from one cheek to the other, looking at me with slightly foolish eyes. She was not an imaginative child. No doubt, to her and her father the latter's work seemed banal, dirty, and tiring, and nothing more similar to one household move than another household move. Later I discovered that if Florence accompanied her father every Saturday, it was only because her mother went out cleaning that day and there was no one to look after the little girl at home. So her father took her along.

Both father and daughter began to consider me a trifle mad to endow their life with so much glamour.

I had asked the big pale-blond man countless times if he wouldn't take me too. He always looked at me for a moment as at some sort of curiosity—a child who perhaps wasn't completely normal—and said, "If your mother gives you permission . . ." and spat on the ground, hitched up his huge trousers with a movement of his hips, then went off to feed his horses or grease the wheels of his cart.

The end of the moving season was approaching. In the blazing heat of summer no one moved except people who were being evicted or who had to move closer to a new job, rare cases. If I don't soon manage to see what moving is like, I thought, I'll have to wait till next summer. And who knows? Next summer I may no longer have such a taste for it.

The notion that my desire might not always mean so much to me, instead of cheering me, filled me with anxiety. I began to realize that even our desires are not eternally faithful to us, that they wear out, perhaps die, or are replaced by others, and this precariousness of their lives made them seem more touching to me, more friendly. I thought that if we do not satisfy them they must go away somewhere and perish of boredom and lassitude.

Observing that I was still taken up with my "whim," Maman perhaps thought she might distract me from it by telling me once more the charming stories of her own childhood. She chose, oddly enough, to tell me again about the long journey of her family across the prairie by covered wagon. The truth must have been that she herself relived this thrilling voyage into the unknown again and again and that, by recounting it to me, she perhaps drained away some of that heartbreaking nostalgia that our life deposits in us, whatever it may be.

So here she was telling me again how, crowded together in the wagon—for Grandmother had brought some of her furniture, her spinning wheel certainly, and innumerable bundles —pressed closely in together, they had journeyed across the immense country.

"The prairie at that time," she said, "seemed even more immense than it does today, for there were no villages to speak of along the trail and only a few houses. To see even one, away far off in the distance, was an adventure in itself."

"And what did you feel?" I asked her.

"I was attracted," Maman admitted, bowing her head slightly, as if there were something a bit wrong, or at least strange, about this. "Attracted by the space, the great bare sky, the way the tiniest tree was visible in this solitude for miles. I was very much attracted."

"So you were happy?"

"Happy? Yes, I think so. Happy without knowing why. Happy as you are, when you are young—or even not so young —simply because you are in motion, because life is changing and will continue to change and everything is being renewed. It's curious," she told me. "Such things must run in families, for I wonder whether there have ever been such born travellers as all of us."

And she promised me that later on I too would know what it is to set forth, to be always seeking from life a possible beginning over—and that perhaps I might even become weary of it.

That night the intensity of my desire wakened me from sleep. I imagined myself in my mother's place, a child lying, as she had described it, on the floor of the wagon, watching the prairie stars—the most luminous stars in either hemisphere, it is said—as they journeyed over her head.

That, I thought, I shall never know; it is a life that is gone beyond recall and lost—and the mere fact that there were ways of life that were over, extinct in the past, and that we could not recover them in our day, filled me with the same nostalgic longing for the lost years as I had felt for my own perishable desires. But, for lack of anything better, there was the possible journey with our neighbours.

I knew—I guessed, rather—that, though we owe obedience to our parents, we owe it also to certain of our desires, those that are strangest, piercing, and too vast.

I remained awake. Tomorrow—this very day, rather—was a Saturday, moving day. I had resolved to go with the Pichettes.

Dawn appeared. Had I ever really seen it until now? I noticed that before the sky becomes clean and shining, it takes on an indecisive colour, like badly washed laundry.

Now, the desire that was pushing me so violently, to the point of revolt, had no longer anything happy or even tempting about it. It was more like an order. Anguish weighed upon my heart. I wasn't even free now to say to myself, "Sleep. Forget all that." I had to go.

Is it the same anguish that has wakened me so many times in my life, wakens me still at dawn with the awareness of an imminent departure, sad sometimes, sometimes joyful, but almost always toward an unknown destination? Is it always the same departure that is involved?

When I judged the morning to be sufficiently advanced, I got up and combed my hair. Curiously enough, for this trip in a cart, I chose to put on my prettiest dress. "Might as well be hung for a sheep as a lamb," I said to myself, and left the house without a sound.

I arrived soon at the mover's. He was yawning on the

threshold of the barn, stretching his arms in the early sun. He considered me suspiciously.

"Have you got permission?"

I swallowed my saliva rapidly. I nodded.

A little later Florence appeared, looking bad-tempered and sleepy.

She hitched herself up onto the seat beside us.

"Giddup!" cried the man.

And we set out in that cool morning hour that had promised me the transformation of the world and everything in it— and undoubtedly of myself.

2

And at first the journey kept its promise. We were passing through a city of sonorous and empty streets, over which we rolled with a great noise. All the houses seemed to be still asleep, bathed in a curious and peaceful atmosphere of withdrawal. I had never seen our little town wearing this absent, gentle air of remoteness.

The great rising sun bleached and purified it, I felt. I seemed to be travelling through an absolutely unknown city, remote and still to be explored. And yet I was astonished to recognize, as if vaguely, buildings, church spires, and street crossings that I must have seen somewhere before. But how could this be, since I had this morning left the world I had known and was entering into a new one?

Soon streetcars and a few automobiles began to move about. The sight of them looming upon the horizon and coming toward us gave me a vivid sense of the shifting of epochs.

What had these streetcars and automobiles come to do in our time, which was that of the cart? I asked myself with pleasure. When we reached Winnipeg and became involved in already heavy traffic, my sense of strangeness was so great that I believed I must be dreaming and clapped my hands.

Even at that time a horse-drawn cart must have been rare in the centre of the city. So, at our side, everything was moving quickly and easily. We, with our cumbrous and reflective gait, passed like a slow, majestic film. I am the past, I am times gone by, I said to myself with fervour.

People stopped to watch us pass. I looked at them in turn, as if from far away. What did we have in common with this modern, noisy, agitated city? Increasingly, high in the cart, I became a survivor from times past. I had to restrain myself from beginning to salute the crowds, the streets, and the city, as if they were lucky to see us sweeping by.

For I had a tendency to divide into two people, actor and witness. From time to time I was the crowd that watched the passage of this astonishing cart from the past. Then I was the personage who considered from on high these modern times at her feet.

Meanwhile the difficulty of driving his somewhat nervous horses through all this noise and traffic was making the mover, whom I would have expected to be calmer and more composed, increasingly edgy. He complained and even swore noisily at almost everything we encountered. This began to embarrass me. I felt that his bad temper was spoiling all the pleasure and the sense of gentle incongruity that the poor people of the present era might have obtained from our appearance in their midst. I should have very much liked to disassociate myself from him. But how could I, jammed in beside him as I was?

Finally, we took to small, quieter streets. I saw then that we were going toward Fort Garry.

"Is that the way we're going?"

"Yes," replied Monsieur Pichette ungraciously. "That's the way."

The heat was becoming overpowering. Without any shelter, wedged between the big bulky man and Florence, who made no effort to leave me a comfortable place, I was beginning to suffer greatly. At last, after several hours, we were almost in the country.

The houses were still ranked along narrow streets, but now these were short and beyond them the prairie could be seen like a great recumbent land—a land so widespread that doubtless one would never be able to see either its end or its beginning. My heart began once more to beat hard.

There begins the land of the prairies, I said to myself. There begins the infinite prairie of Canada.

"Are we going to go onto the real prairie?" I asked. "Or are we still really inside the city limits?"

"You are certainly the most inquisitive little girl I've ever seen in my life," grumbled Monsieur Pichette, and he told me nothing at all.

Now the roads were only of dirt, which the wind lifted in dusty whirlwinds. The houses spaced themselves out, became smaller and smaller. Finally they were no more than badly constructed shacks, put together out of various odds and ends —a bit of tin, a few planks, some painted, some raw—and they all seemed to have been raised during the night only to be demolished the next day. Yet, unfinished as they were, the little houses still seemed old. Before one of them we stopped.

The people had begun to pile up their belongings, in the house or outside it, in cardboard cartons or merely thrown pell-mell into bedcovers with the corners knotted to form rough bundles. But they were not very far along, according to Monsieur Pichette, who flew into a rage the moment we arrived.

"I only charge five dollars to move people," he said, "and they aren't even ready when I get here."

We all began to transport the household effects from the shack to the cart. I joined in, carrying numerous small objects that fell to my hand—saucepans with unmatching covers, a pot, a chipped water jug. I was trying, I think, to distract myself, to keep, if at all possible, the little happiness I had left. For I was beginning to realize that the adventure was taking a sordid turn. In this poor, exhausted-looking woman with her hair plastered to her face, and in her husband—a man as lacking in amiability as Monsieur Pichette—I was discovering people who were doomed to a life of which I knew nothing, terribly gray and, it seemed to me, without exit. So I tried to help them as much as I could and took it upon myself to carry some rather large objects on my own. At last I was told to sit still because I was getting in everyone's way.

I went to rejoin Florence, who was sitting a short distance away on a little wooden fence.

"Is it always like this?" I asked.

"Yes, like this—or worse."

"It's possible to be worse?"

"Much worse. These people," she said, "have beds, and dressers. . . ."

She refused to enlighten me further.

"I'm hungry," she decided and she ran to unpack a little lunch box, took out some bread and butter and an apple and proceeded to eat under my nose.

"Didn't you bring anything to eat?" she asked.

"No."

"You should have," she said, and continued to bite hungrily into her bread, without offering me a scrap.

I watched the men bring out some soiled mattresses, which they carried at arm's length. New mattresses are not too distressing a sight; but once they have become the slightest bit worn or dirty I doubt that any household object is more repugnant. Then the men carried out an old torn sofa on their shoulders, some bedposts and springs. I tried to whip up my enthusiasm, to revive a few flames of it, at least. And it was then, I think, that I had a consoling idea: we had come to remove these people from this wretched life; we were going to take them now to something better; we were going to find them a fine, clean house.

A little dog circled around us, whimpering, starving, perhaps anxious. For his sake more than my own maybe, I would have liked to obtain a few bits of Florence's lunch.

"Won't you give him a little bit?" I asked.

Florence hastily devoured a large mouthful.

"Let him try and get it," she said.

The cart was full now and, on the ground beside it, almost as many old things still waited to be stowed away.

I began to suffer for the horses, which would have all this to pull.

The house was completely emptied, except for bits of broken dishes and some absolutely worthless rags. The woman was the last to come out. This was the moment I had imagined as dramatic, almost historic, undoubtedly marked by some memorable gesture or word. But this poor creature, so weary and dust-covered, had apparently no regret at crossing her threshold, at leaving behind her two, three, or perhaps four years of her life.

" Come, we'll have to hurry," she said simply, "if we want to be in our new place before night."

She climbed onto the seat of the cart with one of the younger children, whom she took on her knees. The others went off with their father, to go a little way on foot, then by streetcar, to be ahead of us, they said, at the place where we were going.

Florence and I had to stand among the furniture piled up behind.

The enormous cart now looked like some sort of monster, with tubs and pails bouncing about on both sides, upturned chairs, huge clumsy packages bulging in all directions.

The horses pulled vigorously. We set out. Then the little dog began to run along behind us, whimpering so loudly in fear and despair that I cried, imagining that no one had thought of him, "We've forgotten the little dog. Stop. Wait for the little dog."

In the face of everyone's indifference, I asked the woman, whose name was Mrs. Smith, "Isn't he yours?"

"Yes, he's ours, I suppose," she replied.

"He's coming. Wait for him," I begged.

"Don't you think we're loaded up enough already?" the mover snapped dryly, and he whipped his horses.

For a long moment more the little dog ran along behind us.

He wasn't made for running, this little dog. His legs were too short and bowed. But he did his best. Ah yes! He did his best.

Is he going to try to follow us across the whole city? I thought with distress. Awkward, distracted, and upset as he was, he would surely be crushed by an automobile or a streetcar. I don't know which I dreaded most: to see him turn back alone toward the deserted house or try to cross the city, come what might. We were already turning onto a street that was furrowed with tracks. A streetcar was approaching in the distance; several cars passed us, honking.

Mrs. Smith leaned down from the seat of the cart and shouted at the little dog, "Go on home."

Then she repeated, more loudly, "Go on home, stupid."

So he had a sort of name, even though cruel, yet he was being abandoned.

Overcome with astonishment, the little dog stopped, hesitated a moment, then lay down on the ground, his eyes turned toward us, watching us disappear and whimpering with fright on the edge of the big city.

And a little later I was pleased, as you will understand, that I did not need to look at him any longer.

3

I have always thought that the human heart is a little like the ocean, subject to tides, that joy rises in it in a steady flow, singing of waves, good fortune, and bliss; but afterward, when the high sea withdraws, it leaves an utter desolation in our sight. So it was with me that day.

We had gone back across almost the whole enormous city —less enormous perhaps than scattered, strangely, widely spread out. The eagerness of the day diminished. I even think the sun was about to disappear. Our monster cart plunged, like some worn-out beast, toward the inconvenient, rambling neighbourhoods that lay at the exact opposite end of the city to the one from which we had come.

Florence was whiling away the time by opening the drawers of an old chest and thrusting her hand into the muddle inside —the exact embodiment, it seemed to me, of this day—bits of faded ribbon; old postcards on whose backs someone had one day written: Splendid weather, Best love and kisses; a quill from a hat; electricity bills; gas reminders; a small child's shoe. The disagreeable little girl gathered up handfuls of these things, examined them, read, laughed. At one point, sensing my disapproval, she looked up, saw me watching her rummage, and thumbed her nose in spite.

The day declined further. Once more we were in sad little streets, without trees, so much like the one from which we had taken the Smiths that it seemed to me we had made all this journey for nothing and were going to end up finally at the same shack from which I had hoped to remove them.

At the end of each of these little streets the infinite prairie once more appeared but now almost dark, barely tinted, on the rim of the horizon, with angry red—the pensive, melancholy prairie of my childhood.

At last we had arrived.

Against that red horizon a small lonely house stood out black, quite far from its neighbours—a small house without foundations, set upon the ground. It did not seem old but it was already full of the odour and, no doubt, the rags and tatters of the people who had left it a short time ago. However, they had not left a single light bulb in place.

In the semidarkness Mrs. Smith began to search through her bundles, lamenting that she was sure she had tucked two or three carefully away but no longer remembered where. Her husband, who had arrived a short time before us, distressed by the dimness and the clumsiness of his wife, began to accuse her of carelessness. The children were hungry; they started to cry with fretful frightened voices, in an importunate tone that reminded me of the whimpering of the little dog. The parents distributed a few slaps, a little haphazardly, it seemed to me. Finally Mrs. Smith found a light bulb. A small glow shone forth timidly, as if ashamed at having to illuminate such a sad beginning.

One of the children, tortured by some strange preference, began to implore, "Let's go home. This isn't our home. Oh let's go back home!"

Mrs. Smith had come across a sack of flour, a frying pan and some eggs while she was searching for light bulbs and now she courageously set to work preparing a meal for her family. It was this, I think, that saddened me most: this poor woman, in the midst of complete disorder and almost in the dark, beginning to make pancakes. She offered some to me. I ate a little, for I was very hungry. At that moment I believe she was sorry she had abandoned the little dog. This was the one small break in the terrible ending of this day.

Meanwhile Monsieur Pichette, in a grumbling anxiety to be finished, had completely emptied the cart. As soon as everything was dumped on the ground in front of the door, he came and said to Mr. Smith, "That's five dollars."

"But you have to help me carry it all in," said Mr. Smith.

"Not on your life. I've done all I have to."

Poor Mr. Smith fumbled in his pocket and took out five dollars in bills and small change, which he handed to the mover.

The latter counted the money in the weak glimmer that came from the house and said, "That's it. We're quits."

In this glimmer from the house I noticed that our poor horses were also very tired. They blinked their eyes with a lost expression, the result of too many house movings, no doubt. Perhaps horses would prefer to make the same trip over and over again—in this way they would not feel too estranged from their customary ways. But, always setting out on new routes, toward an unknown destination, they must feel disconcerted and dejected. I had time, by hurrying, to fetch them each a handful of tender grass at the end of the street where the prairie began.

What would we have had to say to each other on our way back? Nothing, certainly, and so we said nothing. Night had fallen, black, sad, and impenetrable, when we finally reached the old stable, which had once seemed to me to contain more magic and charm than even the cave of Aladdin.

The mover nevertheless reached out his hand to help me down from the cart. He was one of those people—at least I thought so then—who, after being surly and detestable all day, try at the last moment to make amends with a pleasant word for the bad impression they have created. But it was too late, much too late.

"You're not too tired?" he asked, I believe.

I shook my head and after a quick good night, an unwilling thank you, I fled. I ran toward my home, the sidewalk resounding in the silence under my steps.

I don't believe I thought of rejoicing at what I was returning to—a life that, modest as it was, was still a thousand miles away from that of the Pichettes and the Smiths. And I had not yet realized that this whole shabby, dull, and pitiless side of life that the move had revealed to me today would further increase my frenzy to escape.

I was thinking only of my mother's anxiety, of my longing to find her again and be pardoned by her—and perhaps pardon her in turn for some great mysterious wrong whose point I did not understand.

She was in such a state of nervous tension, as a matter of fact—although neighbours had told her I had gone off early with the Pichettes—that when she saw me it was her exasperation that got the upper hand. She even raised her hand to strike me. I did not think of avoiding punishment. I may even have wanted it. But at that moment a surge of disillusionment came over me—that terrible distress of the heart after it has been inflated like a balloon.

I looked at my mother and cried, "Oh why have you said a hundred times that from the seat of the covered wagon on the prairie in the old days the world seemed renewed, different, and so beautiful?"

She looked at me in astonishment.

"Ah, so that's it!" she said.

And at once, to my profound surprise, she drew me toward her and cradled me in her arms.

"You too then!" she said. "You too will have the family disease, departure sickness. What a calamity!"

Then, hiding my face against her breast, she began to croon me a sort of song, without melody and almost without words.

"Poor you," she intoned. "Ah, poor you! What is to become of you!"

Robert Kroetsch   EARTH MOVING

It had begun to snow finally and, though no trucks rattled empty down the trail from the plain above the valley, Mrs. Kubichek, standing now on the rusty tracks at the hillside entrance to her small underground coal mine, ventured a private smile. Even when she saw a man on foot coming up from the valley bottom, she seemed to ignore him and started around the hoist engine and tipple, and she walked carelessly along the path toward her shack. But she saw the man come past the empty bunkhouse and noticed when he waved.

"What are you doing here?" she called.

Jake the Miner had plagued her for fourteen years. He spent his life panning and sluicing for gold in the worthless mud of the Battle River, and so far he had earned nothing but a mocking nickname. To keep himself alive until he struck it rich he trapped muskrats, cut willow fence posts, rustled an occasional calf from a local rancher before branding time, dug coal for a day or two—or, when he was really hard put, he set up a still and cooked a batch of moonshine. And in twenty years of assembling and concealing his piece of copper tubing and an old cream can, he had never found a better hide-out than a deserted room in the Black Jade Mine.

"What are you up to?" Mrs. Kubichek repeated.

This time Jake was within hearing distance. "I thought you might need an extra man."

"You never in your life came near a place when there was work to be done."

Jake grinned and set down the gunny sack he had been carrying. He was wearing a faded blue denim smock that showed holes in its four pockets, his pants and rubber boots were spattered with dry grey mud, and cocked forward on his head, its brim laden with snow, was a badly weathered straw hat. "What's the matter?" he said. "No work?"

"There'll be lots of trucks by morning," Mrs. Kubichek said. "My boys'll be back from the strip mine wanting their old jobs again."

Jake looked at her as if surprised that she didn't laugh at her own joke. "You haven't sold a truckload in a month."

"Wait until it turns cold."

"For God's sake, it's snowing!" Jake held out his ragged arms as if to catch an armful of flakes and show her. "So here you sit with picks and shovels while that outfit across the river is loading coal with draglines."

"Wait until morning," Mrs. Kubichek said. "There'll be trucks lined up clear back to the powder shack."

"They don't have to line up at the strip mine. They get loaded and off they go, and they sell their loads and come back for more."

"Go on! Get the devil going!"

"I'm going," Jake said.

"You're going! Ha! You got no place to go. After all these years you got nothing but a log cabin and two blankets."

"Where are *you* going now?" Jake's small weathered face, beneath the straw hat that was too big, wrinkled into a grin again.

"You go!" Mrs. Kubichek said. She pulled the hood of her heavy woollen plaid parka closer around her face. Her voice now was as frantic and yet as quiet as the snowflakes that twisted down out of the sky. "The next time you show your nose around here, I'm calling the police. I raised a family while you haven't even looked after yourself."

"I brought you a couple partridges," Jake said. He picked up a bottom corner of the gunny sack, dumped out the two birds at her feet, and turned away.

The wind died down before evening, and as the sky cleared the temperature began to fall. All night Mrs. Kubichek lay and listened for the sound of truck brakes, the curses of men stepping down from warm cabs. In other years the truckers from the wheat farms and the prairie towns for fifty miles around had come to her mine for coal. They would arrive during the night, park their trucks in the loading line, then go to the tar paper bunkhouse outside the mine entrance: there they would kick off their boots and sleep fully clothed on the wooden bunks or sit drinking coffee and whiskey and play poker until the mine opened and their turns came to load. All night Mrs. Kubichek listened, hoping as she and her husband had hoped that night over twenty-two years before, after the day he dug and loaded and hoisted out of the mine the first ton of coal that was his own.

A coal miner and a coal miner's son, her husband left the big mines up in Crow's Nest Pass when he was laid off in the thirties. He vowed that his sons would not know such an experience, and he brought his wife and three sons out of the mountains, down onto the flat Alberta plains. He set out to find a store, a homestead, a construction job—anything but a coal mining outfit. And he came, by chance or instinct, to the Battle River.

Here he found an unexpected valley, a sudden valley, as if the frost of winter or the drought of summer had one night split the land. He explored the dry horseshoes, grown over with spruce and tamarack, crossed the dry flats and searched up the ravines and coulees, matted with saskatoons, poplars, and chokecherry bushes. He drove his spade into the reddish-grey eroded valley walls, always watching, always seeking. And when he found what he sought, he dug a slanting shaft down into the clay hillside and marked a trail across the prairie from the nearest town to the valley's edge—and he was again a miner. Eight years later, to the day, the mine that was his own killed him.

Now Rachel Kubichek lay and listened for the first trucks that had always come with the cold weather to buy coal. She listened impatiently, afraid for her pride in the mine and in her family, afraid for having laughed even when the strip miners offered her sons summer jobs. From across the valley tonight she could hear the clank of bulldozers peeling off the acres of clay, the grunt of a dragline scooping up four tons of coal at a swing.

She waited impatiently through the night, and when at last the sun rose, bursting the horizon's long seam, she touched her stockinged feet to the cold worn linoleum and hurried to the kitchen door. Across the valley there were new droppings of clay on the snow-covered mounds. There were columns of smoke rising stiffly into the sky above the strip mine. There was the distant clatter and noise as of magpies circling down onto carrion.

And at the Black Jade Mine the ground was white with snow, and the snow was banked and drifted and as new and old and trackless as Pre-Cambrian rock. At the loading chute, there were no trucks.

The strip miners had arrived unannounced one morning shortly after the first spring thaw. They had torn down a barbed wire fence, had moved into a stubble field, and half an hour later, with bulldozers and power shovels, they were digging their own valley. On the wide prairie horizon they were building their own hills.

Mrs. Kubichek called it the labour of fools—moving sixty feet of waste to lay bare a seam of coal. "Wait until it snows," she told her three sons, early in the summer. "Then we'll have trucks to load. Then they'll come hightailing back to us." And she had scoffed too heartily—for evening came now, on the day after the first snowfall, and still no trucks arrived.

When it was eight o'clock Rachel took the coal scuttle and went out to the mine to start the water pump and to feed the mine horse that was not supposed to leave the mine all winter. Snow had begun to fall again, but she could still find the path to the mine. She stopped at the hillside entrance to light her carbide cap-lamp. A cold wind was blowing from the north, and she hurried down into the warmth of the sloping shaft. Two hundred feet inside, at the bottom of the slope, she stopped and listened. She could hear water trickling, and her impulse was to start the pump. But first she would feed the horse.

She walked back to the room where the horse was stabled and dipped a pailful of oats out of a small bin. Then she heard the horse's rhythmic munching. Quickly she went to the feed box.

The horse had been fed.

"Joe!" she called, remembering her son who had most delighted in feeding the horse.

Her voice echoed back to her from the dark, timbered corridors and from the silent rooms. Nearby, a handful of coal dust whispered down from above a timber, cutting a shadow through the light from her cap-lamp.

She set down the coal scuttle and stepping between the slippery grey ties that led through the tunnel to the rooms she followed the track along which the horse had so often pulled five loaded coal cars to where they could be hooked onto the hoisting cable. She looked into each room—at the picks, the drills, the empty coal cars, the heaps of clay bone. Becoming a little frightened, she picked up a shovel.

Then she looked into the last room under the air shaft and saw him; a man sitting on a pile of hay, his boots off, his stockinged feet up against a small fire that flickered beneath a five-gallon cream can.

A coil of copper tubing curled from the lid and ran through a bucket of water, and at the end of the tube an empty whiskey bottle caught the slow drip, drip of alcohol.

Jake was toying with a lump of coal.

"What did I tell you?" Rachel demanded.

Jake had heard her coming and now he held up the lump of coal so that she could see it. On the lump was preserved a patterned outline.

The fossil glistened black and was clean of dust. It had a familiar look—almost like the tropical fern that Rachel kept hanging in the window of her living room. "So what?"

"Maybe things change."

"Change, you say?" Rachel remembered at that instant what Joe as a schoolboy had told her years before: this very bed of coal had once been a tropical inland sea. She thought of the winter above her, of the broad, snow-buried plain, and a picture came to her mind from one of Joe's school books: a painting of a luxuriant lagoon, of trees that were not poplar or spruce or balm of Gilead, of strange lizard-looking birds, of tropical ferns, of dinosaurs as huge as draglines, scooping up the green slime.

"No," she said. "How could they, Jake?"

"These new strip miners," Jake said. "They'll pay three dollars for a bottle of stuff that's been run through charcoal or a loaf of bread."

"Stuff!" Mrs. Kubichek pointed at the cream can like a mother pointing at a broken window. "What's this?"

"It ain't the best batch," Jake said. "Threw in too many potato peels—wait!"

Suddenly Mrs. Kubichek had raised up the shovel she was holding: before Jake could move, the shovel smashed into the cream can and upset it.

The spilled mash put out the fire, and Jake stumbled clear of the swinging shovel as the lamp on Mrs. Kubichek's cap cut wild arcs through the dark. Tubes and bottles fell with a clattering, splintering violence: echoes pounded back from the corridors. Then suddenly she was finished, and Jake, trying to keep his stockinged feet away from the hissing coals, was feeling in the darkness for his boots.

In silence, bending against the long incline, they started up the two-hundred-foot slope, Mrs. Kubichek in the lead. In a moment the sound of the horse's steady munching was gone. The sound of trickling water faded, but still there was no square of light ahead of them. They climbed onward, occasionally catching at a mine timber to help themselves along, and after a while the damp warm air was replaced by air that was dry and cold.

At the surface Mrs. Kubichek stopped and stared about her. The snow was coming down more heavily now. The wind had become stronger. After putting out her lamp—chiefly to inconvenience Jake—she could not, for a moment, make out the path, nor even her earlier footsteps. In the darkness she could not see the bunkhouse near the mine entrance. It seemed to her that she was walled in.

Then across the valley she noticed headlights raising snow-drifted pillars against the dark sky. Bulldozers, their yellow bodies lost in the snow, were swarming over the new hills. Even while the wind swirled into a blizzard, while the snow came in torn, driven fragments, men were labouring, defying the night.

After she caught her breath Mrs. Kubichek spoke. "My boys," she said, hesitantly, preparing to try the new words on her dry lips, "—they do the blasting over there."

"Good," Jake said. "That's good money." He raised his hand in a faint gesture and started down the path.

"Jake," Mrs. Kubichek said.

"Sure."

"I'll bet you didn't eat," Rachel said. "I'll go get you some supper."

"I can eat in my cabin. I got some soup I made yesterday."

"How about some roast partridge and some wild cranberry sauce? You'd have time to go start your fire."

"My mash is spoiled, probably," Jake said.

"I got some sugar in the house. Left over from canning."

Jake shrugged. "Even then. I'll have to get a new container." He started again down the path.

"I got an eight-gallon cream can," Mrs. Kubichek called. "Come on over to the shack."

"You sure?" Jake said. "Eight gallons?"

"Come on," Mrs. Kubichek said. She waved her hands through the snowflakes as if to shoo them away. "I don't think you charge them enough, Jake."

"I haven't even got any empties," Jake said.

"There are all kinds out behind the bunkhouse. A regular little gold mine."

Jake cleared his throat but didn't speak. He reached up and tapped the straw hat more firmly onto his head.

"You need a light?" Mrs. Kubichek said.

"I think I can make out," Jake the Miner said.

Mrs. Kubichek chuckled deeply. "You think," she said. "You figure, Jake, we could soak them three-fifty for stuff that's been run through a loaf of bread?"

Edward McCourt   CRANES

                                         FLY

                                         SOUTH

"They fly all night," the old man said. "First you hear a sound far off and you figger it's thunder—and it gits louder and nearer, and soon it's like a freight train passin' right over your head, and if there's a moon they fly across it and the night gits dark—"

"But I tell you I saw one!" Lee said. "Honest, Grandpa. Out at Becker's slough. I was looking for ducks—and all of a sudden—"

"Ain't no whoopin' cranes nowadays," the old man said disconsolately.

Lee spoke very slowly now, trying hard to be patient. "At Becker's slough. Honest. I saw the black tips of his wings just as clear!"

"And you feel like you want to go, too," Grandpa said. "Breaks your heart almost, you want to go that bad, when you hear the thunder right over your head—like a big, long freight train passin' in the nighttime."

His voice rose in an unexpected harsh croak. "At Becker's slough, you say? A whoopin' crane—a real, honest-to-gosh whooper? Boy, I ain't seen a whooper for forty years!"

"There's only twenty-eight whoopers left in the whole world," Lee said. "They fly south in the fall clear to Texas."

141

"Me, I'm going south, too," Grandpa said. "You can set in the sun all winter and see things besides flatness. Man gets mighty tired of flatness—after eighty years." His voice trailed off. He fell back in his chair and closed his eyes.

Lee remembered what his mother had said. "Grandpa is a very old man, Lee; he mustn't ever get excited." He knew a moment of paralysing fear. Maybe Grandpa was dying; maybe he was already dead! "Grandpa!" he shouted hoarsely. "Wake up, wake up!"

A convulsive shudder twisted the shrunken body in the chair. The old man stood up without laying a hand on the arm rest of the chair, and his voice was loud and strong. "Boy, I got to see it. I tell you I got to!"

Lee stared, fascinated and irresolute. "But Mum says—"

The old man's voice lost its tone of loud authority, dropped into feeble wheedling. "Aw, come on, boy. Ain't nobody goin' to see us. Your paw's workin' in the far quarter and Ellen she's off to a hen party somewheres. We can slip out and back just as easy."

"But it's three miles. And Mum's got the car."

Grandpa wrinkled up his face. "We got a horse and buggy, ain't we?"

"But the buggy hasn't been used for years and years," Lee protested. "And the harness—"

The old man caught up his stick from beside the chair. Fury chased the cunning from his puckered face. "You git along, boy," he screamed, "or I'll welt the hide off you!"

Lee retreated to the door. "All right, Grandpa," he said placatingly. "I'll hitch Bessie up right now."

Grandpa had a hard time getting into the buggy. But the moment he reached the seat he snatched the lines from Lee's hands and slapped the old mare's rump with the ends of the lines. Bessie broke into a startled trot and Lee held his breath. But Bessie slowed almost at once to a shambling, reluctant walk, and Lee felt a little easier. Maybe the buggy wouldn't fall to pieces after all.

They drove along the road a little way and turned off to a trail that wound across bleak open prairie. Grandpa stared straight ahead, and his eyes were bright. "Like I say, boy, they go south. Figger they see the Mississippi from a mile up. Sure like to see it myself. Will, too, some day."

The old man's chin dropped toward his chest. The lines fell from his fingers, and Lee caught them just before they slipped over the dashboard.

"Thanks, boy, for takin' me out. Maybe we'd better go home now. I'm tired—awful tired."

The boy's throat tightened. "We're near there, Grandpa," he said. "You can see the slough now."

"Ain't no whoopers any more," the old man mumbled peevishly. "Gone south."

Lee swung Bessie out of the rutted trail into the shelter of a poplar grove. He eased the old man down from the buggy and slipped a hand under his arm. "Come on, Grandpa," he urged. "We'll make it all right."

They advanced slowly from behind the sheltering bluff into the tall grass that rimmed the borders of the slough. The sun dazzled their eyes, but the wind blew strong and cold across the slough, carrying with it the rank smell of stagnant water and alkali-encrusted mud. Grandpa huddled under his great-coat.

"What are you doin' to me, boy?" he complained almost tearfully. "You know what Ellen said. I ain't supposed to go out without she's along."

"Down, Grandpa—down!"

The old man crumpled to hands and knees. "Where is it, boy? Where is it?" His voice rose in a shrill, frenzied squeak.

"Come on—I can see his head!"

Something moved in the long grass. For a shuddering moment the boy lay helpless, beyond the power of speech or movement. Then his body jerked convulsively to life and he leaped to his feet and his voice rang wild and shrill.

"Grandpa—look—look!"

He wheeled to clutch at Grandpa, but the old man already stood upright, staring out of dim, fierce eyes at the great white body flung against the pale sky. "Great God in heaven!" The words were a strange, harsh cry of ecstasy and pain. "A whooper, boy—a whooper!"

They stood together, man and boy, held by an enchantment

that was no part of the drab, flat world about them. The great bird rose steadily higher, the black tips of his wings a blurred streak against the whiteness of his body. He swung in a wide arc, flew high above the heads of the watchers by the slough, then climbed fast and far into the remote pale sky. For a minute or more he seemed to hang immobile, suspended in space beyond the limits of the world. Then the whiteness faded, blended with the pale of the sky, and was gone.

The old man's fingers were tight on the boy's arm. Again the harsh cry burst from his lips—"Great God in heaven!"—the cry that was at once a shout of exultation and a prayer. Then the light in his eyes faded and went out.

"He's gone south," Grandpa said. His shoulders sagged. He tried to pull the greatcoat close about his shrunken body. "They come in the night and you hear a sound like thunder and the sky gits dark—and there's the Mississippi below and the smell of the sea blown in from a hundred miles away . . ."

Lee's mother led the boy to the door. "He's raving," she said, and there were tears in her eyes and voice. "He's so sick. Oh, Lee, you should never—"

At once she checked herself. "The doctor should be here soon," she whispered. "Tell your father to send him up the minute he comes."

Lee fled downstairs, away from the dim-lit, shadow-flecked room where the only sounds to break the heavy silence were Grandpa's muttered words and his hard, unquiet breathing. Grandpa was sick—awful sick. He had no strength left to lift his head from the pillow, and his eyes didn't seem to see things any more. But he wasn't crazy; he knew all right what he was saying. Only no one except Lee understood what he meant. He did not regret what he had done. No matter what happened he was glad that Grandpa had seen the whooper.

"He just had to see it," he said stubbornly to his father. "He just had to."

His father nodded slowly from behind the paper he was pretending to read. "I know, son," he said. And he added, a queer, inexplicable note of pain in his voice, "Wish I'd been along."

Lee fell asleep on the couch after a while. When he awoke much later, he was alone in the living room and the oil lamp on the table was burning dimly. He sat up, instantly alert. The house seemed strange and lonely, and the noises which had troubled him even in sleep were still. Something had happened. You could tell.

His mother came downstairs, walking very quietly. Her face was set and calm. He knew at once what she had come to say. Her fingers touched his hair, to show that what he had done didn't matter any more.

"Grandpa is dead," she said.

Suddenly her voice choked and she turned away her head. A moment of anguish engulfed him. He couldn't bear to hear his mother cry. But when at last he spoke, the words sprang clear and triumphant from his throat.

"He's gone south," he said.

STRANGE
LOVE

Dorothy Livesay   A WEEK IN THE COUNTRY

"Jenny's got a beau! Jenny's got a beau!" Elizabeth was chanting, beneath the dining-room window. As soon as Jenny's flushed, shiny face appeared behind the lace curtain, Elizabeth made off. It was fun to tease Jenny, but dangerous too; Dickon might get too embarrassed and just go away.

Elizabeth went around to the front and sat on the fender of his Model T Ford. She rather wished Dickon hadn't come to town with his car this week, so that he and Jenny could go for a jitney ride; and take Elizabeth with them. Now that there was a street-car strike in Winnipeg many servant-girls like Jenny took their half-day off by riding around town in a jitney beside their beaux—some of them young soldiers just back from the War. Elizabeth could think of nothing nicer than riding in a jitney, unless it was going to see Charlie Chaplin or Billie Burke in the moving-pictures.

But that June there was much more excitement in store. As the weather grew warmer the news father brought home from the Free Press made the grown-ups faces look cross and tired. People didn't laugh or joke any more about the strike. And mother stopped going down-town. Father had seen a street-car turned right over, on Portage Avenue. Then, one morning, all the bread and milk wagons stood idle in the

148

yards. Elizabeth and Jenny had to walk to a citizen's depot to get milk. "General Strike" they heard people saying, horrified.

Mother decided it was time now for Elizabeth to be packed off to the country. "It's nearly the end of term, so it won't hurt her to miss school." She turned to Jenny with her plan: "If Dickon comes to the city this week, perhaps you could have a little holiday, and take Elizabeth to your folk's farm. Dickon wouldn't mind?"

"I guess not." Jenny didn't sound very eager.

"You'd like to visit with your mother for a week or so, wouldn't you?"

"Oh yes. I'd like real well to see them. It's just . . ."

"Just what?" Elizabeth demanded. Nosey Elizabeth.

"Oh, nothing . . . sure, I'll ask Dickon." Jenny promised. Elizabeth jumped up and down, not knowing what it was like "in the country" but imagining all of Jenny's family to be like herself, plump and rosy with shining nut-brown hair.

They were all ready that Saturday evening when Dickon came driving along the street in his floppity Ford. The top was pushed down and it seemed to bounce at every bump. Dickon drew up with a grinding sound and climbed out carefully. He wore a shiny black suit and a red striped tie; but his face, so rough and red from the sun, did not seem to fit his clothes.

"Hello, Dickon!"

"Hello, Liz." He had that kind of a smile that made her feel warmed up.

"We're all ready packed, Dickon! I'll tell Jenny!"

When they started out, waving good-bye to mother, Jenny held Elizabeth between her and Dickon. She had on her sailor hat, and a motoring veil that flopped in Elizabeth's face. As soon as they were out on the prairie, on the narrow black dirt road, Dickon stopped the car. "Tuck her in the back seat. She'll rest better."

"Oh she's all right here, aren't you, Elizabeth?" Jenny squeezed, almost poked her.

"I don't care." She felt sleepy already.

"There's a rug back there." And Dickon slid her over onto

the slippery black leather. The top was still pushed back, and she could watch the sky slowly fading from blue and mauve into the long twilight.

It was pitch dark when she woke, hearing voices. The auto seemed to have stopped alongside a poplar bush. Ch-rump. Ch-rump. Frogs, was it? Overhead the sky was like a huge sieve, showering stars. Jenny's voice came to her, murmuring from the front seat.

"No Dickon, please. Not now, please!" And Dickon the tongue-tied was saying. "What's the matter, Jen? You used to like a kiss."

"Not just now."

"Last year—"

"This isn't last year."

"Everything's just the same, to me."

"Well, I can't help it. I feel different. Living in the city . . ."

"I see." He was quiet, and then he came out with it, strong: "You'd better tell me, Jenny! Is there another fellow?"

"No! There's never been anybody else but you that I've gone out with. Honest. It's not just that, Dickon. It's just . . ."

"What?"

"Oh, I dunno. Maybe getting back to the farm . . ."

Elizabeth felt the long silence stretching between them. Then the frog chorus arose and enveloped all the night. Dickon began to fuss with the engine. He had to get out and crank before they were off again, speeding into the cool country.

"Nearly home," Jenny murmured, leaning towards the back seat. But Elizabeth pretended she was asleep.

She awakened with a bump. No sound of the engine. Darkness and voices. Jenny was shaking her, saying: "Here she is, Bessie!" Small warm hands seized hers. "Welcome to the farm!" Someone held a lamp over the doorway and as she entered, wrapped in encircling arms, she saw Bessie's golden brown eyes smiling into hers. Sleepily she felt her clothes being taken off. Soon she was lying in a big double bed with Bessie beside her.

"We can be downstairs in the best room," Bessie giggled,

" 'cause we're both nine. The rest of the kids have to sleep up in the attic." Then Bessie's candle was blown out and they lay alone in the surrounding night.

In the morning it was Sunday. Dolly, an older sister, pounced on their bed shouting: "Sleepy heads! Sleepy heads! Come on, Bessie. It's time to make the tea."

"Tea and crackers, Sunday treat," Bessie explained. And Elizabeth forgot to say, 'I'm not allowed to have tea.' She drank hers blissfully, dribbling the cracker crumbs all over the bed.

"Never mind," Bessie said. "We'll shake 'em out and air the bedding—you and me together, eh?" Bessie was only just nine but she knew how to work. Elizabeth's fingers trembled, she struggled all day to keep up. "Come on, Liz, it's easy," Bessie encouraged, carrying a pail of water from the pump to the trough. "And then I'll show you the new piggies, and my own baby calf. Fred's his name."

Chores and play, play and chores. It seemed all part of the same life. Elizabeth, sniffing it up like some new comfort never before enjoyed, was astonished at the way Jenny complained: "All that work churning butter, ma! And in the city you just run over to the store."

"Somebody has to churn the butter," was all Mrs. Moffat said, mildly. She smiled tolerantly at Jenny, steaming over the wash-tub. "It's such hard work you have to do, mother . . . no washing machine. And it takes so darn long." Mrs. Moffat just laughed, including Elizabeth in her look. Yes, it took time. Yet the farmer found time, between his jobs, to tease the girls and to toss baby Laura high in the air.

"Ouch! Rained in your pants again. Why don't you go out in the proper place and water my seed bed, eh—you rascal?"

Laura was always wet, but nobody minded. Fun to be Laura, riding on the manure sledge, pulled by a horse. Fun to be Bessie and Dolly, starting off Monday morning for school, swinging their lunch pails. How they laughed and waved, clambering onto the school wagon, pulled slowly up and over the hill by two white horses.

Elizabeth was alone now, till nightfall. She hung around the kitchen for a while, watching Mrs. Moffat kneading dough while Jenny stood by, sighing for baker's bread "delivered right to your door." Elizabeth said nothing, just sniffed the yeasty scent and thought of the moment when the knobbly crusts would burst from the oven, filling the kitchen with fragrance. Mrs. Moffat paused long enough to put a cookie in her mouth, and a book of fairy stories into her hand. Then Elizabeth thought of the old deserted buggy beside the barn: a good place to read. She climbed up into it happily, imagining herself a fairy princess on the way to a ball. Lost in reading, it was a long time before she noticed the sun had climbed higher and was beating down upon her head. The letters danced on the dappled page, sizzling heat strafed her head.

"That'll be enough o' that there sun!" the farmer called, passing by with a pail on either arm. "Come to the cool side o' the barn, girlie, and play in the dirt with Laura."

In the evening the farm came awake again. After a supper of ham and fried potatoes the children swarmed outside for games of tag, hide-and-seek, prisoner's base. The excitement of games! Elizabeth found she had to run, shrieking and panting, till her throat was as hot as a pipe-stem. She tried hard to catch the ball thrown to her; but her fingers trembled, she missed. But no one said (as her own father did), "Butter fingers!" And soon Bessie's arm was flung around her shoulder. "Let's go say goodnight to Fred." Gently they walked, arm in arm, cooling off as the prairie night wrapped itself round them.

"Let's just go tiptoe," Elizabeth dared to suggest, "and see if your calf is asleep."

"They'll all be sleeping."

When they reached the barn Bessie unfastened the bolt softly and they slipped into the gloom, into the smell of straw and manure. Dull thud of a horse's hoof, cows chewing their cud: these were the only sounds. Bessie beckoned and Elizabeth followed on tiptoe to Fred's stall. Chuckling, they stooped to rub his nose: Elizabeth tripped and nearly fell over into the stall. Right away she was petrified by a voice from the loft above: "What's that noise?" Bessie stiffened, put a finger on her lips. Then they heard a man's voice murmuring: "Just the beasts below."

"It's Dickon," Bessie whispered, half giggling. She took Elizabeth's hand and they stood stock still, tight together.

Dickon spoke again. "Aw please, Jenny, you don't have to go yet!"

They could not hear a reply, only a scuffling in the loft. Bessie could hardly hold herself in, trying not to giggle. Elizabeth was trembling, her mouth dry.

"It's a long way I walked from my place, just to go home again."

"But honestly, Dickon, Ma'll need me for the separating; I'll come back after," Jenny promised. "Now let me go, quick!"

Bessie, choking with laughter, seized Elizabeth's arm and led her on tiptoe to the barn door. "Hurry," she whispered. Elizabeth stumbled on the sill and nearly fell. They fled rocketing out the door and through the barnyard, running for dear life. In the first field they plumped into a haystack, exhausted, letting their laughter loose in the sweet prickly comfort of the hay.

When they could talk, Elizabeth choked, "Gee, what if they heard us?"

"It wouldn't matter," Bessie told her. "We kids used to peek at them last summer. Dickon lives all alone, y'know, on his Dad's old farm. He has nobody to look after him. But Ma says he's too shy to ask Jenny to marry him."

"He didn't sound shy tonight." That set them giggling again. But after they had crept home and slipped into bed Elizabeth whispered, "But why is Jenny so mean to him?"

"She's not mean!"

"She is so! She's always trying to get away from him."

"Is she? I dunno. I guess maybe she doesn't want to get married. She doesn't like the farm . . . but I do!"

"So do I. And I'd marry a farmer!" Elizabeth smiled into the dark, where she could imagine so clearly the face of Dickon: red and crusty with sandy tufted eyebrows looming above such blue eyes. Blue as . . . as cornflowers . . . sky . . . She fell asleep, still smiling.

When tomorrow came it proved to be a day for housecleaning at Dickon's farm. Jenny took the horse and gig, with Elizabeth and baby Laura up beside her. Ahead of them stretched the straight prairie road with upturned black loam stretching for miles on either side. All else was sky, blue, with puffs of cloud at the brim; and the sound of meadowlarks. It was a happy morning. Only Jenny sat heavily holding the reins, saying nothing.

Elizabeth looked up at her, hesitant; observing the rounded bloom of her cheeks, her ginger-coloured hair struggling to be free from the prim knot at the back; her brown eyes that could flash, her mouth that could pout. Why wouldn't she talk?

"Is it a long way to Dickon's house, Jenny?"

"About three miles."

"I'm glad we don't have to walk . . ." Elizabeth watched the horse's tail twitch as he clopped along. "Is it a nice house —Dickon's?"

"Nothing to get excited about." Jenny pulled the reins tighter.

"Are you going to get engaged to him, Jenny?" As there was no answer she started to say it again, more loudly; but Jenny's clouded face choked the question. They did not talk again until they reached the poplar bluff that served as gateway to Dickon's farm.

The old frame house was sagging, crouched to the earth, unpainted and curtainless. But the barn looked stronger, sturdier, as if it knew the feel of footsteps, touch of hands. While Jenny went into the house to start a fire and clean up, the two children wandered about. Around the barn there were no animals to look at. The chicken house they peered into was empty and untidy; swallows swerved in the gloom of a shed. A tightness . . . she felt a tightness in her throat. Poor Dickon, with no one to look after him! He was far off in the back field today, behind his team. He did not seem to know they were there.

"Is Dickon coming here for dinner?" Elizabeth asked, hungrily hanging around the kitchen door.

"No," said Jenny. "He takes his lunch pail out to the fields. Here, I brought some sandwiches for you and Laura."

They munched them, deep in the unshaven grass, pouring themselves drinks of water from the rusty pump. "Sp'ash, sp'ash," cried Laura, and Elizabeth obediently pumped great squirts of water over her bare feet. Then she jumped into the puddle herself, letting the mud ooze through her toes.

"Here," said Jenny, weakening. "You can take this thermos of tea to Dickon."

Elizabeth wiped her feet on the grass with alacrity, fumbled for her socks and sandals. Then she and Laura trotted off along a muddy lane, on and on through the shimmering sun to Dickon.

He was sitting in a bit of shade by a poplar bluff, eating his lunch. "Well," was all he said. "Well, well." And then, "Thanks, kiddies."

Elizabeth glowed, but she did not know what to say, standing stiffly before him. "Jenny is cleaning up for you," she offered.

"Yes," he replied. "Real nice of her, isn't it?"

"It needs cleaning," said Elizabeth.

"It does that."

"It needs a woman around, I guess." She half laughed, making it sound casual like. But he did not answer. He just looked a long way off across the flat fields. Since apparently that was all he was going to say, and he had finished his tea, Elizabeth picked up the empty thermos. "G'bye then."

"G'bye, Liz." He smiled his rare smile, his blue eyes crinkling. She went back to Jenny in a golden dream, scarcely noticing that Jenny asked no question about Dickon; nor did she look his way when the buggy, homeward bound, passed near his field.

Before Elizabeth's time was up there was a picnic in the bush beside a creek; and a visit to a neighbouring farm. But most days curved in an arc of steady sun, black shade. In the evening, breathless after a game of tag, Elizabeth and Bessie would climb onto the field gate and swing slowly to and fro. Elizabeth always looked along the lane to see if there was anyone coming—a man in blue overalls, it might be, and a blue shirt. But Dickon never came.

"Jenny was cross as two sticks today," Elizabeth told Bessie. "I bet she's sorry she was mean to him."

"Jenny likes the city—shows, and jitneys and things," replied Bessie, who had never been there.

"And I like the country!" Elizabeth sang it out.

"I'm glad. Wisht you could always stay with us."

"So do I." Strange, she had not felt homesick yet.

But the day arrived when the farmer came driving his team home at noon, with Dickon beside him.

"Dickon!" Elizabeth ran to greet him; then hung back, shy. He really looked pleased to see her, and swung her up in his arms. Elizabeth blushed and kicked, so he set her down quickly, saying: "Why I do believe the kiddie's put on weight here!"

"You bet she has." Mr. Moffat smiled. "Too bad she has to go back."

"Go back?" Jenny echoed Elizabeth's question, suddenly appearing from the kitchen door.

"Yep. Strike's over," Dickon told them.

"They say things will be rolling again by Monday," said the farmer. " 'Bout time, too."

"Did the men win?" Jenny wanted to know.

"What's that to you? I dunno. Jones passed the word over the fence to Dickon. They've quit, that's all we know. Them ringleaders arrested."

"Well, I guess your mother will want you home again, eh, Elizabeth?" Mrs. Moffat patted her shoulder.

"Oh, I don't think Mummy would want me *yet*," Elizabeth asserted, casting a hopeful glance towards the farmer and his wife as they stood in the farmhouse doorway.

"Naturally Elizabeth will have to go back to her folks." Mrs. Moffat smiled firmly, putting an arm around her shoulder as they all moved inside. "Though I don't see why Jenny should have to go back so soon. She's entitled to a holiday."

They all turned to look at Jenny.

"I've had my holiday," she said.

Dickon, just inside the doorway, flushed red, moved awkwardly from one foot to the other. He managed to ask her, "Do you want me to drive you to Winnipeg tomorrow?"

"Yes, please," she said. Then she went straight to the stove and began carrying hot dishes to the kitchen table.

"Well, sit down, sit down, Dickon," urged the farmer. "Can't waste time eatin', this time o'year."

On Sunday, after the heavy afternoon dinner, good-byes had to be said. Elizabeth loitered through the barnyard with Bessie; then Bessie packed her suitcase for her and tucked into it a sprig of 'everlasting'—"So you won't forget me, Elizabeth."

"Oh thanks." She was almost choking.

"Maybe Elizabeth can come back some day," the mother said, softening and giving her a last hug. Then she was up into the front seat, between Dickon and Jenny. Everyone waved white handkerchiefs, even little Laura in her daddy's arms. Bessie ran to close the farm gate after them.

"Don't forget, Elizabeth! Don't forget!"

Elizabeth felt dry and empty. Some day, she was certain, she would return to the farm and marry Dickon and really look after him. He wasn't really so old; only twenty-four! Sitting there in the car beside him, with Jenny on the outer side, she felt as if Dickon really belonged to her. She began to chatter away faster and faster, talking to him about the farm.

"You don't like the city, do you, girl?" said Dickon. He called her 'girl' now, not 'kiddie.' "Well, no more do I. No more do I." And he pressed his foot on the accelerator, hard.

Jenny said nothing, all the dusty way home.

Stephen Scobie   STREAK
                  MOSAIC

1

– Prairie? Did you say prairie?
  – No, I said priority.
  – Oh. Sorry.
  – But I could say it for you, if you liked.
  (And if I had, how would I have said it, then? Something
flat, connected with grain. Something monotonous I slept
through on the train. A word surrounding 'air'.)
  – Say it.
  – Prairie.
  – That's not the way to say it.
  – You say it.
  – Prairie.
  (Yes, you could hear the difference.)

That's how we met, and it was in Vancouver. Outside the
window were mountains. They stared at you every day, the
North Shore Mountains, Seymour, Grouse, and always the
same side, like the moon. The far side was wilderness; I lived
there for years and never saw it. While, like a rising tide, a
slow flood, houses crept up the familiar face. The mountains,
there every day, so painfully, incredibly beautiful: you would
think *some*thing would rub off on the people, *some* feeling
for beauty . . .

158

To her, they just filled up air. She said it was a walled city, emotionally under siege. She wanted the walls to fall down, and all that empty air come rushing in. The city exploding to meet it. The limits broken. Into the outside, limit-less. Air.

– Open the window.

This is just one morning, watching her. Her naked body moves against the light. Her feet upon the floor in a firm stance. Ready for long strides. Her arm flung out across air, to the curtain. Pushing it back, wider, as if there were more space to push it to: a whole prairie. Light spilling around her body, edging its curving lines. No sudden mountains, just a gentle expanse. Her skin eager for wind. Her hair like grain.

She opens the window and a mountain comes in.

I lift the sheets and she spreads over me.

– What is it?
 – Nothing.
 – No, you're worried. You're moody. It's something.
 – O.K. But I don't know. It's not you.
 – I love you.
 – It's not you, I said that. It's not you.
 – It's us?
 – Well, it's everything. The city.
 – You mean it's the prairie.
 – The mountains.
 – "In the mountains, there you feel free."
 – Bullshit.
 – Eliot.
 – I know. It's still bullshit. Anyway, that's one of these fake old women talking. Don't sidetrack me with quotations.
 – O.K., it's the mountains. And an absence of prairie. You're homesick.
 – God!
 – I'm sorry, I didn't mean that lightly.
 – O.K. But anyway, I'm not homesick. I don't want to go back. At least, I don't think I want to go back. Hell, I don't know. Do I want to go back?
 – You'd feel better? More free?

– You can get trapped there, too.

– You can get trapped anywhere.

– There it's the sky, here it's the mountains. No, I'm not kidding myself. I came away because I was fucking bored to fucking death. I know that. I know that.

– You're not bored here, are you?

– It's not a question of boredom. It's not a question of art galleries and decent movies. It's not even a question of people. I could have met you back there.

– Uh-uh. I'm not prairies. Lived all my life in Vancouver.

– So what?

– So this, you couldn't have met *me* back there. There's no one *like* me back there. You remember what you told me? The first twenty years of your life, you never saw a mountain. Never saw the sea. I mean, Christ, what does that *do* to people? I lived by the sea all my life. Vacations on Vancouver Island. Camped at Long Beach. I mean, what did you think about, when you read about the sea? When you were in school, reading a poem, and the poet was talking about the sea, what did you think of? What kind of image came into your mind?

– Photographs. Movies. Maybe grain moving, in a large field. Things like that.

– Your mind must be so goddamned *horizontal!*

– That's your diagnosis?

– Damn right it is. What's a horizontal mind doing in Vancouver? Every time it turns around it hits against a highrise.

– Like you. You're vertical?

– Hey, parts of me are.

– Highrise?

– Turn out the light, will you? Can you reach it?

– O.K., you can come in now.

I didn't know what to expect. Three weeks we'd been together, this was the first time I'd been to her apartment: an attic, really, in one of the last old houses in Kitsilano. Apartment blocks going up (vertically) all around.

What she'd put on was an artist's smock, once white, smudged with paint in horizontal streaks. (I'd begun to notice, a lot, what was horizontal, what was vertical.) And paintings all around the walls, stacked canvases, one on the easel. I felt uneasily as if I were in a movie set. Archetypal artist's studio, reality copying cliché.

The paintings were, of course, horizontal. Horizon-tall. Most of them absolutely simple: a horizontal line close to the foot of the canvas, one solid block of colour below, another above; but very subtle colours. Very precise colours.

– I abstract them, she explained. There are lots of colours in grain. This one's an early colour, wheat about three weeks before it's ripe. That sky is a sunset green: yes, green, there's sometimes green in the sky, just tiny streaks and suggestions. Only I take that one shade and extend it over the whole sky, the whole block of colour. I've never seen a sky like that, of course, but I'm sure it could happen. Anything could happen to prairie skies.

I saw one painting different. (It looked more vertical.) A Mondrian in shades of gold, entitled "Streak Mosaic."

– This is seen from above?

– That's right. You fly over the fields, they look like that. Or at least I guess they would, I've never flown myself.

– I like the title.

– It's a disease.

– What?

– It's a crop disease. Streak mosaic. Look, that colour there—that's it. The whole field's useless, the grain will never ripen, never come to maturity. This field here, next to it, is healthy. There's no reason for it. It just happens sometimes. Next year, the same field could be perfectly O.K.

– And the farmer?

– There's nothing he can do about it. By the time it shows, it's too late. His horse'll know about it before he does.

– Is this a new painting?

– No, it's an old one. Before I met you. Do you like them?

– They're tremendous.

– Crap. They're unoriginal. They're exercises. I'm just beginning, I've a long way to go. I mean, what could be more clichéd? The prairie as horizontal lines. I even drew these lines with a ruler. At least I might have done them freehand, got a few waves and lumps into them. The prairie isn't as flat as that, not really.

— That's what everyone says. But isn't the prairie just what you think it is?

— Uh-uh. No. The prairie's itself. It's a sky magnet. It pulls you upwards, into the air. When I was a kid, I had this tremendous urge to fly. There was so much sky, I kept jumping into it. Icarus was born on the prairies, I bet he was.

— But you never did fly.

— No. I came down on the train.

And then two days later she didn't show up for a date. I went round to her place and confronted the landlady. She'd gone. She'd packed up and left. No messages. No forwarding address.

She'd left only one painting behind.

2

— Where you headed?

— Dry Mud. (Absurd, the name of her town. I'd laughed for ten minutes straight when she told me.)

— Thought so. This road don't go anyplace else.

The hitch-hiker climbed in the front seat beside me. I'd driven over 1200 miles alone, it seemed about time for some company. He was a kid in blue jeans and a checked sports shirt; it looked like he was starting to grow his hair long.

— Do you live in Dry Mud?

— All my life.

— What's it like?

— O.K., I guess. It's a place. Don't figure it's too much different from other places.

He spoke horizontally. I thought, goddamnit, I've got to get this horizontal/vertical thing out of my head! There must be other ways of thinking about life. But he did speak horizontally, that was the only word you could use. Long vowels, long pauses between words. Clipped t's and d's sticking up like telegraph poles, along a flat horizon.

– It's a pretty small place, I guess?

– Depends what you call big.

I thought, in a small town everybody knows everybody else. Should I ask him about her? Whether she's come home?

The car veered suddenly, lurched, bounced, stopped, settled. A flat tire. As if there weren't enough things flat around here.

– Hey, you look tired. Been driving long? Let me fix it. I'm good at fixing things. Go stretch your legs.

So I got out, went over to the side of the road, sat down and looked at the sky. The kid was whistling between his teeth, working slowly but efficiently. There was plenty of time. I looked at the sky.

So the prairie isn't really flat? Maybe. But it sure is flat around Dry Mud. I'd never seen country so flat. I'd never seen so much sky. Nothing to hold you down. It looked like one of her paintings: I could see the shades of blue, resolving obsessively into monochrome, one massive block of colour. It was unreal. I began to feel, this is unreal. This doesn't exist, it's a movie. Who ever heard of a town called Dry Mud anyway? It's all ridiculous. I've fallen inside one of her paintings. I know these colours. (I am these colours.) I know that shade of wheat over there. . . .

– Hey, that field over there. It's diseased, isn't it?

The kid looked up from tightening the bolts. Looked at the field. Narrowed his eyes. Looked back at me.

– You some kind of scientist?

So I guess I was prepared for Dry Mud itself. Another movie set; just like her studio, totally unreal. The archetypal cliché prairie town. Main street with buildings down one side, one big grain elevator on the other. All the stores with false fronts.

I asked the kid if he knew her. Sure he knew her. She left for the coast a year ago. No, she hadn't come back. What would she come back for? Her folks were dead. Nothing for her here. What would she want to come back for?

I dropped him on the main street, spun the car round in the dust in front of the grain elevator, and started quickly back.

I didn't want to look at the rears of the buildings. I was afraid they wouldn't be there.

Two hours later I was still driving and I hadn't come to anywhere and that was all wrong. There should have been some small town, a crossroads, *some*thing. I must have missed a turn-off. But goddamnit, there hadn't *been* any turn-off! Anyway, the fuel gauge said zero, so I pulled over to the side of the road and stopped. Took a look at the map. Wondered where I was. The landscape had no distinguishing features.

O.K., so it wasn't flat. There was a gentle rise to my left. A single, totally improbable tree stuck out of a field to my right. The sun had started down. I looked up into the big sky, and I felt what she called the magnet. The top of my head flipped off. I was being pulled upwards. I wanted to fly.

I laughed at myself and got out of the car. Kicked up the dust in the road. Looked up again. Ribs of cloud were riding, high, high in the sky. I had an acute sensation of its dome shape, but I couldn't pinpoint where the inside surface was. A crazy thought came into my head.

It didn't go away.

I laughed again, and got back into the car. Got out again. Climbed up onto the roof of the car. Surveyed the landscape from that height. Flapped my arms and jumped off.

– Son of a *bitch!* I rolled over in the road, clutching at my ankle. Tried to stand up, and couldn't. Sat there watching it swell.

The kid arrived about half an hour later, in a beat-up panel truck, with a case of beer and a big can of gas.

– Figured you'd end up stuck. Saw you take the wrong turn at the edge of town. Say, what'd you do to your ankle?

– I think it's sprained.

– Too bad. Want a beer?

– Sure.

So we sat together, leaning against my car, and consumed a slow beer. It was getting steadily darker.

– Where does this road go, anyway?

– Nowhere.

– Nowhere at all?

– Used to be a few shacks at the end of it. Ain't nothing now. Used to be a mine for something, but it ran out. Nothing here now but wheat.

– For a road going nowhere, it's in pretty good condition.

– Yeah, well, it's kept up. It's useful. You can bring in the crops, it's easier driving than stubble. A road don't have to go somewhere to be useful.

(A pause, while I appreciated the symbolism.)

– Well, I sure didn't get anywhere.

– Were you trying to?

– I was looking for that girl, I explained. Dropped everything. Walked out on my job, bought a second-hand car, drove through the mountains. Just like that. Because I thought maybe she came back here. Now look at me.

– How'd you do it?

– What?

– Your ankle. How'd you manage to bust your ankle driving a car?

– Well, I'd stopped and got out. (Another pause.) Well, I . . . This is stupid, you know, I . . . I jumped off the top of the car.

– Looking around?

– Trying to fly.

The kid laughed.

– Doesn't it ever get to you, I asked, sometimes? The prairie, all this sky?

– I live here.

– That makes the difference?

– Hell, it's only fields. What would I do with a mountain anyway? I'd probably shovel it flat.

– O.K. Or climb it. But here there's nothing to *do* with it all. It's just air. Try to fly, you end up like me. Or down like me. You can't climb the sky, there's too much of it.

– There's only what there is.

– Suppose you went away? What would you feel about it then?

– I ain't going away.

– Yes, but suppose.

– No good supposing. What would I want to go away for?

– That girl. She went away.

– Yeah, but you think she came back.

– I don't know. Maybe. Maybe not. Maybe all she wanted was for me to come out here. Maybe she's waiting for me in Vancouver. Or else I won't see her again. How can you tell? Streak mosaic. One field ripens, one field doesn't.

The kid in darkness, barely visible, tilting his head to drink.

– I guess that's for you to figure out, he said.

– I guess so.

– Well, me, I don't figure she'll be coming back out here. Can't really say I knew her. Danced with her a couple of times. She was O.K., but she left. Most people said she would. What's more (he laughed) she took the right turn leaving town.

A chink as he threw his bottle away. Mine was only half-empty. The ankle suddenly started to hurt like hell.

Victor Carl Friesen   OLD
                            MRS. DIRKS

Old Mrs. Dirks lived on the outskirts of a small prairie town. Her house had but two rooms, had never been painted, and was not very warm in cold weather. Each winter she banked snow against the gray walls to increase the insulation. From a woodpile behind her barn she hauled huge loads of unsplit firewood to the house. For this purpose she used an old round tub to which she had fastened a short length of rope. Even piled high, the tub slid easily over the snowbanks so that Mrs. Dirks, without too much trouble, could keep her house warm. In fact, she usually kept it hot, stuffing one piece of wood after another into the Quebec heater which served the two rooms. Rosie Dirks was seventy-five years old and, like most elderly people, she needed extra warmth to be comfortable. When she was not working, she sat beside her stove.

Her husband, one would have thought, might have done the outside chores. He was still living—but not with her. And he had not been for forty-eight years.

Mr. Dirks had grown up a very shy young man. Merely talking to a girl, or *of* a girl, made him feel ill at ease. Then when he was twenty, the woman who was to become his wife had smiled at him after a church service. He had felt more ill at ease than ever, for it seemed to him that he was obligated to marry the woman. His shyness might have prevented his carrying out any such decisive act, but she took the lead and

167

made things easy for him; she was five years older than he.

Rosie had smiled at several young men before Mr. Dirks came along and, since nothing had happened, she had been getting worried. In her day twenty-five was considered middle-aged. In a land just emerging from a pioneer era, children stopped school in their early teens and started working as adults. By the age of sixteen a girl was marriageable.

Rosie had been marriageable for nine long years; she had not been what the neighbourhood women called "pretty." As a young woman she had a bad complexion, noticeable particularly on her forehead. Her nose, although not ill-shaped, was rather long, and she had a protruding lower lip. When she smiled this lower lip might have made her look sensual had she been pretty otherwise, but as it was it made her look as if she were complaining. And an observer would readily assume she was, for until her twenty-fifth year, no man had paid her court.

Rosie had not given up hope—keeping herself slim, avoiding the matronly stoutness that wives soon ate themselves into after marriage. Rosie had not been over- or underweight, but her figure, like her legs, tended to lack shape. One thought of straight, smooth tree trunks when one saw her legs. But she was physically strong—still an admirable quality in a wife.

Rosie's courtship with Mr. Dirks quickly ended in marriage. The bride with her blushing groom moved into a neat little home, and for a while they were quite happy. Rosie worked hard, cooking and washing and sewing. Tending to a husband was a pleasure for her; she sang as she clattered pots and pans in preparing meals.

Mr. Dirks was overcome with all this attention. He felt like a rich man even though he had no steady work. A good-paying job would come, and meanwhile he had his Rosie. He sat about the house with his shoes untied and waited for his meals.

Mr. Dirks's shyness vanished in time, and his wife could not have foreseen the result. He began to talk freely with people that he met in town, including the women; women are drawn to a recently married man. These women were attractive, more attractive than his wife, and he came to enjoy bandying words with them. When he ventured to say something naughty, they laughed and were embarrassed. He began to think that he had charm and wished he had not married such a homely wife.

In time his flirtations turned to philandering. He came home late at night and did not bother making excuses to Rosie; he did not say anything. Then one night he did not come back at all. A short time later Rosie had a letter from him, with no return address, saying that he had sold their house and that he was going away. She never saw him again.

Rosie Dirks by this time was not unhappy to be rid of spineless Mr. Dirks. But a small kernel of bitterness was there, bitterness that she could not keep her man. This feeling she was determined not to show and pushed it back into a dark corner of her mind. Her lower lip, however, protruded more than ever. Her complaining look became fixed.

Shortly afterwards Mrs. Dirks moved to her present home on the edge of town. "Life is real, life is earnest," she had read in a poem somewhere. There was not anything in life to smile about, she had decided. She had a living to make, and she set to do so in earnest. She kept a cow, a red and white Guernsey which each summer she picketed in a nearby ditch to graze, and she kept chickens and geese. The cow's milk which she did not use herself she poured into one-gallon syrup pails and sold in the town. She soon had a few regular customers. They felt sorry for this solemn woman who appeared before their door every day.

The chickens and geese were Mrs. Dirks's greatest blessing. They provided eggs and meat, but it was the companionship they gave which she most valued. They gathered about her when she flung out grain from her held-up apron. Whenever she went out, even to walk into town, a few chickens would come running up. "I've nothing for you now. Go 'way," she chided them. But she liked their attention.

On a warm summer's day when she left her outside door open, a hen might hesitantly put one foot on the sill and, moving her head slowly to one side, then the other, with bill agape, try to fathom the mysteries of the interior of a human dwelling. With much deliberation the hen would eventually step over the sill and step down inside, still looking about, as if awed by her own accomplishment. Mrs. Dirks would laugh out loud in spite of herself, and the chicken would scurry out.

The geese were the aristocrats of the barnyard, waddling about like fat burghers, necks stretched out, heads looking down on their world. They were very class-conscious, always together, usually apart from the chickens. Sometimes in the evening Mrs. Dirks would stand outside her kitchen door and sing, not from happiness but from habit; she used to sing when Mr. Dirks was still around. At such times the geese would tilt their heads upward, wondering at this strange sound.

The townsmen also listened—and shook their heads. Mrs. Dirks did not have the pleasantest of voices; her songs sounded like the wail of the world's suffering, keening high over the town. "Poor, lonely Mrs. Dirks," they thought. They did not know that she laughed at her chickens—her face was so grim when she was uptown. They did not know that she had geese to sing to.

Mrs. Dirks was too practical-minded to allow herself to become sentimental about her fowl. When she wanted a chicken dinner, she carried a squawking hen to the chopping block at the woodpile. When she wanted to sell a dressed goose to the town's butchershop, she tucked a fat goose under her arm and, bending its neck into a loop, cut through the loop with a few powerful strokes of a sharp butcher knife.

So passed the years. Mrs. Dirks grew old, and her townsmen grew old with her. She continued to live aloof from them, not caring that most of them now drove cars instead of horse-and-buggies. She walked before; she walked now.

She did not care about contemporary fashions. Her dresses were longer than the mode, invariably gray or brown, and cut from heavy, coarse cloth, even in summer. She sewed them herself, generally making them too large so that they hung shapelessly about her.

Her hair she did herself too. Once a week she opened the bun at the back of her neck and combed out the long hair, now streaked unevenly with gray. The hair hung down almost to her waist and made her look like a pagan crone. She did it up carefully each time and set in two brown combs, a present from her husband many years ago. She had lately started to wear them again.

When she was uptown, the townspeople did not notice her hair or her combs. They noticed her thick dresses and the rest of her clothes. Ever since she got old, Mrs. Dirks had taken to wearing men's long underwear the whole year through. These she bought unashamedly in the town's general store. She was not going to catch her death of cold, she told the clerk. Over the legs of the underwear she wore brown cotton stockings and on her feet a pair of felt slippers. She never wore shoes, not even when she went shopping. "Poor Mrs. Dirks," the townspeople thought. "She should really have someone living in her house to look after her."

It was in her seventieth year that a strange thing happened to Mrs. Dirks—strange when one considered her general appearance. She began to imagine that she was sexually desirable and that she always had been. When men peered after her on the street, noting her outmoded clothing, she thought they longed for her; wanted her. "You dirty old men," she said to herself as she straightened her posture and strode off as briskly as she could.

One day some town women paid a call on Mrs. Dirks. One brought some jam and fresh buns. They felt sorry for the old woman and hoped to cheer her up. Mrs. Dirks did not often get company, particularly such happy company. She did not quite know what to make of it—of the small talk and the social laughter. She looked astutely at the faces of her guests and wondered if they had some ulterior motive. Could they know about their husbands' desires for her, she wondered.

On another day some teenage boys crossed the corner of her yard. They had hoped to find something usable in the junkyard behind her barn, but none of the boys had wished to ask the old woman for permission to look. Now they were looking without permission. When Mrs. Dirks saw them, she hurried outside, shaking her apron at them angrily. She had her suspicions about teenage boys anyway, and here they had come onto her yard. One was bareback; another was wearing only walking shorts. "What do you *want?*" she shrieked out.

"Have you no shame?" The boys fled in dismay, not understanding the import of her question.

At night when strange noises occurred outside her house, perhaps the wind rattling a loose eavestrough, or a tree branch brushing against a window, Mrs. Dirks thought that some men were trying to peep under the blinds at her. She kept her door locked and a good fire going in the heater. Warmth always gave a feeling of security.

Sometimes when she was already in bed and under warm blankets and she heard a thumping noise outside, she fancied that her long-gone husband was passing through town and was trying to play a trick on her. Then she would sink off to sleep.

One summer afternoon a vagrant appeared at Mrs. Dirks's door. He was an old man and had the run-down appearance of most derelicts. The one-day's growth of white stubble on his hollow face was set off by what seemed a permanent sunburn. When he smiled, his face was creased with wrinkles; he had no teeth. His clothes, denims rolled up at the cuff and an old suit coat, were dirty and had probably been slept in. He was asking for work to earn a meal. "I'll split some wood," he said.

Mrs. Dirks peered knowingly into the man's face. 'Men!' she thought, 'you're all alike,' and she remembered the ones in town who stared after her. She stood firmly on the threshold of her house and grasped each side of the door frame in her old hands. She had the entrance to the house effectively blocked. But Mrs. Dirks had no intention of turning the man away. She was far too crafty for that. She would get some wood split and let the man inside for a meal, but that would be all. She grew excited with her little scheme.

When she was back inside, she could hear the thumping sound of the axe striking the blocks of wood. She got busy herself, heating coffee and frying some eggs and potatoes. Walking between stove and table, she stopped to look at herself in the mirror on the wall. She patted the bun at the back of her neck firmly as she thought of her scheme, then absently smoothed the wrinkles in her forehead. She set the table for two.

"Don't bother to close the door," she told the man when he came in. "It's hot today." As the meal started, neither said anything, each awed a little by the other's presence. He had not counted on eating with her; she was trying to figure him out. Had he heard about her from those men in town, she wondered. 'Men!' her mind was saying, but what she said out loud was, "You been here long?"

She continued with other casual questions, but as with most women no small talk is ever really casual. Mrs. Dirks was proving to herself her supposition that this man had designs on her. But he would not fool her. She had her own scheme, and she looked through the open doorway.

The man thought his hostess was simply being friendly. He had more eggs and potatoes, then sat back to finish his coffee. He pushed his chair back from the table.

She got up quickly and poured him some more coffee. It was a long time since a man had sat opposite her at table. Strange how the years had gone! She glanced at the doorway again. A hen was approaching. "Where did you say you were from?" she asked.

As he answered her, she without thinking handed him the little wine glass, used to hold the toothpicks. She stopped short. They both looked at each other a little dismayed and then started to smile—he laughed outright—for of course he had no teeth. Mrs. Dirks's lower lip protruded as ever in her smiling. But she was embarrassed. She looked at the open door, and—thank God!—the hen had started to enter. Her little scheme was working.

"Ach! my chickens!" she cried, jumping up. "Shoo! away with you!" and she ran after the surprised fowl. The bird tried to take wing, then scuttled for the flock. "Hey! hey!" Mrs. Dirks called, fluttering her apron, and then ran and hid behind the barn. She had got away from that man safely.

The man watched the commotion through the doorway. He thought the woman was looking after the fowl behind the barn. When she did not come back after a while, he stepped outside too, and saying "Thanks for the meal" to the empty yard, he walked away to the centre of town.

In the beer parlour he asked some of the men there who

the woman was who lived on the edge of town. He remarked on her friendliness and her sense of humour. "Tried to give me a toothpick," he laughed, and he opened his mouth wide for the onlookers so that they could see his shrunken gums.

Word spreads quickly in a small town, particularly when news is broadcast in its most democratic institution, the beer parlour. The townspeople had not been aware that old Mrs. Dirks had much kindliness or a humorous side. Perhaps they had never tried to see these qualities.

The next time Mrs. Dirks came uptown, the people stared at her harder than ever. Was this the same Mrs. Dirks? She seemed to walk with a renewed vigour, or had they just never noticed it before? Her dress too was different. It did not seem as shapeless, and in this surmise the people were right. Something had prompted Mrs. Dirks to wear for once a dress made when she was younger—and slimmer. It fitted her better now than when she had made it, for she tended always to cut her dresses so that they hung in folds about her.

"How that woman has persevered!" the townswomen remarked, nodding to each other. "Still managing to take care of herself! She probably has become quite happy in her home over the years."

The men had to agree with the womenfolk—after these matters had been talked over at home. They observed the old woman with fresh eyes when they saw her. Mrs. Dirks's scrutinizing glance at each of the men's faces spoke of an alert woman who was still keenly interested in life. "Hello, Mrs. Dirks," they said with reawakened cordiality, smiling broadly. "Nice day today." Some of the men tipped their hats.

Mrs. Dirks wore a strange smile in greeting, but she did not say anything. 'Dirty old men,' she thought again, and she strode off home. She could feel her long underwear under her dress, and she was thankful for that.

At home, Mrs. Dirks sat at her table for a mid afternoon lunch. Through the open doorway the sun shone in warmly. Some hens stepped inside over the sill as they were wont to do when their mistress was eating, for she would toss a few crumbs to the floor for them to peck at. It was a homely scene; an old woman with some chickens about her. Mrs.

Dirks did feel quite happy then, for the sedateness of the chickens when they came inside the house always made her smile.

But sometimes when the door was closed, so that no one would possibly see, and Mrs. Dirks sat at her table—she wore a different smile on her face. Her lower lip protruded more than ever; and she was not thinking of chickens at all.

Rudy Wiebe DID
JESUS
EVER LAUGH?

Around this apartment at least they haven't stuck in trees for
birds to sit on and try to sing. Just bushes to keep you off
the patch of grass too small for a gopher and then up blank
like a north end coulee in fall, twenty stories cement straight
up and down, maybe seventeen apartments on each, say
around twelve or thirteen hundred in all; you know, a grey
slab box with metal windows. In twelve or thirteen hundred,
a place like this, there should be one. One at least. You'd
think so, wouldn't you, but you can't count on it; I've tried a
few. Football and hockey games aren't worth the snot you
blow waiting and the late movie's absolutely blank. Nothing.
There's too much of this people coming out now trying to
jack themselves down after some man's north end been flip-
ping through the sheets. It's just nothing like it was.

You'd think a place the size of Edmonton (four hundred
and fifty thousand friendly people says the sign on the Calgary Trail), it's amazing with that number of people and all
that preaching flushing through their heads how few there
really are in the whole city. At least the few I've seen, and
I spend my time looking. I'm never not looking and I know;
there are but few. Bars and nightclubs have always been like
you know, hopeless. The biggest encouragement I ever had

176

about Edmonton was I found two within four feet of each other at the Willingman Brothers Incorporated Evangelistic Revival last year when they come out at the Gardens. In broad daylight! By the time I could move they had both disappeared and I nearly lost them, both. They say Billy Graham is coming next fall, but it's probably too much to pray for.

So that's why I was on apartment blocks now, in broad daylight. Waiting actually isn't too bad there sometimes, with the clouds down and November wind prying in where the liner's torn away on the old Lincoln's doors. It's a beautiful car yet, better every year. I can see it black, from here. I work it over with hard wax at least once a week, you know really sweat it with elbow grease like I always did. All the soft parts in it are about gone and I've got these nice hard boards shoved under the seat covers where I sit. On days like that I can sit, watching and waiting, wherever I've parked and I'll get numb slowly till there's no feeling in me at all and I'm just sunk down, eyes along the bright black edge of the hood, watching. Not feeling a thing, just eyes, waiting.

But this fall's been bad; the summer was cold and rainy but now in October the sun shines as if it's gone mad and Edmonton was prairie. The leaves come gliding off the trees and it's warm and people walking around without coats. It gets so you—I—can't sit at all; all of a sudden I have to get out even when I have a good parking space and the meter doesn't have to get fed. I just have to get out, walk around in the sunshine if you can imagine that, I have to rub behind my knees where the edge of the board cuts. It's terrible; I stand there feeling my blood move, the warm air washing over my face. It's so bad then I even forget the words.

But today, no sunshine. I could sit in the car easy just off the corner where this poured slab was sticking up, holding the concrete clouds. A few dozen had gone by, in and out, but they were no good. One glance will always tell me, I never need more. You're watching and waiting; it seems like all my life now I've spent like this, watching and waiting and there always being so few, so few, for weeks it's hanging in your mind there aren't any left anywhere in the world and then it happens like it always has who knows how it's almost past before you suddenly know and you wonder how many you maybe missed just like that because you were hopeless even while you're sitting up, slowly, careful, feeling it, letting it soak into you again as you're looking and moving, always like first time at that circus and dead-white up high against the canvas the white leg starts out, feeling slowly along something you can't see but it must be there while the drum rolls and you tighten, slowly, and then so sudden you haven't seen the move she's standing complete, alone, white arms crossed out, standing up there above everything on nothing, though you know there has to be a wire. I was on the sidewalk, standing, and walking then. Not fast, just enough to stay behind, feeling the tightness work me like a beautiful dull ache towards the grey block, under the grey porch, and the tune was there, the words and tune too right there as if I was soaked with it

> *Leave the dance with me sweet Sally,*
> *Come with me just*

walking just fast enough to stay behind because a woman with a heavy bag of groceries will not, of course, walk very fast.

With only one bag the outer door was no trouble; she swung that easily and I was slowing down so I wouldn't come up and show I had no key by not offering to open the inner one (wear a tie and always move calm, that's all) but it was all fine, of course, just fine as it always is if you've been able to wait long enough: a man in black pushed out that minute and held the door, she didn't have to bother with a key. I went in fast and caught the door as it started shut after her. I nodded but the man was past and didn't even grunt; he went past without a look at his best deed for the day. When I see him again, I'll thank him.

Two steps up to three closed elevator doors; there was a rubber rug on the floor, and the little lobby off the front door had three bile-green couches and a coffee table with a comic book ripped like some kids had been tearing their hair out there. A blown-up kodachrome saved wallpaper on one wall. Mountain lakes! I can't stand them. Where we waited for the

elevator was a trough of dark broad plants with flowers stuck
in sandpails. The flowers were big as my fist and cold, just
beautiful.

The middle elevator thumped and five people came out,
one a woman with a wiener-dog on a string and two girls.
Their stockings were mottled white so their legs looked like
dead birch sticking in a puddle, but the rest of them—ugh—
they were ugly, so smooth and round-faced with long straight
hair the way you see them now wherever you look in the
world. And tight skirts so short when they sat they'd show
to the crotch, their boobs sticking out, it was obscene,

> O look it's grey out.
> I said bring your coat.
> This lipstick doesn't match it.
> O look it's so grey.
> I said bring your coat.
> But my ear-rings . . .

their stick legs tapping along the rubber rug, twitching their
bandage of a skirt.

She had pushed her floor and I leaned over the panel to
push the same one, just in case she was looking. But she
wasn't, of course. Why should anybody look at me? They
never do, especially in elevators where there are more than
two people; even when there are only two. People in cities
don't look at each other; their glance slides over, like the man
standing beside me with a face as if he'd slept maybe two
minutes in some can last night and nicotine all over his cigarette fingers, letting the smoke curl at me. That's just the way
it is, always, somebody's cancer blowing into your face, you
can count on it like the sun rising

> *. . . with me just once more.*
> *Follow me tonight, we'll take the boat from shore.*
> *I will keep you warm, sweet Sally,*
> *In your dan*

the door was open and she going, I almost hummed it away.
But of course I was moving (even if I'd lost my arm in the
door) following like a gentleman, and turned left as she turned

right, the hall carpet under my feet and one glance at a door number as she walked down the lighted hall—1808—and wheeling after her, only three strides behind when she stopped by a door, fumbling in her shoulder purse, and just beside her as the top of the grocery bag split from her tilt and movement, split so I can stick out my hand for the box of Tide sliding out, grab the whole grocery bag, like a gentleman, just perfect, it is absolutely just perfect.

"O—" then softer, "o—thanks, that—yes, thank you," reaching.

I might as well hold it now, you open up.

"O, yes, of course," the key is out as she hesitates, "it usually," and in the lock, "I should have put it down," turning, "but usually I usually manage," the door clicks and she looks up from its little movement, her hands coming up to take the bag and she'd have touched my hands doing it if I hadn't jerked away, my shoulder swinging the door in—don't for god's sake don't not yet—so I can hardly get my mouth open,

I—I m-might as well—as well c-carry it in.

Her glance flickers up at me in the dim hall light and I step in fast—don't give her a chance not a chance—1815— and in the little hall with the white plaster walls and the kitchen straight ahead my heart slows, settling back even as I hesitate, as I keep my back to her still somewhere in the doorway or maybe the hall,

Where would you like it, please?

like a gentleman delivery boy. The hesitation is all I need, just a little pause you see, little things always will happen but you cut through them with calm direct action and they're no problem. Then just take a deep breath and away you go.

"Anywhere I—on the kitchen counter—my mother-in-law, you needn't—"

No trouble at all, I might as well, and among the dirty dishes I thrust the bag, I might as well, careful with two egg-marked plates, turning to her in perfect calm and look. Now. The big move left. It's starting to roll and a man in black goes past in the hall behind her but doesn't so much as glance, it's starting as I start to the door. Her face loosens like she pulled a cord. She shifts sort of sideways, smile and words start slow, then burst as she opens just a little in relief,

"That was—oh, very kind, of you, I was downstairs washing and the detergent ran out so I hopped down to the grocery while my mother-in-law was . . ."—ooo lady you've got a long way to go—I'm hearing her, I guess, where she stands aside against the coat closet in the grey apartment hall, talking, shifting as I move so there's thirty inches between us, steady, as I reach for the door and she is back between the kitchen's dutch doors, separating them, the light (a momentary break of sunshine outside?) from the window like bullets spraying from her black solid lovely shape as I turn from closing the door and slipping up the door chain without so much as a little rattle, can lean back then against that closed door; and look. The song really rolling now

> . . . *Sally*
> *In your dancing gown,*
> *Warm as the tropic sea*
> *Far from the lights of t*

rolling so I have to wrench myself erect or right then and there I'll be already into the chorus!

She is making a sound; I don't hear quite and her face is in shadow as the light fades again, but her hand goes slowly up to her throat, first one and then the other. I'm standing solid now, weight even on my two feet and everything back under control; I always have to watch that, when the first stage ends. Once after too long I got rolling so strong I—well, spilt milk.

Excuse me, I move to see the lashes on her eyes. You talking to me? She's now against the kitchen counter and her hands drop. Just my right height for a woman, five foot six. Her voice, well, there've been better, but not bad. With other things, the voice is fringe benefit.

". . . the—the faintest idea who you are. I thanked you for your" her arm lifts a little; she has nice motion that way; "and now, go."

Of course not.

She hasn't a touch of make-up and her eyes dead grey, as

they have to be. Not a speck of colour in her eyes. Her face going like stone, she turns, very nice, and walks past the table off the kitchen and around the partition into the living room and while she is still far enough away not to get hurt by something flying I put a bullet through the telephone. The silencer cost me but it's the best you can get; the shot is no louder than a kid falling on its head out of its highchair; the noise is the telephone flying apart on the bookshelf, what's left of it crashing to the hardwood. The bell clangs as it hits, something sizzles

We are all alone, sweet

but I can cut that one easy. Her move rushed me a little and I'm already in the second verse. That's not so good.

You shouldn't of made me do that. Take this out so quick. I put it away. Rushing don't help a thing.

Her back is like you pulled a lever and turned her to rock, half-tilted against the bookshelf. After a while her little finger starts to jerk back and forth a little on the spine of a book lying there; it looks like a Bible, lying with bits of black telephone on its black cover.

Where's Mother-in-law?

Her finger stops; after a while she whispers, not turning, "Mother-in-law?"

Yeah. When we come in. Where's she?

"She—she lives in Vauxhall, three hundred miles—"

That's okay, I was born in Alberta, I know enough about Vauxhall. All right. Would you kindly show me around, you know.

"Show you. . . ."

Just take it easy, around the apartment I mean, that's all.

She wheels so fast I think she's ready for something and look up from her ankles quick, but she's just on the edge of crying to judge by her face. That's no good at all; is she the wrong

"Please, oh please, for the love of—"

Don't do that! and she stops very fast. You know how I can't hold my hand with a voice like that and I have to talk fast. Just don't do that, talk like that. Businesslike, like you'd be with the repair man, okay? Now show me the apartment.

She's looking at me and her face hardens again—I knew it she's the cream the real solid kind who pick it up fast—slowly hardens out of her other expression. She walks ahead of me, voice stripped like she's selling the place,

"You—saw the kitchen, dining area, living room. This is the hall closet."

That's handy, right by the door. I'm standing back a bit, looking forward mostly to be polite; hall closets don't do much for me.

"Every apartment has them there"—atta girl edge in your voice edge—"and this is the storage area, small but conven . . ." she's got the door open and with a twist before I start to see it she's half inside and I've got to grab her, get both my hands out and actually grab her! Yank her before she's inside and the door slammed behind her and who knows what they've got in

> *all alone, sweet Sally,*
> *Far from the dance on shore,*
> *Where your lovers wait to*

that far into the second verse and not ten minutes with her. She's rushing me, that's all I can say, she's a good one, the best maybe but she's rushing me and I can't say anything at all when I break myself out of it and get my face and hands more or less calmed down again (sometimes I've never had to use my hands at all, you know that) and she's staring at me from where she's spread against the dim wall in the hallway, staring up till I can finally get my face quiet and my hands down. My jaw unlocked.

It's that door, that one. Don't you make one move.

It was her fault, that TV trick with the storage room, and she knows it. I have the one closed bedroom door open without taking my eyes off her, bent back, hands still spread from where she caught herself, back against the wall. The shades are drawn, it's even nicer dark in there, but I've got to see sharp now so I reach in with my left hand and flick on the light. An instant is enough; a grey bun of hair on the bed facing the other way and a quilt over the shoulders. The quilt helps. There's hardly a twitch and its done in a flick, no different from putting two into the dummy out on the range so fast and tight the sergeant can't yell a thing because if he's got two bits to his name he can cover both holes. The song and tune holding it right on

> *lovers wait to hold you close once more.*
> *But you'll dance again sweet Sally*
> *As you glide on down*
> *Down, down in the sea far*

though I'm still a little angry she pushed me so fast. It's not really right and when I think about it later it'll be such a waste, so fast now. You really should have time to think about it all, step by step. Appreciate. Well—I've put it away, and my hands are free again. The door's shut.

Into the living room, you can sit on a chair, all right?

I knew she was right; she gets herself straightened up, it takes time but she does and she walks quite steadily into the living room and makes it fine to the armchair beside the bookshelf. The couch across the room for me. Just fine. Beautiful in fact.

You understand of course it's never happened this fast before, so much and so fast. I would never have dreamed to find anyone who could handle it the way she does, that would have been out of the question to imagine seeing I had such terrible waits even finding anyone. Oh, the waiting I've done, sitting, my body going dead sitting, or sometimes walking a little, waiting outside all those buildings in a place the size of Edmonton, four hundred thousand and how can it be I couldn't, didn't find anyone, no one after you, and you— ah-h-h—just sitting here across from her with her slim legs decently together and skirt over her knees even when everything has exploded as it were in her usual life, to sit there and face me again with a dark solid face like rock and I don't have to begin anything. She will keep facing me I know without a word and her face set until I'm good and ready to start. When I'm ready.

There is, of course, no reason in the world why a human being should laugh.

I stop there like usual; I'm so sure now I don't have to bother at all timing it, that she'll butt in. She sits, her arms down along her thighs but she is not slumped. She does not blink and I am sitting right where her eyes seem to meet, although they don't seem quite to see me. She's alive and perfectly inert the way one can only dream and even then knowing you'll wake up before you can taste it all but there's no waking here, not now

> *Down, down in the sea*
> *Far from the lights of town, Michael row*

but that's trouble, the last verse starts like the chorus and if I don't watch that—you remember don't you—I'll be on in the chorus at last before the last verse because the first words are the same, and then it's been wasted all! All! But now I sense it of course right away, the second word in the last verse is 'weep' and I pull up. With someone like this I can probably keep this going—well I can try again can't I—the complete song, every verse, she looking like she is, so I cut the song and continue. At my leisure.

The problem with laughing is it makes you forget. You relax and the bad you've done you begin to forget it. Right away. That's wrong, you see. Don't you. You shouldn't just be able to forget about what you've done wrong. You should have it right there in front of your thinking all the time, know every wrinkle of it. Not wash it away with a laugh or a grin or a big-laugh and slap on the back. You gotta keep it in front of you all the time and that's the biggest thing that's wrong with laughing because it washes it out, you relax and it's gone, right out of sight and out of mind and that shouldn't happen like that outa sight and outa mind which is where laughing gets you because people should just hafta see and keep on seeing and staring right in the face every bit of everything bad they've done ever done . . .

Her expression has changed, and it's just as well because it breaks up my talk. Maybe she said something? I know, I was stumbling already, repeating myself. That's another thing that usually happens when it's so long. I repeat and then I'm going in circles. I know that, you don't have to—it's hard to stop, like some other things, unless you get help and here again she's got it. Just the look is enough and I can get stopped. No problem; start again.

You know these men nowadays call themselves theologians and call people to a new morality and call God dead? No doubt you've heard all about that, you can't get away from it hardly unless you plug yourself up, eyes, ears, nose, every-thing—well, God's dead for them, sure, because they've laughed him to death. There's just nothing left sacred and serious but somebody cuts her up laughing. Can you think of anything they don't laugh at now? I could give you ten minutes and you couldn't think of nothing, bright as I know you are. The Devil in the Snake got Eve to eat the apple by cracking a joke about God and the Devil's been laughing ever since. You laugh and you don't keep the proper things down no more—you get rid of them, right. The stuff's got to be kept down, down where it belongs and not laugh it away, and whatever you do you've got to be able to face it, square face to face and face it right out, and not once do you laugh it away easy. You do every bit you do dead sober, you live a godly, righteous and sober life like the Bible says, right. A righteous and sober life, facing everything you do without . . .

She may have been saying something again. I can't be sure of course, because I was explaining to her, but she may have been saying something because I see now that her mouth is moving and it may have been moving and it may have been probably moving for some time. Her hand has definitely moved; she has the Bible in her hand now and is brushing the bits of black telephone off, holding it clutched in front of her with her eyes closed like sleep, but her lips move.

Right like the Bible says. I know you're a Bible reader, and I base my life on what the Bible says too. I don't always do right, I know that, and I've been punished, don't think I haven't, but I'm never getting punished because I didn't know and didn't care I was doing wrong. I'll know it before any-body else. The trouble with the world that walks past every day is they don't know they're doing wrong and they don't care if they did because they're so busy laughing it away.

Everything's laughed at. People are always looking around, hoping to see something they shouldn't see, something to laugh. Women wear clothes—not you but there're plenty right in this building with you, you've seen them, showing things God never meant to be shown and people look and look and laugh to cover up the evil spinning in their heads when they look. Smiling everywhere, just notice it sometime. It isn't right and I've got the proof for it. You know the final proof?

I wait, like I always can afford and I know from this one I'll get response. But I'm too relaxed, and the verse comes

> *Michael weep for dear sweet Sally*
> *Down in the deep blue sea,*
> *Hang your head and cry down by the gallows tr*

thanks heavenly God she's been saying something again, though I haven't heard it, and her staring mouth moving helps me cut across to her and hear her saying, aloud

". . . ever done, what have I ever done to anybody that you—"

Heyhey now, I've got to jump in here fast. I can't have over-estimated her, but dear God! Now that is no question for us sitting here like this. Don't do that, don't do that at all.

And she stopped, of course. She sits there motionless again, holding the Bible, her fingers dead white along the edges. The darkness has come in more from outside and someone I know is walking down the hall. You can hear him even with the thin rug there. This place must be really built on the cheap, and maybe I should have figured that more before. I guess I did but I didn't think of all the possible implications of that, though by now you'd think I'd know better. Mistakes; I keep doing wrong and one of these—cut that!

You've got the proof right there, in your hand. The Bible. The Book of Jesus. You ever read that Jesus laughed?

She doesn't say a word that I can hear. Her eyes are wide, looking, her face rigid and her lips moving but I can't hear a word so I carry right on or I'll be through all the verse and then there's nothing left but the chorus.

No. You never. You'll never read that we know right now,

both of us, Jesus never done it. He healed the blind and wiped off the sores of lepers and threw out devils and whipped moneychangers and told Pharisees they were just so many sonsabitches and he gave the hungry food sometimes. But when did he ever laugh? Eh? You ever catch Jesus laughing? Nosir.

"...talking of Jesus after the unspeakable things you've..." she goes on talking, her face still rigid like it's been cast forever but her hand gesturing down the apartment hall.

The old woman now, right, and she went in sleep. She never knew a thing of it. We should all pray for that. She could have lived to ninety-five, here and in Vaux—the—the medicine, they have, now, and her teeth falling out and not able to control herself and you wiping up the mess. Oh, I know, Jesus raised some from the dead, about three the Bible says, and some relatives thanked him for it but you never read nothing from the ones that was raised, do you? Not a thank you, not from one of them. He never done it for the dead ones, let me tell you, it was the living, just some of them, nagging him. Anyway, if he did it for the dead, why didn't he do it more? Tell me that. There must have been plenty dead with Jesus walking the country and he just raised three. Nosir. There's nothing to worry about the dead. They never laugh. Not even when they come back.

I must have been talking a long time. My mouth feels dry and she has pulled herself back in her chair, as if she were trying to push back as far as she could. Has she been saying something? Perhaps. Maybe that's why for a minute the sun coming in through the slatted window, the big one in the living room where we sit, my body coming back now a bit and relaxing on what once was a good foam-rubber coach but now worn thin and thread-bare, though it's really clean, I seem to have lost where I was. Even the—no—

> *Down in the deep—*
> *Hang your—head and—cry down by the gall*

no, that's there okay. But it's so far gone. I must have been wasting it somewhere, and she's talking too; I can hear her.

I've heard it all before, yeah, he raised three and loved

them all. So in all them hundreds of years since, how many you think he killed?

That's everybody's mistake about Jesus. He had a lot more things in his mouth than love. That's the forgotten Jesus. Like hanging stones around your neck and into the sea with you, down down, or calling a woman that isn't a Jew like him a dog, just like a lot of other Jews do now, just walk down the pawn street and you'll hear. Or that about the sheep and the goats. Everybody lined up, all the nations, great and small it says right here in your Bible, Matthew 25, and the big finger coming out and the voice, 'You sheep right,' and 'You goat left.' That's judgment, and sheep and goats sliding right and left without even a snicker anywhere. Dead sober, dead, and the goats knowing dead sure why they're going. They know why. Because compared to a sheep a goat's a LAUGHER.

Sheep   the range flat grey powdered rock dusted in hollows to grey chewed root   sheep-like clouds, white on grey-green, white in the streaky blue   the horizon so far and straight the hills turning on a shimmer of griddle heat   sheep like clouds, sheep whitish pancakes fuzzing grey in the heat, frying flat, speckled under the specks of hawks stuck on the blue for gophers   above hawks and sheep and flat grey to the horizon end in sky hang vultures, flat, sailing like mobiles hung on strings hooked nowhere over the impossible level of sage and stubble gnawed grey by sheep and gophers and the unending sun   soft at the flat edge of it, gentle a little but slowly hoisting itself higher and higher to burn over the gaunt woolly sheep panting against each other, sides thumping in the heat till their backs merge in the shimmer of flat earth sweating greyness and light under the mobile of vultures endless turning turning   sheep. The goat standing in the one patch of shade   beside the sleeping-wagon   alone in a herd of sheep   no female to chase in a small surge through the flat back. and a momentary lunging elevation female of his kind   always erect already in whatever shade, on whatever elevation, a sweat-spot beside the wagon or a stone large enough for two front hoofs   head erect, horns curled back   chewing   standing and chew-

ing endless under the mobiles   chewing with a twist to his
mouth, head turning from the panting sheep smeared flat
over the land   facing ahead, a twist in his mouth   the
flat blazing earth flimmering   in heat
   . . . where's the girl?
   She stops what she has been saying to me; whatever it all
was. Her mouth just stops and she is looking.
   "Excuse me?" she says finally. "Please!"
   Your girl? She at school now I guess? She just stares. Over
there, the picture. I see everything. How old is she?
   "It was, just last, fall, before she started school, just last,
we got that picture . . ." She's staring at me now and the
expression on her face is changing again. She is looking at her
wristwatch and her expression is changing as I watch, her
fingers slowly kneading the smooth leather of the Bible.
   In the dark northern lights come and go   washing out
the stars in colour with their slow twitch   alone in a world
so flat it bends backwards   the goat's white tail flickers
      you can step off into stars   his black head nodding.
He coughs.
   ". . . finally dressed, it was such a hurry. And like I said
when we finally got there, after all the fuss of the accident
right in the underpass, it wouldn't have really caused any
trouble if it hadn't happened right in the underpass, we almost
cancelled everything, but Jake said it couldn't be helped, it
wasn't his fault and Mama had come from Vauxhall to see
her start school so why go through all that again but we were
all so upset it came out stiff upset by the accident she's usually
such a happy little girl the photographer tried everything and
even got out his jack-in-the-box but she didn't want to laugh.
He tried everything and Jake almost choked but she just
couldn't seem . . ."

   down by the gallows

her mouth stops. And then her face breaks. Breaks like when
a hammer hits a dried-out clod of southern Alberta gumbo

   tree
   Michael weep for

She is screaming. Sitting perfectly motionless holding the Bible in front of her, staring at her wristwatch, screaming. "God my God my God, that horrible song, stop it! STOP IT!"

I told you she was the right one. The song is in my head of course, I've of course never sung it out loud again and I wouldn't, you know that, even with her, but she knows. She's that kind

dear sweet

she's on her feet, screaming, moving *her dancing* coming toward me, her hands set like claws *Drifting in the tide* too fast! It's too fast, she's coming too fast, reaching *the lights of town Michael row the* but it's too fast! I can't finish! I just can't jam it all in so FA-A-A-A

The blanket from the shelf in the hall closet covers her easily. Even the Bible lying there, spread out. I shouldn't have counted on her that much, depended so much. Sitting so still, talking so long and perfectly normal—weren't you talking about your life, all those growing up things, don't you remember?—I should have expected she'd break and got it finished. But it was so comfortable, at last. That was my mistake, I know, but we have to have time or it doesn't do any good. You taught me that, too. And this almost worked, you can't say it didn't, till you had to spoil it but it worked— well, it's a minute to four—all afternoon? She was better than anyone, since. In a place the size of Edmonton, to find so few! But there's still the little girl. Is there?

I'm sitting erect on the window sill eighteen floors up. There's no balcony, this place is too cheap, and there's not even a screen but my head is very steady on heights so it is not dangerous at all. The black bridge, beautiful with black heavy steel, reaches over the valley, low water glinting here and there under the sodden clouds. Apartment blocks stick up all over but the black level line is the best thing about the best thing about the valley, a line straight across the green hollow, though now in late fall the leaves are finally gone there is mostly grey left. They are gone. The valley, the river, the road and the spidered trees, the sideway and the parking lot approach below. All variations on grey.

Four o'clock so it must be very close to the time. The sun pretty well gone. A black spot of man comes out from under the porch and cuts across the grey, passing behind my black Lincoln. I sit. She'll be coming soon. Has there been pounding on the door? I listen but then, how can you tell? The song hanging there, waiting, still waiting to be finished finally. Flat Vauxhall. Is someone pounding? Is there?

Or is it a knock? Ah-h-h-h-h-h

FAMILIES

W. D. Valgardson   DOMINION DAY

It was two o'clock before I saw Monica's relatives turn into the driveway. They were to have arrived at twelve and I had convinced myself that this year they weren't going to spend Dominion Day with us. Monica, having much more faith than I, had covered the salads and the jellied chicken with Saran and put them at the back of the fridge.

Ever since we moved to Eddyville five years ago, Monica and I have faithfully driven to Winnipeg at Christmas to share dark fruit cake and port wine with her Great Uncle and Great Aunt, Fred and Fern Harper. Every July first they return the visit and bring Brenda and Hughie Aldridge, their niece and nephew. Although the visit is only for the afternoon, it is still something of an event. Eddyville is only seventy-five miles from Winnipeg, but all through April, May, and June, there is a constant flow of letters.

I was pulling chickweed from among the crushed rock of the driveway as the car pulled up to the corner of the house. I stood to greet them and Uncle Fred nodded to me from behind the wheel. At eighty-three he's as clearheaded as some of our relatives who are half his age. His only infirmity is that his hands tremble when he's not holding onto something. The traffic department has tried to take his license away from him every year since he turned seventy-five, but the most they have managed is to restrict him to driving with his glasses on.

He's tall and thin with two flat, brown moles on the front of his head where his hair has been reduced to a few stray wisps.

Aunt Fern was huddled against the door. She is two years older than Uncle Fred. During the five years they have been coming, she has slipped further and further into senility. She sleeps a lot, but she also has periods when she becomes quite agitated. Uncle Fred calms her by taking her for a ride in the car. When the ride begins, she either falls asleep or sits staring directly ahead and every few minutes, repeats, even in the dead of winter, "Aren't the trees beautiful today."

If she becomes agitated when Uncle Fred is not feeling well enough to drive around the city, he parks the car in front of the house so the wind will carry the exhaust away. Then he helps Aunt Fern into the front seat and starts the motor. There they sit under the elms until she becomes calm.

Uncle Fred rolled down his window. No one else moved so I leaned over and said, "Hi, Uncle Fred. Aren't the others going to get out and visit for awhile?"

Aunt Fern was unaware that the car had stopped. She stared at the glare of the dashboard.

Brenda sat behind her aunt. At forty-five, because she had not married but has made a business career for herself, she is held up to the women of the family as a symbol of success. She's a secretary in a collection agency. In spite of the fact that she tends to be plump, she is an attractive woman. Her hair is a dark chestnut with only the slightest sprinkling of grey.

Hughie was sitting beside her. If he ever straightened up he would be over six feet tall, but his shoulders are so pulled in that they are rounded and he walks and sits with a notice-able stoop. He has a large, hooked nose and a narrow face. Although he's fifty, he has never held a job. His pastimes are listening to the radio and memorizing slogans which impress him. Some time ago Brenda gave him a tape recorder so he could tape the radio programs and play them back for any saying he wanted to learn.

Brenda, with the look of disdain she adopts the minute she leaves the city limits, got out. She looked like she was step-ping into ice water. After going around the back of the car, she opened her brother's door with "Be careful, Hughie. There's gravel and you might slip and hurt yourself."

Every time they come she says the same thing. I was annoyed. I was going to ask her if she thought I should pave the driveway to make their yearly visit safer, but just then Monica appeared. Monica's an enthusiastic person and when she took over her relatives with a burst of questions about their health and their winter's activities, I felt better. I relaxed as I watched her standing among them, her shoulder-length hair set off with green ribbon that matched her skirt and blouse, and her body rising slightly forward on her toes as if to catch their answers before they melted into the air.

It took Uncle Fred nearly five minutes to ease Aunt Fern out of the car. Once on the grass she crouched over her heavy black walking stick until Uncle Fred put his hand on her shoulder and led her into the house.

My annoyance subsided. It had been quick to rise because I had wanted to barbecue steak while Monica and I watched the Dominion Day activities that were taking place in the school yard. The stream that runs between our back yard and the school's property is twenty feet wide, just the right distance to insure our privacy and still be narrow enough to let us see everything that goes on. What I would have liked was to have stripped down to my shorts, packed a twelve of beer into a bucket of salted ice, and lain on the deck chairs while the steaks cooked. However, the old people's stomachs were not up to cold beer and because they had false teeth, we were going to eat jellied chicken.

I helped herd them into the dining room. After we were settled around the table, Monica brought the food. And Fern came far enough out of the stupor brought on by the car ride to nod at me.

As usual, Hughie had chosen the seat between his aunt and sister.

"Would you like some potato salad, dear?" Brenda asked. Hughie, his hands folded decorously in his lap, said yes. Brenda dabbed some potato salad onto his plate.

Brenda listed everything that was on the table, including the salt and pepper. After his plate was full, Hughie waited in silence. Noticing that he had not started eating, Brenda oh-deared him twice and cut his chicken into fork-sized bits.

The conversation was mostly between Uncle Fred and Monica, with Brenda and myself adding an occasional comment. Someone eventually mentioned the high cost of living. Hughie jumped in with "Always save your pennies. If you save your pennies, dollars save themselves. It's not what you earn, but what you save that counts."

Aunt Fern and Brenda nodded their agreement.

I have never been able to decide whether or not Hughie deserves sympathy. Two doctors have said there is nothing physically wrong with him. He's not particularly intelligent, but considering the fact that he's never gone to a full year of school, he's not particularly stupid either.

One story Monica's relatives never give over telling is about Hughie's first attempt to ride a bicycle. He had been let outside for the afternoon, and being eleven or twelve, had tried to ride a bicycle that had been left on the boulevard. His mother had looked out of her bedroom window just as he fell down. To punish him for endangering himself and upsetting her, she restricted him to the house for three weeks and to the yard for another three weeks. By that time snow had fallen and bike riding was over.

Hughie learned his lesson well. His mother has been dead ten years, but whenever he sees someone riding a bicycle he clicks his tongue in disapproval until he is asked what is the matter. Then he launches into a lecture on the dangers of bicycle riding. If he isn't asked, he becomes angry and sulks.

As Hughie ate his chicken, he leaned so close to his plate that his nose was in constant danger of being smeared with potato salad. When he finished, he put his hands in his lap and sat absolutely still. After a minute or so, Brenda noticed him and said, "Would you like something more, Hughie?"

"Yes," he replied.

She reinventoried what was on the table. At potato salad and chicken, Hughie said yes. Brenda dabbed some of each onto his plate.

Aunt Fern noticed that something was happening. She pushed her head over Hughie's plate and peered nearsightedly at the food. She ducked her head closer and for a moment I thought she was going to be struck by Brenda's fork. Aunt Fern noticed the danger. As she pulled her head back, she said, "Don't eat too much. You'll make yourself ill."

No one spoke for the next five minutes. Then Aunt Fern twisted her head from side to side and said, "Clean your plates. Don't waste anything. Waste not, want not."

Hughie had finished everything on his plate except a piece of chicken skin which he had pushed to one side. He was waiting to be offered dessert, but when Aunt Fern spoke, he picked up his fork and popped the chicken skin into his mouth. He looked around for approval. Not getting it because his aunt and sister were eating, he sat up straighter and primly repeated, "Waste not, want not."

After the ice-cream was finished, I suggested that we all go outside and sit in the back yard. Slowly, as though we were following a coffin, we shuffled out into sunlight so bright it hurt my eyes. I went to the garage for a canopy to set up over our guests.

In the school yard clusters of people constantly formed and dispersed. Here and there reds and yellows and oranges made bright spots among the blue and grey suits and dresses. A baseball game was being played in one corner of the field. In the opposite corner the childrens' races were being run. The monotone of the announcer called "Twelve and under. Twelve and under. Collect at the starting line. Will all those twelve and under please collect at the starting line." A record of *The Maple Leaf Forever* was playing at the grandstand. Through the other noises the constant harangue of the basemen rose and fell as they tried to unnerve a procession of batters.

The baseball players reminded me of the wooden dolls with wires in their backs which we used to shake so that their arms and legs would wave wildly in a grotesque dance. Despite their constant chatter, the players stood perfectly still until the ball was hit. Then they rushed about in a momentary paroxysm of action only to stop and return to their former positions.

Aunt Fern, her mouth gaping, fell asleep. Brenda noticed

her aunt and started to the car for a blanket. She was half-way there when Hughie asked her to bring a blanket for him.

Uncle Fred looked at Hughie, then at me. It was eighty above. Hughie noticed our expressions and huddled further down in the wicker chair so that his stomach bulged. Without looking up, he said, "Us old people have got to look after ourselves. We get sick awful easy. Dr. Hoskins told me to watch myself pretty closely."

"What happened to Dr. Johnson, your folk's doctor?" I asked. "I thought you went to him."

"If he knew more, maybe they would still be here. I've been so sick and tired since he sent me to the rehabilitation centre that I've nearly died. I was going to be rehabilitated every day. I had to wait for the bus and the shelter's not heated. It's a miracle I didn't get pneumonia. You don't know how cold it gets in the city in winter. Some days it was so cold that I couldn't wait. I had to go home to bed."

His explanation was interrupted as Brenda started tucking an afghan around his knees. While she fussed at his feet, he craned his long neck toward me, and said, "When I called the doctor he would never come until the afternoon. The last time, he said I had to come to the office from then on because I really wasn't sick." He took a deep breath before saying with some satisfaction, "I know when I'm sick."

I wished I could have heard exactly what the doctor had said. More curious than ever, I asked if the new doctor was helping.

"Oh, yes," Hughie replied. "He knows more than any doctor I've met. Of course, he's a specialist. It costs Brenda more to have him, but Mother always said you get what you pay for. Quality makes the difference."

I was going to do a little more prying, but I saw Monica's disapproving look. When she disapproves of something she presses her lips together ever so slightly and a dimple forms on her chin. Instead of asking any more questions I stood up and invited Uncle Fred to walk to the stream with me. We had been standing on the stream's edge for less than a minute when he said, "The doctor should have kicked his ass all the way to the bus stop."

It was so unexpected that I laughed out loud. Uncle Fred kept a straight face, but the skin around his eyes crinkled and the line of his mouth softened. He raised his hand just past his shoulder and flicked a stone into the stream. The skin of his hand was darkened with brown irregular patches and ridged heavy blue veins. A small blue bruise from a burst vein marred the skin between his thumb and forefinger.

"It's not his fault, really," he said, "but there are times he makes my foot ache. His mother nursed herself to death. When she died we cleared out her bedside table. I counted one hundred and fourteen different kinds of pills. Some had been there so long you could barely read the writing on the labels."

"How sick was she?"

He shrugged. "It depended on who came to visit. If you didn't make much money, she was dying. If you made a respectable amount, she sent down a note. If you made as much as her husband, she asked you upstairs to the bedroom and you got to sit on a footstool and talk to her. If you made more, she came downstairs. Dressed in black, of course, but she came. She spent her entire life practising dying."

A red-winged blackbird fluttered onto the stem of a blue flag and he added, as though it explained everything, "They both came from England in fourteen. He was a remittance man."

I was interested in Uncle Fred's description of Hughie's mother. According to the other members of the family, she had been a woman moulded into a paragon of virtue through suffering. None of them ever mentioned her name without appending 'saintly.'

We moved along the bank with the casualness of sheep grazing, stopping here and there to look at the soft browns and greens and greys of the ground and grass and water. There was nothing intense about it, but rather a confidence, an absorption in the looking that precluded talking. I was surprised to find that the water wasn't blue. It has always been blue when I have glanced across it from the yard, even when the water was low in the fall and grey fence posts strung with moss and the black mounds of muskrat houses were revealed for all to see. At those times I had wondered how anything like the posts and mounds could not have been dyed blue by their immersion.

Now the water was brown and grey and green when I leaned over to watch the water bugs skid from stem to stem. I took three steps back and the water turned blue. I stepped forward and the surface changed again. Somewhere, I thought, there is an invisible line, the passing of which lets me see the water as it really is.

I looked at the ground. It was black loam roughened by the hooves of the last owner's dairy cows. He had moved them into a field half a mile down the road and I had seen them with their black and white faces, crowding against the fence. Now, the ground was covered with short green grass that never grew enough to need cutting. Closer to the house the grass was coarser and grew ankle deep in seven or eight days.

A bottle floated by on its side. Uncle Fred threw a stone at it. A white spurt appeared just in front of the bottle, making it wobble slightly. I bent down and dug a stone from the edge of the stream.

"Too much lead," I said, threw my stone, and hit the water two inches behind the bottle. We walked along throwing rocks until the bottle was out of range.

As we were coming back, Uncle Fred pointed and said, "There's another one." He reached into the reeds and lifted out a green whiskey bottle. He poured the grey water out and plugged the neck with clay. After we had both collected a handful of stones, he flipped the bottle upstream. It made a graceful arc, disappeared below the surface, then reappeared. We threw wildly at first.

"Don't let it get away," Uncle Fred said as the bottle went past us. We followed along the bank, hurling stones and hard lumps of clay encrusted with gravel. It looked like the bottle was going to escape unharmed and leave us defeated, but then it was caught in an eddy. It spun slowly in a circle. We threw together.

The stones went to their mark. We both shouted "Mine!" as the green glass shattered. For a second the large end turned up, its sharp edges throwing off sparks of sunlight. Then it filled with water, leaving circular ridges of light and dark on the surface as it sank. We turned from the bottle to look at each other and for a moment shyness overcame us both.

We stood there smiling at each other long enough for the first ripple to break against the bank and for the announcer to shout through his loudspeaker "Adult competitions will begin in fifteen minutes. Will those entering the one hundred yard dash come to the starting line."

Uncle Fred looked like he was going to say something, but Hughie's shadow pierced the patch of light between us. He stopped well back on the stream's edge and said, "Uncle Fred. Uncle Fred. There's an awful lot of clouds over there. The wind's starting to blow. It might rain."

Hughie was right about the change in the weather. Ragged black clouds were building over the lake. The breeze was just strong enough to stir the tips of the swamp grass.

"Thank you, Hughie," Uncle Fred replied. "We'll leave in a few minutes."

I expected Uncle Fred to return to the house immediately. Instead, he waited until Hughie had shuffled away, then snapped off the head of a last year's bullrush. Plucking the tufts of tan-coloured seeds from the head, he held them out for the wind. The breeze was erratic and some of the seeds flew back and struck him, but most of them settled among the reeds and on the open water. When the stem was bare he stood watching the crowd mill about the field.

A young girl's high-pitched squeal of laughter reached us. We saw her dart back and forth among the groups of adults who were standing and talking. She was wearing a short pink dress and had long, pale blonde hair. Two boys of fourteen or fifteen were chasing her. They caught her and with bursts of excited giggling they struggled with her until she walked into the crowd holding their hands. Uncle Fred flipped the dry stalk into the water and turned toward the house.

Something about the way he had hesitated on the edge of the stream had moved me. I said, "You'll have to come and stay with us a couple of days. I'll arrange to be free. We'll drive around the countryside. The stream is beautiful further up where the land is slightly rolling. The sheep keep the grass cropped so close you'd think someone mowed the banks."

Without stopping, he said, "When you get to be my age, you can't afford to be coy and wait for a second invitation. If you'd really like me to come, I'll come. But it won't be for awhile."

As he spoke, he looked at Aunt Fern. "She needs a lot of care. She can't do anything for herself at all. It's not so bad when she doesn't know what's happening, but when she's herself, she cries."

He stopped beside Aunt Fern's chair and put his hand on her shoulder. I looked down. Her skin was thin and fragile and had the same blue cast that the inside of a Belleek cup has when the sun shines on it. For a moment I had the fleeting feeling that if I touched her, my fingers would shatter the skin and bone and leave dark unfillable holes. The vein at her temple and in the curve of her neck beat so slowly that the motion was barely visible.

As Uncle Fred's fingers rested on her shoulder they stopped trembling. "She used to be very beautiful," he said.

Abruptly, he shook my hand. "Thank you for having us. It's good to be around young people. If you never see young people, you begin to think the entire world is old. Next month I'll get the port wine for Christmas."

Our hands gripped briefly, but the pressure of the handshake stayed with me. Uncle Fred woke Aunt Fern and led her into the house.

We had tea and cucumber sandwiches, then safely arranged in the car, our guests disappeared down the highway. I took a beer to the stream's edge and sipped it as I watched the races.

The black clouds over the lake were moving landward. The wind was stronger but still unsteady, first flattening the grass one way, then another. Dust devils spun on the worn patches of the school yard. The wind and the crowd excited me. All at once I wanted to plunge into the crowd and feel it rubbing and bumping against me. I wanted to elbow my way through the noise and the faces and join in the mile race that was being announced. It was a long race, the longest of the day, and few people entered it. I had run the mile in high school and now I wanted to run it again, even if it was only for the first few laps.

I waved at the window and caught Monica's attention.

I pointed at her, myself, the celebration. Monica shook her head and lifted a soapy cup. I jabbed my finger at her and myself, refusing to accept her reply. There was always time to wash dishes. Dominion Days come and go so quickly. When she came, I took her hand and started for the bridge. I walked so quickly that once or twice we stumbled on the uneven ground.

Sheila Watson   THE
BLACK
FARM

We miscalculated our Uncle Daedalus. When a man has trafficked in light and colour and softness he may tire of them at last. He may see God, not in the port-hole lights of heaven, but in the black keel which nightly bearing down on him forces him back below the coloured fishes of day's flood, or, deeper still, into the eyeless sockets beneath the sea itself.

I looked for a motive after our uncle had destroyed himself. When he began to build the Black Farm I thought he was playing one of his foolish tricks and that he would succeed somehow; and success, as my brother Oedipus was quick to point out—not without some ambiguity since he had meddled more than anyone suspected in the affair—needs no justification but itself.

You would have to know our Uncle Daedalus to understand. He was, as Oedipus said, sculptured all round and broadloom from ear to ear. He had, Oedipus said, a split-level mind. He wanted the best of both worlds and revenue besides. He talks of vistas, but his windows are shopkeepers' windows built for display, Oedipus said. He buys and sells view lots in a cemetery. He cuts down trees so that his foolish pansies can smile and wink for a day. He can leave nothing as it is.

Our mother made excuses for our uncle.

After all, she said, the turkey carpet on which we took our

first steps has worn thin. The marble basin in the bathroom is cracked.

Replacement is a law of life, Puss admitted, but what does our uncle care for that. Replacement for him is a sales factor —nothing more.

It's curious, our mother said, how often self-made men come on truth through the back door. Daedalus picked up what he knows like agates off a beach. No one bothered about his education. He was the youngest of the boys. What could he do, she said, except to busy himself with things?

He has done his best to make the world a better place to live in, Puss's wife said.

Better than what? Oedipus asked.

Well, better, she said, than it was when I was a girl. He's made the world better for children. I can remember being jabbed with a button-hook when my mother got me into my leggings.

True enough, Puss said. He's tried to persuade the world that he's made it jab-proof and hole-proof and scratch-proof, that it's crush-resistant and heat-resistant and stainless; but he ignores lemon juice and the Siamese cat. He forgets the catechism and original sin.

Our mother raised her eyebrows.

Original sin is not a subject for the dinner table, she said. I remember the catechism I learned and probably Daedalus does too, although his education was neglected. Yet before we leave the subject, she said, may I ask if acknowledgement of man's limitations must become a counsel of despair? You have, she said to Oedipus, no sense of proportion. Must a man live naked because he was born naked?

Job had something to say about that, Oedipus answered.

Refrain from quoting him over your cheese, our mother said. He went clothed himself before the days of his misfortune and after, too, I think.

She turned to me. When are you going for your holiday? she asked.

Oedipus rolled the stem of his glass between his thumb and middle finger. If a man could only take a luxury cruise to Eden, he said.

Our mother raised her chin a little.

Europa writes, she said to me, that your uncle has been buying up the land around her.

Buying up the hills? I asked. I didn't think he'd follow me beyond the telephone and the hydro.

It is not likely that he will, our mother said. At bottom I think his investment is some scheme to help Europa. He's always been more or less attached to her since he left home as a boy though she tried to spank him once for tying fire-crackers to the cat's tail. He destroyed a good deal from innocent curiosity your father used to say. He lived, your father said, in the nursery of the imagination.

And like Jack climbing the bean-stalk of success he depended on his native wit to defend him from the ogres which people the universe, Oedipus said.

He was as simple as Dick Whittington, our mother said, and as successful.

She put her napkin down beside her plate and rose. Puss's wife followed her into the living room.

When I think of our uncle, Oedipus said, walking the earth as if he'd been cast by nature for some top-echelon role on the stage where Operations Anthropos has gone into the twentieth century of recorded production I can only wonder that he's not booed from the stage.

I must admit that I hoped by visiting Europa to escape for a bit into Eden myself. I was prepared to find the serpent of course, curled squat about some flowering branch. He's the necessary tension in any Eden. It's the shock of finding him in an aspidistra that can't be borne, or turning him up in a pot of African violets. I wasn't prepared, however, despite my mother's comment, to find my uncle or to be followed by him. I could, if I wanted to, level an inkpot any day at the devil, but before the dove-like simplicity of my uncle I was powerless. I had no recourse against him but retreat.

Europa met me and drove me into the hills. I saw no difference in her. She was simply and magnificently old as a tree is this season and next.

I've come, I said, because I want to get away from it all. I need to let the old Brahma bull in me loose for a little. I can't stand the maze. I'll compound any day for a simple barbed wire fence.

The hills hunched indifferent shoulders about us.

They resent intrusion, Europa said. She pointed to some thistles in a field of hay. Somehow or other, she said, they resist exploitation. They revenge themselves in the end.

I asked her about Daedalus's speculations.

It was one way of saving the hills, she said. I couldn't buy the land myself, so I asked Daedalus to help. His buying the land will protect it from others, she added. It is still in the family. I am sure he'll never want to live here himself; the hills will be free for a generation at least.

When we reached her verandah we turned to look at the sweep of the land. Light burned along the grass and flamed up the thin stems of the poplars. It licked over into the dark coulees and smouldered in the thick mat of wolf willow.

We drank raspberry wine together.

I like to think, Europa said, that I live without the help of Daedalus and his friends but I can't forget poor Thoreau and his axe.

After I had changed my things she helped me saddle.

You won't get far by yourself, she said, but I've a cow to milk and sandwiches to make. Keep to the black path and turn back at the soggy spring. You can't miss either.

I rode off without comment.

Mind the gates, she called after me, and don't bring back a bouquet of deadly camus.

I'll leave that for Daedalus, I answered. He could probably distil it into something innocently sweet as Adam's rib.

I let the horse jog off with me. The thought of my uncle was enough to upset me.

I followed Europa's instructions. And when I got back I unsaddled and turned the horse into the upper pasture. But when I walked into the house there he was—Uncle Daedalus sitting in one of Europa's hand-made chairs and sipping a glass of raspberry wine.

Those who know . . . he was saying. My entrance interrupted him.

How did you get here? I asked.

The question's not how I got here, but why I came, he said. When I heard you were coming I couldn't resist coming too. I keep my ear to the ground, he said.

What a preposterous picture language can evoke, Europa said. You mean you keep your hand on the telephone. But you won't be able to here.

I don't know that I want to, Daedalus answered. Although remember, he added, I'm a born innovator and could change all that if I wanted to. I turned the city into a little country with my planting areas and my barbecues. I could change the hills I suppose. You've no idea, he said, how my planting areas and barbecues took on.

I'm sure, Europa said. Human beings have a curious passion for picnics and potted plants.

Our uncle looked at her approvingly.

You've got the idea, he said. There's no limit to human desire. But human beings don't know what they want. They sleep and dream but they leave it to men like Freud and me to find out what they are really dreaming about. They sleep, he said, and dream; but they sleep on rubber foam now instead of straw.

You'll sleep on a felt mattress here, Europa said, and if your feet are cold at this altitude you can warm them on a hot brick. We keep our traditions in the hills.

Are you sure? Daedalus asked. Do you begin to make bread by putting a handful of loose hops in a muslin bag?

Europa ignored his question. I still pick wild strawberries, she said, on my knees among the bluebells and bedstraw. I've crawled on my knees over the better part of a quarter section. Everyone should do it sometime in his life. There are some pleasures, she said, that you can't buy.

Not many, Daedalus said. Besides if you have a passion for picking strawberries you can grow them in a barrel in your own patio. Some of the new varieties are tremendous, he said. In no time at all we'll have single berries as big as a saddle of mutton.

I'm surprised that you remember that symbol, Europa said as if she were cutting off the solid white fat and putting it at the side of her plate.

You're in cattle country, I reminded my uncle. Mutton is not esteemed here and lamb even less since it frolics into muttonhood at last. A hogshead of mint sauce wouldn't sweeten the thought.

Europa silenced me with a gesture.

I was thinking, she said, how intractable mutton is in large pieces. I should have thought you would have discarded the idea of saddles and haunches when you and your colleagues advocated a pressure cooker for every stove and a garbage disposal unit for every sink.

You may laugh if you like, Daedalus said. There's not much unpleasantness in the world that can't be chopped and minced and drained away. As a matter of fact no one wants to be bothered with saddles and haunches. I can hardly remember the cuts myself. It's funny, he said, how ideas slip back into a person's mind.

I'm old fashioned, Europa said. I know the power of naphtha soap and ammonia, of borax and banana oil, of peroxide and javell water. I've used Fuller's earth, and sour milk and molasses, but grass stain and blood stain and mildew persist.

Your reagents are mere makeshifts, Daedalus said. It is easy enough to set everything right with a little detergent and some household tools.

So that I could live every day, Europa said, as if I had never lived before.

Daedalus looked at her.

No, he said, so that you could live every day as if you had just begun and everything was ahead of you.

I feel as if everything is ahead of me here, he said. I own all the land now except what still belongs to you. And I could make an offer for that too that you mightn't like to turn down.

I'm getting tired of gadgets, he said, even the big ones. I've made my money, he said, and now I want to spend it. After all a man's only got a limited time to spend what he has before he dies. I might divide the land up and start a sort of hill city here for people who were tired of the plains.

How could you do that without making more money? I asked him.

Where would I go? Europa asked.

Uncle Daedalus sat back in his chair.

I don't suppose you're different from the rest of the world, he said. Most people want a change; most people want a new model after a bit unless they have a taste for antiques and it's not usually the people who have heirlooms who want them. Take the prairies, he said. People there wanted to climb off their tractors into their cars after they'd thrown away their wagon wheels to bring in the tractor. We sold them machinery until they didn't want it anymore; till they got to hate it the way a man hates a nagging wife. We'd saturated the market as the scientist would say. There wasn't much we could give them after we'd given them the combine except a trip to Bermuda or a winter at Palm Springs. So we did and started a reverse reaction. We converted half a ton of tractor seats into household chairs and a carload of wheels into chesterfield frames and we sold them to people who'd only seen wheat ground into flour or steers cut up into roasts and steaks and roped down under cellophane in the groceteria. We've sold the West to thousands of people, he said. I could sell the hills if I wanted.

I couldn't help interrupting him.

As Puss says you've been buying and selling sentiment for years, I told him. You've done a bargain basement business in hearts and flowers. Now you're going to sell men back the simplicity you've cheated them out of just as you sold them back barbaric masks and patterned prayer rugs.

Uncle Daedalus put down his glass.

You forget the time factor, he said. We're selling some things to some people for the first time. If you'd never had freedom there might be something in trying to buy it by the half acre. If you'd always trimmed your nails and listened to dull sermons you might want an African mask or a genuine prayer rug.

In my day it was brummagen brass, Europa said.

Daedalus ignored her.

Oedipus was spoiled, he said. There are people who make

up their minds to be satisfied with nothing. In the end a man might as well take them off his mailing list. There are enough people with built-in needs, he said, to make people like Oedipus of no account at all.

Europa picked up the lamp to go for some sandwiches. I didn't wait for them. I went to bed. The next morning I got her to drive me down to the station.

He'll ruin you, I said.

She only laughed. I'm rather fond of Daedalus, she said. He was an amusing boy. Since he didn't know what others knew he was always drunk with the wonder of the commonplace.

When I got home I called Oedipus on the telephone.

I thought you'd gone beyond the phone and the hydro, he said.

But not beyond the grapevine and the moccasin telegraph, I answered. Nor for that matter beyond the power of automatic transmission. Uncle D. pulled in just behind me.

Trying to look as rustic as a mallard in a cord shirt and slacks no doubt, he said.

He's more like an osprey, I said. The mallard keeps its feet tucked up.

I'd give anything, Oedipus said, to have been squatting in a duck blind when he flew over. I'd have winged him, he said, and I'd do it yet if I could hold the sights firm.

You never would, I said.

And in the end there was no need because Daedalus destroyed himself. I think now with shame of the lightness of our conversation and the narrowness of our apprehension. I would like to forget. I am of slight build with too little steel in my bones to bear the weight of truth. I see now dimly that Oedipus railed at our uncle because he saw in him what I think poets have called his own antimask. He railed. Then he interfered. But to do him justice he was left shaken by the whole affair and his own part in it.

The first news of our uncle's decision came from Europa. I have persuaded Daedalus, Europa wrote, to consolidate his holdings. I have convinced him that subdivision is the symbol of death. He has certain prejudices which I have found it difficult to overcome. If subdivision is the symbol of death he argues, perhaps some must die so that others may have life more abundantly. But it is a demonstrable fact that no one ever found abundance of life in a six-foot plot.

For once, Oedipus said laying down the letter which had been addressed to our mother, Daedalus may have lost a victory for a truth he can hardly understand. It is not until the coping closes round us that we begin to live. Could it be that our uncle is developing a sense of values other than those chalked up in the broker's window?

You jump to conclusions, I said to Puss. I don't trust our uncle's prejudice any more than I trust Europa's analogy. The amoeba reproduces by the simple process of division.

Puss groaned.

And you call that life, he said. The daughters of Amoeba shall inherit the earth.

I'm sure, I said, that Uncle Daedalus won't lose it.

I was wrong. He did, but not as one might have thought from incompetence or greed and not at once. He became possessed instead of possessing and all that is left now is the ruin of the Black Farm and the memory of a man who perished in a night he had created for himself.

After Oedipus had read our mother's letter he borrowed his wife's convertible and drove up to see Daedalus, who was still staying with Europa. He said that Europa's talk of death had upset our uncle completely. I was quite right, he said, the old fellow is really beginning to realize that there are eternal verities. But habit is strong. He talks wildly about building some sort of showplace on his property, some monument for posterity—something unusual and striking—the house black, all the fittings black, black flowers in the garden, black hens on the roost, herds of black cattle, black dogs on the lawns, and, in contrast, everything reserved for the master gold so that he may shine like a wrought monogram on a rich velvet ground.

I've told him, Oedipus said, that he's stood behind a stall in the market place too long; he has wasted his money and squandered his ingenuity in the great toy shops of the world. He has spent his life like a magician in various transformations. Now that Europa has persuaded him to consolidate his holdings into an estate I have advised him to devote his skill and his money to the discovery of values and the pursuit of truth. This is the very thing I would do myself, Oedipus said, if I had the time and the money.

I found it difficult to think of our uncle with an estate of any kind. Whatever his ancestors had been, he could certainly have no real conception of himself as a country squire or even as a gentleman farmer. If he succeeded in carrying out the idea of the Black Farm he would be nothing but a Sancho Panza with a kingdom of blackamoors. I found it ludicrous to think of him, too, as searching for truth with his assembly-line tools and weighing what he found in the grocers' scales of his past experience. However, Oedipus's visit seemed to set him in motion. Up to that time he had moved about his affairs sometimes by oscillation, sometimes by rotary synthesis. Now he assumed direction. And his imagination, set going by Oedipus, carried him by a sort of jet propulsion into a darkness as black as Pluto's acres.

The difficulty, he said to me when he met me in town one day, is to find true black. I used to live by a decorator's chart. What the experts said was good enough. Since I've started my project, he said, I see quite plainly that you can't change a blonde into a brunette by dyeing her hair. Colour, he said, can't be rubbed on. It's the thing itself. It's curious, he said, where real thought takes one.

He looked for horses, dogs, and hens—all of uniform blackness—without much success. He had no trouble in finding gold. He bought himself a palomino. The sun only altered the quality of its fire, which in winter glowed with a little more warmth, in summer with a softer brightness. Brief as a horse's life is, though, he was not himself to live long enough to test the real quality of the gold. For the time being he had no quarrel with it. But his black horses faded and the slightest gall patched them with white.

He explored blackness in all its manifestations. I don't know where he came by his information. Probably he read in the public library for our mother saw him there one day surrounded by encyclopaedias and guides to science and the arts which I think he had never turned over before except for information incidental to his business. He had as we knew a wealth of knowledge about Roman brick and Botticelli caps and other trivia connected with his ventures.

Now he was becoming global in his research. He began to import materials for the farm. Since he could find no suitable wood for his house he sent to the Black Pasture quarries in Northumberland for marble. When the marble had been raised on its foundations he found that the surface reflected the green of the trees and the crimson of the evening sky. He cut down the trees but the sky was beyond the reach of his workmen. He imported black cocks from Asia only to find that they had white wing patches and vermillion eyebrows. He hired boys to trap blackbirds for him but the birds' beaks were gamboge yellow and the females various shades of brown. He sent to India for black buck but the young males when they were unloaded from the plane were yellowish fawn and would, he found on further inquiry, deepen into black only with age. He collected black nightshade, which poisoned him with its leaves and blossomed into flowers as white as innocence.

I have set myself to find a natural uniformity, he said, against which my person might shine with the glory of heaven. Nature resists me at every turn.

Europa told us that he had imported servants from Haiti and the heart of dark Africa, but that the whites of their eyes were a continual distraction to him. The Labrador dogs, too, which lay about his door, stared at him out of amber eyes. She thought, she said, that the whole enterprise had been a whim and harmless—an innocent fancy which would keep him busy and save the hills from exploitation for a while at least.

He had stopped going to the library and remained, as far as any of us knew, in the marble house which continued to reflect the sky. He was, the report came, under the tutelage of one of his white-eyed servants making excursions into black magic. If nature would not co-operate with him he would find ways of exacting submission from her.

He had ordered a number of black earthenware pots. Europa had seen the bill of lading at the station when she drove in to pick up a saddle she herself had ordered. And while she was still in the station one of the servants had ridden in on Daedalus' palomino to pick up the *govi* as he called them for his master. She herself had taken them in the car despite the man's protests, fearing, as she said, that he would break them. It had given her a start, she said, to see the black man on a palomino like a devil riding the sun.

Daedalus, she felt, had not been pleased to see her when she drove in with the pots; but she had stayed long enough, she said, to drink a very bad cup of tea which one of the servants finally brought. She had asked him what he intended to do with the pots and he had remarked succinctly that he was going to have a family reunion. She reported that he looked thin and pale and generally out of sorts. She had asked him why his man had referred to the pots as *govi*. He had hedged a little and then become voluble, almost incoherent, in his speech.

A single one of the pots, he assured her, had more value than a university education—certainly more value than anyone would set on the scraps of information he had managed to pick up in his various projects. The whole family, he said, had scorned him because, although he had been successful in practical affairs—more successful than any of them—he had no sense of value. These men of mine, he said, can summon into these pots all our ancestral *loa*—the active spirits of our race. Once I have them in these pots behind locked doors I can extract from them in a moment more knowledge of eternal verities than Oedipus ever dreamed up under his rose bushes. Ghede has already chosen me, he said, the eternal figure in black.

Who, wrote Europa, is Ghede? I am afraid that Daedalus's financial worries and his isolation are having a serious effect on his constitution. I thought, she wrote, that he was simply playing with magic as a child plays with tinker-toy or the chemistry sets which are sold at Christmas in most department stores.

Who, echoed our mother, is Ghede?

He is, said Oedipus, death at the cross roads. He stands at the intersection of time and eternity. He is corpse and phallus, king and clown. He introduces men to their own devil. He is the last day of the week and the cross in every cemetery. He sings the song of the grave digger.

Next Europa reported that drums were beating incessantly in the hills. Her amused tolerance had become concern. She had ridden over to see Daedalus but the black servants had refused to let her pass through the black marble vestibule into the house itself. The master, they said, had left orders not to be disturbed. She had seen the palomino cropping grass in the pasture, but had noted nothing else except the frightful mess made by the felled trees which had sheltered the house, and a black rooster fattening in a pen where Daedalus had intended to build a marble patio. All was quiet; but as she rode through the gate into what had once been her old lease she heard the drums chuckling behind her.

With her letter came one from Daedalus himself addressed to Oedipus. It was written in white ink on what seemed to be the folded page of a cheap photograph album. The message was brief:

The god of the abyss has spoken. All black is white.

There are no eternal verities.

Oedipus stood holding the paper.

He has cried out to the god, Oedipus said, but the echo of his own voice has drowned the answer. I must drive down and put an end to this business.

But that very night Daedalus set fire to the long grass in his pasture.

Margaret Laurence   HORSES OF THE NIGHT

I never knew I had distant cousins who lived up north, until Chris came down to Manawaka to go to high school. My mother said he belonged to a large family, relatives of ours, who lived at Shallow Creek, up north. I was six, and Shallow Creek seemed immeasurably far, part of a legendary winter country where no leaves grow and where the breath of seals and polar bears snuffled out steamily and turned to ice.

"Could plain people live there?" I asked my mother, meaning people who were not Eskimos. "Could there be a farm?"

"How do you mean?" she said, puzzled. "I told you. That's where they live. On the farm. Uncle Wilf—that was Chris's father, who died a few years back—he got the place as a homestead, donkey's years ago."

"But how could they grow anything? I thought you said it was up north."

"Mercy," my mother said, laughing, "it's not *that* far north, Vanessa. It's about a hundred miles beyond Galloping Mountain. You be nice to Chris, now, won't you? And don't go asking him a whole lot of questions the minute he steps inside the door."

How little my mother knew of me, I thought. Chris had been fifteen. He could be expected to feel only scorn towards me. I detested the fact that I was so young. I did not think I would be able to say anything at all to him.

"What if I don't like him?"

"What if you don't?" my mother responded sharply. "You're to watch your manners, and no acting up, understand? It's going to be quite difficult enough without that."

"Why does he have to come here, anyway?" I demanded crossly. "Why can't he go to school where he lives?"

"Because there isn't any high school up there," my mother said. "I hope he gets on well here, and isn't too homesick. Three years is a long time. It's very good of your grandfather to let him stay at the Brick House."

She said this last accusingly, as though she suspected I might be thinking differently. But I had not thought of it one way or another. We were all having dinner at the Brick House because of Chris's arrival. It was the end of August, and sweltering. My grandfather's house looked huge and cool from the outside, the high low-sweeping spruce trees shutting out the sun with their dusky out-fanned branches. But inside it wasn't cool at all. The woodstove in the kitchen was going full blast, and the whole place smelled of roasting meat.

Grandmother Connor was wearing a large mauve apron. I thought it was a nicer colour than the dark bottle-green of her dress, but she believed in wearing sombre shades lest the spirit give way to vanity, which in her case was certainly not much of a risk. The apron came up over her shapeless bosom and obscured part of her cameo brooch, the only jewellery she ever wore, with its portrait of a fiercely bearded man whom I imagined to be either Moses or God.

"Isn't it nearly time for them to be getting here, Beth?" Grandmother Connor asked.

"Train's not due until six," my mother said. "It's barely five-thirty, now. Has Father gone to the station already?"

"He went an hour ago," my grandmother said.

"He would," my mother commented.

"Now, now, Beth," my grandmother cautioned and soothed.

At last the front screen door was hurled open and Grandfather Connor strode into the house, followed by a tall lanky boy. Chris was wearing a white shirt, a tie, grey trousers. I thought, unwillingly, that he looked handsome. His face was angular, the bones showing through the brown skin. His grey eyes were slightly slanted, and his hair was the colour of couchgrass at the end of summer when it has been bleached to a light yellow by the sun. I had not planned to like him, not even a little, but somehow I wanted to defend him when I heard what my mother whispered to my grandmother before they went into the front hall.

"Heavens, look at the shirt and trousers—must've been his father's, the poor kid."

I shot out into the hall ahead of my mother, and then stopped and stood there.

"Hi, Vanessa," Chris said.

"How come you knew who I was?" I asked.

"Well, I knew your mother and dad only had one of a family, so I figured you must be her," he replied, grinning.

The way he spoke did not make me feel I had blundered. My mother greeted him warmly but shyly. Not knowing if she were expected to kiss him or to shake hands, she finally did neither. Grandmother Connor, however, had no doubts. She kissed him on both cheeks and then held him at arm's length to have a proper look at him.

"Bless the child," she said.

Coming from anyone else, this remark would have sounded ridiculous, especially as Chris was at least a head taller. My grandmother was the only person I have ever known who could say such things without appearing false.

"I'll show you your room, Chris," my mother offered.

Grandfather Connor, who had been standing in the living room doorway in absolute silence, looking as granite as a statue in the cemetery, now followed Grandmother out to the kitchen.

"Train was forty minutes late," he said weightily.

"What a shame," my grandmother said. "But I thought it wasn't due until six, Timothy."

"Six!" my grandfather cried. "That's the mainline train. The local's due at five-twenty."

This was not correct, as both my grandmother and I knew. But neither of us contradicted him.

"What on earth are you cooking a roast for, on a night like this?" my grandfather went on. "A person could fry an egg on the sidewalk, it's that hot. Potato salad would've gone down well."

Privately I agreed with this opinion, but I could never permit myself to acknowledge agreement with him on anything. I automatically and emotionally sided with Grandmother in all issues, not because she was inevitably right but because I loved her.

"It's not a roast," my grandmother said mildly. "It's mock-duck. The stove's only been going for an hour. I thought the boy would be hungry after the trip."

My mother and Chris had come downstairs and were now in the living room. I could hear them there, talking awkwardly, with pauses.

"Potato salad," my grandfather declaimed, "would've been plenty good enough. He'd have been lucky to get it, if you ask me anything. Wilf's family hasn't got two cents to rub together. It's me that's paying for the boy's keep."

The thought of Chris in the living room, and my mother unable to explain, was too much for me. I sidled over to the kitchen door, intending to close it. But my grandmother stopped me.

"No," she said, with unexpected firmness. "Leave it open, Vanessa."

I could hardly believe it. Surely she couldn't want Chris to hear? She herself was always able to move with equanimity through a hurricane because she believed that a mighty fortress was her God. But the rest of us were not like that, and usually she did her best to protect us. At the time I felt only bewilderment. I think now that she must have realised Chris would have to learn the Brick House sooner or later, and he might as well start right away.

I had to go into the living room. I had to know how Chris would take my grandfather. Would he, as I hoped, be angry and perhaps even speak out? Or would he, meekly, only be embarrassed?

"Wilf wasn't much good, even as a young man," Grandfather Connor was trumpeting. "Nobody but a simpleton would've taken up a homestead in a place like that. Anybody could've told him that land's no use for a thing except hay."

Was he going to remind us again how well he had done in the hardware business? Nobody had ever given him a hand, he used to tell me. I am sure he believed that this was true. Perhaps it even was true.

"If the boy takes after his father, it's a poor lookout for him," my grandfather continued.

I felt the old rage of helplessness. But as for Chris—he gave no sign of feeling anything. He was sitting on the big wing-backed sofa that curled into the bay window like a black and giant seashell. He began to talk to me, quite easily, just as though he had not heard a word my grandfather was saying.

This method proved to be the one Chris always used in any dealings with my grandfather. When the bludgeoning words came, which was often, Chris never seemed, like myself, to be holding back with a terrible strained force for fear of letting go and speaking out and having the known world unimaginably fall to pieces. He would not argue or defend himself, but he did not apologise, either. He simply appeared to be absent, elsewhere. Fortunately there was very little need for response, for when Grandfather Connor pointed out your shortcomings, you were not expected to reply.

But this aspect of Chris was one which I noticed only vaguely at the time. What won me was that he would talk to me and wisecrack as though I were his same age. He was— although I didn't know the phrase then—a respecter of persons.

On the rare evenings when my parents went out, Chris would come over to mind me. These were the best times, for often when he was supposed to be doing his homework, he would make fantastic objects for my amusement, or his own —pipecleaners twisted into the shape of wildly prancing midget men, or an old set of Christmas-tree lights fixed onto a puppet theatre with a red velvet curtain that really pulled. He had skill in making miniature things of all kinds. Once for my birthday he gave me a leather saddle no bigger than a matchbox, which he had sewn himself, complete in every detail, stirrups and horn, with the criss-cross lines that were the brand name of his ranch, he said, explaining it was a reference to his own name.

"Can I go to Shallow Creek sometime?" I asked one evening.

"Sure. Some summer holidays, maybe. I've got a sister about your age. The others are all grownup."

I did not want to hear. His sisters—for Chris was the only boy—did not exist for me, not even as photographs, because I did not want them to exist. I wanted him to belong only here. Shallow Creek existed, though, no longer filled with ice mountains in my mind but as some beckoning country beyond all ordinary considerations.

"Tell me what it's like there, Chris."

"My gosh, Vanessa, I've told you before, about a thousand times."

"You never told me what your house is like."

"Didn't I? Oh well—it's made out of trees grown right there beside the lake."

"Made out of trees? Gee. Really?"

I could see it. The trees were still growing, and the leaves were firmly and greenly on them. The branches had been coaxed into formations of towers and high-up nests where you could look out and see for a hundred miles or more.

"That lake, you know," Chris said. "It's more like an inland sea. It goes on for ever and ever amen, that's how it looks. And you know what? Millions of years ago, before there were any human beings at all, that lake was full of water monsters. All different kinds of dinosaurs. Then they all died off. Nobody knows for sure why. Imagine them—all those huge creatures, with necks like snakes, and some of them had hackles on their heads, like a rooster's comb only very tough, like hard leather. Some guys from Winnipeg came up a few years back, there, and dug up dinosaur bones, and they found footprints in the rocks."

"Footprints in the *rocks*?"

"The rocks were mud, see, when the dinosaurs went trampling through, but after trillions of years the mud turned into stone and there were these mighty footprints with the claws still showing. Amazing, eh?"

I could only nod, fascinated and horrified. Imagine going swimming in those waters. What if one of the creatures had lived on?

"Tell me about the horses," I said.

"Oh, them. Well, we've got these two riding horses. Duchess and Firefly. I raised them, and you should see them. Really sleek, know what I mean? I bet I could make racers out of them."

He missed the horses, I thought with selfish satisfaction, more than he missed his family. I could visualise the pair, one sorrel and one black, swifting through all the meadows of summer.

"When can I go, Chris?"

"Well, we'll have to see. After I get through high school, I won't be at Shallow Creek much."

"Why not?"

"Because," Chris said, "what I am going to be is an engineer, civil engineer. You ever seen a really big bridge, Vanessa? Well, I haven't either, but I've seen pictures. You take the Golden Gate Bridge in San Francisco, now. Terrifically high—all those thin ribs of steel, joined together to go across this very wide stretch of water. It doesn't seem possible, but it's there. That's what engineers do. Imagine doing something like that, eh?"

I could not imagine it. It was beyond me.

"Where will you go?" I asked. I did not want to think of his going anywhere.

"Winnipeg, to college," he said with assurance.

The Depression did not get better, as everyone had been saying it would. It got worse, and so did the drought. That part of the prairies where we lived was never dustbowl country. The farms around Manawaka never had a total crop failure, and afterwards, when the drought was over, people used to remark on this fact proudly, as though it had been due to some virtue or special status, like the Children of Israel being afflicted by Jehovah but never in real danger of annihilation. But although Manawaka never knew the worst, what it knew was bad enough. Or so I learned later. At the time I saw none of it. For me, the Depression and drought were external and abstract, malevolent gods whose names I secretly learned although they were concealed from me, and whose evil I sensed only superstitiously, knowing they threatened us but not how or why. What I really saw was only what went on in our family.

"He's done quite well all through, despite everything," my mother said. She sighed, and I knew she was talking about Chris.

"I know," my father said. "We've been over all this before, Beth. But quite good just isn't good enough. Even supposing he managed to get a scholarship, which isn't likely, it's only tuition and books. What about room and board? Who's going to pay for that? Your father?"

"I see I shouldn't have brought up the subject at all," my mother said in an aloof voice.

"I'm sorry," my father said impatiently. "But you know, yourself, he's the only one who might possibly—"

"I can't bring myself to ask Father about it, Ewen. I simply cannot do it."

"There wouldn't be much point in asking," my father said, "when the answer is a foregone conclusion. He feels he's done his share, and actually, you know, Beth, he has, too. Three years, after all. He may not have done it gracefully, but he's done it."

We were sitting in the living room, and it was evening. My father was slouched in the grey armchair that was always his. My mother was slenderly straight-backed in the blue chair in which nobody else ever sat. I was sitting on the footstool, beige needlepoint with mathematical roses, to which I had staked my own claim. This seating arrangement was obscurely satisfactory to me, perhaps because predictable, like the three bears. I was pretending to be colouring into a scribbler on my knee, and from time to time my lethargic purple crayon added a feather to an outlandish swan. To speak would be to invite dismissal. But their words forced questions in my head.

"Chris isn't going away, is he?"

My mother swooped, shocked at her own neglect.

"My heavens—are you still up, Vanessa? What am I thinking of?"

"Where is Chris going?"

"We're not sure yet," my mother evaded, chivvying me up the stairs. "We'll see."

He would not go, I thought. Something would happen, miraculously, to prevent him. He would remain, with his long loping walk and his half-slanted grey eyes and his talk that never excluded me. He would stay right here. And soon, because I desperately wanted to, and because every day mercifully made me older, quite soon I would be able to reply with such a lightning burst of knowingness that it would astound him, when he spoke of the space or was it some black sky that never ended anywhere beyond this earth. Then I would not be innerly belittled for being unable to figure out what he would best like to hear. At that good and imagined time, I would not any longer be limited. I would not any longer be young.

I was nine when Chris left Manawaka. The day before he was due to go, I knocked on the door of his room in the Brick House.

"Come in," Chris said. "I'm packing. Do you know how to fold socks, Vanessa?"

"Sure. Of course."

"Well, get folding on that bunch there, then."

I had come to say goodbye, but I did not want to say it yet. I got to work on the socks. I did not intend to speak about the matter of college, but the knowledge that I must not speak about it made me uneasy. I was afraid I would blurt out a reference to it in my anxiety not to. My mother had said, "He's taken it amazingly well—he doesn't even mention it, so we mustn't either."

"Tomorrow night you'll be in Shallow Creek," I ventured.

"Yeh." He did not look up. He went on stuffing clothes and books into his suitcase.

"I bet you'll be glad to see the horses, eh?" I wanted him to say he didn't care about the horses any more and that he would rather stay here.

"It'll be good to see them again," Chris said. "Mind handing over those socks now, Vanessa? I think I can just squash them in at the side here. Thanks. Hey, look at that, will you? Everything's in. Am I an expert packer or am I an expert packer?"

I sat on his suitcase for him so it would close, and then he tied a piece of rope around it because the lock wouldn't lock.

"Ever thought what it would be like to be a traveller, Vanessa?" he asked.

I thought of Richard Halliburton, taking an elephant over the Alps and swimming illicitly in the Taj Mahal lily pool by moonlight.

"It would be keen," I said, because this was the word Chris used to describe the best possible. "That's what I'm going to do someday."

He did not say, as for a moment I feared he might, that girls could not be travellers.

"Why not?" he said. "Sure you will, if you really want to. I got this theory, see, that anybody can do anything at all, anything, if they really set their minds to it. But you have to have this total concentration. You have to focus on it with your whole mental powers, and not let it slip away by forgetting to hold it in your mind. If you hold it in your mind, like, then it's real, see? You take most people, now. They can't concentrate worth a darn."

"Do you think I can?" I enquired eagerly, believing that this was what he was talking about.

"What?" he said. "Oh—sure. Sure I think you can. Naturally."

Chris did not write after he left Manawaka. About a month later we had a letter from his mother. He was not at Shallow Creek. He had not gone back. He had got off the northbound train at the first stop after Manawaka, cashed in his ticket, and thumbed a lift with a truck to Winnipeg. He had written to his mother from there, but had given no address. She had not heard from him since. My mother read Aunt Tess's letter aloud to my father. She was too upset to care whether I was listening or not.

"I can't think what possessed him, Ewen. He never seemed irresponsible. What if something should happen to him? What if he's broke? What do you think we should do?"

"What can we do? He's nearly eighteen. What he does is his business. Simmer down, Beth, and let's decide what we're going to tell your father."

"Oh Lord," my mother said. "There's that to consider, of course."

I went out without either of them noticing. I walked to the hill at the edge of the town, and down into the valley where the scrub oak and poplar grew almost to the banks of the Wachakwa River. I found the oak where we had gone last autumn, in a gang, to smoke cigarettes made of dried leaves and pieces of newspaper. I climbed to the lowest branch and stayed there for a while.

I was not consciously thinking about Chris. I was not thinking of anything. But when at last I cried, I felt relieved afterwards and could go home again.

Chris departed from my mind, after that, with a quickness that was due to the other things that happened. My Aunt Edna, who was a secretary in Winnipeg, returned to Manawaka to live because the insurance company cut down on staff and she could not find another job. I was intensely excited and jubilant about her return, and could not see why my mother seemed the opposite, even though she was as fond of Aunt Edna as I was. Then my brother Roderick was born, and that same year Grandmother Connor died. The strangeness, the unbelievability, of both these events took up all of me.

When I was eleven, almost two years after Chris had left, he came back without warning. I came home from school and found him sitting in our living room. I could not accept that I had nearly forgotten him until this instant. Now that he was present, and real again, I felt I had betrayed him by not thinking of him more.

He was wearing a navy-blue serge suit. I was old enough now to notice that it was a cheap one and had been worn a considerable time. Otherwise, he looked the same, the same smile, the same knife-boned face with no flesh to speak of, the same unresting eyes.

"How come you're here?" I cried. "Where have you been, Chris?"

"I'm a traveller," he said. "Remember?"

He was a traveller all right. One meaning of the word *traveller* in our part of the world, was a travelling salesman. Chris was selling vacuum cleaners. That evening he brought out his line and showed us. He went through his spiel for our benefit, so we could hear how it sounded.

"Now look, Beth," he said, turning the appliance on and speaking loudly above its moaning roar, "see how it brightens up this old rug of yours? Keen, eh?"

"Wonderful," my mother laughed. "Only we can't afford one."

"Oh well—" Chris said quickly, "I'm not trying to sell one to you. I'm only showing you. Listen, I've only been in this job a month, but I figure this is really a going thing. I mean, it's obvious, isn't it? You take all those old wire carpet-beaters of yours, Beth. You could kill yourself over them and your carpet isn't going to look one-tenth as good as it does with this."

"Look, I don't want to seem—" my father put in, "but, hell, they're not exactly a new invention, and we're not the only ones who can't afford—"

"This is a pretty big outfit, you know?" Chris insisted. "Listen, I don't plan to stay, Ewen. But a guy could work at it for a year or so, and save—right? Lots of guys work their way through university like that."

I needed to say something really penetrating, something that would show him I knew the passionate truth of his conviction.

"I bet—" I said, "I bet you'll sell a thousand, Chris."

Two years ago, this statement would have seemed self-evident, unquestionable. Yet now, when I had spoken, I knew that I did not believe it.

The next time Chris visited Manawaka, he was selling magazines. He had the statistics worked out. If every sixth person in town would get a subscription to *Country Guide,* he could make a hundred dollars in a month. We didn't learn how he got on. He didn't stay in Manawaka a full month. When he turned up again, it was winter. Aunt Edna phoned.

"Nessa? Listen, kiddo, tell your mother she's to come down if it's humanly possible. Chris is here, and Father's having fits."

So in five minutes we were scurrying through the snow, my mother and I, with our overshoes not even properly done up and our feet getting wet. He need not have worried. By the time we reached the Brick House, Grandfather Connor had retired to the basement, where he sat in the rocking chair beside the furnace, making occasional black pronouncements like a subterranean oracle. These loud utterances made my mother and aunt wince, but Chris didn't seem to notice any more than he ever had. He was engrossed in telling us about the mechanism he was holding. It had a cranker handle like an old-fashioned sewing machine.

"You attach the ball of wool here, see? Then you set this little switch here, and adjust this lever, and you're away to the races. Neat, eh?"

It was a knitting machine. Chris showed us the finished products. The men's socks he had made were coarse wool, one pair in grey heather and another in maroon. I was impressed.

"Gee—can I do it, Chris?"

"Sure. Look, you just grab hold of the handle right here."

"Where did you get it?" my mother asked.

"I've rented it. The way I figure it, Beth, I can sell these things at about half the price you'd pay in a store, and they're better quality."

"Who are you going to sell them to?" Aunt Edna enquired.

"You take all these guys who do outside work—they need heavy socks all year round, not just in winter. I think this thing could be quite a gold mine."

"Before I forget," my mother said, "how's your mother and the family keeping?"

"They're okay," Chris said in a restrained voice. "They're

not short of hands, if that's what you mean, Beth. My sisters
have their husbands there."

Then he grinned, casting away the previous moment, and
dug into his suitcase.

"Hey, I haven't shown you—these are for you, Vanessa,
and this pair is for Roddie."

My socks were cherry-coloured. The very small ones for
my brother were turquoise.

Chris only stayed until after dinner, and then he went away
again.

After my father died, the whole order of life was torn. Nothing was known or predictable any longer. For months I lived
almost entirely within myself, so when my mother told me
one day that Chris couldn't find any work at all because there
were no jobs and so he had gone back to Shallow Creek to
stay, it made scarcely any impression on me. But that summer, my mother decided I ought to go away for a holiday.
She hoped it might take my mind off my father's death. What,
if anything, was going to take her mind off his death, she
did not say.

"Would you like to go to Shallow Creek for a week or so?"
she asked me. "I could write to Chris's mother."

Then I remembered, all in a torrent, the way I had imagined
it once, when he used to tell me about it—the house fashioned
of living trees, the lake like a sea where monsters had dwelt,
the grass that shone like green wavering light while the horses
flew in the splendour of their pride.

"Yes," I said. "Write to her."

The railway did not go through Shallow Creek, but Chris
met me at Challoner's Crossing. He looked different, not only
thinner, but—what was it? Then I saw that it was the fact
that his face and neck were tanned red-brown, and he was
wearing denims, farm pants, and a blue plaid shirt open at
the neck. I liked him like this. Perhaps the change was not
so much in him as in myself, now that I was thirteen. He
looked masculine in a way I had not been aware of, before.

"C'mon, kid," he said. "The limousine's over here."

It was a wagon and two horses, which was what I had

expected, but the nature of each was not what I had expected. The wagon was a long and clumsy one, made of heavy planking, and the horses were both plough horses, thick in the legs, and badly matched as a team. The mare was short and stout, matronly. The gelding was very tall and gaunt, and he limped.

"Allow me to introduce you," Chris said. "Floss—Trooper —this is Vanessa."

He did not mention the other horses, Duchess and Firefly, and neither did I, not all the fortnight I was there. I guess I had known for some years now, without realising it, that the pair had only ever existed in some other dimension.

Shallow Creek wasn't a town. It was merely a name on a map. There was a grade school a few miles away, but that was all. They had to go to Challoner's Crossing for their groceries. We reached the farm, and Chris steered me through the crowd of aimless cows and wolfish dogs in the yard, while I flinched with panic.

It was perfectly true that the house was made out of trees. It was a fair-sized but elderly shack, made out of poplar poles and chinked with mud. There was an upstairs, which was not so usual around here, with three bedrooms, one of which I was to share with Chris's sister, Jeannie, who was slightly younger than I, a pallid-eyed girl who was either too shy to talk or who had nothing to say. I never discovered which, because I was so reticent with her myself, wanting to push her away, not to recognise her, and at the same time experiencing a shocked remorse at my own unacceptable feelings.

Aunt Tess, Chris's mother, was severe in manner and yet wanting to be kind, worrying over it, making tentative overtures which were either ignored or repelled by her older daughters and their monosyllabic husbands. Youngsters swam in and out of the house like shoals of nameless fishes. I could not see how so many people could live here, under the one roof, but then I learned they didn't. The married daughters had their own dwelling places, nearby, but some kind of communal life was maintained. They wrangled endlessly but they never left one another alone, not even for a day.

Chris took no part at all, none. When he spoke, it was

usually to the children, and they would often follow him around the yard or to the barn, not pestering but just trailing along in clusters of three or four. He never told them to go away. I liked him for this, but it bothered me, too. I wished he would return his sisters' bickering for once, or tell them to clear out, or even yell at one of the kids. But he never did. He closed himself off from squabbling voices just as he used to do with Grandfather Connor's spearing words.

The house had no screens on the doors or windows, and at meal times the flies were so numerous you could hardly see the food for the iridescent-winged blue-black bodies squirming all over it. Nobody noticed my squeamishness except Chris, and he was the only one from whom I really wanted to conceal it.

"Fan with your hand," he murmured.

"It's okay," I said quickly.

For the first time in all the years we had known each other, we could not look the other in the eye. Around the table, the children stabbed and snivelled, until Chris's oldest sister, driven frantic, shrieked, *Shut up shut up shut up.* Chris began asking me about Manawaka then, as though nothing were going on around him.

They were due to begin haying, and Chris announced that he was going to camp out in the bluff near the hayfields. To save himself the long drive in the wagon each morning, he explained, but I felt this wasn't the real reason.

"Can I go, too?" I begged. I could not bear the thought of living in the house with all the others who were not known to me, and Chris not here.

"Well, I don't know—"

"Please. Please, Chris. I won't be any trouble. I promise."

Finally he agreed. We drove out in the big hayrack, its slatted sides rattling, its old wheels jolting metallically. The road was narrow and dirt, and around it the low bushes grew, wild rose and blueberry and wolf willow with silver leaves. Sometimes we would come to a bluff of pale-leaved poplar trees, and once a red-winged blackbird flew up out of the branches and into the hot dusty blue of the sky.

Then we were there. The hayfields lay beside the lake.

It was my first view of the water which had spawned saurian giants so long ago. Chris drove the hayrack through the fields of high coarse grass and on down almost to the lake's edge, where there was no shore but only the green rushes like floating meadows in which the water birds nested. Beyond the undulating reeds the open lake stretched, deep, green-grey, out and out, beyond sight.

No human word could be applied. The lake was not lonely or untamed. These words relate to people, and there was nothing of people here. There was no feeling about the place. It existed in some world in which man was not yet born. I looked at the grey reaches of it and felt threatened. It was like the view of God which I had held since my father's death. Distant, indestructible, totally indifferent.

Chris had jumped down off the hayrack.

"We're not going to camp *here,* are we?" I asked and pleaded.

"No. I just want to let the horses drink. We'll camp up there in the bluff."

I looked. "It's still pretty close to the lake, isn't it?"

"Don't worry," Chris said, laughing. "You won't get your feet wet."

"I didn't mean that."

Chris looked at me.

"I know you didn't," he said. "But let's learn to be a little tougher, and not let on, eh? It's necessary."

Chris worked through the hours of sun, while I lay on the half-formed stack of hay and looked up at the sky. The blue air trembled and spun with the heat haze, and the hay on which I was lying held the scents of grass and dust and wild mint.

In the evening, Chris took the horses to the lake again, and then he drove the hayrack to the edge of the bluff and we spread out our blankets underneath it. He made a fire and we had coffee and a tin of stew, and then we went to bed. We did not wash, and we slept in our clothes. It was only when I was curled up uncomfortably with the itching blanket around me that I felt a sense of unfamiliarity at being here, with Chris only three feet away, a self-consciousness I would not have felt even the year before. I do not think he felt this sexual strangeness. If he wanted me not to be a child—and he did—it was not with the wish that I would be a woman. It was something else.

"Are you asleep, Vanessa?" he asked.

"No. I think I'm lying on a tree root."

"Well, shift yourself, then," he said. "Listen, kid, I never said anything before, because I didn't really know what to say, but—you know how I felt about your dad dying, and that, don't you?"

"Yes," I said chokingly. "It's okay. I know."

"I used to talk with Ewen sometimes. He didn't see what I was driving at, mostly, but he'd always listen, you know? You don't find many guys like that."

We were both silent for a while.

"Look," Chris said finally. "Ever noticed how much brighter the stars are when you're completely away from any houses? Even the lamps up at the farm, there, make enough of a glow to keep you from seeing properly like you can out here. What do they make you think about, Vanessa?"

"Well—"

"I guess most people don't give them much thought at all, except maybe to say—*very pretty*—or like that. But the point is, they aren't like that. The stars and planets, in themselves, are just not like that, not *pretty,* for heaven's sake. They're gigantic—some of them burning—imagine those worlds tearing through space and made of pure fire. Or the ones that are absolutely dead—just rock or ice and no warmth in them. There must be some, though, that have living creatures. You wonder what *they* could look like, and what they feel. We won't ever get to know. But somebody will know, someday. I really believe that. Do you ever think about this kind of thing at all?"

He was twenty-one. The distance between us was still too great. For years I had wanted to be older so I might talk with him, but now I felt unready.

"Sometimes," I said, hesitantly, making it sound like *Never.*

"People usually say there must be a God," Chris went on, "because otherwise how did the universe get here? But that's ridiculous. If the stars and planets go on to infinity, they could have existed forever, for no reason at all. Maybe they weren't ever created. Look—what's the alternative? To believe in a God who is brutal. What else could He be? You've only got to look anywhere around you. It would be an insult to Him to believe in a God like that. Most people don't like talking about this kind of thing—it embarrasses them, you know? Or else they're not interested. I don't mind. I can always think about things myself. You don't actually need anyone to talk to. But about God, though—if there's a war, like it looks there will be, would people claim that was planned? What kind of a God would pull a trick like that? And yet, you know, plenty of guys would think it was a godsend, and who's to say they're wrong? It would be a job, and you'd get around and see places."

He paused, as though waiting for me to say something. When I did not, he resumed.

"Ewen told me about the last war, once. He hardly ever talked about it, but this once he told me about seeing the horses into the mud, actually going under, you know? And the way their eyes looked when they realised they weren't going to get out. Ever seen horses' eyes when they're afraid, I mean really berserk with fear, like in a bush-fire? Ewen said a guy tended to concentrate on the horses because he didn't dare think what was happening to the men. Including himself. Do you ever listen to the news at all, Vanessa?"

"I—"

I could only feel how foolish I must sound, still unable to reply as I would have wanted, comprehendingly. I felt I had failed myself utterly. I could not speak even the things I knew. As for the other things, the things I did not know, I resented Chris's facing me with them. I took refuge in pretending to be asleep, and after a while Chris stopped talking.

Chris left Shallow Creek some months after the war began, and joined the Army. After his basic training he was sent to England. We did not hear from him until about a year later, when a letter arrived for me.

"Vanessa—what's wrong?" my mother asked.

"Nothing."

"Don't fib," she said firmly. "What did Chris say in his letter, honey?"

"Oh—not much."

She gave me a curious look and then she went away. She would never have demanded to see the letter. I did not show it to her and she did not ask about it again.

Six months later my mother heard from Aunt Tess. Chris had been sent home from England and discharged from the Army because of a mental breakdown. He was now in the provincial mental hospital and they did not know how long he would have to remain there. He had been violent, before, but now he was not violent. He was, the doctors had told his mother, passive.

Violent. I could not associate the word with Chris, who had been so much the reverse. I could not bear to consider what anguish must have catapulted him into that even greater anguish. But the way he was now seemed almost worse. How might he be? Sitting quite still, wearing the hospital's grey dressing-gown, the animation gone from his face?

My mother cared about him a great deal, but her immediate thought was not for him.

"When I think of you, going up to Shallow Creek that time," she said, "and going out camping with him, and what might have happened—"

I, also, was thinking of what might have happened. But we were not thinking of the same thing. For the first time I recognised, at least a little, the dimensions of his need to talk that night. He must have understood perfectly well how impossible it would be, with a thirteen-year-old. But there was no one else. All his life's choices had grown narrower and narrower. He had been forced to return to the alien lake of home, and when finally he saw a means of getting away, it could only be into a turmoil which appalled him and which he dreaded even more than he knew. I had listened to his words, but I had not really heard them, not until now. It would not have made much difference to what happened, but I wished it were not too late to let him know.

Once when I was on holiday from college, my mother got

me to help her clean out the attic. We sifted through boxes full of junk, old clothes, schoolbooks, bric-a-brac that once had been treasures. In one of the boxes I found the miniature saddle that Chris had made for me a long time ago.

"Have you heard anything recently?" I asked, ashamed that I had not asked sooner.

She glanced up at me. "Just the same. It's always the same. They don't think there will be much improvement."

Then she turned away.

"He always used to seem so—hopeful. Even when there was really nothing to be hopeful about. That's what I find so strange. He *seemed* hopeful, didn't you think?"

"Maybe it wasn't hope," I said.

"How do you mean?"

I wasn't certain myself. I was thinking of all the schemes he'd had, the ones that couldn't possibly have worked, the unreal solutions to which he'd clung because there were no others, the brave and useless strokes of fantasy against a depression that was both the world's and his own.

"I don't know," I said. "I just think things were always more difficult for him than he let on, that's all. Remember that letter?"

"Yes."

"Well—what it said was that they could force his body to march and even to kill, but what they didn't know was that he'd fooled them. He didn't live inside it any more."

"Oh Vanessa—" my mother said. "You must have suspected right then."

"Yes, but—"

I could not go on, could not say that the letter seemed only the final heartbreaking extension of that way he'd always had of distancing himself from the absolute unbearability of battle.

I picked up the tiny saddle and turned it over in my hand.

"Look. His brand, the name of his ranch. The Criss-Cross."

"What ranch?" my mother said, bewildered.

"The one where he kept his racing horses. Duchess and Firefly."

Some words came into my head, a single line from a poem

I had once heard. I knew it referred to a lover who did not want the morning to come, but to me it had another meaning, a different relevance.

Slowly, slowly, horses of the night—

The night must move like this for him, slowly, all through the days and nights. I could not know whether the land he journeyed through was inhabited by terrors, the old monster-kings of the lake, or whether he had discovered at last a way for himself to make the necessary dream perpetual.

I put the saddle away once more, gently and ruthlessly, back into the cardboard box.

Wilfred Watson   THE LICE

1

There was a certain bishop of Edmonton who greatly deplored the behaviour of his congregation and of the people of Edmonton, whom he thought guilty of covetousness and greed, envy, sloth, drunkenness, gluttony and lechery, anger, vanity and pride. He would often talk about this matter with his two priests, especially with the younger, whom he loved. But they preferred to think of their congregation as being materialistic. No, no—said the bishop. He liked to call materialism, he said, by its older names. He would roll off on his tongue the Latin terms for the seven deadly sins: *superbia, invidia, iracundia, accidia,* etc. etc. When the people of Edmonton's actions deserved these labels, he wouldn't neglect to apply them, he told his subordinates. That is what these labels were for.

He preached a good many powerful sermons on the subject of the deadly sins. One Lent he preached a series beginning, Pride, and going on through the list of sins till he got to the last. His congregation took these tongue-lashings in a tolerant way. They—the serious people among them—agreed with their bishop about the nature of sin; but though they felt he was right to preach about the utter holiness of God and the deplorable filthiness of sin, they felt that the bishop didn't rightly understand the tenacious nature of sinfulness. How could he? He was a saintly-minded man, and had mastered his passions and appetites. It was easy for him to resist temptation—and besides, he was a priest, and not only that, getting on in years. He couldn't comprehend how difficult it is for the non-clergy, even when they had a mind to, to cure the sinfulness of Adam in our natures—especially with this demon of materialism attacking us from the radios and television sets, from the newspapers and the motion-picture houses, from magazines, advertising mail and shop windows.

Mr. Dobbs, a good Christian, though heretical on the difficult topic of birth control, said as much to the bishop one day. If only, he ended up by exclaiming, the people of this diocese could be made to *see* their sins—in all their ugliness —as you have described it—then, perhaps, father, then, perhaps . . .

The bishop thought deeply about what Mr. Dobbs had said to him . . .

But no way to show his flock the nature of sin came to his mind . . .

If only sin *could* be made visible.

If only . . .

At length, he decided to take his difficulty to God.

If only, he said in his heart, God would make the sin of each sinner in the diocese into a hunchback, why, how many souls would be saved for the New Jerusalem, saved in fact from terrible damnation. If only . . . He shivered a little at the thought. Suppose his own hump were uglier and fatter and more conspicuous than the lump of sin on the backs of his flock? Suppose he himself were, in spiritual pride, uglier and fouler than any of his congregation? It would be for the good of his own soul, he decided, if any condition of sin in him were made manifest.

So the bishop worded an outright prayer, as the spiritual leader of his flock, to God, that the sins of his congregation and of himself, should be made visible to himself and to all of them.

Then he fell asleep.

The next morning was Sunday. It was, the bishop saw

when he awoke from dreamless sleep, a glorious clear fresh sunny morning. The sun sang in the sky like an angel. The blue sky sang. The trees seemed to be wearing a fresher green than usual, as if they had been washed with rain during the night—perhaps they had—but no—the ground was dry. It was the sun shining through the marvellously clear air of Edmonton, that made everything so clean and bright.

In church, when the bishop turned round to look over the new clothes and the clean faces of his congregation, the people themselves seemed newer and brighter and more colourful than ever before. The gay hats of the young girls . . . the red dresses . . . the shirts and trousers and jackets of the men . . . even the blacks of those who had come decently garbed in black . . . seemed to glow with the colour of the morning and of the sun outside.

A sombre thought struck the bishop. Perhaps there had been another of those false "sales" at the Westmount shopping centre . . . and this new look . . . this freshness was simply just that. It was then that the bishop remembered his thoughts about hunchbacks and his prayer to God the night before.

He glanced at the shoulders of his flock to see if his prayer had been—but no, and he said a 'Thy will be done' to himself, rather hastily. A terrible fear struck him. He wriggled his shoulders. They seemed, as he did so, rather odd. He squeezed his elbows to his side, trying to feel his back. He looked round, and finally, put his hand to his shoulder, as if—and this, he realized glumly was a deceit, a hypocrisy—he were adjusting his clothing. But no . . . his terrible prayer . . . God in his mercy . . . who sees all issues . . . had . . . in his wisdom . . . seen fit not to grant. *Non sum dignus . . .*

Introibo ad Altare Dei—*Adjutorium nostrum in nomine Domini*—I will go into the altar of God—Our help is in the name of the Lord . . . the bishop had got so far in the saying of the order of mass. And the confession was over, *Confiteor Deo omnipotenti, beatae Mariae semper Virgini* . . . I confess to almighty God, to blessed Mary ever a virgin. . . . The bishop had got as far as the absolution: *Misereatur vestri omnipotens Deus, et, dimissis peccatis vestris* . . . May almighty God have mercy upon you, and forgive you your sins . . .

It was then that the bishop's eyes fell upon the crucifix on the altar, for at this point he had to turn to the altar and say, silently,

Take away from us our iniquities, we beseech thee . . .

The words turned to ice in his throat.

For, streaming from the crucifix . . . was . . . terrible thing to see, a swarm . . . yes, swarm of some sort of insects . . . No, not streaming from it . . . but drawn to it . . . as if to a magnet . . . which was sucking them in . . . insects . . .

The bishop didn't know what to think. He wasn't sure what he ought to do . . . He prostrated himself, burying himself for a time in prayer . . . Then he stood up before the crucifix . . . and yes . . . it was insects that were hanging in clusters there . . . as if a swarm of bees had alighted . . . as if the blessed crucifix were their queen . . . but, *domine misere,* it was not bees, but some small loathsome insects . . .

Lice . . . said the bishop. *Lice* . . . And then, in an instant the meaning of the miracle—for it was a miracle that his eyes were glazed by—dawned on him, as clearly as if an angel had told him. God had chosen his own way to make the sins of his congregation (and perhaps the sins of the people of Edmonton, too) visible to the eye of sense; he had chosen to turn these foul loathsome wickednesses, evil thoughts, covetousnesses, cupidities of the flesh, into lice polluting the crucifix.

Even when this realization had punctured its way into his mind, the bishop, like someone who has received a telegram of great importance, understands it, but remains unbelieving, put (or rather pushed) forward his arm, and stretched his finger out to touch one of the hideous things . . . The insect was crushed by the doubting Thomas finger, and a drop of blood smeared—polluted the altar-cloth. Polluted? Ought he, the bishop fearfully checked himself, to conclude, *polluted?* Might not this blood be the blessed blood of the Redeemer of mankind? He sank feebly down upon his knees again, and hid himself in a state between trance and wordless prayer.

Not knowing what they should do, his priests and his acolytes, who had seen almost in the same instant (but with far less comprehension) what he had seen, came towards him, fearing that he had been overcome. But he pulled himself together, and signalled to them to turn to their ritual places.

And he went on, as if instructed by God Himself, in this emergency, with mass. He didn't realize what he was saying. In his mind two ideas were in conflict—swinging backwards and forwards like an irresistible pendulum, which swayed him with its motion. He thought: a miracle, a miracle. But his next thought was: these sins have been turned into *lice*. As far as the glory of the one thought raised him up, the shame of the other sucked him down.

There were hanging to the crucifix, it seemed to him, all sorts of small noxious pestiferous blood-sucking insects. There was the common louse. There were bed-bugs, flat and stupid-looking discs of redness; and every sort of louse. He had seen—once, on the farm he was brought up on, a chicken-house hanging with ropes of chicken fleas; and he thought of the pecked rumps of these sorry infected fowl—their featherless backs bleeding where other chickens with no less melancholy backs, had beaked them, pecking at lice, but beaking through the skin. But no sight as horrible as the one before his eyes.

When the *credo* was over, he went down to the communion rail, and stood facing his flock. Casting his eye over them, as a shepherd counts his sheep, or as a father casts his eye over his children, he marvelled at their shining faces, at their shining clothes, at their shining presence—the light seemed to come from within them—they seemed like a churchful of angels, not people. The other swing of the pendulum compelled him. He didn't know what to say to them. It certainly wasn't a time for preaching. At last the words came, almost of their own.

"My children, turn round your heads and look at one another."

Surprised, they didn't at once obey him, but stared straight and fixedly at him.

"My children, look at one another."

Shyly, first one and then another turned round to look at his neighbour, and then, catching his neighbour's eye, turned back in a puzzled fashion to the old priest. It seemed to them he stood there in front of them like a shining angel.

"My children," he said over again, with smiling patience, "look at yourselves—turn round and look at yourselves. Take a good look at yourselves. It is a *good* look, isn't it?"

Less shyly this time, they did as they were told, and then turned their eyes back to the priest.

"What is it," he asked them, in the softest voice—in a voice not louder than a whisper—"what is it you see—what do you see?—You see," he told them, "the beauty of holiness adorning each one of you."

He stood silent for a long time.

At length he found words to tell what had happened. "God has performed a wonderful miracle. We think in our hearts that there aren't any more miracles performed in this twentieth century after Christ's birth—we think God has lost the ability to do a miracle. But behold, God has performed one. God has shown each of you the beauty of human beings, even in this shape we stand in—it is a beautiful shape, if it isn't made ugly by sin."

He paused. "Look round you at yourselves again." They still didn't understand him, but they looked around about them, as he told them to.

"And now," he said to them, in a voice sepulchral and low—the voice of one buried in the grave, "look at the crucifix on the altar . . ."

Look at the crucifix on the altar . . . when he said this low-voiced injunction a second time, all their eyes were trained on the crucifix.

None of them could see clearly what it was that had darkened, had clouded over, the shining silver of the cross . . . and the bishop explained to them what had happened. As he spoke, the vision of brightness which he saw resting upon them, vanished.

In thrilling fatherly voice he implored them to gaze on the miracle, and see how God had made visible their sins to them, in the form of lice . . . *lice* which he had caused to infest the crucifix, nasty, loathsome, bloodsucking creatures, lice . . . fleas . . . and *bedbugs* . . . and this was why . . .

His voice trailed away into inaudibility, mere imploration. But everyone in the church understood what he was trying, and unable, to say.

2

When the news of the miracle spread to the world outside —as it very quickly did spread, a nine-day's wonder resulted.

The Edmonton *Journal* gave the miracle front-page headlines, and for several weeks reported daily on the ebb and flow of the swarm of insects to be seen clinging to the cross of the church. *Time* wrote up the miracle in a leading article, honoured the bishop with a cover portrait, and commented on the remarkable reticence he displayed—indeed, complained of it. In truth, he wasn't interested in this sort of fame. *Life* sent photographers to him, but the bishop refused them admittance to the church. Whether they did take photographs surreptitiously, or whether they manufactured them, photographs of the miraculously infested crucifix appeared, in the current issue of *Life*.

Even as far away as Rome, notice was taken of the "miracle of Edmonton," as it was soon called. The Vatican was bound to take an interest in it, for, as may be expected, scientists of a sceptical turn of mind asked to be allowed to test the validity of the alleged miraculous happening. The bishop, however, refused to allow them access to it. They challenged him in the name of truth. There was no lack of witness to the truth, he said. Many eyewitnesses of unimpeachable veracity testified to what had happened—and all that sceptics wanted to do was to find some way of throwing doubt on the occurrence.

The editor of the Edmonton *Journal* held the bishop's stand to be right. An editorial appeared which took the bishop's part against the scientists—this editorial pointed out that the saintliness of the bishop had done more for Edmonton in the way of publicity than anything else in the city's history, with the possible exception of the victories of the town's football team, the Eskimos. To this editorial, a University of Alberta classics professor replied caustically, in a letter, that he, for one, didn't want Edmonton to become another home of superstition, like Lourdes, in France.

As for the bishop, he withdrew his skirts with remarkable dexterity from all these unsavoury arguments about what had happened.

His heart indeed was set elsewhere.

And the next Sunday after the appearance of the lice, he rejoiced to notice that the swarm on the crucifix had very noticeably diminished. He might have attributed this lessening (or so I am inclined to think) to a waning of the force of the miracle. But he believed, as a result of their sins being made visible to them, his congregation had been at some pains to resist the temptations of sin; and that the crucifix was a gauge of their success.

When he spoke to them in church, that was what he said. "My children, I rejoice to see that . . ."

In a low voice, he begged them to try with all their hearts to continue the improvement of the past week . . . he knew that a long-settled-in habit of vice couldn't be cured in a few days . . . but God was helping them . . . and he said he looked forward to the time when the crucifix would be completely free of lice which still clung to it in swarms . . .

It is difficult, however, for human beings to resist temptation for periods of longer than a few days, even when all the world has its eye on what is happening; and the second Sunday after the miracle occurred showed a marked increase in the swarming lice.

The bishop in a reproachful voice recalled to his flock what was happening. They looked at his reproachful figure sadly, as if they were all signifying to him, we can't help it, but . . . we are flesh and blood, merely. They received what he said to them in patience, at least. It was not so on the *third* Sunday after the miracle. To the bishop, with anxious eyes on the crucifix of the church as a true gauge of the sinfulness of his people, it seemed, on this third Sunday after God had spoken to them with the plague of lice, as if his flock was more sinful than ever they had been.

His voice, though he tried to modulate it, was petulant. It bit into the air like an iron rasp. He was not heard in patience.

People in the church stalls fidgeted and squirmed. It was as if one and all were shrugging their shoulders. When he called on them to look at their shame, visible as lice on the crucifix, they didn't raise their eyes, but looked away almost defiantly. He sensed their hostility.

I must not lose patience with them, he told himself. Human nature, he reminded himself, is very very weak. It was natural for his flock to relapse in this way. He must go out to them, as a father, in loving confidence. He stood at the door of his church, after mass, and tried to give each of them his personal assurance of his belief in them . . .

Person to person, some of them relented of their stiff attitude in church. But others openly rebelled. One of them went so far as to ask, how can we be sure, reverend father, that what has happened to the cross is a sign from God, and not an insult from the devil. Another church member said, was it really a good thing to be able to see one's sins in so dramatic a fashion. He wasn't speaking for himself, mind you, father—but wouldn't it tend to harden people's hearts and make them brazen—just as a prostitute is turned into a brazen huzzy by the outward, open wickedness of her life of vice?

The good bishop shook his head. No, no, he said. We must take it as a miracle from God. If it is a miracle, how can it work for evil?

One of his priests ventured to speak to this question. The younger of the two (the one he loved particularly) observed that, if the result of the manifestation of lice on the crucifix did cause *more* sinfulness, then ought we not to conclude that it was, on this very argument of the bishop, one of the works of the devil?

No, no, no, said the bishop in anguish.

The younger priest held his tongue until the bishop had gone, and then observed, to the other priest, that "we must conclude this, mustn't we?"—"I don't know what to think," said the elder of the two.

The bishop however, received instructions from his superior, the archbishop, that it was plain, from the scandal of the "miracle," that the "miracle" must be adjudged "no miracle." He must therefore have the cross cleansed of the "miraculous" lice, which were, in all probability, due to some natural cause, and to be accounted for as some unusual but perfectly *natural* plague.

This intervention of his superior was perhaps brought about because some professors of science at the University had examined specimens of the infestation, as they called it, and had pronounced upon the nature of the insects making up their "sample," obtained with a genuine zeal for truth but in an unlawful way. All were such varieties of bloodsucking vermin as could easily be found in Edmonton. There was no satisfactory explanation forthcoming as to how they occurred where they did in such numbers. However, according to one wag, a rough estimate of the number of insects on the crucifix could be made; and hence, a count of the number of sins committed in Edmonton.

Moreover, an analysis of blood taken from some of the lice was made. The reports about this analysis were conflicting. Not all the samples were said to be human blood; and more than one type of human blood was detected. It could not be maintained then that the blood in the lice was the blood of the Saviour, as the bishop was said to suppose. All in all, these investigations didn't completely prove the miracle to be a fraud, but they left considerable room for speculation.

With a sad heart, the bishop ordered the crucifix to be cleansed of the lice infesting it. What his hopes were, may be expected. He was consequently most despondent when, after vigorous disinfection, the cross was once more free of lice.

He went to his room and prayed, not for another miracle, but simply prayed—wordlessly he opened his heart in passive obedience to God. He remained in prayer for most of the night. When the next morning—it was Wednesday morning —he again went into the church, he didn't dare raise his eyes at once to the cross.

When he did so, he saw it was clean—as clean as the cleaning people had left it. He realized that what had occurred might easily be taken as a defilement of the church—that the church might have to be re-consecrated. The archbishop indeed had gently hinted as much in an exchange of letters.

On Thursday, the crucifix was still free of infestation. And so it was on Friday. And on Saturday.

On Saturday morning, the Edmonton *Journal* reported what had taken place in the church during the week: the cleansing away of the lice infesting the crucifix. Though asserting his belief in the sanctity of the bishop, the editor urged his readers not to draw hasty conclusions from exceptional circumstances. Perhaps, this strange happening might prove to be, not a supernatural event, but one of those many natural miracles that our age has provided, and its solution a feather in the cap, not of religion, but of science.

But when, on Sunday morning, the bishop, about to say mass, raised his eyes to the cross, there, lo and behold, were the lice clinging to it, as if it had not been subject to the activities, on the Tuesday before, of the vermin exterminators.

He wanted to cry out, then and there, Look, O ye of little faith, the lice have returned—your sins and mine have again been made visible. But he made no allusion to the repetition of the miracle, as he thought, or to the re-infestation of the crucifix, as most of his congregation thought. He learned that they thought so, as he spoke to them after mass.

They seemed to be daring him to assert that the crawling insect life on the crucifix was, in fact, a miraculous manifestation of their sins.

He held his peace.

By doing so, he earned the approval of his younger priest (the one he loved), who remarked to his brother priest that he thought the bishop had shown wisdom and discretion in maintaining silence in the face of the return of the plague of lice.

The bishop again ordered the exterminators into the church. But Monday, Tuesday, Wednesday, Thursday, Friday and Saturday—though they exerted all their efforts, the exterminators had no success. They were this time unable to cleanse the cross of its vermin. Nor could they find any natural cause why it should be infested.

They did spray the sanctuary and the body of the church with quantities of an insecticide having deodorant properties.

The smell of the lice had become extremely unpleasant—as the younger priest said to his confrère, "God is not only making our sins known to our eyes, but to our noses." The odour of the spray which the vermin-exterminators used rather enforced the stench of the vermin (they seemed unable to kill) than eradicated it or covered it up. As one entered the church, a strong suspicion of violets made one's nose quiver. But this scent of violets quickly changed to a strong whiff of carrion. It was as if, in a flower garden, you were hit by an overpowering smell given off, say, by the putrefying body of a dead animal, a dead cat or dog.

Because of this smell, and for other reasons, I should have thought that there would have been no congregation on the following Sunday, but such was not the case. The fact is, an angry congregation makes a full church.

The bishop, for his part, flatly and without emotion (still calling his flock, "my children") re-asserted his belief in the miracle. He said that they were right to be ashamed of what had happened to the crucifix, but, though this shame was a good thing, they were wrong to think there was no way to end the pollution of their church.

The church was polluted by sin.

It could be purified by fighting against sin, and God had helped to make this fight easier, by showing them their sins.

The bishop was nevertheless conscious all through mass of the hostility of the people.

After mass, very few spoke to him, but one forthright, golden-hearted old woman spoke out her mind. "I think it is a miracle, father. But it is a very hard one for human flesh and blood to stomach."

"God will provide us with strength."

"It is a very hard thing, reverend father."

3

All that next week, the bishop reflected on what she said to him. He wondered if he had been too fanatical in his zeal to reform his flock. He recalled to mind how he had asked for the miracle, the wonderful vision he had had of his people, that first morning, when the miracle had come, and the unhappy aftermath. Was God judging *him?* He felt very despondent.

Little by little, however, he began to repair his morale. He chided himself for lacking courage, he blamed himself for lack of faith—he blamed himself, too, for not realizing that he must face a desperate struggle with the forces of evil. He also reminded himself that he had an ally in God.

After all, the bishop told himself, he was the shepherd of his flock, and the good shepherd lays down his life for his sheep. He himself must give up his life for his sheep, if need be.

By Saturday, a course of action shaped itself in his brain. That night, he again prayed articulately to God.

Thy will be done, O Lord—but, if possible, let the pollution of the cross with the sins of my flock cease—even if the lice could infest me—yes, yes, the shame of the polluted cross is too great for them—let the lice infest me . . .

So he prayed.

The next morning, Sunday morning, he knew that his prayer had been answered, there was no doubt of that. For he himself was covered with the lice. He was torn between thankfulness to God, and the bodily torment of the plague of vermin.

In church, he saw that the cross was free. As he heard mass being said, he began to wonder if he had the strength to undertake the task he had asked for. After the *credo,* he went to the altar rail, and again stood before his flock.

"By miracle," he told them, "it has pleased God to show us all, my children, how our sins hurt His Son. But here is another miracle. He will now show us, such is His will, how His priest is hurt by the sins of His people—your sins, my children."

There was neither joy nor reproach in the bishop's voice. He spoke in a factual manner. Having finished speaking, he divested himself of his clothes, down to the waist. Then he held his arms up above his head, so that all in the church could see how the lice which had clung to the crucifix, were now transferred to him.

He walked down the centre aisle of the church and back again, all the time holding his hands above his head.

Then he drew his clothes about him.

He felt, during the rest of that Sunday, and through the other days of the week following, that what God had made happen He had made happen for the best. There was, he believed, a great decrease in the number of lice crawling over his body. He was by no means free from the physical discomfort of them. The comforting thing was, the lice had decreased.

On the following Sunday, he once again experienced the joy he had known, in a surpassing degree, on the day of the first miracle.

It seemed to him that the people in the church were shining with a new cleanness—especially the faces of some of the girls and young women of the congregation seemed to be lit up with the light that must once have shone in the Garden of Eden, the garden of aboriginal innocence . . .

But, immediately after mass had been said, he sensed a relapse. He knew there must be some retrogression—his experience of human nature told him that. But he suspected from the great increase in the number of lice on his body that the increase had been disappointingly great.

Throughout the following week, the lice on his body increased. In fact, on Sunday, he could hardly bring himself to go to mass.

But he did.

And once again, he stood up before the people, and stripped off his clothes, and showed them his body covered with lice.

"My children," he began, but he got no further.

An unprecedented thing happened.

A woman near him interrupted him. "The smell, father"— this was as far as she got and stopped surprised at herself. "It's the smell of sin—it's your smell, my children," the bishop answered her.

A loud arrogant male voice took up the woman's complaint.

"I'm a Christian, but it's not sanitary for you to appear

like this, father . . . you ought not to come into church like it . . ."

A chorus of voices took up the protest, and soon everybody joined the hubbub.

"You ought to be ashamed of yourself, father, coming to mass like this . . ."—"Stay at home, father, until you are fit to be seen in public . . ."—"This isn't any miracle, father, it's just filth . . . . How can we expect our kids to keep clean and wash the backs of their ears and comb their hair, father, if you come to church all covered with lice?"—"Be off with you, father, you're lousy . . ."—"Go and wash, father."— "Take a bath, father."—"Wash yourself in Lysol, father."

"Shut up," a girl shouted out hysterically.

The bishop steadied himself on the rail of O'Brien's pew, and wrote with his finger in the dust—for the wind had filled the church with the summer dust, which hung over the city like a cloud, and, sifting into the church, made all the woodwork gritty to touch.

A boy's voice whined from the back of the church, "Go de-louse yourself in the river Jordan, father."

"My children," the bishop began again, "these are your sins . . ."

"No, they are lice, father."

"They look like lice, father."

"My children," the bishop wept . . .

"Off with him."

"Out of the church with him."

"Chase him out."

With the women, girls and children screaming denunciation or encouragement, the male sheep of the bishop's flock pushed out of their stalls, and, approaching their half-naked shepherd, began to butt him out of the church.

His priests ran to help him into the bishop's residence, which was adjacent. Once in, he threw his discarded clothing across a wooden library table, and then searched in the pocket of his jacket for a packet of cigarettes—it was a packet of Player's he had bought as long ago as the week before the *first* miracle. He hadn't smoked a cigarette since then.

He fumbled with trembling fingers at the packet. Approving

this indulgence, one of his priests (the younger one he loved), reached into his own pocket for a booklet of matches, tore off a match, and stood waiting to light the bishop's cigarette. But when the bishop got his box of smokes open, he found the half-filled package swarming with lice. They clung to the cigarette he started to extract, and he pushed it back into the contaminated container.

"Have one of mine, father," urged the younger priest, and offered him a cigarette of his own.

"No, no—no thank you, my son."

"A smoke will do you good, father."

"I will have one of my own," he told his priest. And he extracted the cigarette he had just rejected, tapped it so that the lice clinging to it dropped back into the box, and put the cigarette to his mouth.

The priest lit the cigarette.

But the lice had crept into the tobacco, and the stench of burning insects made the smoking of the cigarette impossible.

The bishop butted it.

As he did so, an upboiling of emotion, a tide burning hot and freezing cold by turns, seethed through every blood vessel, every artery and vein, every capillary, every fibre of his flesh. His skin contracted under its covering of vermin. What he experienced was a recognition. He knew . . . at this moment . . . with absolute certainty . . . that he was picked out to be a martyr . . . and, too, he knew that his suffering . . . the passion of his martyrdom . . . was now begun.

"Lord," he said, "I am afraid. But let your will be done."

He stood up erect, a sense of glory swelling within him, and pulling at his stiff, slack, aging skin—a sense of glory made trebly delicious to his senses by the itching of the lice which clung to him and were sucking his blood. His skin was aflame. If only the world knew, he thought to himself—it was for nothing so sensually delicious as this, that men lusted after the caresses of harlots, and gave up their immortal souls for the embraces of adultery.

Yet it was an agony.

Embarrassed, awkward, his two priests stood beside him, not knowing what to do, or what to advise. The younger priest was thinking over a course of action. They were both startled when the bishop spoke to them in a voice of command.

"Read to me."

"Read *what* to you, father?"

"Read to me from the scriptures."

"Wouldn't it be better," the younger priest presumed to say, "if you tried taking a shower—I'm thinking of your personal comfort," he added, for he saw the look kindling in the bishop's eye.

"Read to me from the scriptures," the bishop ordered him.

"Yes, father, what shall I read?"

"From the last chapter of the Book of Isaiah," decided the bishop. *Sion deserta facta est. Jerusalem desolata est . . . quomodo si cui mater blandiatur*—but as one who comforts his mother. I will comfort you . . .

He understood now, as the younger priest read to him from Isaiah—he grasped now with the firm-handed grasp of inner comprehension, the meaning of the phrase, *vicarious sacrifice.* He . . . God was going to accept him . . . as a sacrifice for his flock. Because of the shepherd's love for his sheep, the sheep would be saved—what foolish sheep they are! But this, it seemed to the bishop, at this moment, was the most precious of the truths of Christendom. With this imperfect coin of our lives, we can buy the lives of others, and save them from . . . and so perfect ourselves . . . Yet as he thought these words, he realized that he had never loved his congregation. At best, he tolerated them. Indeed, he had *despised* his flock, he had, hadn't he, in trying to purify it—make it what it wasn't? Now he knew the formula. He must offer himself. And God had accepted his pretended love for his people, as *if it had been a real living love.* Or was God showing to him his own worthlessness? No, that was an anthropomorphic idea. Rather, God was taking him at the word of his lips, and overlooking the empty hollowness behind that word —the emptiness of his heart. The bishop recalled the exemplum, the little medieval sermon anecdote, of Pers, the usurer. Pers, the usurer, had never done a charitable deed in all his life. But once he had flung, not *in* but *out* of charity, in anger, a loaf of bread at a starving woman. This act of violence had been reckoned—after the system of accounting of heaven— as a good deed to the credit of Pers, the usurer.

"Now let me be for a little while," the bishop said to them, adding, gently, "my sons." He went up to his room. When the younger of the priests visited him after a short lapse of time, he found the bishop collecting together his belongings.

"You are leaving us, father?"

"You have been making arrangements for me to leave you, haven't you, my son?" The apparent clairvoyance of the bishop disturbed the priest.

"Something must be done soon, father."

"Yes, my son. I'm collecting my personal things together. But I shan't, I think, have much use for them."

The priest bowed his head, and left.

4

Later in the day, the bishop agreed, with no fuss, without a single objection, to a proposal of his younger priest. It was that he should leave his see, leave Edmonton, and go into retirement. If he did agree—all the arrangements, said the younger priest, had been made. An unoccupied farmhouse had been put at the bishop's disposal by a member of the congregation, on account of the great scandal the church was suffering. It was provided with bed, table, chest of drawers, other simple furnishings, and the owner wanted no remuneration for it. Nearby, there lived an old woman who had agreed to look after the bishop—she was unfortunately a Presbyterian, but otherwise of unexceptionable character. The arrangement, the younger priest had admitted to the older priest, seemed almost to be a providence of God. "But will he be persuaded . . ." the older man had wondered. "Ah, yes . . . that's our difficulty," said the priest whom the bishop loved. It had proved, however, to be no difficulty at all.

After all the arrangements had been made, there did occur *some* difficulty in getting the bishop transported out to his new house. No taxicab would agree to accept the lice-ridden churchman as a fare. No one in the bishop's congregation seemed anxious to transport the bishop out there—partly from shame, for no one wanted to be the person chosen to drive the bishop away from the fold; partly, too, there was fear of infesting the car in which the verminous bishop would have to ride.

Put to some pressure, finally one church member offered his car and his services as a driver. It was understood that the car should afterwards be fumigated thoroughly at the church's expense. If the driver of the car picked up any of the vermin on his own person, he too was to be compensated. Some simple precautions were taken. A stout white heavy cotton sheet was draped over the back seat, and another sheet was stretched across between the back seat and the driver's seat— so that the driver would be shielded as much as possible from infestation. Oddly enough, the lice seemed to prefer the bishop to the car or its driver, for none of them (so I was told) were afterwards found either on the driver's person, in the back seat upholstery, in the armrests, in the lining of the car roof, or under the floor-mat. "Isn't that miraculous," the driver said to the younger priest, who had been largely responsible for these arrangements. "Very remarkable," was the answer.

A fairly large crowd gathered at the bishop's house to witness his departure. The police were present, in case of trouble. But there was no demonstration. His farewells were much abbreviated. The elder priest offered to come and live with the bishop. But the bishop, with his eye on the younger priest, whom he loved, wouldn't hear of it. Both priests, he said, were needed in the church. A few intransigents from his congregation assembled a small group of children with fir boughs, which were to have been flung under the car as it drove away. But though the little mites waved their fir boughs faintly at him, no boughs were cast under the front of the car.

The crowd was rather sheepish. They knew the bishop knew they were glad he was leaving. So they merely stood about stupidly. Only one jaundiced teenager called out, with a voice of brass and ashes, "Come back, father, when you've got rid of the lice."

"That will never be," said the bishop, but he spoke to himself merely.

When the bishop had departed, the archbishop from afar caused the church to be re-consecrated, as he had beforehand decided to do.

5

The Presbyterian widow who was to look after the bishop discovered him standing alone in the kitchen of his new house. She had seen his car arrive, and came down "to be of use," she said. She was shocked by the fact that he was unescorted by friends, came, in fact, unaccompanied except for the driver, who, as soon as the bishop had alighted, and his few possessions been put in the house, fled down the road like a juvenile with a stolen car and with a few drinks under his wind breaker. Her good honest Presbyterian heart revolted at what she believed to be the treachery of the bishop's flock. "And they call themselves God's Christians," she exclaimed angrily to herself, "why, I wouldn't treat a dog so. The dirty Catholics . . ."

She tried to make the bishop feel at home and cared for. But the bishop was not responsive. The woman herself felt strange in his presence, and supposed he must feel strange in hers. As for his affliction, she resolutely closed her eyes to it. She did, however, take pains to assure him that there was a hot bath for him, whenever he wanted to avail himself of it. (The house had propane gas, and the younger priest had arranged to have a new cylinder of gas attached.)

After the bishop had seen where everything was, came introductions.

"What shall I call you, sir?"

"My flock called me 'father,' " the bishop told her.

"Very well, sir, 'father' it is from now on."

"And what shall I call you?" the bishop asked her.

"M'name is Mrs. McGinis. You can call me that, if y'like,

sir. But the lads at the ranch, well they call me mom, or mother . . . guess I am older than you, sir, if'n we took a count of our years."

"Then if you wish it—I will call you . . . mother," said the bishop.

"There's some lovely nice hot water in the tank," were her parting words, to which she added, very self-consciously, "father."

"Thank you, thank you," said the bishop.

She went away muttering curses against the Pope, Cardinal Sheen, monsignor the archbishop, and all Roman traitors— "leaving the old man alone, like this. The dir*r*ty Dogans, the dir*r*ty Dogans."

6

All day, the bishop's heart had been anesthetized by inner misery. But as soon as the Presbyterian widow had left, his feelings began to awake. As long as his heart had been numb, he hadn't noticed the torment of the lice. Now that his heart revived, stirred first of all by the solicitude of Mrs. McGinis, and especially by the flowers she had set out for him at his table, desk, and bedroom altar, he could feel the agony of the lice. He tried to school himself not to scratch at his hands, arms, limbs, or trunk. But every now and again he lost control of his fury, and clawed savagely into his flesh, until the futility of scratching wearied his fingers.

He sat down at the table to eat the meal arranged for him by his part-time housekeeper. But as he reached for the potato salad, cold meats and pickles that Mrs. McGinis had left him, lice from his body dropped on to the plate of food, and though he tried to brush them away, they seemed viciously intent on getting into his food and contaminating it. At length, he got up from the table without eating. He made tea, but he drank none, for it too was spoiled by lice falling into his cup.

He took off his clothes, because the suffering was less when he was almost naked. He stood up, because the vermin were most bearable in that position.

He was almost caught in half-naked state by Mrs. McGinis, when she called later on in the evening to see if all was well.

After she had gone, he did eat a very little food, and drink a sip of tea. He lay down on his back on his camp-cot, and at long last, very late at night, slept a little. He couldn't pray. All he could do was to keep asking, out of his affliction, *How long, O Lord, how long?*

The next day, he tried taking a bath. But though many of the vermin were drowned in the very hot bath he poured himself, his suffering wasn't lessened, for the water made his skin more tender to the biting of the blood-sucking insects. He couldn't dry himself, because the chafing of the towel set up an intolerable itching. As he stood dripping onto a towel, he decided that bathing was a luxury he couldn't repeat. Anxious not to offend Mrs. McGinis, he was bothered by the state he left the bathtub in. As much as he tried to wipe it clean of vermin, fresh ones fell into it. Finally, he abandoned the task (—an odd fact this, considering that all the reports I have had of the matter suggest that the lice were attracted to him as if to a magnet.)

On the night of the second day, he slept early and long. Next morning, he awoke greatly improved in his mind. He was able to pray; and he prayed for strength. When he had finished his prayers, he encouraged himself by thinking how glorious it was—his terrible fate. He had wanted to cure his sheep of their sins by showing them how ugly they were. But he was doing something better. He was actually helping those who couldn't cleanse themselves. He was taking to himself their iniquity. Certainly not in love—in wilfulness . . . but . . . God, he felt sure, was accepting his pitiful effort *as if* it was a true sacrifice. In desperation, he had said, let the sins of my flock come to me *as lice*. It was only half a promise, but God had insisted that he keep it. This was the thought which steadied his heart.

But later that day a relapse occurred. The afternoon was sunny and hot, the humidity in itself trying. He took off his clothes. He tried to pray, but couldn't. He shut himself up in his bedroom and wouldn't see Mrs. McGinis, who nevertheless called out to him, when she left, about the availability of bathwater . . . And why didn't he take a nice bath? He would feel so much better, she was sure . . .

Finally, his endurance broke.

O God, he prayed, *let me be rid of these accursed lice, so that I can return to my church. Don't punish me with them any more. I've had enough. O God, let me be set free of this torment.*

He fell into a long sleep.

In the morning, all the lice were gone.

7

He couldn't at first believe either his eyes or his skin, over which he kept running his finger. He immediately threw himself into a great tub of water, and bathed himself with wonderful enjoyment. He was amazed to find that his skin was completely rid of irritation. He gave himself a marvellously revitalizing rub-down with the bath towel. He shaved, a thing he hadn't been able to do. Then, feeling like a new man, he had an excellent breakfast, drank two cups of instant coffee, and smoked three or four cigarettes.

When Mrs. McGinis came about eleven o'clock in the morning, she said to him, "Why, father, you look as if you'd taken on a new lease on life!—I see you've had a bath," she added, glancing in at the damp towels in the bathroom. "I told you it was all that was needed—it's the simple remedies that work. Nothing like soap and water. You see," she told him, "you have another nice hot bath tonight. Keep them at bay it will."

She insisted on changing his bedsheets. "But—why, you haven't soiled them at all," she said.

The next morning he took another bath.

He wondered how long he ought to wait before going back to his church. A day—or two days? He seemed so useless, just waiting around in the farmhouse. He smoked cigarettes, given to him by the younger priest as a farewell gift. He ate his meals. He thought of how surprised his congregation would be, to see him again, so quickly. There would be no reproaches. It might be that he would love them better than he had done hitherto, because of the bond of failure between them—he had failed and they had failed. There would be mutual forgiveness. As he conceded his failure, as, putting it on like a new garment, he got somewhat more used to it, his need for the *community* of the church became more insistent. He must get back right away.

But at the end of the day, he discovered one thing: he *could never go back.* It would require just as much courage of him, to think out the new philosophy of life going back would require ... the excuses ... the new goals ... that ... Ah, just as much ... as staying.

That night he didn't sleep at all. By morning, he found himself, with his new vitality, hating his cleanness. He bathed himself contemptuously. If only, he said to himself, I still had the lice—better the torment of the lice, than the emptiness of what I am now.

He didn't dare pray.

But, by that evening, he could endure himself no longer. *O God,* he prayed, *let the lice return to me. Forgive my weakness. Let the lice return, if it is your will, let the lice return ... non sum dignus, domine, sed ...*

He fell asleep. When he awoke, it was morning. The lice had returned. They were much worse than before.

8

So much worse were they, that before the evening of that day was come, he had again prayed that the lice leave him. In the morning, he was again free of them. He couldn't hesitate now—he mustn't play fast and loose like this. He packed his handbag. He prepared to leave. He would go back and love his flock, this would be the meaning of all that had happened ... for him and for them, for they in return would love him too.

But when he was ready to leave, his decision wavered again. He unpacked his clothes, he decided to stay. He paced up and down the farmhouse, into and out of all the rooms of it, like a caged tigress, her cubs taken from her and her dugs full of milk. He saw that he couldn't live in this state of irresolution, but it was a long time before he could once again bring himself to pray. It was early the next morning before he could pray. But then, a little before two-thirty a.m., he was able to. *Let the lice return to me. Let the lice return to me.* He then slept for an hour or two. When he awoke, they had come back, Back, and much worse than they had been on their second return. He took off his night clothes and lay for a long time naked on his bed.

The lice seemed to be multiplying. They were gnawing in his arm-pits—he tried to clean them out. If he rested on his back, they crawled across his belly. They crawled across the small of his back, if he lay on his belly. They got into his groin, and, into his ears—he had already put wads of cotton wool into his ears, to keep the lice out, but they worked their way past that barrier. Into his ears. What lies, the thought shrieked across his brain, are my people breeding now? The vermin crawled into his anus. They crawled across his scrotum, and got into the folds of the *glans penis.* What sodomy are they now committing, he cried out, as he scratched at his rectum . . . what fornication or prostitution or pimping or adultery am I suffering for now? The lice crawled over his hands—cupidity, cupidity, he told himself. . . .

They crawled into his navel—across his teats—into his eyes—into his mouth, even. . . .

When Mrs. McGinis called promptly at eleven a.m., she found him completely naked. But it wasn't his nakedness that horrified her, it was the sight of the true deformity of his condition, which, till now, had been more or less hidden from her. Good honest woman that she was, she shrieked with terrified disgust, when she saw *that.* All her fear of him turned into vituperation and reproach. "Why don't you do as I told you?" She threw the bathroom door open.

"Do as I tell you," she screamed. "Get in there and bathe yourself until you are clean again."

He shook his head piteously

"Look, father. You're going to obey me. Into that bath."

He shook his head.

"Goddam you," she shouted, "do as I say."

When she found that he wouldn't or couldn't do as she ordered him, she banged her fist down on the table. "Very well, father. Very well. If you won't take steps to cure yourself, it's the last you'll see of me. Good-day. Good-day." She slammed the door, and went muttering to herself up the path.

The bishop knelt down to pray. *Lord, have mercy upon me,* he murmured . . . *but, O God, if I pray to be free of the lice . . . and I will pray to be free of them . . . have mercy upon me . . . don't ever listen to my prayer. Don't ever listen to my prayer. Let the lice be with me.* When he had said this prayer, he felt, for a moment of bliss, as if this resolution had carried him up into the seventh heaven of paradise . . . as if his martyrdom was completed.

He was able to say the Lord's Prayer, and to make a brief act of contrition. *My God I love thee.*

But then the torment started again. He kept shrieking, take the lice away, take the lice away, take the lice away. Then he would stop from sheer exhaustion. And then one thought would gnaw in his brain: what is the use of it? Isn't it all entirely useless, like mountain-climbing, aren't I like the mountain-climber, who only keeps on to get to the top, because he has engaged himself to get to the top? Again the bishop would moan, take the lice away, take the lice away. Then again his outcry would exhaust itself, and he would think, I'm like the Anaconda serpent which has swallowed too large a deer and can't let go of it because inward-curving snake-teeth have trapped both the snake and the victim. He was, the bishop told himself, the snake and God, the deer. He couldn't spit God out, if he wanted to. He also thought, these lice will purify me, but how can they help my flock, how? They continue as they were. Then once again the bishop would begin to keen, take the lice away, take the lice away, take the lice away . . .

Then his mind could think no more. He could only rage. Far across in the McGinis ranchhouse, they could hear him roaring. Mrs. McGinis put in a call to Edmonton, but could get no one at the church. When, however, the next morning, there was complete silence, the good woman again telephoned, and asked that someone be sent to the bishop's assistance . . . because . . . she was afraid of the worst . . .

9

It was at the eleventh hour that the bishop gave up the ghost. His friends, summoned on the next day, did not arrive at the farmhouse until the next morning after that. They saw then a third miracle, if the lice on the crucifix was considered as one miracle, and the lice on the bishop himself, another. What they saw was, out of the mattress of the camp-cot a thick turf of a marvellously green new grass growing. On, or rather in, this grass, were the remains of the bishop. All the lice were gone, and only his skeleton was seen, at first. There was absolutely no sign of any vermin, no flea, no bedbug, no louse of any kind.

Summoned by the Presbyterian-minded Mrs. McGinis, it was the police who made a second discovery. One was a constable and the other a corporal. The constable *observed* that death couldn't have been recent. The corporal, however, *looking* more closely at the bishop's remains, saw that, within the bony cage of the churchman's ribs, the heart and other chest organs were still fresh and new.

At this, the clergy were filled with fear, for they knew what had happened *must* be a miracle. "I'm afraid," said the constable to the corporal, "there has been foul play."

These policemen were to be present at the performance of yet another miracle.

The first to discover the bones, the younger priest (whom the bishop loved in particular), when he perceived what had happened, drew back. He didn't want to look at the miracle. It was there. He was convinced that it had happened. But there was nothing inside him to receive it. I am like a barren woman, he thought. The bridegroom comes into me, and I don't conceive. He smiled to himself, thinking what would a psychologist make of a celibate Roman Catholic priest using such imagery? He went into the bathroom. When he had made water, he put his hand to the hot water tank. It was, of course, warm. Then he went into the kitchen, and there he saw the carton of cigarettes, which he had given the bishop as a parting gift. He saw how many the bishop had smoked. And thinking of what he had *done* for the bishop (for besides the cigarettes he had out of his own pocket arranged to have the cylinder of gas attached, so that there could be hot water always available for the bishop's use), he was ashamed of *how little* he had done.

Pushing his way through the others who were still wondering at the bishop's remains, and pushing aside the policemen, who speculated as to the possibility of a crime, he flung himself down before the bishop, seized the bishop's hand, and wept, Forgive me, father.

It was then that the final miracle occurred, before the very eyes of the police. A great swarm of vermin appeared to descend upon the bishop's heart, as if to devour it.

Seeing this, the younger priest fainted away. When he had been carried into the kitchen, laid on the floor, and restoratives given, some one of the party noticed that the lice had consumed the bishop's remaining vitals, and that the skeleton was now completely free of the organs inside it.

But when they looked for lice, there were none to be found.

Bibliographical Notes

Victor Carl Friesen (1933-   ) was born on a farm near Rosthern, Saskatchewan, and still lives there every summer. He has taught in schools and universities and his eclectic interests are shown in the articles he has published: on Thoreau, the Fort Carleton Trail, the flight of the ruffed grouse, among others. What concerns him most in his fiction is "the commonplaces in the lives of ordinary people." His stories have been read on CBC "Anthology," and printed in *Canadian Forum*; "Old Mrs. Dirks" appeared originally in *Queen's Quarterly* (Fall 1971).

Frederick Philip Grove (1872?-1947). Although critics are no longer agreed about when or where Grove was born, it is known that he was born somewhere in Europe and by 1912 was teaching in a country school in Manitoba. No one has written so extensively and so powerfully of the Canadian pioneer as Grove in his five prairie novels; they have a kind of austere massiveness. "The First Day of an Immigrant" is one of several stories he left in manuscript and now made available by the collection *Tales from the Margin* (1971), edited by Desmond Pacey. It appears to have been the opening chapter of *Settlers of the Marsh* (1925), and discarded in the final version of that novel.

Henry Kreisel (1922-   ) was born in Vienna, and after some years in England, settled in Canada. He is now academic vice president of the University of Alberta. He has published two novels, *The Rich Man* (1948), and *The Betrayal* (1964), and a number of short stories. In them there is often a detached observer who, as the story progresses, discovers that when he truly understands what is happening, he can be detached no longer. "The Broken Globe" first appeared in *The Literary Review* and was reprinted in *The Best American Short Stories 1966*.

Robert Kroetsch (1927-   ) was born in Heisler, Alberta, and has lived "alternating between various parts of the wilderness and various universities." Between long bouts of writing he presently teaches at the State University of New York, Binghamton. He has published three novels and the two set in Alberta, *The Words of My Roaring* (1964), and *The Studhorse Man* (1969), are ribald picaresques of ordinary men made giant by their passions, both sensual and cerebral. "Earth Moving" first appeared in *The Kansas City Review* (Spring 1960), as "Defy the Night."

Margaret Laurence (1926-   ) was born in Neepawa, Manitoba, and now spends almost equal time writing at her homes in Canada and England. She first gained world attention with her stories about Africa in the late 1950s. Three of her subsequent novels and the Vanessa MacLeod stories collected in *A Bird in the House* (1970) are either set in or involve persons who came from a Manitoba town whose name she invented: Manawaka. Her continuing exploration of the people of this town may be part of her own coming to grips with her past, as she has implied, but it is also bringing into being some of the finest fiction written anywhere. "Horses of the Night" first appeared in *Chatelaine* (July 1967); it is the sixth of eight long stories in *A Bird in the House.*

Dorothy Livesay (1909-   ) is known primarily as a poet whose first collection of lyrics was published in 1928 and who continues to write poems of warmth and beauty. Her *Collected Poems* will be published in 1972, but she is also a teacher of writing and has written many articles of literary criticism. During the 1940s she wrote a cycle of stories about her own childhood in Winnipeg, where she was born. "A Week in the Country" is one of these; it has been read over CBC Radio but has not appeared previously in print. Her awareness of the social sickness of a changing world is evident in all her writing.

Edward McCourt (1907-1972) came to Alberta from Ireland as a boy and since 1944 has taught at the University of Saskatchewan. His extensive writings include literary studies, travelogues, biographies, fictionalized histories for young readers, and novels and short stories. His best-known novel is *Music at the Close* (1947), and a widely re-published story "The White Mustang," in *Canadian Short Stories*. "Cranes Fly South" was first printed in *Weekend Magazine* (April, 1955.)

Ken Mitchell (1940-   ) was born and grew up in Moose Jaw, Saskatchewan. He received his M.A. degree from the University of Saskatchewan (Regina Campus) in 1967 and has been teaching courses there in Canadian literature and creative writing since that time. He has written articles, radio and T.V. plays, documentaries, short stories and a novel, and he won first prize in Ottawa Little Theatre's national competition for a one-act play written in 1971. "The Great Electrical Revolution" first appeared in *Prism international* (Spring, 1970).

W. O. Mitchell (1914-   ), born in Weyburn, Saskatchewan, and growing up in Florida, has lived much of his life near Calgary. *Who Has Seen the Wind* (1948) is the classic Canadian novel of a boy growing up; *Jake and the Kid* (1962) is a collection of stories based on several hundred episodes first heard on CBC Radio and continues his chronicle of prairie life in folksy, tall-tale humour style. "Hercules Salvage" is from his forthcoming new novel.

Frederick Niven (1878-1944) was a Scot born in Chile who finally settled in Nelson, B.C., in 1920. He made his living writing travel books and novels, many ephemeral, but a big exception was *The Flying Years* (1935), a novel of Canadian prairie history as one man, Angus Munro, experiences it between 1856 and 1914. Other western novels are *Mine Inheritance* (1940) and *The Transplanted* (1944). Though they are often weak in overall structure, isolated parts of his novels can be superb. "Indian Woman" is from chapters 4 and 5 of *The Flying Years*.

Howard O'Hagan (1902-   ) was born in Lethbridge, Alberta, and besides writing has had careers as a McGill student, Australian real estate salesman, New York and

Buenos Aires publicity man, and Rocky Mountain guide. His novel *Tay John* (1939) is built around the legend of the Yellowhead Pass. "The Tepee" reconstructs a story he heard an eighty-year-old trapper named Montana Pete tell in his cabin on the Little Hay River one January night in 1934; a story lived decades before. It is told in that context in *Wilderness Men* (1958), and also appears in his collection *The Woman Who Got on at Jasper Station, and Other Stories* (1963).

Sinclair Ross (1908-   ) was born near Prince Albert, Saskatchewan, and from his experience as a banker in many parts of the West during the 30s and 40s came the finest novel yet written about the prairies, *As For Me and My House* (1942). His moving short stories of the same period have been collected in *The Lamp at Noon and Other Stories* (1968); their situations are usually blackly ironic, their characters oppressed and thwarted despite their strong dreams. For some reason "A Day with Pegasus," which shows a very different picture of farm life, is not included in that collection. It is here reprinted from *Queen's Quarterly* (Summer 1938).

Gabrielle Roy (1909-   ) is perhaps the French-Canadian writer best known to English readers. She was born in St. Boniface, taught school and then moved to Montreal. She has written realistically of the city poor in *Bonheur d'Occasion (The Tin Flute,* 1945), and of the poor in wilderness Manitoba with a tender lyricism in *La Petite Poule d'Eau (Where Nests the Waterhen,* 1950). "The Move" is the third of four interconnected stories in *La Route d'Altamont (The Road Past Altamont,* 1966); the book reflects strongly her own childhood and growing awareness.

Stephen Scobie (1943-   ) came to Canada from his native Scotland in 1965, studied in Vancouver and since 1969 has been teaching at the University of Alberta. He has published one collection of poems, *In the Silence of the Year* (1971), and two others will be out shortly; he has also exhibited poem-prints in Vancouver and Buenos Aires. His story "The White Sky" was read on CBC "Anthology" and is published in

Fourteen Stories High (1971). "Streak Mosaic" is published here for the first time.

Wallace Stegner (1909-   ) was born and has lived most of his life in the United States, but from 1914-20 his family homesteaded in Saskatchewan south of the Cypress Hills. An evocation of this land is found in one of his many books, *Wolf Willow* (1962), which he subtitles "A history, a story, and a memory of the Last Plains Frontier." "Carrion Spring" is one of the fiction sections. The same country appears in many of his stories and also his novel *The Big Rock Candy Mountain* (1943).

W. D. Valgardson (1939-   ) grew up in Gimli, Manitoba, near where he was born, and studied at the Universities of Manitoba and Iowa. He now teaches at Cottey College, Nevada, Missouri. He has published poetry, but is establishing his reputation as a story writer concerned with ordinary people in situations that push them back upon themselves. One of his stories, "Bloodflowers," was first published in *Tamarack Review* and has been selected for *Best American Short Stories 1971*. "Dominion Day" is from *Fiddlehead* (Spring 1971).

Sheila Watson (1919-   ) was born in New Westminster, B.C., and taught public school in the Cariboo country before coming to the prairies with her husband Wilfred Watson. She teaches at the University of Alberta. She is best known for her novel *The Double Hook* (1959), a beautifully structured ballad in prose about peasants in an isolated valley which for evocative imagery and polished language has few equals. One of her published short stories is "Brother Oedipus" *(Queen's Quarterly,* Summer 1954), whose title character also appears in "The Black Farm." "The Black Farm" was originally published in *Queen's Quarterly* (Summer 1956); its allegories echo *The Double Hook*.

Wilfred Watson (1911-   ) came to British Columbia from England at the age of fifteen and to the prairies in the early 50s. He is a Shakespeare and modern media scholar at the

University of Alberta, is respected for his poetry *(Friday's Child*, 1955), but most widely known as a dramatist. *Cockcrow and the Gulls* (1962), *O Holy Ghost Dip Your Finger in the Blood of Canada and Write "I Love You"* (1967), and *Let's Murder Clytemnestra According to the Principles of Marshall McLuhan* (1969), are some of his plays, and they are as vivid and bizarre as their titles. All have been staged, none published. "The Lice" originally appeared in *Prism international* (Fall 1960).

Jon Whyte (1941-   ) lives in his home town of Banff, Alberta, where he sells and publishes books. He has studied medieval literature at the University of Alberta, film-making at Stanford, and his major writing interest now is to unearth for Canadians "the troves of richness our heritage does afford." A section of his long poem "Homage, Henry Kelsey" appeared in *White Pelican* (Summer 1971). "Peter Pond, His True Confession" is printed here for the first time.

Rudy Wiebe (1934-   ) was born near Fairholme, Saskatchewan, and moved to southern Alberta as a boy. Two of his novels, *Peace Shall Destroy Many* (1962), and *The Blue Mountains of China* (1970), portray the Mennonite people; *First and Vital Candle* (1966), explores the white Canadian relationship to Indians. Two recent stories with an Indian-white theme are "Where is the Voice coming from?" *(Fourteen Stories High,* 1971), and "The Fish Caught in the Battle River" *(White Pelican,* Fall 1971). "Did Jesus Ever Laugh?" is from *Fiddlehead* (March-April 1970).

Ethel Wilson (1890-   ) was born in South Africa and has made her home in Vancouver since she was eight; she has had a long and distinguished career as a writer of fiction. Her stories often begin with seemingly ordinary people in very ordinary situations; ironically, gently satiric, they tend to move quite beyond the usual "realistic" experience until suddenly the reader finds himself pushed into a frightening beyond. "A Visit to the Frontier" first appeared in *Tamarack Review* (1964); it is not included in her collected stories, *Mrs. Golightly and other Stories* (1961).